To Patrick

One of the most talented musicians I've ever had the pleasure of meeting let alone

THE ROGUE MOUNTAINS

jamming with.

Yes I know I spelled jamming with I'm back there. I'm on my 3rd bourbon.

Joshua Tarquinio

To Dick,

One of the most talented musicians I've ever had the pleasure of jamming with. Let

Yes I know I spelled jamming wrong. I'm back there with. It's on my 3rd bourbon.

[illegible signature]

TRIGGER WARNING

This story contains descriptions of suicide.

If you're at risk, read no further and talk to someone. They'll even let you text.

https://suicidepreventionlifeline.org/

1-800-273-8255

ISBN-13: 978-0-9992402-1-2

To Alyssa

PROLOGUE

The Revelation came and went, but it wasn't the end of all things. It wasn't even as encompassing as advertised. The Earth was still spinning, most of it untouched, when the battle ended. Mankind was still alive. There was still electricity, and cars, and music, and all the other things that came with civilization. There were still jobs to do and things to invent. Children still went to school, grew up, got married, and had families. People continued to be born, although what happened after death was in question.

Since the Events of Pittsburgh, mankind found itself as religiously confused as he'd ever been. If the Final Battle *had* truly happened, and man still existed, then where was God? Was God still here? Did It leave? Did the rapture happen and if that were the case, were the billions of people still left on Earth damned? Maybe God *was* still around, but working out the planet's next iteration.

Some people had their faith strengthened by the Events. Others had theirs destroyed. The vast majority were the same as they'd ever been. They thought there might be something out there, but right now they had to go to work so they could feed their family. The one thing no one disagreed on, however, was the existence of monsters.

Humans weren't the only ones that survived. When the dust settled on the Events, the surviving beasts and beings from Hell and the other planes found themselves trapped with humans in the physical realm.

Some were lucky. Some were able to blend in with society. They took regular jobs and lived out their days.

Many joined sideshows, which had seen a resurgence in popularity. One forward-thinking entrepreneur even managed to put together an entire circus full of creatures from the other planes. They toured the world astounding and horrifying.

The lesser beasts were hunted, caged, and studied, but they couldn't be contained. They escaped the city, through the rivers and through the woods. They proliferated and spread out. Of those that went south, some found a trio of mountains that had escaped the Appalachian range. And some of the creatures that found the mountains settled there and infested them.

The Rogue Mountains, as they were called, had little in the way of foothills. The tree-covered giants were islands in the gently undulating plain. Some said the mountains were the edge of the East. Some said they belonged to the Midwest. The people of Brothers, Pennsylvania, the hunting and farming town cradled at the base of the mountains, didn't tend to worry about what their region was called. The topic rarely came up since the monsters moved in. Miles from any highway, Brothers had one main road, a hotel, a general store, and not much else.

This story begins 23 years after the Events of Pittsburgh, 22 years after the creatures found the Rogue Mountains, and 21 years after Ariana Coleman was born.

CHAPTER 1

The woods were dead silent. Even Tempest's hoofbeats were muted in the dewy leaves, like she was tiptoeing. She'd been making these treks for about five years, since Ariana Coleman was 16. The human girl had the small town blues, among other things. Got her kicks from ringing death's doorbell and running. Tempest was used to it, and if she'd been able to talk, would've said she enjoyed the thrill too.

The sun, still behind the mountains, lit the sky enough to see, even in those woods where the leaves had begun to change and fall. Ariana preferred the dull blue glow to the contrast of a sunny day. In those woods, where death took many forms, every stark shadow was a potential threat.

Tempest got that feeling—that innate sense of danger animals get when a predator is near—and she stopped. She stopped and gave a stamp, which she and Ariana decided a long time ago was her way of warning her human.

Ariana stroked Tempest's mane and asked, "Where is it, girl?" The human held her breath and looked around, first for familiar shapes and then for movement...

Nothing yet.

The girl clicked her tongue which was the signal (they had decided) to proceed with caution and be prepared to turn tail. Reins in the left hand, Ariana slid her right hand over the grip of the Smith and Wesson Model 19 on her hip.

Tempest took a few more steps and stopped again. Ariana's fingers closed on the handle of her sidearm. An alarm went off in her bones.

Ariana drew her gun as a hunner dyer emerged, shrieking, from under a swath of leaves and dirt. Tempest reared, brandishing her hooves.

Hunner dyers most closely resembled carpenter ants, though they were only slightly smaller than men. They had six legs and their bodies were segmented. Their abdomens were proportionally small, allowing them to walk and stand on their hind legs. Their thoraxes appeared to have human-like ribs on the outside. Patches of coarse hair grew randomly. Their heads contained a loose ring of 24 black eyes, a pair of fangs like a tarantula, a long, retractable middle tooth, and a needly tongue for extracting whatever the tooth exposed.

"Hunner dyer" was not the creature's proper name. It's just what everyone called it. Ariana and Tempest had seen and killed a ton of them; shriek, click, bang. This time, however, as Tempest's hooves came back down, Ariana hesitated. This time she felt different. This time she felt like a bully; like she had just walked into the creature's home with the express purpose of killing it for no reason. That was exactly as it always had been. Why it bothered her now, she didn't have time to speculate.

The hunner dyer lunged. Tempest turned and ran without a cue from Ariana. They beat a path back across and down the hill. Though the monster gave chase, it couldn't keep up with the horse. It was far behind by the time they reached the fence.

Ariana's nerves balanced on a pinhead as she dismounted and opened the gate. She smiled at the feeling as her hand shook on the gate latch. This was what she came for—the adrenaline rush.

The hunner dyer shrieked again. It had cleared the last hump and was on its way down to torture and kill Ariana and her companion.

The girl threw open the gate and led Tempest through. The monster descended, kicking up leaves and shrieking every few breaths. Its movement was sloppy, as if it didn't know how to run. It was neither a crawl nor a gallop, but something in between. Its clawed forelimbs waved and reached, only touching the ground when it needed the balance.

Ariana slammed the gate closed as the monster slammed into it, giving the girl a good look at about ten of her own reflections in its onyx black eyes. It ran its tooth through the fence, reaching its limit an inch from Ariana's throat. The girl flinched and fell backward.

This was an unusual situation for Ariana. Typically, she would have shot the monster when it first appeared and left it deeper in the woods. The fence itself was never meant to hold the creatures of the mountains back, only deter them from the areas where people live. Ariana had never seen what would happen if a monster were given incentive to find a way over or through the fence.

She wished the creature away as it rammed and beat at the fence. She wished for it to get tired and go away. Then she thought she might have to kill it anyway, just to make sure it didn't come back.

The hunner dyer made her decision easy. It looked up, ran its forelimbs along the top of the fence, then began to crawl up. It got one more shriek out before Ariana blew its head off. The gunshot tapered off through the valley, leaving Ariana and Tempest in dead silence once more.

The adrenaline sat in Ariana's veins like stale coffee in a day-old pot. She wondered if that would be the end of that thrill—one of the few thrills she had in her podunk, one-horse, middle-of-bumfuck-nowhere town.

She opened the gate again and tied a rope from Tempest's saddle to the carcass. Couldn't leave chum by the gate. Girl mounted horse and they dragged the dead bug into the woods before heading home.

Away from the scant foothills, an old refrigerator truck puttered up to an old picket fence around an old farmhouse. The truck door slid open and Reggie Adams slid out, drumming a pencil on his clipboard. His curly black hair billowed and bounced as he bobbed to the song in his head. He popped open the side door, hopped in for a moment, and then dropped back out with a small package wrapped in butcher's paper.

Rick Jenkins greeted Reggie at the door. Rick was one of the old timers. Been living in Brothers since before the whole Pittsburgh thing, before that mess made its way to the country. That was always the way though, Rick knew—everything starts in the cities and works its way out, whether countryfolk like it or not. Though neither Rick, nor anyone else for that matter, expected what they got. He thought the changing times would've meant dealing with kids and their long hair and devil music. Instead he had an infestation. It put things in perspective. With monster-infested mountains a stone's throw away, Reggie's hair was less of an affront to Rick than it could have been.

"Morning, Rick," Reggie said with a smile.

"Reggie," Rick nodded. "I don't know how you're so bright-eyed and bushy-tailed after playing music all night."

"I got a little nap. I'll get the rest when my route is over. I'm used to it." He handed the package over saying, "Five pounds of ground wood devil, right?"

"Sounds about right to me."

"Solid. Just sign right here for me."

Rick signed and handed the clipboard and pencil back to Reggie. "You know," asked the elder, "I always wondered. How often you attract any them creatures, driving a meat bus around like that?"

Sometimes Reggie wondered that himself. That truck was on its last leg. He, nevertheless, responded as he always did—with confidence and good humor. "Ah! Well... Difficult as it may be to ascertain by the humble exterior of this fine machine, the refrigerator contained within not only keeps the fare fresh, but well sealed. And if all else fails, the exhaust fumes will repel just about anything." Reggie patted his sidearm and said, "I've never even had to draw this thing."

"Say, that's pretty—watch out!" Rick pushed Reggie to one side and drew his own gun. He took aim at a hellcat that was sprinting toward them. Reggie covered his ears and watched. The gun wobbled in Rick's hand. He was getting older, but not too old. And it certainly wasn't the first time he'd had to deal with a hellcat.

The creatures looked like bobcats, but bigger and mangier. Their eyes glowed and flickered with hellfire whether at night or on a bright sunny day. They made no noise as they ran, creating a sensory dissonance in anyone unfortunate enough to see one bearing down on them.

Rick's shot rang out and dropped the hellcat 20 feet from the porch. The old timer kept his eyes on the beast as he holstered his weapon. When he was satisfied it wasn't going to get back up, he turned to Reggie and said, "Never had to draw, huh?"

"That's right," Reggie said with a smile and gesture at Rick's gun. "Plus, most people around these parts don't like to stand around talking with raw meat in their hands. Did you want me to take that?" He pointed at the hellcat.

"Please," said Rick.

Reggie flipped the pages on his clipboard to start on a new form. "And do you want to sell it, have it processed, get it mounted?"

"I'll take five pounds of it. Ground is fine. Make it easy."

"You sure? The tenderloin on these is almost as good as beef. Just smaller. You can do like little filet mignon medallions. Little butter, little garlic... mmmm, mm!"

"Heh, all right then. I'll take five pounds ground and a tenderloin. Sell you the rest."

"Excellent choice, sir!" Reggie said, filling out the order. "Excellent choice, indeed. Here is your receipt. And I'll bring you the difference on delivery. Sound good?"

"That'll be fine, Reggie. Thanks."

"Cool, cool."

Rick helped Reggie load the carcass into the truck. Once it was closed, Reggie took a spray bottle and spritzed a few blood streaks left on the exterior. He said to Rick, "A little bit of bleach helps keep the monsters away too."

The truck fought itself awake and backfired its displeasure. Reggie waved to Rick and pulled away. He only had a few more stops before he could head home and sleep.

When the truck had gone, Rick looked to the three mountains in the distance. The overcast sky reached down wisps to stroke them. The mountains used to be beautiful. They used to beckon. Back in the day, Rick's chief motivation was to give himself as much time as possible to hike or hunt those mountains. They used to be havens for such things. Now they loomed, foreboded, and forbade. They were home to escapees of what everyone thought was the all-time final battle. They were gargoyles, demonic sentinels.

Rick realized he hadn't looked behind himself lately. He wheeled with a hand on his gun.

Nothing.

A couple of farmhands rode tractors in the field behind the house.

Jeremy Crawford was jarred awake by one of his mother's nervous tics. He took a deep breath and looked at the clock: 2:30pm. Pretty close to four hours of unbroken sleep. He'd take it. Despite it being upright in a chair, it was a deep and solid sleep. He felt rested and tongued the film out of the corners of his mouth.

Connie, Jeremy's mother, twitched and chuffed in her bed in a dream state akin to the line between Purgatory and Hell. Whenever Jeremy left the room, the nightmare would return and push Connie's dreams into torture.

The young man took another deep breath, then moved to the edge of the bed. He took Connie's hand and said, "Mom. Mom," startling her awake. Or maybe only half awake. Maybe Connie only *feigned* half awakeness so as not to have to think or talk or burden Jeremy or herself too much.

"Mom, come on. You should get up and move around a little

bit. Get some food."

Connie stared. Afterimages of her nightmares played on the ceiling; visions of gory death, torture, and loss burned into her memories. Like so many times before, Connie wondered how much more she could take. She didn't know how she had made it as long as she did.

Jeremy gave her hand a tug and helped her sit up. She shambled to the kitchen while Jeremy went to the bathroom to relieve himself and get a shower.

There wasn't much in the fridge. There hadn't been since the nightmare, since the role of caretaker flipped at the Coleman house. Fortunately, Connie and Jeremy were friends with Kelly Karasek, the owner of the nearby Foothill Hotel and Bar. Kelly usually made sure to send some food home with Jeremy at the end of the night.

Connie slouched at the table, thousand-yard stare, turkey club between her hands. With no saliva to help, she chewed her first bite for a few minutes. She heard the water running in the shower—a sign of life in a house, formerly a home, being eaten by time before her eyes. She remembered the day she put up the now-peeling wallpaper with her husband, James. She remembered how they bickered over it. She remembered how he let her have her way and how he said it didn't look half bad after it was up. She remembered the squeeze and smile he gave her. Then she cried, because she knew the nightmare would ruin that for her next. But as much as it hurt to sleep, it hurt even more to be awake.

Jeremy had barely rinsed the shampoo out of his hair when he heard Connie screaming. He sighed and shut the water off. He pulled on a bathrobe and walked out, cleaning the fog from his glasses with his sleeve. "Twenty minutes!" he said. "Was all I needed."

Rounding the corner into the kitchen he saw Connie curled up on the floor next to the table, the sandwich a few feet away from her, and the nightmare. The gremlin-like creature sat on Connie and looked up at Jeremy. It was furry, with a pair of short round canines poking out over its lower lip. It turned its bulbous eyes to Jeremy with the ignorance of a house cat as Connie screamed and trembled beneath it.

"Go on!" Jeremy shooed. "Get outta here!"

When it didn't move, Jeremy stomped toward it. It vanished.

Jeremy cleaned up the sandwich while Connie calmed down. He put the sandwich back in the container and the container back in the fridge. Then he wiped the mayonnaise off the floor with a dish towel and balled it up on the counter.

He woke up Connie again.

"I'm sorry," she whispered. "I'm sorry."

"Yeah I know," he said, helping her to her feet. "Listen, I gotta get some clothes on. You think you can stay standing here for five minutes? Or even better, walk around a bit?"

Connie's eyes were closed but she nodded and got out a weak "y-yes" as she held the doorway for support.

She didn't walk around, but she did manage to stay standing and awake until Jeremy returned. He helped her to the bed, where she fell right back to sleep and right back into the dream state that wasn't quite Hell and wasn't quite Purgatory.

Jeremy set up a stool and began to quietly write and practice music with his guitar.

This was the majority of Jeremy's daily routine.

After Laura Krause's parents died, the silence in the house clung like slime. The house itself seemed to die, or sleep, or freeze in place. Laura didn't watch TV or listen to the radio. It was a struggle to get a signal on either of them anyway. She had only her laundry to do and mostly ate at the Foothill Bar where she worked.

The silence was not deafening, as some say. It was abysmal, depthless. Every footstep was a gunshot. Every creaking floorboard was a wail. The chair rubbing across the floor, the spoon clanking against the bowl, the cereal crunching in her head, the slurping of tea and the smacking of her lips were a cacophony which, by the time she finished breakfast, nearly drove her mad on a daily basis. On a particularly stressful morning, it caused her to fling her bowl against the wall.

Laura wondered if the house would seem less quiet if it were smaller. She rarely spent any time in the sitting room, except to dust. It hadn't changed much since her parents died. It was a museum with no visitors, curated but aging. There wasn't much in it that was hers; nothing she *felt* she could claim ownership to, anyway. On the occasions she did look in, it was usually to reinforce its image in her memory. Someday soon she'd be moving to the city for work and she wouldn't be bringing much with her.

It was almost 6:00 p.m. by the time she finished her breakfast. The sun was gone and it was time to go to work. The ceramic bowl hitting the stainless sink basin resounded like a bell. The floorboards groaned their goodbyes and she silenced it all with the thud of the door.

The outside was more of a comfort. There was noise—crickets and breezes—but it was different than the noise in the house. There was room outside. The world was alive and breathing.

Steen's General Store was atypical as far as general stores go. High corrugated walls topped with razor wire circled the parking lot and made the store feel more like a compound. One way in. One way out. It sat on the edge of town, if such a point could be defined, furthest from the mountains, and therefore saw little in the way of stray monsters. To Pete Steen and his patrons, however, the walls contained relief. No one had to be on guard at the store. Along the walls was stacked everything from firewood to tractor parts. *Inside* the store was... well, name it.

Pete Steen thought himself a great salesman. He didn't have much in the way of references though. Most of the people who went to him already knew what they wanted, but in Pete's mind, he'd upsold them all.

"Lemme ask you something, Steve," Pete said. "How long you up there on that tractor?"

"Pete," said the farmhand, "I'm just here for spark plugs."

"How long?"

Steve sighed and said, "Hours."

"Uh huh. Uh huh. And how do you feel when you come down? Tired? Achy? Sore ass?"

"Yeah, I guess."

"What if I told you I had something that would make your John Deere as comfy as a Cadillac?"

"I'd say comfort costs money I don't have."

"Now, now, that all depends on how much your comfort's worth to you."

"Just the spark plugs, thanks."

"Steve, let me show you this baby over here. Now *this...* is FarmCo's new universal tractor seat with adjustable suspension. See this little doohickey here? You push that thing down and you won't feel a single bump. Like riding on a cloud. Everybody says so."

"You sell a lot of these then?"

"No. It's too hot! The suppliers can't even keep ‘em in stock. I was lucky to get this one. And look, yellow vinyl." He counted on his fingers, "Reflects the sun so it doesn't heat up too much in the summer. And if it gets dirty, all you gotta do is hose 'er down. Made, as all the best things are, in the good ol' US of A."

"Mmhm. How much?"

"These babies are going for $75 a piece at major retailers, but I can let 'er go to you for $50."

"That sounds like a pretty good deal."

"But only if you act now."

"Just the spark plugs, Pete."

"Coming right up."

As Pete rang Steve up, Ariana entered. The shop owner saw her out of the corner of his eye. Her curly red mane was hard to miss. The already jovial shop owner beamed as he called out to her.

"Hey Pete," Ariana replied. She didn't realize her polite smile was genuine.

"We sure appreciate your business, Steve," said Pete, handing the farmhand his change.

"Well I don't really have much of a choice," said Steve. Then he realized that might have sounded rude, so he added, "Then again, even if I did, you've already got everything anyway."

"Ha! You be careful out there now."

"Thanks, Pete. You too." Steve gave Ariana a polite nod as he left.

Pete came out from around the counter, smiling wide at the girl. She'd been coming into the store since she was "knee-high to a grasshopper" as he would say. In his eyes, she never got any bigger.

"Ariana! How are you? How's your dad? How's Tempest?"

"Everybody's fine. Just fine," Ariana said.

"Good. Good. Say, what time is it? Shouldn't you be at the Foothill getting set up?"

"We don't start for a while yet. And my amp's already there. I really only take my bass with me."

"Fantastic. Well, what can I do for you?"

"Dad just asked me to pick up a bag of chicken feed."

"She *needs* the *feed,*" Pete said, rubbing his hands together. "Maxi!"

Pete's son Maxwell appeared from an aisle, pad and pencil in hand, saying, "Seriously, I hate when you call me that. It makes me sound like a—Hey Ari."

"Hey there, Maxi," she winked and smirked with schadenfreude. Ari didn't dislike Max. He was just an easy target. Teasing him was another one of her releases.

Max was tallish and thinnish, but the way his clothes clung to him, he looked overly both. He kept his short brown hair neatly slicked back and his face baby smooth. His head bent slightly forward, as if he'd rather stoop at all times than watch out for the next low bridge. Awkward as he may have appeared, Max was well spoken, with a mind as sharp as his jawline. No nonsense when it came to managing the store.

"You know, Ari," said Pete with a devilish smile, "Maxwell here is still si—"

"What'll it be, Ari?" Max interrupted.

His embarrassment was delicious to her. "Just a bag of chicken feed's all."

"Ari!" said Pete startling her to attention. "We just got this new chicken feed all the big farms are using right now. It's made with all the usual stuff *plus*, it's got these ancient Aztec grains mixed in. Bunch of proteins and *em-zymes* and whatnot." He knew how to pronounce it, but he liked making Max roll his eyes. "Like a super food! Your chickens'll be laying ostrich eggs! I'd about guarantee it."

"Ostrich eggs, huh?" Ari was entertained as usual by Pete's antics.

"Dad, you can't just *say* stuff like that," said Max.

"Oh come on, *she* knows what I mean," said Pete.

"It's just a bad habit to be in. One of these days somebody's going to sue you for false advertising, or get hurt."

Pete waved his hand in Max's face and said to the girl, "What do you say? May not get ostrich eggs, but they will be bigger... eggs *and* chickens."

"I don't know, Pete," said Ariana. She and Paul weren't exactly living high on the hog.

"I tell you what," Pete said, putting a hand on her shoulder. He looked around to make sure nobody was too near, then murmured, "I'm gonna give you a bag of the super feed at the same price as the regular. You give it a try and we'll see what song you're singing next time. How's that?"

Ariana hated smiling. She was more comfortable in her malaise. The bar was low there. Still, the old man was charming and incorrigible. It forced the corners of her lips up and away. She shook her head in a vain attempt to shake off her amusement, then shrugged and said, "What do I have to lose?"

Pete's eyes sparkled as he clasped his hands together. "Fantastic!"

"That's like the whole markup, Dad," said the ever-pragmatic Maxwell.

"It's an *investment*, Maxi. *And* it's for one of our best customers. I think we can afford to look the other way on a buck-fifty. Now be a gentleman and put the feed in her car while I ring her out."

Max rolled his eyes. There he was; 27, degree in pharmacy, balls cut off in front of one of the hottest girls for miles. Not that he ever thought he had a chance with Ariana... or that they were even compatible. Still, it was the principal. He gave Ariana a nod and a polite smile, then went off to do his task.

Pete almost whispered as he led Ariana to the register. "He's a great kid, Ari. A little too by the book sometimes, but he's got a good head on his shoulders."

Ariana blushed and pushed a coil of hair behind an ear.

"Plus, he's heir to all *this*!" Pete said throwing his hands up.

Ari put both hands on the counter and said, "Pete."

He mirrored her position.

"Just the feed today," she said.

Pete smiled and pointed at her saying, "*Today... Today,* she says." He pushed a few buttons on the register and the drawer popped open. "Two bucks," he said. "*Today* it's just the feed. *Tomorrow,* who knows?"

Ariana gave him $2 and a smile, saying, "Thanks, Pete."

"Ooh, wait! Don't forget." He ducked behind the counter.

"Pete, I'm 21."

"Not to me you're not." He returned with a jar of lollipops and held it out to her. It wasn't just a jar of lollipops, though. It was nostalgia. Every time Ariana reached in, she pulled out another memory from her childhood, when life was simpler, when she was happier.

She took a grape one, put it in her jacket pocket, and gave it a pat. "Thanks, Pete," she said and turned to leave.

"Any time, Ariana. Come back any time."

She wasn't even out the door before Pete was talking to someone else about garden tools. A sinking feeling came over her as she stepped outside. Had she forgotten something? She had paid... She had her keys... She had her bass... Max just closed her hatchback with the feed inside...

"You okay, Ari?" Max asked.

"Yeah," she said. "I just feel like... I'm forgetting something."

"He did charge you *something* for the feed, didn't he?"

"Yes, *Maxi,* he did. I don't know, something just feels... off."

"Well if it's anything to do with us, he'll be at the hotel later as usual."

"Yeah, how come *you* never come out? It's like the one and only thing to do around here."

"I'm usually pretty tired by the time we close up... and *somebody* has to keep track of inventory." Maxwell could've added a lot more to the list but didn't want to take a chance of offending Ariana or shutting down whatever small opportunity he might have had with her. He liked things quiet. She was partially responsible for the noise. He didn't care for all the smoke and he didn't drink much. He was one of very few people in town with a higher education. He was also one of very few people in town who bothered to read recreationally and, as a result, didn't expect much in the way of conversation there.

"Why don't you treat yourself tonight?" Ariana said. "Inventory will be what it is anyway. Come out and see us, Max."

He said, "Maybe. We'll see," but he'd already made up his mind to go. A look at her jeans was incentive enough. Pragmatic as he may have been, he was still a man.

CHAPTER 2

Any other night, the crickets would have been background noise—an endless one-note song that lulls the sleepy and annoys the restless. Any other night, the ceaseless stridulation would be no more than a mating call. For Del Ballantine, however, the crickets were a cover—a veil that allowed his dangerous prey the upper hand. As he strained his ears, the chirping seemed to grow louder and inspired him to pause and consider the nature of the cricket.

Every living thing has a function. For insects, the function tends to be to break down matter into smaller parts, to return things to the dust they came from. They're also food for other living things, allowing *them* to fulfill their functions and maintain the balance of nature. Lastly, they mate, create more of themselves so the species can continue performing its function. The mechanics of mating vary little despite the myriad of ways in which animals attract each other. Some creatures puff up. Some fight. Some, like the cricket, make noise. As he arrived at that thought, Del Ballantine realized humans do all of those things. He began to wonder if it meant anything for us in the grand scheme—if we're special, if we're a sort of sum total of everything over which we supposedly hold dominion. There his thought train stopped and he returned to the cricket, the tiny little bug that makes so much noise. It has no bones. He could crush it with his pinky—wipe its existence from history and erase its children from the future. Its brain is so small it can't even contemplate its own existence. All it knows is hop, eat, chirp, mate, and survive. It knows all that. A cricket is born and it hops off looking for food. Instinct, they call it—nature. When a human is born, it needs years of supervision just to make sure it doesn't get itself killed. The human brain is more complex than a cricket's though. Humans have to learn how to balance six feet of meat on two little feet. They have to learn thousands of words to be able to communicate deep and complex ideas. The cricket rubs its wings together to attract a mate. Why? Instinct, they say. It just does. That's its nature. Some humans never learn how to rub their wings together. Like all things human, the process isn't usually so simple.

Del Ballantine supposed that, as beings of this Earth, humans must be subject to the same basic nature as every other animal, including the cricket. We must eat, mate, and survive. Anything we do, whether good or bad, must lead back to one of those things. But are we so simple, or do our complex minds give us a complex nature? Is our nature beyond our scope, or is it right in front of us? Is the fact that we are able to contemplate things beyond us evidence of there being more to life? Or have we evolved beyond all the universe has to offer? Are we looking for a higher meaning where none exists?

Ballantine decided there that humans must have two natures, an instinctive and a sophisticated. One nature drives us to survive and procreate. Another, higher one, pushes us into using our talents. That's what must pull some people to science and others to labor, some to politics and others to religion. "That must be it," he thought. "A higher, more complex nature. It makes some people artists and some people doctors. It makes me a monster hunter."

A snapping twig at his 6:00 position pulled him out of his reverie. A shuffle in the leaves at his 12:00 flipped his fight-or-flight switch, but he flipped it back. Panic would be his enemy. A living stench wafted across him from 9:00, curling his upper lip. There was a guttural rasp at his 3:00, and then... crickets.

One last time, Del Ballantine rolled his fingers along the grips of his Colt 1911 pistols—.45's. They're not exactly hunting weapons, but if he hoped to bag more than one wood devil tonight, he'd have to allow his prey in close. A long-range rifle would only allow him one, maybe two kills before the rest of them took off. This way, alone in the dark, with a fresh smear of his own blood across his forehead for bait, it seemed as though he'd attracted four... and that would do.

There was a flash and a hiss as the 3:00 wood devil tripped one of Ballantine's wires, igniting a flare he'd hung from a branch. Before Ballantine turned, the red glow allowed him a glimpse of the 12:00 devil.

Wood devils looked like undead satyrs. They had humanoid torsos, shaggy lower halves, cloven hooves for feet, claws at the ends of their fingers, and a goat-like head with horns and a goatee, but their eyes were front set and pale. Their teeth were all spikes, and their three-inch canines hung out of the folds of their upper lips. They were skinny and sickly, but agile and springy.

As Ballantine raised his weapons and turned, the wood devils bared their teeth and drowned out the crickets with their hollow throaty hissing. Strands of drool cascaded from their gaping maws. Their soulless eyes bulged and glistened like pearls in the light of the flare.

As he twisted, Ballantine raised a pistol each to the wood devils at 12:00 and 3:00.

BLAM!

Two shots rang out as one. The bullets smashed through the devils' torsos, knocking them back, exploding their chests, and ripping apple-sized holes in their backs.

The flare at 9:00 (now behind Ballantine) ignited. Still turning, shifting his weight and pivoting with thoughtless precision, he took note of the 6:00 devil's position, but kept his head turning to sight in the braying 9:00 devil as it lunged.

BLAM!

Again, two shots rang out as one. The 9:00 devil was struck center mass and knocked backward out of the air. The other bullet ripped through the 6:00 devil's right arm, severing it just below the shoulder.

The devil's shriek bristled every hair on Ballantine's head. It lunged, tripping another wire, igniting another flare. The hunter adjusted and fired one last time, exploding the devil's chest, knocking it back into a heap of stinking flesh.

From the first flare to the final shot, the whole exchange took less than five seconds. This wasn't Del Ballantine's first rodeo. He was on a mission to do his part in ridding the Earth of the invasive species left over from Pittsburgh.

He holstered his guns and unsheathed his hunting knife. He would have to work quickly, before the flares ran out—before all that blood in the air attracted more than he'd be able to handle.

The knife squished.

The flares hissed.

The crickets chirped

Because the hunting was better at night, Ken's Taxidermy and Meat Processing tended to be open during the wee hours. Situated in the foothills of Devil's Mountain, the only indication it existed was a little wooden sign at the base of a windy tire-rutted driveway. Del Ballantine didn't see it until he was already passing by, so he had to make a three-point turn and head back.

His truck jolted and jostled up the rocky uneven ruts and into the thick of the woods. It was one of those driveways that was long enough to make him rethink whether or not he even had the right place. He felt like an intruder. The trees stood like menacing guards, wrangling him in, reminding him he wasn't going anywhere.

It looked like a park-where-you-can situation as the driveway opened up to a swath of flat dead grass before the house/business. The left half of the building was a mobile home. The right was the processor, a mess of a structure that looked like it was put together with whatever they could find; 2 x 4s, plywood sheets, tarpaulins, duct tape, nails here, screws there. A work light hung from an extension cord above an uninviting door. Ballantine guessed that must be the entrance he needed. He parked his old beater next to a shiny new pickup with all the fixin's: extended bed, extended cab, lift kit, winch, fog lights, you name it.

He got out of his truck and dragged two wood devil carcasses by their horns out of the back. As he neared the processor door, it swung open at the hand of a tall man's silhouette.

"Oop! Pardon me," came the silhouette's very proper English accent. "I'll get out of your way." The silhouette stepped out under the work light and held the door. He wore a very smart-looking leather outback hat, with the right side of the brim snapped up and the chinstrap loose. The sleeves of his spanking new camo fatigues were rolled up to his substantial biceps. The shiny leather boots that laced halfway up his shins didn't have a spot of dirt on them, which as far as Ballantine could tell, meant the man must have somehow been able to walk without touching the ground.

"Oh my," the man said appraising Ballantine's haul. "Quite the take for you tonight, eh?" The brim of the hat cast a black mask over his eyes, but his perfect smile sparkled like jewels in the harsh work light.

"I guess," said Ballantine. He wasn't very happy with his take at all. It took him longer to get to town than he would've liked and that had set him back. "Thanks," he said as he walked through the door.

"Cheerio then!"

As the door swung shut behind him, Ballantine took a moment to wonder how that stranger would get his gigantic truck back down the driveway. Then the atmosphere inside the shack hit him. He'd been in a lot of meat processors, some worse than others. This one was worse than others.

The smell of rotting meat hung stagnant and biting in the thick, humid air. The place was cluttered to the fill line with stuffed and mounted creatures both earthly and otherwise. There was a black bear, a few squirrels, and an owl. There were wood devils, shug monkeys, a hellcat, and even a few gremlins. At the back of the room, Ken Adams, Reggie's father, was skinning a wood devil.

Ken was about 50 years old by Ballantine's guess. Sweat

dripped from the folds of his brow as he worked. Between his blood-stained smock, the latex gloves, and the monster on the table in front of him, he looked a little like a mad scientist. As he flayed with expert speed, he threw an unimpressed glance at Ballantine's haul, then at Ballantine, then back to his work.

"I'll sell you that one I already stuffed for $350," Ken said. "Otherwise, it'll be $550 for each of them, and it'll be a couple days."

"Huh?" said Ballantine. "Oh no, I don't need a trophy. Just here to sell the meat if I can."

"You can. Let me just..." Ken dug his fingers under the tabled devil's scalp and started yanking. The squelching skin punctuated their conversation. "So you just passing through, or you staying a while?"

"Actually, I'm more of an exterminator."

"Of wood devils?"

"Of anything that wasn't here before what happened in Pittsburgh."

"Anything?"

"Anything."

"Like gremlins and hellcats?" Ken asked.

"I've got my share."

"Trolls and fairies?"

"I've gotten a lot of trolls. Fairies are nothing to worry about though."

"Witches?"

"Three."

"That all?"

"There aren't as many out there as you'd think."

"Maybe. Maybe there are more out there than you realize."

"Maybe. You know something?"

"Maybe," Ken finally got the skin off the wood devil's face and took a breath. "It's tough with the horns. You mind bringing them over to the cooler for me?"

Ballantine, still dragging his kills, followed Ken to the walk-in cooler. The sterile cold was a welcome reprieve for both of them.

"I pay $2 a pound," Ken said, heaving a devil onto a scale. "$220 for this one. Next time, leave the guts in and we'll get you some more money."

"You use the guts?"

"You can use everything, man. Well maybe not you, but *somebody* can. We grind up the horns and hooves, dry out the stomach and intestines... Shit, we even bag up the hair. Send it all to Pittsburgh to sell to the tourists. Usually, it's the Chinese buying the weird stuff."

"You said you might know something about a witch."

"I might. I might not. It's all legend anymore. Haven't even heard about her for years. If she's still there, she's keeping to herself."

"Where?"

"Damn, you just rolled into town, didn't you?" Ken took the other devil and heaved it onto the scale. "$224. You killed these suckers on Devil's Mountain, right? Well, the witch is on..." Ken raised his eyebrows at Ballantine.

"Witch's Mountain?" Ballantine finished.

Ken laughed as they left the cooler and said, "You catch on quick."

"Clever names."

"They got real names. Been about 20 years since all them things moved in though. People been naming the mountains after them since. 'Goin' huntin' Devil's Mountain.' 'Don't let your kids play on Witch's Mountain.'"

"And the third mountain?"

Ken took a moment to reminisce before saying, "The Cave Worm's Mountain."

Ballantine had never heard of a cave worm. A younger Del would've assumed silly local superstition, but he'd been around long enough to know never to assume. "What can you tell me about this cave worm?"

"What, you think you gon' get it? You see all these stuffed animals I got in here? You think I have the time to just put together display models? These are all for people who heard about the thing, didn't listen to a damn word anybody told 'em, and went and got themselves killed before they could pick up their orders. If you go after the cave worm, you ain't... coming... back."

"Why?"

"How am I supposed to know, man? I'm here. The I-don't-know-how-old rumor is that it does, like, a telepathy thing. Pulls you in like gravity. Stops you controlling yourself and just makes you walk to it." Ken looked out into nowhere as if remembering. "You can tell you're getting close when the woods go quiet. No birds, no squirrels, no shug monkeys, or hunner dyers. The closer you get, the less you feel like turning back. That's how you know you should. When those woods get quiet and you don't want to go home anymore, go the fuck home while the choice is still yours. Better yet, go the fuck home now."

"You seem to know plenty about this thing."

Ken fixed his narrowed eyes onto Ballantine's, took a few moments to decide how much to say, then said, "One man made it back. He's fucking insane now. He came back, said just enough for us to put all that together, then lost the rest of his goddamn mind. That's how I know about it. You want to find out for yourself? Go ahead. You ain't the first tough guy to get his ass eaten. You won't be the last either."

"Easy there, partner. I never do anything without foolproof preparation."

"Yeah, I've heard that too."

The door to the mobile home opened to reveal a beautiful, fair-skinned brunette who looked to be about 20 years old.

"You about ready for some lunch, baby?" she said, stepping into the shack. She wore short cutoff shorts, a loose tank top, and a necklace.

After her figure, it was the necklace that caught Ballantine's eye. The little green jewels sparkled in the shadows as she padded over to the men. Ballantine thought for a moment the jewels were, in fact, glowing, but decided there was probably just some optical science behind it that he didn't understand.

"Baby," said Ken, "shouldn't you be inside?" He cast a sidelong glance at the mesmerized monster hunter.

"Oh baby," she pouted, "this is as close as I get to getting out."

"Yeah, but still—"

"But, but, but," she jibed. "Chalk it up to cabin fever."

As she stepped into better light, Ballantine stole a glance at her tenting nipples before being taken by her eyes. He'd seen beautiful eyes before. At least, he thought he had. But these sparkled as vibrantly as the jewels she wore. These were deeper than the rest. These told him nebulous stories of hopeful love.

If her eyes were the lure, her smile was the hook. Ballantine was dumbstruck. He'd never seen anything like it.

She extended an elegant hand, saying, "I'm Jenny."

Ballantine snapped out of it, glanced from Ken to her as he took her hand, and said, "Dallanti—Ballantine... Del Ballantine." He kicked himself, shook it out, then went on the offensive. "That's a really pretty necklace you got there."

"Thank you," she smiled and pressed her fingertips to it, at which point Ballantine noticed the wedding ring on her hand. "I got it from my mother."

"Lucky girl," he said. Then he looked at Ken and said, "Lucky husband too."

"Don't I know it," Ken said. Then he said to Jenny, "Look baby, why don't you fix me a plate and I'll be right there."

"Sure thing, baby," she said. "It was nice to meet you, Mr. Ballantine."

"Nice to meet you, Jenny."

The door closed behind her, shutting off the tingle in Ballantine's heart and taking a little extra with it.

Ken counted out the money and asked, "So how long you gonna be in town, Mr. Ballantine?"

"As long as it takes."

"$440... one, two, three, four. Heh. Guess you'll be staying a while, then."

"You think?"

"Take you all year and a team to get all them wood devils, and they'll probably just migrate anyway. Plus, you'd never get all the ones on Witch Mountain, assuming she's still there."

"Why?"

"She got the whole thing spelled. You can hike and hike but never gain any ground. Walk an hour, walk a day. Soon as you turn around, you'll see you never went anywhere."

"No getting through it?"

"No. No getting through it. Now go on, hunt your devils, and your hellcats, and your gremlins. Just make sure you get 'em to me before you go after the witch or the cave worm. Be a shame if they all went to waste."

As Del Ballantine drove to the hotel, his thoughts bounced from the cave worm, to the witch, to Jenny. Jenny... what was a girl like that doing with an old timer like Ken? Mail-order bride? He's doing good business. Couldn't rule out a trophy wife. Couldn't rule out a witch and a spell either. “Keep your guard up, Del,” he thought to himself. But what would a witch like her want with him if she could go anywhere and have anybody? And as for the cave worm, he's never met an adversary who didn't have a weakness. There's always a way. To believe otherwise is to accept defeat before working on a solution.

CHAPTER 3

The Foothill Hotel and Bar was, like Steen's General Store, a compound of sorts. The property, which contained the hotel and its parking lot, was surrounded by an eight-foot wall. There were gates on all sides, but the front one saw the bulk of the work. It was usually left open. During the night, when the beasts were most active, it was manned.

Depending on the time of night it would either be Joe Markovich or Dave Kovak taking watch. Both of them were retired; not much use on a farm anymore, but they could still handle a gun and a gate. Joe would get there around sunset and, before taking his post on the rusty folding chair, walk the lot to make sure no "critters" had stowed away. Though the hotel was nearer the mountains than Steen's General, it wasn't subjected to many more visits from stray monsters. Joe or Dave typically only had to kill a hell-critter every once in a while. Kelly, the owner, gave them each $20 per night, but the peace of mind was priceless.

Many of the patrons came for that very thing—the chance to relax. The strong would come for a beer and leave. The weary would find reasons to prolong their stay. That's not to say everyone who stuck around was weary. The Foothill Hotel and Bar was the only such place for miles, and the Trinity band (made up of Jeremy, Ariana, and Reggie) was the only thing they had for entertainment.

Dave Kovak was at the gate when Ballantine pulled up. The old-timer pushed a hand down repeatedly to signal for the hunter to slow down. Ballantine thought his speed was fine. He gave a polite wave to the gatekeeper before almost slamming into a parked car. Did he have the right place? When he checked in earlier, he couldn't imagine the parking lot ever filling up. Now it was packed, and here he was, trying to squeeze his little pickup truck in between a couple of monstrous ones.

As he turned the key, the rumble of the engine gave way to the bass of the band inside. He looked up at the hotel in an effort to gauge the effect of the noise on the rest of the building. Seeing as he was staying on the second floor, it didn't look like he was going to be getting much sleep until the band finished.

Ballantine had checked in in the early evening before setting out to hunt. The Foothill wasn't a modern hotel by any standard. It made the hunter think of the hotels of the Old West, saloon on the bottom, rooms on top. He didn't know those places still existed. He reminded himself of how far out in the country he was, then decided he probably shouldn't be too surprised.

There had only been a few pickup trucks in the lot when he arrived, making him think the word, "HOTEL," on the sign might have been a relic. The unattended concierge desk was just inside the door. The bar, at which a few regulars sat, lay immediately ahead. It was three sides of a rectangle, attached to the kitchen wall on the left, and it stuck out a little more than halfway into the room. Against the wall on the right were little square tables covered with plastic red-and-white-checkered tablecloths sporting the usual salt, pepper, sugar, and ketchup containers. A few people sat at those, eating dinner. Beyond the bar was an open area with some larger tables that could be moved for dancing or events. In the corner was a small stage with a PA system and a drum set. To Ballantine's left, just before the bar, was an opening that led to the staircase.

He had seated himself at a barstool two down from a haggard and frail-looking man who never looked up from his coffee. The hunter had tried to make small talk with the man while he waited for help.

"That's some drive into town, huh?" Ballantine said.

The man mumbled something the monster hunter couldn't quite make out.

"I was starting to think I got bad directions until I saw those mountains."

Again, the man mumbled something unintelligible.

Ballantine decided the man was having a rough day and wasn't in the mood for conversation, so he got to the point. "Don't suppose you know if management's around, do you?"

The man raised his sandpaper voice. His lips and teeth and tongue shaped consonants and vowels, but failed to arrange them into anything that resembled English. His eyes were a prisoner's. He took another sip and set his cup down hard enough to slosh out a dribble.

Behind the bar, the kitchen door swung open and Kelly stepped out. She was a blond woman, about 50, whose overall appearance was indicative of someone who ran a hotel and bar all by herself. She wore her hair in a ponytail to keep it out of her baggy eyes and off her cratered cheeks. Under her black Foothill Hotel and Bar t-shirt, her old bra was more of a tradition than a comfort as the elastic had months ago stretched to its limit. At least it kept her breasts in front of her. The equator of her paunch gave her high-waisted jeans just enough ledge to cling to.

"Okay Sam," she said to the man. She turned to Ballantine and said, "That's Sam. He doesn't say much."

"Sorry about that," said Ballantine to both of them.

Kelly waved off his apology and asked him his business.

Ballantine said he was in town for hunting and could use a room if she had one.

She showed him upstairs to a room on the second floor. It was a bare-bones deal. There was a twin bed, a chair, a dresser, a closet, and a lamp and a clock on a nightstand. The bathroom was at the end of the hall, and he'd be sharing it with the one other tenant on his floor. If it was occupied and he had an emergency, he could use the one in the bar. Otherwise, she'd prefer not to have to clean the vacant third floor's bathroom any more than was necessary.

The band turned out not to be as loud as Ballantine had expected. It was too loud for normal conversation, but not so loud that one couldn't be had with raised voices. The locals around the bar stared at Ballantine as he entered—sweaty, bloody, and dirty. There wasn't anything uncommon about a sight like him walking through that bar, but other than the band, new faces were the closest thing the people of Brothers had for entertainment. So they stared at him as he looked the place over again. Couple of small tables open. Sam still on his stool against the wall with a pair open next to him. The three-piece band in the corner doing some kind of folk/country/funk/rock concoction Ballantine thought might have been a little too progressive for the audience. Then he remembered the town probably didn't have a whole lot of options for bands. The bass player was a cute redhead. Cute for all he could tell from across the room, anyway. Great hair: thick, curly, and swept over from the right to the left. The white-haired guy Ballantine recognized from the general store joked with the waitress and nudged his clerk.

Ballantine caught eyes with Kelly behind the bar. She nodded. He waved and went upstairs.

The floor buzzed on every other beat. Then the tempo changed and it buzzed for longer than it didn't. Then the time signature changed and the floor buzzed irregularly. Ballantine dropped his gear off in his room and headed for the shower.

The tile floor was already wet when he stepped in. Someone had beaten him to it. He hoped for hot water and got it. All in all, it wasn't the worst shower he'd ever had. The nozzle had good pressure, and the spider up in the corner seemed to be keeping the bugs away. The sight of the dirty water swirling into the drain was therapeutic.

He stepped out into the hall and saw a taller, well-built, and well-dressed man coming out of the room across from his.

"Well," said the man with a very proper, very familiar English accent, "don't you clean up nice."

Ballantine humored him with a smile and an, "I have my moments."

"Tell me, I know you probably aren't keen on conversation in just your towel, but will you be heading downstairs at all? I should very much like to buy you a drink and speak with you about your impressive take tonight. Two wood devils is quite the challenge."

The more exterminators, the better, was Ballantine's philosophy. He said, "Sure. And I got four tonight. Not two," then closed his bedroom door behind him.

The band played on, covers interspersed with originals and improvisational jams. Some of the lyrics came so quickly, they were on to the chorus before Ballantine had picked out five words. The locals, entertained as much by the Brit's accent as they were by his stories of travel, disengaged him to look at Ballantine as he entered. Taking a cue, the Brit turned around, smiled at the monster hunter, and gestured to the seat between Sam and himself.

Ballantine pulled the stool a couple of inches away from Sam and had a seat. Kelly put a bar napkin down in front of him and asked what she could get him.

"Whiskey on the rocks," he said.

"Single or double?" she asked.

"Si—"

"Give him a double," the Brit said, "of the good stuff. This one's on me."

"Thanks, man."

"You want food?" Kelly asked.

Ballantine realized he should eat and said, "Sure. Got a menu?"

"No. We can make you pretty much anything, though: chicken, beef, fish... other. Wood devil is cheapest. It's what most people do. And we make it better than anybody else."

"Wood devil burger, then?"

"Mushrooms and gravy?"

"Is lettuce/tomato possible?" He hated the texture of mushrooms.

Kelly nodded and asked, "French fries or frog goblin legs?"

Frog goblins were named because of their proximity in appearance and habit to frogs. At a glance, it was easy to mistake one for another. They both lived near water. They had long, strong legs and small, weak arms. They tended to crouch when at rest and make great leaps when on the move. They mostly ate bugs, but were known to attack rodents on occasion. Frog goblins had little fangs that could puncture human skin, but they hadn't attacked anyone in years. Not since humans figured out how to deal with them.

"French fries, please," said Ballantine. He wasn't in the mood for frog goblin legs.

Kelly leaned her head into the kitchen to shout the order at the cook.

"Well," said the Brit, "now that the important things are out of the way, I'm Nigel. Nigel Carrington."

"Del Ballantine," he said as they shook hands.

"Del... Delbert? Delmar?"

"Delaney."

"That was my next guess. Delaney Ballantine. Strong name for a strong man."

"Del's fine. And what's your story, Mr. Carrington?"

"Please, Nigel. Nigel's the name and game is the game, ha, ha! I travel the world looking for the thrillingest hunts. I tell you I was disappointed by the relative ease with which I was able to take down a wood devil. Mind you, I was still happy to have been able to hunt it, but it gave me no more thrill than a lion or tiger which, up to now, were the most dangerous game I've hunted. I thought at least I'd get a nice trophy out of it. But as I left the lodge and saw you hauling two, my imagination went wild. Now there's a thrill! *There's* the next challenge. Bagging more than one of a creature whose pack takes off once you've nailed one and then returns in greater numbers if you haven't left the scene in time."

"You say you got two?" asked one of the men next to Nigel.

"He got four, he tells me, Rick. Rick, Louis, and Andy, this is Del Ballantine—Master Hunter, no doubt."

The three of them looked like farmers. Rick Jenkins, who sat at the corner of the bar, next to Nigel, wore a John Deere hat on his head and broken blood vessels on his nose. He looked to be the oldest of the three—pushing 60. Louis Malone, on the other side of the corner, had black hair, a goatee, and olive skin tinged red. Both he and Andy Tumpkins wore white tank tops. Although they weren't young, they were younger than Rick. Andy's overbite came with a diastema between each of his teeth. He had short red hair and bright pink cheeks.

"Four?!" Rick said.

"Bullshit," sang Louis.

Ballantine chortled into his glass, said, "Believe what you want," then took a sip. It was the good stuff alright.

"What he say?" asked Andy, who was a little too far away to hear with the band playing.

"He said he killed four wood devils tonight," said Louis. "And I'm calling bullshit."

Andy laughed and said, "Yeah, right."

"I ain't trying to impress you," Ballantine said.

"Could've fooled *me*," said Louis.

"You're doing that yourself."

"You didn't kill four wood devils!"

"Gentlemen! Gentlemen!" Nigel waved his hands, accidentally caught Kelly's attention, said, "Yes, another beer, please," then turned to Louis. "Perhaps Mr. Ballantine has some wisdom he'd like to share with us. After all, people used to be sure the world was flat, didn't they?" He turned to his left and said, "Now then, Mr. Ballantine, what was it? Special traps I imagine, yes?"

"You could say that," Ballantine said.

"I should've thought so. What did you use? Bait and snare? Dig a pit? Claymore mines? Ha, ha!"

"Myself."

"Bullshit!" said Louis.

"Do go on, Mr. Ballantine," said Nigel, giddy at the thought of using himself as bait.

The "master hunter" cast his eyes at his empty glass. Nigel took the hint. He waved a finger at Kelly to order another, then wriggled in anticipation.

"They take off when you fire at long range, right?" Ballantine said.

"Indeed," said Nigel.

"And they don't group close enough together to kill more than one with one shot, right?"

"Indeed!" Nigel's inflection rose with his excitement.

"So you have to lure them in close to you."

"Said the lunatic," Louis said.

Andy laughed. He didn't really hear the conversation. He just knew he supported Louis' opinion.

"I didn't say it was for everyone," Ballantine said.

"How do you get them in close to you?" Nigel asked.

"Same way you lure them anywhere—blood. Smear some on your skin, sweat through it, let the wind pick it up. They'll come right to you, surround you—"

"And kill you and eat you before you can blink," said Louis.

"The trick is to get them close enough for their blood lust to overpower their sense of self-preservation, but at the same time, have them far enough away that you can get your shots off. You gotta be perfect though. I'm not recommending it to any of you."

"Because you didn't do it."

"Easy, chief. I got nothing to prove to you. I just answered a question."

"Indeed, Louis. Whether Mr. Ballantine is lying or not doesn't affect you in the long run. However, I did see him, with my own eyes, dragging two freshly dead and gutted wood devils into Ken's Taxidermy not two hours ago."

"Gutted?" said Rick. "You know they pay—"

"—for the guts too," said Ballantine, "I know now. Thanks."

Nigel continued, "Anyway, I'm sure he'll have proof enough soon enough."

"Don't hold your breath," said Ballantine.

Louis scoffed.

Andy took his cue from Louis and scoffed too.

"What? Why?" asked Nigel, disappointed.

"First off, I don't usually take trophies."

"And why not?"

"I'm always on the move and I don't have the room."

Louis scoffed.

Andy scoffed too.

"Secondly, I didn't have the time or muscle to get all four back to the truck. Those two you saw were all I could bring back."

"Well, isn't that convenient?" Louis said.

Andy scoffed.

"If I did believe you," Louis said, "I'd say that ain't very sporting of you."

"I do say he has a point," said Nigel. "Not very sporting at all."

"I'm not in it for the sport," said Ballantine.

Louis said a little too emphatically, "Tell us, oh master hunter, what you *are* in it for, then."

Del Ballantine set his empty glass down and said, "Eradication."

Kelly laid his burger down and asked if he wanted another drink.

"Just a beer this time, thanks," he said.

"Eradication?" Nigel said.

Louis laughed and said, "What, you think you're just gonna come in here and clean house?"

"Worked out okay in the last ten-or-so towns," Ballantine said to his burger.

Rick interjected, "Say now, this town gets a lot of business from people coming to hunt wood devil."

"Judging by the amount of people renting rooms here, I'd say you and I have different ideas about the words 'a lot.' Besides, I'm sure you'll get just as many when the deer repopulate."

"Back up," Nigel said. "Last ten towns. Have you been eradicating that long?"

"What are you?" Louis asked. "Buffalo Bill?"

"Who's Buffalo Bill?" Nigel asked.

Ballantine explained, "A guy who helped put bison on the endangered species list when they were building the railroads in this country. Pissed off a lot of Indians too."

"Well then, don't you think you might, uh, piss off the locals? I mean it isn't very sporting to just go and exterminate game."

"It isn't game!" said Ballantine, slamming his burger down. "It's an invasive species! Do you know what the difference is? People used to be able to leave their homes unarmed! We used to be at the top of the fucking food chain. Worst we had to deal with was an errant bear or mountain lion... and even those were easy enough to avoid. Now we gotta worry about wood devils and hellcats... wyverns, witches, cave worms..."

The other men looked up from their drinks at him. Even Sam turned to look at Del Ballantine.

"Did you just say you've hunted wyvern?" Nigel asked.

Ballantine took a bite out of his burger and said with a bulging cheek, "Yeah."

"Might I ask where?"

"You might," Ballantine said before swallowing. "But you wouldn't find any there now."

"Who told you about the cave worm?" Rick asked.

Ballantine got the feeling it was supposed to be a secret, so he just said, "You know these small towns. Word travels fast."

"You ain't thinking of going after it are you?"

"Not yet. Looks like I'll be in town a while though. Anything I should know?"

"Yeah, leave it alone! If it doesn't kill you, you'll lose your mind like..."

Ballantine watched their eyes flick over his shoulder.

"What's a cave worm?" Nigel asked.

"Cave worm?" came a smoky female voice from behind Ballantine. "That old story?"

Ballantine was no stylist, but even he could tell her hairdo was a little behind the times. Vibrant and blond, it reminded him of Marilyn Monroe's hair. It was wavy and bouncy, but tight, its restrictive perfection belying the blitheness for which it strove. Her clothing choices spoke to youth, but that's about where they ended. Where Ballantine was from, women her age didn't show off their legs in short denim skirts, even if they *were* as nice as hers. They didn't wear tight tops and push up their tits anymore, even if they *did* still have the body for it. They didn't paint their faces as much either, but that wasn't to say she looked cartoonish. It was just more than Ballantine expected from any of the women in this town. She was aging well, though. Her big blue eyes sparkled like new. Her cheekbones were high and pronounced, creating shadows below, accentuating the slight droop of her heavy lips. Everything about her, along with the lighting in the bar and the blue stones on her ears, conspired to distract from the telltale lines around her eyes and mouth, creases on her neck, and the dappling on her décolleté.

Nigel decided she'd been a hard 10 in a past life. The Brit put her at about a 7.5 now. He was a little younger than the monster hunter and still concerned himself with the 10-point scale. Ballantine's scale was simple. He either would, or he wouldn't. In this case he thought, "I might."

"Why you gotta go telling tall tales to tourists, Rick?" she said.

"He's the one who brought it up," Rick said, pointing.

"What's a cave worm?" Nigel asked again.

"Really?" she said to Rick, ignoring Nigel. "And who might he be?"

Ballantine decided he'd had enough questions for one night and said, "Just a tourist looking to shoot a wood devil here or there."

"Nonsense!" said Nigel. "This is Del Ballantine, the prolific monster hunter!"

Ballantine boiled inside for letting himself get roped into conversation.

"...slayer of wyverns...," Nigel continued. "...who, this very night, exterminated not one, not two, not three, but four, yes four, wood devils on a single hunt. The Buffalo Bill of monster hunters."

"And of course," Louis said, "he has no proof to back up any of it."

"My, my," the blond said.

"Well I believe him," Nigel said. "I saw him with the two devils and that's a feat in itself."

She extended her hand to Ballantine and said, "I'm Jessica. Jessica Waters."

Ballantine wiped the salt and wood devil juice off his fingers and took her hand saying, "Del Ballantine."

"And Nigel Carrington at your service, madam," said the Brit, taking her hand between both of his own. "The pleasure is entirely mine."

"Such a gentleman!" Jessica said. She raised her eyebrows at the three farmers and said, "You boys paying attention? You'd get a lot farther in life if you acted like him."

"Ain't that hard to get far with *you,*" said Louis.

Andy almost shot his beer out of his nose. He kept it in, but it was burning up where it shouldn't have been. He spent the next couple of minutes trying to snort it back down.

"Louis," Nigel said, "where I'm from, we treat a lady with a little more dignity."

"Yeah?" Louis said. "But how do you treat *whores* where you're from?"

Nigel smacked his hand on the counter and stood up sharply. Louis slammed his beer down and shot up in his seat. He suddenly realized Nigel's physique outmatched his. He hoped the Brit was softer than he looked.

Kelly had been watching Jessica since she walked in and shouted, "Hey!" so loudly the band almost stopped. She pointed at Nigel, then down at his chair. He sat. She stuck her finger in Louis' face and said, "This is the only bar for 25 miles. Do you want to get banned for fighting?"

Louis' pride didn't let him answer.

Kelly moved on to Nigel and said, "There's no fighting in my bar, you got me?"

"Loud and clear, Kelly," Nigel said. He was mortified for having, as he saw it, lost his temper like that.

As far as anyone can remember, Kelly had never liked Jessica.

The only reason she hadn't banned her from the bar was so she could keep some kind of an eye on her. As Kelly's eyes fell on Jessica, the owner's mouth curled into a sneer. Her hand trembled as she pointed, saying, "...and you..."

"Kelly," said Jessica, "I didn't do—"

"I don't care!" Kelly's voice broke over the last word. "If there's any more trouble and you're near it, you're outta here!"

"Okay!"

"And I know I told you not to come within ten feet of my husband!"

Jessica craned her neck to see Sam on the other side of Ballantine. Kelly had told her a long time ago never even to look at him and she had obeyed. He was always in the same chair, so it had been easy enough. She would make note of the figure in her periphery and never glance at it, closing her eyes or casting them down if she needed to cross close by. It would've hurt her to look anyway. It hurt now. Sam used to be strapping, rugged, and handsome like Mr. Ballantine. He had arms like pythons and a chest like a tree trunk. Now he was a skeleton in a bag of skin. His hair was greasy and dull. Stray whiskers glimmered on his gaunt jaw. He drooped over an Irish coffee like a wilting bluebell. Jessica's nostalgic bubble popped, forcing tears into her eyes.

"Don't look at him either!" Kelly's own eyes welled.

"I'm sorry! I didn't see him there with Mr. Ballantine—"

"He's *always* right there! Keep it moving... like you always do."

Jessica forced her chin up and made her way to the low-top nearest the band. She tried to focus on the music. They were singing a song about not being able to go back in time to change things. It wasn't what she needed to hear. Her head was a bingo machine. Memories of rights and wrongs bounced around with shoudas and couldas, rattling her head, pounding her heart, pushing up more tears.

A tap on Jessica's shoulder made her jump.

Laura Krause, the young waitress, stood over her with a gin and tonic, Jessica's usual. A bewildered Jessica took it instinctively, although she didn't remember placing an order. Laura pointed across the bar where Nigel raised a glass and a corner of his mouth. She mirrored his half smile, raised her glass, and took a sip. The drink was good. She raised her glass again to thank him. He returned the gesture and the two went back to their respective business.

The gin and tonic tasted like Christmas. That's why Jessica liked it. As much as she liked spring, and as hard as travel was in the snow, Christmastime had always calmed her. She wasn't even Christian. She just enjoyed the fantasy of peace on earth and good will toward men. That was her escape from the life for which she had almost no one to blame but herself: Christmastime, gin and tonics, and the blanket of snow that silenced the world.

She tuned back in to hear the beginning of a song about "living in a small town even though you feel like you're meant for more." It was more tolerable to Jessica. She had just begun to bob her head along when a younger man with lust in his eyes sat next to her and offered her a bar napkin for a tissue. She smiled graciously and dabbed her eyes.

He said his name was Bobby. He was handsome—baby faced. Apart from the callouses on his hands, the rest of his skin was soft and tan. His deep-set eyes boasted experience he didn't know he didn't have, but that didn't matter much to Jessica. She took it all ways. At the very least, she was happy she could still attract the attention of a man so young—a boy. After all, this town wasn't completely dead. There were girls his age to chase—girls more supple, more nubile... but then again, girls who wouldn't do *half* the things an experienced woman would. Girls his age weren't as sure a lay as Jessica, either.

She used to be ashamed of it. It used to make her feel cheap to look in a man's eyes and see nothing but his lust, to know he only cared more about what he could put *in* her mouth than what came *out* of it. It had made her feel like a bucket of slime being felt up, turned on, and penetrated. She had felt the town's eyes on her, judging her wherever she went. She had wanted to tell them she couldn't help it, that it wasn't her fault.

Then one day, the shame ceased to bother her. It was like a

virus that had run its course. She had woken up and felt fine. The daggers in other women's eyes couldn't touch her. The grimy clutches of the men became strong and comforting. The arrows of degradations both whispered and shouted no longer found their mark. Guilty pleasure became ecstatic rapture. She had accepted herself, and she had been happier for it.

Jessica sniffled, sighed, smiled, and said, "Well, what a gentleman."

She did with Bobby as she'd done with so many others. She flirted with him. She laughed at his crass jokes. She let him buy the drinks and put his hands on her. She let him slide his nose behind her ear and tickle her neck with his breath.

The two pretended they were only semi-visible, sitting just outside the throw of the tin cans Kelly called stage lights. Jessica liked that spot. It was a little darker than the rest of the bar, and it was far enough away from Sam. She never had to feel bad about how little the men really cared to talk to her there, because the band was just loud enough to make talking a chore anyway. Plus, it always gave her the opportunity to tease Jeremy Crawford, the singer/songwriter/guitarist she'd never been able to seduce.

CHAPTER 4

Jeremy was aware of Jessica's interest in him, but he never had too much of a problem with her. Things were uncomfortable for a while at first. She didn't take his rejection well. Such a thing rarely happened, and when it did, it didn't last long. The more he resisted, the harder she tried, until one night when she forced herself on him.

It had been out in the parking lot as the bar closed. Jeremy had just put his guitar in the back seat and turned around in time for Jessica to press him up against his car. She kissed him and ground her hips against his saying, "Come on, baby. I know you want it. You're a man, after all."

Jeremy pushed her away saying, "Get offa me!"

"*Hey*!" came Kelly's voice from the doorway.

Jessica backed away from Jeremy with a look that said, "Someday," then left.

Since then, however, Jessica's flirtation with Jeremy was little more than playful banter, passing catcalls Jeremy brushed off as "Jessica being Jessica." As long as she wasn't accosting him or interfering in his business, he didn't mind her so much.

That's not to say Jessica was shallow. She genuinely felt for him, mostly because of his sick mother. Everyone did. If she thought she had more than her body to offer him, she would have offered it. She threw him a wink and a smile while Bobby ran his nose through her hair.

Jeremy half smiled, shook his head, and kept singing. He couldn't help being a little bit flattered, even though he knew the woman would fuck anything with a pulse. He *was* a man, after all.

The song broke into an instrumental part and Jeremy stepped away from the mic. He turned to join the rest of his band.

Ariana stared a thousand yards past the stage lights, bobbing her head, spaced out in the groove. Her thick scarlet curls waved like a heavy flag in a light breeze. She wore her bass so high that it cradled and accentuated her right breast, inspiring some of the men at the bar to regularly remark, "She's the only reason I come here."

Jeremy hoped Ariana would go home with him that night. She'd been going home with Reggie a lot lately and the singer was feeling left out. Ari didn't want anything complicated and had made it clear from the very start that neither of the boys had a claim to her—that she would do what she wanted, when she wanted, with whom she wanted, and that if either one of them had a problem with it, then they were done.

Jeremy didn't want to complain, but he was getting frustrated, and not just sexually. He'd been fed up with the town for a while. He watched the days tick by as he did the same things over and over, never getting anywhere—never getting anything more done than a new song written. Sure, he knew songwriting was nothing to sneeze at, that he was doing something comparatively special. Every time he finished a song, he thought about how all the other people in town were content to do the same job every day until their time ran out. He considered himself lucky, and allowed himself a brief celebration before sinking back into the frustration of wasting away in a two-bit town. Kelly, his friends, and a few bar patrons here and there would compliment him on his work, but he took it with a grain of salt. What do they know? What are they going to say to one of their only musicians? "Actually, you suck?" "I didn't like that one?" "We're thinking of going a different direction with our entertainment?" And back down into disgruntlement he went.

Reggie's charisma and positivity helped keep Jeremy going. The drummer charmed everyone. Nobody stayed sad or angry if they talked to Reggie long enough—even if they were angry at Reggie. He was a master of rapport, a fountain of positivity, and if all else failed, his grin alone was contagious.

To Reggie, life was a little boat adrift in the ocean of time. There were crests and valleys, storms and doldrums, murky waters and crystal-clear lagoons. People could paddle all they wanted, but the ocean would do what it wanted to do, and someday it would eat the boat. Nobody makes it to land. The philosophy relaxed him. If he didn't get something he wanted one day, maybe he would the next. There was no telling what was on the other side of the next crest. Whatever it was, was coming for him either way, and he considered it part of the fun of life.

Ever the social butterfly, Pete Steen chatted his way around the room. He asked about this person's family and that person's recent purchase. "How's she doing?" "How's the thing I sold you working out?" Although he invested himself in every conversation, he always kept an eye and an ear on the band. Everyone was special or interesting to Pete, but in his eyes, the band itself was even more special. That's how he always said it—"Even more special." "Supernatural" would be the word he would have settled on if it had come to him. In all his years, he'd never seen anything like the band. In reality, *no one* had.

Pete worked his way through almost as many drinks as people. His gesticulations grew wilder. His laugh became more boisterous. His eyes more twinkly.

Max hovered near enough to Pete to not look aloof, but far enough away to not have to join in any conversation. He wore his black-leather bomber because it wouldn't retain the stink of smoke as long as a fabric jacket would. Since he didn't like to be drunk and would be driving, he nursed a rum and Coke for the better part of their visit. There were really only two people in the room he would've cared to have a conversation with. One was busy on stage, and the other was busy serving tables.

Laura wouldn't have minded his conversation either. She did Max the courtesy of a quick "hello" and "howyadoing" earlier in the night, but otherwise didn't have time for people with full glasses who weren't hungry. “One of these days,” she thought. One of these days, she'd talk to him some more. She'd *have* to if for no other reason than to maintain her sanity. That was one of the thoughts her mind circled back to throughout the night. “One of these days, talk to Max. When? At the store. He's busy then. And I'm at work the rest of the time. We had time once, though. Because I *made* time. What if we got married? I'd probably end up working in the store. Can't have that. Didn't go to school for nothing. Getting out of this town. When? Hell if I know. I'm gonna go crazy soon though. Wish I had someone to vent to. Max would be good. One of these days I'll talk to Max.”

"Thanks everybody," said Jeremy into the microphone. "We're gonna take a little break and get some lubrication. Back in a bit."

A few people clapped as the band hopped down from the stage. They hadn't made it three steps when the jovially inebriated Pete Steen appeared in front of them, arms outstretched.

"You guys were *fantastic*!" he said. "I mean, really."

The band deflected the compliment with downcast smiles. Pete did this every night—got drunk and told them they were the best thing he's ever seen.

"You're the best thing I've ever seen! And I've been around, you know."

"We know Pete," said the amused Jeremy.

"You tell us every night," said Ari.

"Now, now," said Reggie playing along, "let the man speak. He's obviously very knowledgeable and worldly."

"You're *damn right*!" said Pete, putting a hand on Reggie's shoulder, partially out of thanks, partially for balance.

"Come on, dad," said Max. "Time to go."

"Now, now, now," Pete said, waving everyone off, "I'm serious now. You kids are something special. Need to get yourselves on to something bigger and better than *this* dump."

"I *heard* that!" Kelly called from the bar.

"You know what I mean!" Pete called back, flipping a hand at her.

The hotel owner rolled her eyes and half smiled.

Reggie patted Pete on the shoulder.

Jeremy said, "Glad you enjoyed it, Pete."

Ariana got that sinking feeling she had at the store earlier. She caught eyes with Max and said, "Get home safe."

As father and son turned to leave, Reggie looked around and patted his pockets.

"What's up?" asked Jeremy.

"Feels like I'm forgetting something," Reggie said.

"Beer?"

"That's probably it."

Dave Kovak watched from his folding chair as the Steens came out of the bar. It was the most interesting thing he'd had to look at in a while. Max stopped Pete in an open area of the lot and patted his dad's chest.

"You wait here while I get the car," Max said. "We're packed in like sardines."

As Max walked away, Pete tried to pat his shoulder but missed.

Pete's last words were, "Did we pay the tab?"

He was checking his pockets to make sure he hadn't forgotten anything when the hell vulture struck. Up until the Events of Pittsburgh, the Andean condor was not only the largest vulture, but the largest flying bird on Earth. Now that title belonged to the hell vulture. At 33 pounds, the birds weighed roughly the same, but the hell vulture's wingspan topped the Andean's by three feet for a total of 13, perfect for silent gliding. Its head was mostly gnarled beak. Its feet, mostly talon. It bore no feathers, but was covered with marbled gray skin and sparse wiry hairs. Whereas Earth vultures primarily stick to the dead or dying, hell vultures were bred for torture.

Lucky for Pete, he was liquored up. A few of his last moments were spent trying to figure out why suddenly he was face to face with gravel.

Dave jumped up faster than he had in a long time and took aim with his shotgun, but stopped himself short of firing in the direction of the hotel. He drew his pistol as he ran his bowed old legs as fast as they'd go toward a better position.

After a couple of taps, the vulture found the squishy parts on either side of Pete's spine, opened its beak, and dug it in.

Electric fiery pain exploded in Pete's lower back.

Dave took aim, but before he could fire, Max pulled the truck into the way and jumped out, pistol drawn.

The bird clamped its beak and pulled, snapping Pete's spinal cord from its roots, pulling with it yarns of guts that had snagged on it.

Pete tried to stay calm. He clawed weakly at the gravel, afraid to ask himself why his legs weren't working. There was fire in his back and belly. There was blood in his stomach that he couldn't quite throw up. It kept getting caught in his throat and swallowed back down.

BLAM! BLAM! BLAM! BLAM! BLAM! BLAM! click click click click click click...

Max emptied his gun into the vulture's body and it fell dead. He ran to it and pulled it off of Pete. It was awkward, like trying to toss aside a leafy tree branch. He assessed his father's damage as the majority of the bar patrons came out, weapons drawn.

Pete tried to talk but could only gurgle. He made a squeezing motion with his hand. Max took it.

Laura pushed her way through the people saying, "Look out! Look out! I'm a nurse!" However, when she saw the glistening red hole and twisted vertebrae, she lost her confidence and forgot her training, not that it would have helped her anyway.

Ballantine turned to Louis and spat, "*This* is why I do what I do." Then he caught Nigel's eye for assurance. The Brit gave it to him with a nod.

Ariana's sinking feeling gave way to nausea as she stepped around the crowd. Her joints turned to jelly. Her heart climbed into her throat. Her lungs fought to get out of her chest. She was used to this by now. Correction: She *should've* been used to this by now. She had *thought* she was. People got mauled, eaten, taken from this town all the time. It was nothing new. As sure as the full moon comes back around, someone's number comes up sooner rather than later.

So why did tears stream down her face? It had been a long time since she'd cried. Why did she kneel in the gravel? Why did she take Pete's other hand? Why did she sob uncontrollably when she felt that hand relax?

It had been a long time since there was a serious attack at the hotel. A few of the bystanders got a conversation started about other attacks they either saw or heard about from someone who told someone who told someone else. A few others carried the vulture to the incinerator in the basement. Some put their arms around the stoic Max and told him it would be all right. Dave apologized. Max assured him he understood. Jeremy was the first to reach Ariana, who buried her face in his shoulder as he embraced her. Some people said some words. Kelly called the sheriff.

The town of Brothers, being as small as it was, didn't have much in the way of emergency services. It'd been without a doctor since Laura Krause's father died. Brothers relied heavily on Dunkard, its nearest neighbor about 10 miles west. Despite the distance, emergency crews had seen their fair share of the town over the years. Especially Sheriff Landry. He always wished he could do more, but Dunkard had its own troubles.

The sheriff was tall, with kind, weathered eyes and a bushy salt-and-pepper mustache. He had a warmth in his voice that put most people at ease. He used it that night to calm the people one by one while they waited for the coroner.

"You wanna talk, Ariana?" he asked.

She shrugged.

Jeremy let her go and said, "I'll just be inside."

"What's on your mind, darling?" Sheriff Landry asked the girl.

She shook her head to organize her thoughts but couldn't make anything stick. "Just... everything," she said. "I don't know why I'm crying. I don't remember the last time I did."

"That might be part of your problem. Ain't good to hold on to grief... or anger... or anything bad like 'at."

"Yeah well I don't see how it does any good to let it out either."

"Got emotions for a reason, Ari."

"Yeah well, crying doesn't bring anybody back."

"That's not what crying's *for*, darling."

"Crying's useless."

"S'what makes us human." He gestured to where the attack had been. "Makes us better'n them. Makes us better'n we were before."

"Yeah well I'll take being an ignorant fuck over losing the people I care about any day."

"Ha. We all would, darling. Don't work like 'at though. Least of all these days... in this town. Grief is good for you, though. Reminds you what's important."

"And what about anger?"

"Anger is fire. Motivation. You can move mountains if you learn how to use it. But it'll burn you right up if you can't control it."

"Not sure one pissed-off little girl is gonna tear these mountains down."

"Then you haven't learned how to use it yet."

Ariana chewed on his words for a moment, then excused herself to head back inside.

The sheriff ended with Max.

"You okay, son?"

"Fine," Max said, chewing on his lower lip. "Fine. Part of life around here, right?"

"S'one way to look at it. Now I don't know there's anything I can say to make it hurt any less for you..."

"It's fine."

"It's just one of those things that's gonna hurt."

"It's *fine*."

"All right then. You need a ride or...?"

"I'll be fine. Thank you."

"Your dad was a good man. I liked him a lot. For whatever it's worth to you, I'll be praying for him tonight."

"Thank you, Sheriff Landry. Very kind."

The sheriff tipped his hat and left.

Maxwell Steen took one last look at the bloodstained gravel where his father died, then drove home. He'd only just closed the apartment door above the store when he fell to his knees sobbing.

The hall light clicked on. His mother called out to him.

Back inside the hotel bar, Jeremy played solo and somber for a while out of respect for Pete's passing and the people it affected. As was mentioned however, an attack was nothing new. The people, though respectful, were used to it. They bought rounds in Pete's honor, told stories about him, and soon the place was as boisterous as it had been before the attack.

Ariana and Reggie returned to the stage and dedicated the rest of the night to Pete.

The band wrapped at 4:30 a.m. as always, rolling whatever atmosphere remained onto its side, letting everyone know it was getting to be that time.

"Thank you all for coming out and seeing us," said Jeremy into the microphone, "even though we know we're pretty much all you have for entertainment around here. Don't forget to tip your servers. And most importantly, don't forget Pete Steen and everything he's done for this town. Don't forget his family either. I think we all know they're gonna need our love and support. Anyway, thanks again and we'll see you all tomorrow night."

The speakers popped as the PA powered off. Jeremy and Ariana packed up while Reggie went to see Kelly for their payment and complimentary beers.

"Nice stuff tonight," Jeremy said to Ariana.

"Thanks," she said.

"How you doing? Okay?"

"Fine."

"Sure?"

"Fine."

"Okay... How's your dad?"

"He's all right."

"All right, then."

"I'm sorry. I'm just... kinda tired..."

"I know. Me too."

"...of just everything."

"Me too, Ari... me too... You think you might want to come over and... vent?"

Ariana took her time trying to decide, then said, "I don't know. Maybe."

Frustration burned like acid in Jeremy's stomach. "Maybe" usually meant "No." Nevertheless, he maintained his composure, saying simply, "Okay. How's Tempest? You get to run her today?"

"Yeah. A little."

Ariana once told Jeremy she'd fantasized about taking Tempest out riding and not coming back. It was one of the few times Jeremy could remember seeing her eyes sparkle. The rest of the time, they were shrouded in resignation and contempt. He wondered if running away was on her mind now.

"That's good," he said searching for the magic words that would start a conversation with her. "That's good."

"Mmhm," Ariana said as they finished packing.

"Thirsty?" Reggie asked, handing them their beers and envelopes.

Jeremy felt the doors close on his chance at a private conversation with Ariana. He resented Reggie in that moment, but he'd never have the gall to say anything. He knew better than to fight with a friend over something like sex. The three took seats at the bar.

The place cleared out quickly. Rick, Louis, Andy, and a lot of other patrons had long taken off. Kelly and Laura made change and straightened up. Jessica was still flirting with her boy in a dark corner. See-you-tomorrows and get-home-safes sounded through the haze.

"How's your dad's business going?" Jeremy asked Reggie through Ariana's hair.

"It's going good, man, thanks," Reggie said. "It's been a good season. Been running my ass off on deliveries."

"That's great, man. Good to hear."

"How's your mom?"

Jeremy flipped a palm up saying, "Same as always."

Reggie pursed his lips and shook his head saying, "I'm sorry, man. That's really tough."

"It is what it is, you know?" Jeremy decided to break up the gravity of the evening's events by saying, "Anyway, I thought that was a really great set tonight."

"Totally! Ari, you were *so* on tonight. I love when you do that thing where your eyes glaze over and you can just tell you're on planet groove, like BMM-TK!— BM BUDOO-TSKA-BADALADA—BADALAPADOW—BOM, BOM." Reggie laughed and gave Ariana a little push.

The girl tried to fight the smile, but Reggie's personality was, as usual, difficult to resist. Ariana held it in as long as she could, cracked a smile, then spit some of her beer back into her glass.

The acid in Jeremy's gut gave another churn as he anticipated Ariana's decision. His mood took a nose dive. The glass in front of him went fuzzy and the noise around him died off.

"Well," said Reggie. "We're gonna take off."

Jeremy snapped out of his reverie and spun on the stool. His big question—"Why?"—poured through his glasses.

"I know, Jeremy," Ariana said. "I'm sorry. I just... your mom..."

"So?" Jeremy said. "He lives with his parents *too*!"

"Yeah but his parents don't scream in terror all night."

"But what about the smell? That's gotta be just as off-putting—all those animal carcasses."

"You get used to it. Look Jeremy, I understand you're frustrated, but so am I, and if I have to choose between a house with a screaming woman or a taxidermist's, I choose the second one... at least I do tonight."

"And for the last few weeks."

"Okay, you know what, I've already explained more than I needed to. I'm not your toy."

"I'm sorry."

"If you got a problem with the rules, you're a big boy and can do what you want about it. Right?"

Jeremy mimed buttoning his lips and looked at the ground.

"I'm sorry, Jeremy," Ariana said. She put a hand to his cheek, then she and Reggie grabbed her bass and left.

The acid in Jeremy's stomach turned to lumps of hot charcoal, weighing him down. He sat there for a while letting his eyes unfocus and refocus on his beer. Then he realized a beer wasn't enough, so he caught eyes with Kelly and asked for a double shot of Jameson.

She poured him a single and said, "I want you home safe tonight, bud."

"Just like all the other women," Jeremy thought. "Can never get what I want."

He waited until her back was turned, then passed his hand over the shot glass, creating for himself a second, identical shot. Typically, Jeremy was more careful about using his abilities in public. This time, however, his frustration had gotten the better of him. He gave an unaware Kelly one more glance, then quickly drank the extra shot and placed the glass in the shadow of a napkin holder.

Across the bar, Del Ballantine watched Jeremy through narrow eyes while Nigel went on obliviously about legends versus realities. Was the kid a witch? A freak? A demon in disguise? Seemed harmless enough—well liked. Better to just keep an eye on him until he could get a bead on him.

Jessica Waters noticed too. She'd been watching from the shadows when Ariana let Jeremy down. She had been waiting off to the side for her evening boy toy to pay the bill when Jeremy did his little trick. She thought, "Maybe this time," and slunk like a lioness toward a hobbled antelope.

"Hey, Jeremy," she said, putting a hand on his shoulder. "You okay?"

He jumped at her touch, nervous about having potentially outed himself. "I'm fine, Jessica," he said and took a sip of his beer.

She leaned in close and let her hand fall down his back saying,

"You know, my offer's still good if, uh... well, you know."

The breath on his ear, the caress down his back, and the implicit promise turned him on, but couldn't weaken his resolve. He wasn't desperate enough to turn to her. Not yet, anyway. Without taking his elbows off the bar, he gave her a polite smile.

"I know," he said. "And thank you, but I'll be fine."

It might not have been the accepted definition, but she still considered him a friend. Part of it was the small-town factor; they saw each other all the time. But Jeremy never disrespected Jessica, and that meant the world to her. He had turned down her advances a hundred times, but he'd never called her a whore. She hated seeing him as down in the dumps as he'd been lately. She tried to make her lips say something else—the right thing—but they came up empty. Instead, Jessica stroked Jeremy's shoulder a few times, then turned and left with Bobby.

Laura breezed by and took the shot glass Jeremy had hidden.

"Hey Laura," he said.

She stopped and turned, ponytail bouncing.

"You uh, doing anything after this?"

Laura squeezed his arm and pursed her lips.

"I'm going to sleep," she said. "It's been a long day."

"I hear you."

"Proposal," Nigel said to Ballantine.

With eyes still on Jeremy, the monster hunter took a sip and grunted.

"You and I hunt together tomorrow—er—today. I've no doubt you've invaluable tips for me, and I'm sure I've more than a few toys *you'll* love to play with."

It was easier to hunt alone. Safer too. Ballantine didn't want to have to worry about where a friendly was when the beasts attacked. He didn't want to have to save someone as heavy as Carrington from animals whose instinct is to keep its prey alive as long as possible while devouring it. Still, the more people there are killing monsters, the sooner they go extinct. Besides, the guy probably *did* have some nice toys.

"Alright," said Ballantine. "Meet me here bright and early at noon."

CHAPTER 5

The main road through town was neither new nor old. There were cracks and a few indentations, but no real potholes. The secondary roads were dusty with gravel from cheap post-winter repair. Off those roads branched bumpy dirt roads swallowed by grass or trees. There wasn't much that extended from the tertiary roads. What did wasn't usually more than a barely visible pair of tracks.

Bobby turned into the tall grass. He'd have missed the driveway completely if he hadn't been following Jessica. His truck crept along behind hers up the hill, threatening to buck him out of the window as it rolled over the rocks and through the divots. He couldn't imagine having to go up and down that driveway every day.

The path emerged into a small, inclined clearing. The tall grass and Jessica's trailer shone pale blue in the moonlight. Her home was a single-wide with rusty edges and God-knows-what-chewed-through latticework around the base. Behind it, the hill rose into the trees.

They switched their engines off in front of the house and hopped out. Water babbled somewhere in the darkness. As Jessica pushed her key into the lock, Bobby’s strong calloused hand slid up the back of her thigh to squeeze her butt. She shivered and tingled.

"I'm surprised you even need to lock your door out here," Bobby breathed as he slobbered into her ear. He slid his other hand around her waist and up to her breasts to squeeze them. She writhed in his grasp, relinquishing what little inhibition she had left, pressing her ass into his crotch.

A scratching, scraping sound inside the trailer broke Bobby's momentum.

"What was that?" he asked.

"Just my dog," she said, reaching back to pull him in for a kiss.

Scriiiiiiip, scrip, scrip...

"Don't worry," she said, "I've got him locked up."

"Sounds like he's digging his way out."

"You should see that *room*," she laughed. "It's an embarrassment!"

Something about that scratching and scraping didn't sit right with Bobby. His mind hovered in limbo between lust and curiosity. What kind of dog...

"Oh don't worry baby," Jessica said groping his bulge, pulling him back to lust. "I promise he won't getcha." She slid her fingers into his belt and led him inside.

The trailer was humid, with a fishy smell. There must have been about ten medium-sized fish tanks along the far wall, glowing, humming, burbling. Jessica didn't bother with the light. Bobby was able to see the outlines of a chair and a couch as his eyes adjusted before she pulled him away, into the hall, past the laundry cupboard door—

BOOM!

The house shook. The sound of splintering wood fibers and rattling hinges accompanied the impact. Bobby jumped out of his skin at the crash against the door.

"See?" said Jessica. "Safely locked away. Come on now. You didn't come all this way for nothing, did you?"

There was just enough light for Bobby to see her lift her skirt and sashay into the bedroom. It reinvigorated him and got his legs moving toward her. He tuned out the scritch, scratch, scraping noises, remembered he was a man, and decided he'd had enough playing around.

Jessica, by the bed, pushed her hands up her chest and extended her face for a kiss, but Bobby was done with foreplay. He was horny and on edge. He spun her around by her shoulders and bent her over the bed.

Jessica laughed, saying, "Don't be too eager now, baby. Mama wants to enjoy herself too."

Bobby barely had his fly down before he shoved himself inside her. The boy was packing, and his angle hit Jessica's spot just the way she liked. She shivered and moaned as ecstatic stimulation swelled inside her. She tried to buck against him but couldn't get leverage. The feeling of helplessness excited her. It curled her lips and unfocused her eyes. She arched her back to take him deeper. It worked. Her ecstasy built in tiers. He pounded faster, pushing her ever closer to her climax.

Then he slowed down...

...then he grunted...

...then he released...

...and she had been so close.

Bobby buckled up and left without a word, ashamed to admit the scratching, scrupping sounds unnerved him, ashamed he let his dick do so much thinking for him.

Jessica lay facedown and unfulfilled, listening to the sound of Bobby's engine rumbling away. She couldn't say she was too surprised. The young ones tended to be too eager for her own good. He'd be bragging to his friends before long, telling them how he gave it to her so good they shook the house. Then, the next time they saw each other, he'd pretend he couldn't see her. She might leave him alone. She might tease him a little. It would depend on the mood she was in.

Jessica rolled onto her back, gripped her knees, and brought them to her chest. She stayed like that for about five minutes to give Bobby's sperm the best chance. Then she sighed and pulled her vibrator out of the nightstand to take care of her unfinished business.

Scriiiiiiiitch... scrit, scrit... BFF! BFF! BOOM!

"I know, I know," Jessica said. "Mama's coming."

Outside Ken's Taxidermy and Meat Processing, the chirping of the crickets tapered. The thick air held onto the stench of death like an acrid cloud around the trailer. An anomalous breeze found its way through Reggie's bedroom window, caressed Ariana's shimmering face, and died on Reggie's chest.

Ariana flipped her hair to the other side and another breeze wafted across her neck. Her overheating was partially her own fault. She hadn't planned to stay long, so she hadn't taken off her shirt. Sweat rolled down her temples as she rocked her hips a little faster against Reggie's. Her palms struggled for traction on his hairy yet slick potbelly.

...faster...

Reggie's twin bed squeaked and bumped against they-didn't-know-what... they didn't *care* what. Reggie's parents were nice enough to at least pretend the kids had privacy.

"Yeah, Ari!" Reggie grunted.

"Hold on," she moaned. She squeezed her eyes tight as her pleasure welled. She dug what she had left of fingernails into Reggie and shuddered. Stars burst under her eyelids and in her head. Her orgasm overtook her, crashing her hips against him one more time, winding her body tight, and spangling her head with euphoria.

"Okay!" grunted Reggie, lifting the girl off by her hips.

She would've liked a little more time to enjoy the sensation, but she wasn't bitter about it—well, not any more bitter than she was about any of life's *other* disappointments, which were piling up. She was grateful for the escape though, and finished him with her hands.

Outside the window, the world turned pre-dawn blue. Birds chirped. A rabbit hopped along the tree line.

Reggie sighed and draped an arm over his forehead. Ariana wiped her hands on a towel, then laid it over the mess on Reggie's stomach.

"You going now?" he asked. His voice cut in and out.

Ariana gave a few shallow nods.

"You don't have to." He slid to one side as best he could and laid an arm out across the bed—an invitation for her to lie down with him.

"I know," she rasped. She didn't want either of them getting in too deep with each other. What they had was fine—disposable, inconsequential. If it went away tomorrow, she'd feel as indifferent as if she'd dropped a french fry on the ground. If she lay in his arms, she might like it. She might want more, get addicted... attached.

Ariana gave Reggie a pat on the stomach, put her pants back on, and padded quietly out the bedroom door. She was only a few steps down the hall when her malaise caught up to her, hollowing her a little more with every step. Had she lost the thrill of sex too?

"Hey Ari," came Jenny's voice as Ariana left the hall.

The girl had been so close. The door was only five steps to her right. Ahead of her was the sitting area. To the left was the kitchen, where Jenny was leaning against a counter.

"How are you, baby?" Jenny asked.

Uncomfortable. A conversation with the mother of the guy she just had sex with was the last thing Ariana wanted. She wiped her temples with her shirt cuffs and gave herself a quick look-over for evidence of sex.

"Fine," Ariana said. "Tired. I'm just gonna—"

"Oh, please stay and chat for a minute," Jenny said. "I never get any girl time up here."

"Yeah well, that kind of thing happens when you're a recluse," Ariana thought to herself. Snarky as she may have been about it, she didn't have anything against the woman. In fact, she kind of liked her. Ariana thought it might be because Jenny looked and acted so young for her age. Still, she had just banged the woman's son. It wasn't the time to chat, which made each successive step toward the couch feel slimier than the last.

The sitting room was crowded with plants: tall ones in the corners and framing the windows, short ones underneath, hanging ones on the shelves, and succulents covering the coffee table between the couches. The smell of humid earth was a refreshing change to the ever-present tang of decaying flesh.

The women sat opposite each other. Jenny sank back and smiled as she took in the sight of Ariana. The redhead used only the edge of the seat and folded her hands in her lap.

"Look at you," Jenny said. "I can't believe how fast you've grown up."

Ariana pursed her lips and smiled.

"How's the band going, good?"

"It's fine."

"And your dad?"

"He's fine too."

"Good. That's good."

"Uh, look, Mrs. Adams, I don't wanna be rude but..."

"I know. You're tired. This is probably the last thing you want to be doing right now."

"No, no, I do. It's just—"

"I know, I know, Ari. It's okay," Jenny said standing. "You get home and get to bed. I just... like to see you is all."

Ariana was barely a step out of the door when Jenny said, "Ari... uh..." She rolled her eyes around to look for the phrasing. "You know you can... Well, I'd really like it if you... talk... you can talk to me about anything."

"Uh, thanks, Mrs. Adams."

"Call me Jenny, please. And come by any time, especially if you want to talk... about *anything*. I know it must be hard growing up without... I mean, I can't imagine growing up without your mother. I've always *wanted* to..." She cut herself off when she saw the girl's welling tears.

Ariana's mother, Jodi, had disappeared... or left... or been killed after the girl was born. What hurt Ariana the most was how everyone left her in the dark about it, including Paul, her own father. She assumed her mother had packed up and left. Why *else* would anybody lie about it? People were killed in those mountains all the time. It wasn't like she couldn't handle that information, especially now that she was 21.

Ariana was used to burying feelings, but on that day, with the hunner dyer and Pete already weighing on her, she couldn't keep her lip from trembling.

"Oh no, baby," Jenny said, "I didn't mean... Oh!"

Ariana strode to her jalopy and tried to focus on driving to stave off the tears. "Ignition, reverse, turn, drive, turn, don't lose the axle in the driveway..."

Jeremy lived along the main stretch about a mile from the bar. His driveway would've been easy to miss if it weren't for the reflector on the mailbox. Otherwise, the only thing to see was a gravel path sloping slightly through a thicket of sickly spruces. His tires crunched down the narrow drive, past the tall grass, past the rusty old swing set. His headlights lit the front of the house. It looked sad. Awnings over the windows drooped like heavy eyelids. The broken storm door hung open as if mid groan.

Jeremy had left his mother's window open so she could get a breeze. As he turned off his engine, the rumbling was replaced by Connie's moans, whimpers, and cries. He pressed his forehead against the steering wheel, considered driving away again, then grabbed his guitar and went inside.

The old linoleum in the kitchen crackled under his footsteps.

"Aah! Who's there?!" called his mother from her bedroom.

He set his guitar down in the corner and popped open the fridge. Inside was one beer and the leftover sandwich from the night before. Jeremy duplicated the beer and opened it. He didn't really care to drink it, but it had become a nightly habit: come home, think about driving away forever, not do it, guitar in the corner, crack a beer. The beer was getting skunky. He'd have to buy another one soon.

"Get out! Get out of my house!"

Jeremy looked around at the time capsule of a kitchen,

searching as usual for deeper meaning in a room that hadn't changed since he was ten. The peeling wallpaper echoed the siding on the exterior. The rust-spotted refrigerator buzzed on, too old to even know how to die. Above the table in the corner was mounted his mother's collection of rooster-themed dishes. Above the table on the other wall—the wall that ran the length of the kitchen—were hung family photos.

The Crawfords had never had any professional pictures done. These were all snapshots taken by one person or another, birthday parties and camping trips mostly. Jeremy is never more than a few years old in any of the pictures. They stopped taking them after his father James was killed.

CHAPTER 6

Twenty years earlier…

It was noon, and the men of Brothers gathered at the Foothill Hotel bar to discuss their plan of action. A little more than two dozen of them took up the long tables in the back. Kelly Karasek floated from person to person taking orders before the meeting started. She was buoyant, stronger than the feminine ideal—tomboyish, but handsome and with a bounce in her step. It had been a big year for her. She had married Sam, then her father had handed her the hotel.

James Crawford, Jeremy's father, stood facing the men, his back to the bar.

The cool daylight streaming in from the front was broken by Jessica Waters' silhouette. She slunk, dragging a finger along the bar. The five blue gems of her necklace almost seemed to glow in the shadows, stealing one gaze after another.

Noticing the distracted men, James turned to look and stayed to stare. Jessica chose one of the little tables across from the bar in full view of the men. Her perky tits defied gravity. Her pert ass defied imagination. Her tight jeans defied physics. She pretended not to notice the men gawking at her as she sat with her back to the wall and crossed one leg over the other.

Kelly went to take her order, obstructed the men's view, and snapped them back to reality.

"All right," James said, trying to decide how to start. "It's been a year of us doing the same thing and nothing's working. I think it's time we reevaluate our game plan."

"What do you suggest?" asked Sam Karasek.

"Well... I'm open to any suggestions of course, but I think it's time we start thinking about *managing* the problem; learning how to *live* with 'em."

The men buzzed like a shook-up hornet's nest.

"Are you serious?" asked Sam.

James threw a hand up and said, "It's been a *two years*. And all we have to show for it is a bunch of dead men."

"Then we change our tactics."

"To what, Sam? We've swept Mt. Braddock a dozen times and the bastards keep coming back like we never did a damn thing. We can't even *get* anywhere on Mt. Fayette, and nobody who's ever gone to Mt. Liston has come back. So... what can we do?"

After a bit of silence Paul Coleman, Ariana's father, said, "We could start putting up fences."

Many of the men laughed.

Paul continued, red faced, "I ain't saying it's not a big task. I know it is. I also know I stopped losing so many animals when I put up a good one."

"It's the truth," said David Krause, Laura's father. "Barely take a rifle with me anymore when I'm out on his property." David and his wife Sandra had been helping Paul since Jodi disappeared. David was the town's doctor. When he wasn't seeing patients or making house calls, he helped out on Paul's farm. Sandra took care of Ariana in tandem with Laura.

"That's a fine idea, Paul," said James, who then raised his voice to say, "Best I've heard yet."

"What if we advertise?" asked Ken Adams.

"Advertise?" asked James.

"Bring more hunters in. Make this like a tourist thing. That way we won't be doing it by ourselves *and* we'll make some money!"

"That doesn't sound half bad," said Sam.

James chewed on it before twisting his mouth to the side and saying, "I don't know. I think inviting people to hunt monsters could be a liability. And I don't know about you, but I'd rather deal with monsters than lawyers."

"Well, what about the National Guard then?" asked Rick Jenkins. "Can't we declare a state of emergency?"

"Only the governor can declare a state of emergency," said James. "As far as the government is concerned, the closest thing we have to local authorities are ill equipped, and the higher powers have bigger fish to fry. They won't be coming around to us for a while, if they do at all."

"Well, the only idea you *didn't* shoot down," said Sam, "was the fence. And you're gonna need to do better than just that."

"What do you want me to say, Sam? Huh? Maybe we can get a Remington sponsorship? I'm getting tired! I'm getting older!"

"You're not that much older than *me*!"

"I just had a *kid*! All right? I got *him* to think about now! I can't keep going out after these fucking things that want to eat me alive."

"Then what are you gonna do when a stray one comes after your family?"

James had nothing.

"Anybody else here lose a friend on one of those mountains?" called Sam. "I know *I* did. I lost *more* than a few. Good friends. Good *people*. You say you want to coexist with the things that murdered them. Why don't you piss on their graves and fuck their wives? At the rate these things multiply, we're gonna be overrun if we don't do anything. We need to keep pressing."

The men contemplated, but no other solutions presented themselves.

"Look," said James, "maybe we didn't have too many bad ideas here today. Paul, if you want to build a fence, I'll help you. I'm sure there are others here who would too. Maybe we'll start with a few key spots, you know? Start with diverting them before we worry about containing them.

"Ken, maybe you can still advertise, but just do it quietly—word of mouth, and experienced hunters only."

"Gon' take a hell of a lot longer to get enough people up here," Ken said.

"It'll be better than nothing until we come up with a better plan," James said. "And Sam, I'm sure there's no shortage of people who'll stand with you. I will too, if you really need me. Just don't get frustrated and go charging headlong at Fayette or Liston unless you know what you're doing."

James took a seat. The men murmured, then buzzed, then grew boisterous as they discussed their new plans.

Kelly, as if cued, began bringing out the food. She brought Sam his plate first. If she had been able to get her hand around his shoulder, she'd have squeezed it. Instead, she gave it a rub and smiled at him.

Sam looked up at her and calmed down. Kelly always had that effect on him. She had always been strong, never needed anyone. Her strength was the only thing the burly hunter allowed to soften him.

As Sam went to wash his hands, Jessica saw her chance. She'd been after him for a while. Though many of the other men fell like flies for her, Sam was one of few who'd been able to resist. In any other case, she could walk into a room and wait for someone to approach. But with Sam, it was *she* who did the hunting. She was never blatant about it, especially not with Kelly around. She'd bat an eyelash here, twirl her hair there, but Sam never noticed... or maybe he *pretended* not to. She would try to make small talk, but never got much more than a word at a time out of him until someone else stole his attention. It frustrated Jessica and became a challenge for her. Sex was her life. Sam wasn't interested in that with her. Finally, she had something she knew he wanted, and maybe she could use it as a bargaining chip.

The restroom doors stood on opposite sides of a nook in the back wall. Men on the left and women on the right. As soon as Sam's hand touched the door Jessica tapped him on the shoulder.

"I can help you with Fayette and Liston," she said.

Sam turned around to look at her. Her eyes were the deepest blue he'd ever seen. He had never noticed before. They almost seemed to glow in the... He squeezed his eyes shut and shook out his fuzzing thoughts. He knew she was trouble. He knew what she really wanted.

"How?" he asked.

"Too long a story to talk about it here and now," she said. "Come to my place tonight and I'll tell you everything."

"Why can't you tell the others?"

"Because I don't want them getting themselves killed."

"And you're okay if it happens to me?"

"No! I'm telling you because I think you're the only one who can handle it. Mt. Liston is a one-person job. It's also the key to Mt. Fayette."

Sam stared at her, trying to decide if she was just blowing smoke.

"I live just off of Fayette Run road," she said. "Last hill before the mountain proper. I'll keep my dance card clear just for you tonight." Then she winked and went into the women's room.

Sam didn't visit her that night. Whether she had real information for him or not, he could see a mile away that she was playing a game, and he refused to join her.

CHAPTER 7

"I have a gun! Don't come any closer!" Jeremy's mother squealed as his footsteps clopped down the hall to her room. She whimpered, "Pleeeeeease, get out."

He flipped the light switch. Connie lay in her bed, sweating and straining. On top of her chest sat the nightmare. Its bulging eyes reflected the lamplight as it turned its attention to Jeremy. His mother's screams would've given him goosebumps if he hadn't had to deal with them every night.

"All right, beat it," Jeremy said cocking a thumb out.

The nightmare vanished in a wisp.

The screams subsided into wheezes, subsided into whimpers just as they always had as Connie Crawford returned to reality and caught her breath.

When Jeremy was 16 years old, it was *he* who had the nightmare. He dreamed he was there when his father was killed. He dreamed he was too far away to do anything as James was torn open at the stomach by a pack of wood devils. He watched as they gnawed his limbs off and pulled out his guts. Even though it was only a dream, it was vivid enough that Jeremy still remembered the hideous screams and the silent gape on his dream father's face after his lungs had been torn out.

Jeremy had been screaming in his sleep, which woke up Connie.

She burst into his room and threw on the light, revealing the nightmare on his chest. The creature was too deep in Jeremy's dream to vanish immediately back to wherever it lived. Connie, unthinking, charged at it, swinging her fists. In defense, the creature opened its mouth and sank its fangs into Connie's arm, then disappeared.

Since then, Connie's sleep habits were the opposite of normal. She slept most of the time, dreaming horrible dreams, and was awake only some of the time. The nightmare venom marked her. If someone wasn't watching over her as she slept, a nightmare would take her in a second.

Jeremy held Connie’s hand as she emerged from her quicksand sleep.

"Oh Jeremy," Connie said, her face twisting in anguish. "It was so terrible."

"I know, mom. I know," he said for the thousandth time. "It's always terrible."

"I'm sorry. I'm so sorry."

"I know that too. You're always sorry."

"I know you know, but I still have to tell you."

"Well, take a break for a night, huh? Come on. You took care of me by yourself for how many years?" He sighed, but tried not to make it sound like it was because she was a burden. "Least I can do is return the favor."

"I'm sorry," she cried again. "I'm so, so sorry."

"Yeah, yeah, I know. Just calm down. Breathe. You should get up and walk around a bit since you're awake."

"You're right," she said.

Connie put her bony hands in Jeremy's as he helped her to her feet. Her legs felt weaker than she remembered. She realized she was deteriorating and cried again.

"Okay. Okay," Jeremy said, taking her in his arms.

She sniffled and said, "I'm falling apart, baby."

"No you're not. You're just weak from being asleep so long."

"How old am I?"

"I'm not playing this game with you again."

"I can't be 50. It can't have been seven years."

"Time flies when you're fast asleep."

"Oh no, Jeremy. Oh no, no, no..."

Connie buried her face in Jeremy's shoulder as usual. And as usual, he rubbed her back and said, "You're okay." A thousand times he had told her. A thousand times she had let herself be consoled.

Then as usual, in an effort to catch a whiff of normalcy, she asked how things were with Jeremy.

As usual, Jeremy told her everything was fine. "The band sounded good tonight. Kelly had her hands full like she always does."

"Laura Krause still working there?" Connie asked.

"Yeah."

"Shame about her parents."

"Shame about mine," Jeremy thought.

"She still planning on moving away soon?"

"I guess. We didn't really get a chance to talk tonight."

"Mm. Wonder who Kelly'd find to work such crazy hours."

"Oh, I'm sure someone would come along."

"How's Sam? Sam any different?"

"Sam's the same."

"Mm. Well at least we aren't the only ones with problems, huh?"

"Yeah."

"Can I just..." Connie sat on the edge of the bed.

"You should take a little walk," Jeremy said, too tired to care whether she listened to him or not. "Maybe get a little food in you."

She yawned and said, "Oh please, Jeremy, I'm so tired."

"The sooner you fall asleep, the sooner you go back to the nightmares."

Connie's face twisted up again, but no sound came out until she sniffled. "It hurts to be awake," she moaned. "And it's torture to be asleep."

Jeremy was tired of hearing it. "I don't know what you want me to tell you," he said. "Damned if you do, damned if you don't."

Connie slumped over onto her pillow and sobbed. Jeremy, out of habit, rubbed her arm, but he was out of things to say.

A couple of minutes passed before Connie calmed down enough to say, "I can't do this anymore, Jeremy."

"Well it's not like you have a whole lot of options," he said.

She nodded, rolled onto her back, pulled the other bed pillow over her face, and squeaked, "Just press down."

Jeremy yanked the pillow away, revealing his mother's pathetic face, and said, "Are you kidding me?"

"Please," she sobbed.

"You're half asleep. You don't know what you're talking about."

Connie sat straight up and locked eyes with Jeremy. Her eyelids hung as heavy and morose as the awnings on the front of the house. "Please. Kill me, Jeremy." She lay back and closed her eyes. "Set me free." She twisted her face up one more time. "Let me be with your father." She sobbed twice gently, then fell asleep.

Jeremy stood for a long time with the pillow in his hands. Every tic Connie made, every grunt, every squawk was a new thorn raked down his side. Seven years of that. Seven years of trying to sleep through that. Seven years of that affecting a woman's decision about having sex with him. Fuck. Ariana deserved all the credit in the world for putting up with it for *one* night, let alone the many she did. Fuck. She was better to him than she ever needed to be. Who else would want to deal with this? Who else would understand? Imagine what life would be like if he *weren't* dealing with this. He was losing his chance for a partner in this fucked-up world to a guy whose house smelled like death all the time.

"*GAAAHH!!!* Huh... huhhh..." Connie vocalized, twitching on the bed.

As soon as he left the room, the nightmare would return and her tics would change to screams again. Jeremy's emotions took huge swings between pity and indignation. He used to hurt for her, but lately her whimpers often sounded more like whines.

"Suck it up already," Jeremy would think sometimes. "How bad can it be?"

He'd try to remind himself how irrational he was being—that he couldn't possibly understand. It was her burden. He was in no position to judge...

...

"*...gaaaahhh...*"

...

...but all he had to do was press down...

...

...and both their problems would be solved.

...

Jeremy slowly raised the pillow. Butterflies fluttered. His stomach sank. He pictured his mother thrashing beneath him. He pictured her lifeless face when it was done. Images of her in better days flashed through his head.

He whipped the pillow across the room where it rattled the closet and fell to the floor. His bottled emotions got the better of him, as tears pushed their way out of his eyes and ran down his straining cheeks.

Every tic, every moan Connie released was a whine for death that Jeremy knew he couldn't give, one more internal conflict to add to his pile. He didn't have the strength to shovel anymore that night.

He pressed the heels of his hands into his eyes, moaned through his teeth, and turned to leave. He flicked off the light and shambled back up the hall with his hands in his hair. Connie was screaming before he even reached his bedroom door.

CHAPTER 8

Eighteen years earlier…

Two years after the men of Brothers had met to rethink their plan of action, the town was in markedly better shape.

Paul Coleman and company had made headway on the fencing. The mountains were by no means cordoned off, but enough had been built to divert the supernatural wildlife away from people's properties. Attacks on livestock and the raiding of crops had been reduced from a major problem to a mere nuisance.

Ken Adams, in the meantime, had been busy. He traveled to Pittsburgh and made contacts for selling meat and other products. He quietly spread the word about the hunting opportunity. There was never an influx of people that the Foothill Hotel couldn't accommodate, but enough came through that Ken found himself without time to hunt. Heck, if he didn't live where he worked, he'd never see his three-year-old son Reggie.

Since the meeting, Sam Karasek, who still hadn't taken Jessica up on her offer, had never called on any of the men with children regarding a hunting matter. James, Paul, Ken, and David were out. Sam spent those two years tweaking and reworking his plan of attack. Sometimes Ken's tourist hunters helped. Sometimes they hindered. Either way, there was little doubt that Sam's refusal to let up had contributed to Brothers' safety. In fact, he was the most revered man in town. That's why, when the day came that Sam called on every man to help him, they came. Anyone who had any trepidation kept it to himself, even James Crawford.

Sam told the men about a clearing in the woods on Mt. Braddock, which had over time earned the nickname Devil's Mountain. It was about a hundred feet from an overlooking ridge and across a creek. For the last few weeks, he and his followers had been chumming the clearing with things like groundhogs, rabbits, and anything else that was easy to kill, tear open, and chuck over. He said, "If I'm right, there'll be a horde of wood devils down in that clearing tonight and enough blood to make them too stupid to run. It'll be like fish in a barrel. Long as none of you is bleeding, they should leave us alone. Also, if I'm right, it'll be a self-perpetuating culling spot. We'll kill so many tonight, that place will attract them like ants to sugar every night until they're all gone."

Before sunset, a little more than a dozen men drove as far as the mountain road let them. They then hiked a narrow path that cut over a hillside before opening out onto the ridge. The low orange sun reached its spindly rays through the leaves and branches, allowing the men to make an assessment. The creek appeared to be a little over knee deep: enough to slow someone down, but not stop them. Animal bones littered the clearing, picked clean of their meat, broken and drained of their marrow. A sizable pile of freshly killed varmints laid scattered and, of course, bloody.

James and Sam were shuffled to the far right as the men took their positions, lying prone and prepping their ammunition.

"Wait until there are twice as many as us down in that clearing," Sam told them. "Then open fire."

As magic hour fell, the woods rustled with the sound of stalking devils. The light of the deep-blue sky turned everything in the woods the same shade of shadow. The men took aim, searching more for movement than shapes. Then, with a half hour of fading light remaining, a devil descending from the opposite hill caught their eyes. It was exciting, but no more than any other hunt. Then another devil moved across the way. “Two,” some of them counted. Then another moved. “Three.” Then another, and another. “Four, five...” Another... “Six? Or did I count that one?”

The wood devils appeared like stars at twilight. Before the men realized it, the woods around the clearing were teeming with devils, *more* than two dozen. Closer to four dozen. None of the men was prepared for such a turnout. Not even Sam. Half of them looked up from their rifles in disbelief and only snapped out of it with the BANG of Sam's first shot.

They chose their targets and fired at will, crackling atop the ridge, resounding through the forest. After several shots, only about a dozen wood devils lay dead. The moving ones were easier to see but harder to hit, thanks to the ever-dimming sky. More devils, drawn by the thick scent of blood, entered the clearing and were gunned down.

The distant woods sank too far for the men to see in the dark. Visibility shrank to a few hundred feet and closing. Wood devil after wood devil seemed to appear out of nowhere eliciting knowing glances among the men. Sam realized his culling was not going to be as simple as he had expected. They'd have to pull out soon.

A nearby splash needled the men's spines. They turned their attention to the creek to see a wood devil in it, snarling up at them. Sam put a bullet between its eyes before wondering what was wrong. The devils should be mindlessly drawn to the blood on their side.

SPLASH, SPL-SPLASH!!!

The horde had for some reason turned its attention to the men.

"Retreat!" Sam cried, standing and firing at the devils in the water.

The men hopped up and scarpered up the path one by one. Those who remained each took a shot before turning tail. With only a few men shooting, the wood devils cleared the creek and clawed up the embankment.

"Get outta here!" Sam cried to the few remaining men.

Stars pierced the violet sky. The creek frothed in the deluge of wood devils. The shrieks of the blood-lusted monsters were rapiers in the dark.

Sam reached for James' collar but missed as James was pulled down by a devil where he stood. The devil reared back and bared its fangs. Sam drew his sidearm and exploded its head at point-blank range.

James laid there in shock, not knowing if he was okay, already dead, or somewhere in between. Sam holstered his sidearm and swept James over his shoulder. He'd only just made it to the path when James' weight shifted backward and they were both hauled down. Sam rolled onto his back and drew in time to see a shadowy wood devil bore its claws into James' torso.

BANG!

The wood devil's head evaporated in a dark-gray plume.

James moaned weakly as he tightened his stomach, trying to hold himself together.

Sam got to his feet and reached for James, but another three wood devils were already at the fallen man's legs. The burly hunter fired three perfect shots, exploding each of their heads.

The leaves rustled and shrieks pierced the air around them. At that, Sam knew they wouldn't both make it.

"It's okay," James said. He'd been around long enough to know it too. "It's okay."

That was when Sam began to hate himself. He put his last bullet in James' heart, escaped to his truck, and headed back to town. Until the day he died, he never stopped hating himself for that moment.

CHAPTER 9

The Coleman farm was in a basin between a couple foothills. The main road ran the length of the farm and curved away around a hill as it reached the house. Along the other side, at the base of the other hill, ran a creek.

For as much land as Paul had, the farm itself was not large. With only Ariana to help him, Paul produced enough to survive and a little to sell. A couple dozen chickens gave them all the eggs they could want. So many that Ariana couldn't stand the sight of them anymore. They planted plenty, though, but being situated where they were, they tended to have weak harvests. The barn was part stable, housing two cows and Tempest.

As he stepped out of the house, Paul looked up at the barn's weather vane to see that the sun hadn't yet cleared the mountainside to hit it.

"Beat ya again," he said.

He was happy to hear Ariana's engine buzzing on the other side of the hill. Her temper was hit and miss these days, but the way he saw it, he'd rather have her mad at him than not have her at all. With the way the world was, he was just happy she was coming home.

Paul had just opened the barn doors when Ariana flew around the bend and slid to a stop in the driveway. A dust cloud surrounded the car. A bird chirped somewhere. Ariana's muffled scream broke the peacefulness.

Paul went into the barn to ready Tempest. He was on the last strap of the saddle when Ariana stormed in and sloughed off the bag of chicken feed, trying to hide her face in her hair. As she bridled the horse herself, Paul strapped a feedbag to the saddle. Ariana pulled herself up and gave Tempest a gentle kick to get her trotting.

"I'll make your favorite when you get back," said Paul.

"Please don't," said Ariana.

She rode along the path between the fence and creek. The morning sun cleared the hill behind her and sparkled in the fresh dew. The world sang its tranquil morning song while Ariana raged inside. Beyond the fence there was nothing but empty field. The girl kicked, whipped the reins, and with a "YAH!" they were gone.

Tempest's hoof beats were music. The wind roared in Ariana's ears, whipping her problems out the back of her hair. They galloped full speed for as long as Tempest would run, over one hill, through another basin, past Laura Krause's house, then up the next hill to stop at the top.

They could see the horizon from up there. Like so many times before, Ariana thought this time she might do it. This time she and Tempest were going to keep going. Whatever else was out there had to be better than what she had.

But all she could see was farmland... and she already had that.

Sweat rolled down Jessica's head as she squatted next to the hot-water tank in her laundry cupboard. The morning light pushed through the shutters enough to let her know it was well past her bedtime. Her newborn chupacabra bounded about the trailer, excited and curious. Every so often, it would try to lick her face.

"I know, baby, I know," she'd say and gently push it away. "I'm excited too."

Another contraction pulled her stomach tight, forcing a whimper out of her, forcing her to push again over the towel beneath her. As many times as she'd gone through it, it never seemed to get easier. With one hand on a pipe for support, she hiked her denim skirt up to her chest and pressed on her stomach as she contracted again, this time stretching past her threshold of pain. Straining, her face turned red and her eyes rolled back, focusing in and out of the ceiling tiles above. "Almost there," she told herself.

She took a deep breath in anticipation of her next contraction. Then, as it wracked her body one last time, she cried and pushed the egg out gently onto the towel.

The pain gave way to a tidal wave of relief, making Jessica giddy. She doubled over on her hands and knees and wiped the sweat from her head.

The young chupacabra took it as a sign that Jessica wanted to play and bounced over to nuzzle in her hair.

She laughed and reached up to run her hand along its scaly skin.

"Easy! Easy," she said, as she sighed and sat up, then gently positioned the egg near the heater with the others.

"What do you say we name *this* one?" she asked her pup. "How about Bobby Junior?"

Del Ballantine and Nigel Carrington met outside the hotel by their vehicles.

"That's some truck you got there," said Ballantine.

"Isn't it?" said Nigel.

"What kind of engine you got in that thing?"

"No idea, but she's four-wheel drive and hauls ass! So American. Walked into a dealer in New Jersey and said, 'Give me the best you've got.' What do you think?"

"Could probably fit *my* truck in the back there."

"*Ha*! Come look!" Nigel motioned and opened the door. "Hop in! Hop in!"

Ballantine set his bag down and stepped up into the driver's seat. He'd never imagined a truck seat so comfortable. It was springy, yet soft, and there was so much room. Probably rode like a Cadillac compared to *his* rust bucket.

"And look in the back!" Nigel said like a kid on Christmas.

In place of what should have been the backseat, Nigel had added a gun-and-ammunition rack the entire width of the cab. It *did* look like Christmas to Ballantine. There were handguns of different calibers, assault rifles, hunting rifles, an elephant gun, all top of the line.

"An AK-47?" Ballantine asked.

"I didn't know what I'd need for hunting monsters so I brought a little from column A and a little from column B."

"Looks like you got some from C, D, and E too. What is *that*?" Ballantine asked, pointing.

"Ah," Nigel said smiling. "Saw that one, did you? That is my Dragunov SVD military-issue sniper rifle. Best in its class. Shoot the tits off a gnat at 600 meters. Infrared scope too!"

"Infrared?"

"Anything emitting infrared light, like a set of night-vision goggles, shows up on the scope. *Incredible* technology!"

"Doubt we're going to be seeing many monsters that are using night-vision goggles."

"Perhaps not, Mr. Ballantine. But there are things on these mountains that emit infrared light nevertheless. I'll show you when we get there. I've got two sets of goggles."

"Of course you do."

"Of *course* I do!"

"And a Remington 870, I see."

"Good eye."

"Slugs or shot?"

"Couldn't decide. Stocked up on both. What you think?"

"How good a shot are you?"

"Cracking."

"Slugs then. Something gets close enough for you to need a shotgun, you're gonna want to make sure it's dead. Plus, I've run across a few creatures in my time I'm not sure buckshot would've brought down." Ballantine opened a box expecting to find a trove of ammunition, but instead... "Grenades?"

"Yes," said Nigel as though it were normal to bring grenades hunting.

"Maybe I should've just asked what you *don't* have."

"*HA, HA*!!! Indeed. Let me think. An attack helicopter and a bazooka. And only because they wouldn't fit."

As they rode down the main stretch, Ballantine perused the collection of eight-track cassettes in Nigel's center console. The Brit was going all out for his American experience with tapes of everything from Elvis Presley and Chuck Berry, to Aerosmith and the new Lynyrd Skynyrd.

"Feel free to play one," said Nigel.

Ballantine chose Rush's Fly by Night and popped it in. Rush was Canadian, but that was close enough for Nigel.

"So what's first that you'd like to do?" Nigel asked.

"I figure while we've got the daylight we should do a little exploring," Ballantine said.

"Ah, yes! Learn the topography. The ins and outs, as it were. Good thinking. Been down here yet?" Nigel pointed at a dirt road off to the left.

"No," said Ballantine.

"Shall we?"

"Sure."

A rusty road sign stood at an angle on the corner.

"Fayette Run Road," Nigel read aloud. "Didn't Rick say something about a Mount Fayette?"

"He said it was the witch's mountain."

"Ah yes! Then the game is afoot!"

The road cut through a small field before banking and winding into the foothills. Sunlight sparkled through the canopy, dappling the woods beneath.

"I tell you," said Nigel, "these mountains may not be Kilimanjaro, but they're not exactly a stroll in the garden either."

"A mountain's a mountain, huh?"

"Oh, indubitably. But the benefit of *these* mountains is they're not so tall as to induce altitude sickness, not so steep as to require climbing equipment, and not so vast as to require a guide. If it weren't for the teeming hellspawn, I imagine the worst-case scenario would be accidentally leaving down the wrong side."

"You say you've been to Kilimanjaro?" asked Ballantine.

"Twice. Got a lion and a bushbuck the first time. Went back and got an eland. And that was all just on the mountain."

Ballantine had never even heard of two of those animals. "Everything go okay? Nice and smooth?"

"Hm... smoother than Everest."

"What happened on Everest?"

"Avalanche. Took ten men. Including my brother."

"Jesus. I'm sorry, man."

"S'alright."

"But that's what I mean. You can't underestimate mother na—"

"We finished the climb."

"Say what?"

"We kept on. Gerald wanted me to. We made a pact before the climb: conquer, no matter what."

Ballantine wasn't sure how to feel about the revelation. "What about his body?"

"Still there."

"You didn't go back?"

"Oh, I went back all right. Conquered the mountain a second time for him. Tossed a bottle of his favorite scotch over the spot where he went down."

"But you never retrieved his body?"

"My dear Delaney, Everest is not a place anyone can just walk into and retrieve someone; it's every man for himself up there. Nor is an avalanche something that can be cleared with a spade. One might sooner empty a lake with a tea—"

"Look out!"

Nigel looked ahead in time to see a little brown something streak into the road and disappear in front of the hood. He gritted his teeth and stomped on the brake, locking the wheels, skidding, skidding...

...

No thump.

Ballantine drew a pistol and the two men hopped out. Nigel, incredulous, inspected his front end for signs of contact, but found none.

"What was that?" asked the Brit.

"Kinda looked like a dog," said Ballantine, peering into the woods. "But mangy and deformed. Spines down its back. Chupacabra, probably."

"Chupacabra?"

"Or something like it."

"Thought those were more of a Mexican thing."

"They *were*."

"Look there!" Nigel pointed behind Ballantine.

There was a mailbox next to a pair of overgrown tire ruts running up and into the woods. On the side of the mailbox was the faded name Waters. The men took note but said nothing. Ballantine peered off across the street for a few more moments, made sure there was nothing that shouldn't be there, then motioned with his head back to the truck.

"Should we go after it?" Nigel asked as they climbed in.

"Nah," said Ballantine. "Chupacabras don't really attack humans, so they're low on my list. They mostly go after livestock. Besides, they don't come from Hell. I don't have a problem with them unless they make one. A farmer might have a different opinion."

"I don't suppose you'd be terribly offended if I were to bag one."

"Chupacabras know how to hide, man. We're lucky we saw *that* one. I doubt you'll see another in your life. If you bag one, I'll be impressed."

"Challenge accepted," Nigel said with a smile.

CHAPTER 10

As Nigel and Ballantine continued, the road wound for another mile before fanning into a dead end at the base of Mt. Fayette, the largest of the three mountains. An old fence ran as far as the men could see. With its drooping wire, it was more of an inconvenience than a barrier. The gate was a formality. An old sign stood nearby as well, indicating that they were at Mount Fayette and offering a history lesson neither man cared to read.

"What do you think?" asked Nigel as they looked up into the trees.

"It's a mountain, all right," said Ballantine.

"A mountain with a *witch* on it!"

"Easy, partner. Don't mistake danger for a thrill."

"Of course," Nigel said, though he could hardly contain his giddiness at being called "partner" by this American gunslinger. It was *just* like the movies! They were Butch Cassidy and the Sundance Kid, Wyatt Earp and Doc Holiday, John Wayne and Clint Eastwood. The Brit eyed the area for clues. Ooh! Sherlock Holmes and Buffalo Bill. That's it. That's who they were. When Nigel had figured that out, he assessed the mountain. There were trees, rocks, lots of leaves, a small path, and...

...and...

"What else have you got?" Nigel asked.

"Tire tracks," said Ballantine.

Nigel looked over to see his partner looking at the ground.

"Ah, so someone's been here."

"More than a few times. There's a lot of tracks here, but they're all the same zigzag pattern."

"Devil's advocate, but isn't it possible for more than one person to have the same tires, especially in a town so small?"

"Course. But when you consider the tread is wearing low on all the tracks, you're bound to eliminate some people."

"Aha. Naturally." Nigel cursed himself for not having noticed sooner. He wouldn't be so easily taken in again.

"Notice anything else about the tracks?"

Nigel stared hard. He took a little longer than Ballantine had the patience for.

"They're—"

"Nn! Sh! Sh! Just a moment."

...

"I've nothing."

"They're angled, deeper on the inside. Their alignment is off..."

"Damnit," thought Nigel. "He's Sherlock Holmes *and* Buffalo Bill. I'm Inspector Clouseau."

"...which narrows the field a little more. So what do you think, Watson?"

"I'll take it," thought Nigel. "Worn tires, improperly aligned... Whoever was here either doesn't care or doesn't know *how* to take care of his or her vehicle."

"Mmhm."

"They aren't mechanically inclined."

"Likely."

"Like a woman."

"That's a generalization, but sure."

"Did I miss anything?"

"Their business."

"Well they're not coming to Witch's Mountain for *fence* maintenance, I can tell you that."

"Not likely."

"And they said nobody really comes here to hunt because of the spell."

"They did say that."

"So whoever it is must likely have business with the witch."

"*Likely* is your key word."

"I see," said Nigel.

"Come on. Let's go see what else is out here."

The hunters took a left onto the main road toward Devil's Mountain. They passed Laura Krause's house and the Coleman farm before winding back up into the hills. They passed the meat processor and rode another mile or so before coming upon the first of several pull offs around the base of Mt. Braddock.

"Stopped here on my way in," said Nigel. "Not much to see. Looked a bit of a hike so I rode on."

"It *was* a hike," said Ballantine.

"This is where you got your four?"

"Well, up, over, and down a ways, yeah."

"No wonder you only brought back two."

"I tell ya."

The road descended and wound on for another half mile. There were other pull offs, but none worth stopping to inspect. As the road leveled off, the trees thinned. Nigel slowed them down. Ballantine saw that the road carried on across a plain. Nigel hung a left onto a dirt and gravel road, not unlike Fayette Run, that continued along the base of Mt. Braddock.

The road ran level for a half mile, dividing the mountain and the field, then forked. The left branch twisted up into the thick. The right continued along the base. Nigel took the left fork. Gravel crunched beneath the tires and tinkled off the wheel wells. Big stones bounced the big men in their springy seats. The grade steepened, shifting some of their weight to their backs.

"Just up here is where I was last night," said Nigel.

"Brave man," said Ballantine.

The road leveled and narrowed, falling away off the passenger side. Instinctive trepidation pumped Ballantine's heart faster as he looked out his window and what appeared to be straight down to the treetops. Nigel's assertion that he had done it last night was the only thing that kept Ballantine from questioning whether or not the path was actually wide enough.

A pull off appeared on the other side of a great stone and the road widened enough to breathe. Nigel parked, hopped out, and waved Ballantine over.

"Here's where I was," said Nigel as they walked. "You can see we're on a little bit of a peak, which is nice. Gave me the high ground. I tossed my bait down there, set up shop on this rock, waited, waited, waited, then *pow*."

"How many were there?" asked Ballantine, leading Nigel down the bank.

"Three."

"Where'd you throw the bait again?"

"A little further down. I say, it wasn't much fun hauling the carcass up *this* bank. I mean I've carried heavier on steeper, but never with the looming threat of a pack returning. Quite a rush though, I can tell you. Oh, you should be about where I killed it now."

"I can tell," Ballantine said, inspecting the ground. He found a few drops of blood on some dead leaves and a whole mess of hoof prints.

"What are you looking for?"

"Just wanted to see about how many return after one is killed."

"Ah, excellent thinking. So we can know what we're dealing with in case we get caught."

"Yeah." Ballantine furrowed his brow in concentration and took large steps around the area so as not to disturb it as much.

"So how many did those buggers bring back, you think? Ten?"

Ballantine shook his head. He didn't believe his own assessment.

"Fifteen?"

The monster hunter shook his head again. He didn't *want* to believe it was more than that, but the evidence didn't lie.

"How many then?"

"About 20 or 30."

Nigel's mouth fell open and he breathed, "Oh, mama."

Ballantine looked up at him and nodded.

"Could you imagine? That's not a pack. That's a *swarm*!"

They got back into the truck and kept on. Further ahead, the road forked again. The left path went up and in, the right path, down the mountain. The men chose the left path, climbing shallow, rough, and narrow into the trees. Nigel took it easy and hung out of his window to make sure his tires stayed on the path. Four-wheel drive wouldn't be much help on a drop that sheer. Ballantine could almost reach out and touch the mountain on his side.

A half mile along, the path dead-ended at an overlooking cliff. With just enough room, Nigel turned around before turning off the engine. The men got out and stepped to the edge of the cliff. Ahead of them was a 50-foot drop to a slope that continued down into more trees. To their left was the valley along which they had just been traveling. To their right, the mountain rose sharply upward. However, with the trees obscuring, they couldn't tell how much higher it reached.

Oooo*OOO*!!!

The sound echoed from somewhere in the trees.

"What the devil?" said Nigel, taking steps back to the cab.

"Shug monkey," said Ballantine scanning the woods and reaching for a pistol.

Oooo*OOO*!!!

"Dangerous?" Nigel asked.

"Can be," Ballantine said.

"Weapon?"

"If it's just the one, a medium rifle will do."

"And if it's more than just the one?"

Oooo*OOO*!!! Oooo*OOO*!!!

Oooo*OOO*!!! Oooo*OOO*!!!

Oooo*OOO*!!! Oooo*OOO*!!! Oooo*OOO*!!!

Oooo*OOO*!!! Oooo*OOO*!!! Oooo*OOO*!!! Oooo*OOO*!!!

"We gotta move," said Ballantine. "Now."

The severity in the monster hunter's voice rattled Nigel's steady confidence. The Brit hopped in, started the engine, and slammed it into gear. A knock on his back window made him jump. He looked in his mirror to see Ballantine motioning for him to slide the window open. He did so.

"Mind if I borrow your AK?" Ballantine asked.

"Sure," said an atypically shaky Nigel Carrington. "Sure." He popped the AK-47 out of the rack and passed it through the window, then pulled two magazines out of a box. "Sixty rounds enough?"

"Should be plenty."

"Here," he said, reaching for another magazine. "Take 90."

Ballantine smirked as he shoved the extra mags in his belt. "Roll your window up and just focus on getting us out of here," he said.

Nigel became aware of the sweat beading on his forehead. His shaking hand slipped off the window crank twice. When the window was up, he slammed his hand on the steering wheel, both to shake out the nerves and work out his frustration with himself. He was Nigel Carrington: world traveler. He'd hunted the most dangerous animals on earth. Here he was, armed to the teeth, and about to soil himself over a bunch of monkeys. How bad could they be?

Del Ballantine crouched against the truck's rear window for support as it bumped and bounced along the path.

Oooo*OOO*!!! Oooo*OOO*!!!

Oooo*OOO*!!! Oooo*OOO*!!!

Oooo*OOO*!!! Oooo*OOO*!!! Oooo*OOO*!!!

Oooo*OOO*!!! Oooo*OOO*!!! Oooo*OOO*!!! Oooo*OOO*!!!

The shug monkeys appeared first as amorphous black spots blinking in and out of the leaves, shaking the trees, snapping branches. Five of them... Ten of them... Twenty of them... all gaining on the crawling truck.

"How we looking there, mate?" Nigel called out.

Twenty-five of them.

"Fine, Nigel," Ballantine said. "You just keep driving."

Oooo*OOO*!!! Oooo*OOO*!!! Oooo*OOO*!!! Oooo*OOO*!!!

Oooo*OOO*!!! Oooo*OOO*!!! Oooo*OOO*!!! Oooo*OOO*!!!
Oooo*OOO*!!! Oooo*OOO*!!! Oooo*OOO*!!! Oooo*OOO*!!!

Thirty... ish.

"The passenger window is still open!" Nigel called.

"You got a pistol in there?"

"Yes."

"There's your backup plan."

Nigel pulled a .38 special revolver from under his seat and held it tight.

The chorus of howls grew as the creatures swung nearer. They were four feet tall and inky black. Their silken fur billowed like clouds of black smoke. Only the pinpricks of light in their eyes and the glisten of drool on their fangs gave any indication they even had faces or forms beneath. Black leather claws emerged in succession to grip creaky tree branches.

Ballantine squeezed the trigger...

RA-TAT-!!!

...and the nearest looming shug monkey fell in a heap about 50 feet behind the truck.

Nigel checked his mirror for a reference, but saw no monkey.

"I like this gun," said Ballantine. He had experience with AK-47s, but it had been a while. He didn't remember it being so smooth.

"If we make it back alive, it's yours," said Nigel.

RA-TAT... RA-TAT!!!... Two more monkeys fell, but the troop gained and surrounded from the branches.

Ballantine twisted and fired, turned and shot, hit and missed as the monsters disappeared and reappeared behind the trunks. Two monkeys made it overhead and dropped down, forcing Ballantine to spray a line of bullets straight up.

The bodies fell into the bed in front of him. Their force pushed a rear wheel off the side of the path. Ballantine put a foot on the wheel well for support as the back end sank and shifted.

"You're okay!" he called to Nigel. "Just keep on, steady."

Nigel fought his instinct to hit the gas as the back end slugged to the side. He was white knuckled at 10 and 2, pinning the gun in his right hand against the wheel. The only part of him not clenched was his trigger finger.

RA-TAT... RA-TAT...

Oooo*OOO*!!! Oooo*OOO*!!!

Dark blots dropped to the path ahead of the truck, raised their arms, and jumped up and down. Every muscle of Nigel's face twisted as he pushed back against his consummate fear about the open window.

RA-TAT... RA-TAT!!!...

Oooo*OOO*!!! Oooo*OOO*!!!

"Mr. Ballantine!" Nigel called.

Ballantine arched himself up to see, through the windows, the five shug monkeys standing on the path ahead of them. More on the way. He brought down three in the trees above, then twisted around and stood, one foot on the bed, another on the wall.

RA-TA-TA-TA-TA... tck, tck...

The first magazine brought down three of the obstructing creatures, then ran out. Ballantine was removing the empty magazine when a shug monkey landed on the high wall of the bed, jolting the entire truck and sending the back end further over the side. The monster hunter lost his balance and nearly fell out as the rear axle ground along the edge of the path. He dropped his weight, spun, and drew a pistol with his left hand. As efficient as he was with a rifle, the pistols were his home. His left hand snatched the gun, fired through the monkey's head, and re-holstered as fast and precisely as a rattlesnake.

Ballantine pulled another AK magazine from his waistband, loaded the rifle, then stood and spun in time to see the two monkeys on the road charging at the truck. He got one shot off, killing the first monkey. The other one disappeared in front of the hood.

...

No thump. At five miles per hour, it was probably too much to hope for anyway.

BOOM!

The truck shook and the back end slid even further over the

side. The left rear wheel clung feet from the edge as the axle ground on. Ballantine fell to his back in the corner where the bed met the wall. A shug monkey perched above the wheel well on the opposite wall. Two pin dots of light glinted deep in the black well of its face. The creature bared its slick fangs and let out a roar that gave the hunter goosebumps and hollowed the driver's guts.

Ballantine raised the AK to take aim, but another shug monkey landed next to the first one, shaking the truck again. The two monkeys jumped up and down, roaring. Ballantine curled a hand under the lip of the wall to keep from being bounced out.

As the axle dug in and Nigel lost speed, he pressed the gas a little harder. The wheels coughed dirt out the back and down the mountain. The suspension sobbed as the monkeys jumped.

Then the men caught a break. The right rear wheel caught a projecting stone, popped the truck upright and back onto the path. One of the jumping monkeys fell onto the bodies in the bed. The other was able to maintain its balance on the wall. Ballantine had regained himself as well. While lying on his back he fired two through the fallen monkey's head and two center mass on the perched monkey, causing it to fall backward off the truck.

BOOM!

Another monkey landed on the spot from which the last one had fallen. This time the truck held to the path.

The monkey from the road ahead climbed up the front and peered its soulless eyes over the hood at Nigel. It pulled itself up one hand, then one foot, at a time.

"Mr. Ballantine!" Nigel called.

"Busy!" the monster hunter called. He was still on his back taking down the pursuing shug monkeys, trying to fire in between the bumps.

To Nigel's credit, he kept the wheel and the speed steady. The monkey on the front jumped and smashed its fists into the hood, leaving two large dents. Nigel pointed his revolver at it with a "Go on! Go!" It leapt again, put two more dents in the hood, then leaned its face close to the windshield.

Nigel aimed his pistol at the creature, but couldn't mask the fear in his eyes. The monkey snarled, making the Brit jump and recoil at the proximity of its horrendous jaws. Nigel almost pulled the trigger, but decided a barrier like his windshield was best left intact for as long as possible. Then he betrayed himself with a glance at the passenger window. The creature noticed, then crawled over the glass to the roof. Nigel remembered Ballantine was in the bed, likely with his back to the monkey crawling over the top. The Brit fired two shots through the roof, temporarily deafening himself. He looked in the mirror. Ballantine was still facing backward shooting. Monkeys were still falling out of the trees.

The shug monkey on the roof swung through the passenger window feet first. Appearing in Nigel's peripheral as a flash of black, its non-shape devoured the man's courage. He snapped his arm down and turned his head in time to see pin dot glimmers, silvery strands, and leathery claws coming toward him. Terror coursed through Nigel's arm and into his trigger finger.

He never felt the gun kick. The pin dots and silver strands disappeared. The claws fell. The mass of hair slumped against the passenger door. Nigel glanced at the path to make sure they were on track, then pulled the trigger eight more times, firing his last three shots into the black mass before click, click, clicking until he realized he was empty.

The danger had passed, but the fear still stormed inside him. It clenched his teeth and pumped his chest. With nowhere to go, it turned to frustration. Nigel threw the gun on the floor and cried out in release.

Ballantine looked back in time to see the Brit slamming his open palm against the steering wheel over and over. He called out to Nigel but received no response. The monster hunter reached through the back window to tap the Brit on the shoulder, startling him and almost causing him to veer off the path.

Ballantine's smile calmed Nigel's racing heart. The monster hunter said something Nigel couldn't quite make out through the ringing in his ears.

"What?!" Nigel said.

Ballantine's voice was muffled, but audible. "I said, the rest are bugging out! We're in the clear!"

Nigel shivered in his seat and pulled himself together. "Jolly good!" he said. "Jolly good."

When they reached the fork, Nigel put the truck in park to regroup.

Ballantine opened the passenger door and the shug monkey body fell out.

"You wanna help me with this?" he asked.

"S-sure," Nigel said, still coming down from his adrenaline rush. He hopped out and grabbed the beast by its ankles... or its wrists... or one of each. No, they were definitely the ankles. He could tell by the length of the feet compared to the hands. On three, the two of them heaved it into the bed.

"You okay?" Ballantine asked.

"Of course!" Nigel said, a little too forcefully. He crossed his arms behind his back to hide the shaking and looked in the bed to avoid Ballantine's eyes. "My, we got ourselves a nice take didn't we? How many is that?"

"Looks like five or six."

"Wonderful," Nigel said clasping his hands tight. His apprehension wasn't lost on Ballantine.

"You ready to head back?"

"What? Why? Got all this daylight left." Nigel was too insulted and angry at himself to answer any other way. "Onward!"

The pair got back in the truck and Nigel turned left onto the fork they didn't take earlier. The road snaked and bumped slowly down the mountainside, every once in a while branching off to another path. In the interest of covering as much ground as possible, the men left the branches alone, instead simply taking note of how many there were and the condition in which they appeared to be. Ballantine fingered one of the door's bullet holes as he looked out and down the side. He found himself at ease bouncing along inches from the drop off.

Nigel recounted the events in his head: the fear that had

gripped him at the mere sound of the approaching monkeys, how unsteady his hand had been winding up the window, and how he carelessly emptied his weapon into the creature, leaving himself defenseless. It ate at him as he glanced at the placid Del Ballantine. There was no way the monster hunter *hadn't* noticed Nigel's foibles. He was kind enough to say nothing of them though, sparing the Brit's pride. Nigel appreciated that, and found himself with a new level of trust in the man to his right.

"Look, uh, Mr. Ballantine... I'm not... er... I'm sorry if I lost it a bit back there. Not entirely sure what was the matter with me."

"Happens. We made it out. S'all that matters."

"I've been thinking about it. All these years of hunting around the world and I've never been the hunted. You go hunting tiger and they put you up on an elephant, surround you with guides, practically point them out to you. A lion, you can spot from across the savanna—same with elephants, naturally. Indeed, the majority of game that would attack a lone man is the very game that requires a group to hunt anyway, either to guide or help retrieve.

"I dare say, apart from my devil hunt yesterday, it's rare that I've been outnumbered by prey... prey that would pose me a threat, that is. And I've *never* been as up close and personal as today. I've *never* been in a... kill-or-be-killed situation."

"Well, if you're gonna hunt monsters," Ballantine said, "you better get used to being hunted yourself. These things were bred to torture humans. That reminds me, if you end up in a situation where it doesn't look like you're going to make it, you might want to save a bullet for yourself."

"Damnit man, how do you stay so cavalier about everything? I was a bag of jelly back there and you were rock solid. How do you escape the fear?"

"First off, I *do* get scared. Anybody who tells you they don't is either lying or crazy. Best anyone can do is channel it. Secondly, most fear is fear of the unknown. I've dealt with shug monkeys before, so I had an idea of how to handle them. You've never even *seen* them, so *of course* you're going to be afraid. You didn't have any idea how big they were, how they moved, how they attacked.

It's like your first time swimming or skydiving."

"Perhaps with practice, I might learn to channel my fear?"

"There's a lot to be said for practice."

Nigel sighed and smiled.

"Then again," said Ballantine, "my cousin's been practicing guitar his whole life and he *still* sucks, ha, ha."

Nigel's self-confidence sank again. What if he'd been a sham his entire time as a hunter? What if he'd had it too easy, with the benefits of guides and the best weaponry and technology?

The bumpy, inclined path met the relatively smooth, level road along the base. The change was refreshing to both of them—like taking their boots off at the end of the day.

After a few more minutes of driving, they came to a three-way intersection. Ahead of them, the road was blocked by a chained double-swing gate twice the height of the one at Mt. Fayette. The chain was of a hefty girth and dark with oxidation. No simple bolt cutters would be getting through it, nor the padlock. Although it didn't seem as old as the chain, it was rusty enough for Ballantine to wonder if a key would even turn. And then he wondered, "Who has the key, anyway?"

To the right, the road took them out of the woods and onto the plain. They'd ridden it for a couple of miles and were thinking about turning around when it began to bend to the left, putting the Rogue Mountains outside Nigel's window. Ballantine craned and bent around to get a bearing. Out the back window, over the driver's side of the bed, Wood Devil Mountain was rimmed in gold from the evening sun. Ballantine figured they'd only gone about halfway up, earlier.

Outside Nigel's window stood Mt. Liston, the Cave Worm's Mountain. Until then, the only part they'd been able to see from town was the peak rising up between the other two. It looked weathered and depressed, slumped and round, like an old man waiting to die. Sticking up behind was Mt. Fayette, the Witch's Mountain.

"Feels like the bloody dark side of the moon over here," said Nigel. "Wonder how often anybody actually comes through this way."

"Enough that somebody feels like they need to put a gate up, apparently," Ballantine said, pointing ahead.

They came upon another gate. This one was the same as the last, and blocked a road branching off to the left, toward the cave worm's mountain. On either side of the road was a ditch. They parked in front of the gate and got out.

"Funny, isn't it?" Nigel said. "This truck just conquered a mountain. Put a little wire and wood in the way, dig a little trench, and she's completely stymied."

Ballantine leaned against the fence and looked through, sizing the mountain up, gathering all the information he could: rusty chains, rusty lock, no tire tracks. No one had been there for a long while.

"So that's the cave worm's mountain, eh?" said Nigel. "Feels doubly ominous with the gate in the way. How much of the legend do you think is true?"

"I always prepare for all of it," Ballantine said, "and more, if possible."

"And how does one prepare for a foe that wills its prey into its mouth?"

"That I don't know."

"You don't know? The great monster hunter hasn't any experience with telepathic beasts?" Nigel mocked.

Ballantine gave him a razor-sharp stare and said, "My father was *killed* by a telepathic creature."

"Oh my... I-I didn't mean to... I'm terribly sorry."

CHAPTER 11

Twenty years earlier…

Autumn.

Delaney Ballantine had just received his first hunting license. He could have gotten it sooner, but his father Ron refused until the boy had learned enough about survival, tracking, and animal behavior to be able to take care of himself in an emergency.

"You can have all the fancy equipment money can buy," Ron would say, "but it won't do you any good if your gun jams and there's a ten-point bearing down on you. A high-powered scope won't help you see a rattlesnake at your feet. And a shotgun ain't going to lead you out of the woods if you're lost. The most dangerous thing you can do is think you're at the top of the food chain just 'cause you're carrying a gun. Mother Nature *has* never and *will* never bow to man. Best you can do is be prepared... and there's no reason you shouldn't."

Delaney, having had to listen to his friends brag about their kills for the last two years, was hungry for a quality hunt. He wasn't going to sit in a tree and shoot the first thing with antlers to cross his path. He was going to track a ten-point, stalk it, practically walk right up to it.

Black tree limbs clawed at the cobalt sky above the back country road. The air was still. Not even the birds were awake yet.

He swung his feet out of the truck and onto the dewy grass. The air was chilly, but it would be warm by the time they were done. In fact, he thought, he'd probably be sweating as he dragged his deer back. He closed the passenger door only hard enough to latch it. It groaned as it swung, then gave a gentle click.

The boy slung his rifle over his shoulder and shuffled down the bank alongside his father. Del's camouflage hand-me-downs hung on his frame like a sail and threatened to slide off his waist if he didn't attend them. Even with an extra pair of socks, the boots wobbled on his feet. He hated them, but that was all. To him, the early mornings, the cold, wet feet, and the too-big jacket were all as inevitable as a bowel movement, but he didn't like the idea that if he needed to run, he could trip. It seemed to fly in the face of everything his father taught him about preparedness. Then again, Ron didn't seem worried about it. They were together, anyway, and Del trusted his father with his life. Ron didn't like the idea of giving the boy ill-fitting clothes, but new ones weren't really in the budget. Especially, since he would soon grow out of them.

The sky brightened. Father and son searched for tracks, stalking through the woods, trying to make as little noise as possible. A little less than a mile in, they found some, but not what they expected.

"What do you know about these prints?" Ron asked.

"They're deep and far apart," Delaney said. "Two people and a... I don't know."

"What *do* you know?"

"The people were running. Probably chased by whatever made those."

"Go on."

"One's a set of oxfords. The heel is deeper which means it's taller. So it was probably a girl... or a woman."

"Which is it?"

Del furrowed his brow at the tracks. It felt like his brain was lifting weights. "Well... The other set of prints are Chuck Taylors, and not a whole lot of grown-ups wear those. Not a lot of girls either. High school kids, probably."

"And where'd they come from?"

Del squinted in the direction from which the tracks came, but saw nothing but forest. He had to think and remember where they were. "That way is... Darlington Lake?"

"That's right. Or maybe the park. So what's their story?"

"They were at the lake or the park and got chased by whatever *this* is."

"And what do you make of *this*?"

Del thought for a moment, then shook his head. "I don't know."

"What—"

"—*do* I know? Right. Right. There are two sets of four... fingertips?"

"Looks like it to me. Inch-and-a-half pads a couple inches apart. Notice how each one pushed the dirt in a different direction. That's another indicator of fingertips. They're not tightly together like a paw would be... or like its *toes* are. Tell me about the rear prints."

"Four sausage-like toes followed by another pad. Kind of like a person walking on their toes, but longer toes... wider feet."

"Good job," said Ron. "Weight distribution?"

"Hard to say with the different types of tracks. Maybe about even?"

"You're right. It *is* hard to say. Anything else?"

Del wondered what else Ron had noticed. The boy hated to disappoint. He strained his thoughts but came up with nothing.

"It's all right," said Ron. "You did good. I got nothing else either."

Pride flooded into Del for a moment before he realized he still had no idea what made the tracks. He asked his father for his opinion.

"That I don't know," said Ron. "But I know what it's not, and that's a start. Remember to pay as much attention to your surroundings as you do to the tracks. Keep your eyes moving. Take in as much as you can as fast as you can."

They followed the tracks along the crest of the hill, then down to a shallow creek with a wall of shale on the other side. The ground on the bank was soggy and contained deep footprints. A glance around didn't reveal any more.

"What happened?" asked Ron.

Del said, "They ran into the creek."

"Who did?"

Del looked a second time at the footprints and saw only two sets. "Just the boy and girl. They ran across the creek... but there's no way they climbed that wall... and their footprints don't come back out."

"No?"

"So they ran through the creek."

"Which way?"

Delaney racked his brain. He put himself in the situation. Something's chasing him. He hits a wall. Which way does he go? "That way?" he said, pointing downstream.

"Why?"

Del shrugged and said, "That's the way *I'd* go."

"Points for going with your instincts. The creek is running that way and therefore easier to run with. It's downhill. Also easier. Not as easy or quiet as running on land though, so if our guess is right..."

About 15 steps downstream they saw the tracks re-emerge and continue along the bank. A speck of white in the mud caught Delaney's eye. The boy checked his surroundings, then knelt to investigate.

"It's a shoe," Del said. He tugged on it, but the mud held it tight. He adjusted his grip and pulled hard until it released with a squelch.

"Saddle shoe," said Ron, pulling his rifle off his shoulder. "You were right. It was a girl. Better leave it where you found it. Let's move on. And keep your senses sharp." He took the lead.

The gravity of the situation washed over Delaney. On their last few hunts, Ron had made Del do all the tracking. For Ron to take the lead now meant the situation must be serious. The boy readied his rifle like his father, but couldn't do anything about the butterflies frolicking in his stomach. His thoughts went back to his boots. He considered different techniques for running in them if he needed to. And what was this nervous sensation in his arms? Why were his arms restless all of a sudden? What if his hands got weak and dropped the gun? Were his hands weak? They felt weak.

Ron put his hand out behind him and almost palmed the nose of the half-attentive Del. They had stopped at a small cliff where the creek turned into a six-foot waterfall. The sky provided a wash of soft light.

"Stay here," Ron said, his skin turning pale. "Don't look down there. Just keep your eyes on the woods."

Terrifying curiosity pumped through Delaney's heart. He asked, "What is it?"

"Just keep your eyes up. Watch our backs, okay? Whatever's out here doesn't mess around." Ron slung his rifle over his shoulder, made one more survey, then shuffled down the embankment at the side of the cliff.

When Ron had disappeared from view, Delaney refocused himself on his mission. The boy snapped the rifle up and scanned the forest. Ron had always complimented him on his discipline. Del had this under control. He didn't need to see.

"Oh my God." Ron's words floated just over the light rush of the waterfall. They frightened Del—made him sick. His father's voice was weak and desperate, two states in which the boy had seldom, if ever, seen the man. He had to check on him. Make sure he was okay.

Delaney Ballantine, rifle in hand, tiptoed to the edge of the cliff and looked down. Below him, his father stood over the mangled corpse of a teenage girl. The boy disturbed some pebbles, attracting Ron's attention.

"I told you to get back!" Ron yelled, scaring Delaney more than anything.

He scanned the trees for anything abnormal, trying to decide whether or not to remember what he had just seen. Regardless, the image would hijack his dreams for years to come.

The girl was Cindy Cantone, a sophomore at Del's school. They'd crossed paths every day but never really talked. Still, it was someone he knew. She was pretty, pretty enough to be dating Nick Sarnecki, one of the football players. Not anymore, though. Now her guts were all over the woods. There was an eight-inch hole in her belly, through which hung slick, rubbery shreds of intestine and other things Del couldn't identify. There were chunks of flesh missing from her legs and arms. Her skirt and shirt were in tatters, and of course she was wearing only one muddy saddle shoe. She had gaping wounds on her ribs, and her left nipple was gone. Her neck had been eaten down to the vertebrae, which seemed to glow a vibrant white amid the leftover decay. All of it was too surreal for Del to truly believe, like something in a movie.

Except her face. Her face was nothing like a movie. It turned his stomach. Aside from a couple of nicks, Cindy’s face was still in one piece. It was the way it lay, lifeless, like a rubber mask. He'd been to funerals before, but only for old people. Every time he'd ever seen a dead *young* person, they were only ever playing, like on a TV show or when playing army with friends. They still had life in their face. They still had color. Cindy's face was pale blue and completely slack. It melted on her skull like cheese on a pizza.

Sheriff Mike Capaldi had only just gotten off the phone with Marjorie Cantone, Cindy's mother, when Ron and Del walked in.

"Sheriff," Ron said.

"What brings you by, Ron?" Mike asked. He already knew it was bad news. He could tell by the way Ron walked, his complexion, and the timbre of his voice.

"We found a body in the woods," Ron said. "Teenage girl. Del here says she's Cindy Cantone, a girl from school."

"Bad?"

Ron nodded.

"Anything else for me?"

"She may have been with her boyfriend at the time. Nick Sarnecki?" Ron looked at Del for confirmation.

"Jesus."

"But we're not sure where he is. Looks like he got away."

"Not for long," the sheriff said, standing.

"Sheriff, Nick didn't kill her. Something else did."

"What?"

"Can't be sure. Never seen tracks like these before."

"Something from Pittsburgh?"

"Could be."

"Christ. All right. Can you take me to the body?"

"Sure can. Okay if I drop him off at home first?" Ron asked, pointing at Del.

"What!?" said Delaney.

"You don't need to be seeing that again."

"I *found* it."

"I really need to get there as soon as possible, Ron," said the sheriff. "Can his mother come get him? He'll be safe enough here."

"Probably."

The sheriff handed Ron the phone. Del's rage built with every whir of the dial.

"Hey, Beth, it's me," Ron said. "Everything's fine. I just need you to come pick up Del from the sheriff's office if you can... He didn't do anything. We came to file a report and now I have to go help the sheriff... We really have to get moving. I'll tell you about it later. Or Del can tell you... Okay, thank you... I love you too... Bye."

Del took a deep breath to protest, but Ron pointed at him and said, "Don't." And when Ron said "Don't," he meant it. Del's mind raced for an argument. It had to be good. It had to be sound. It had to be a knockout... and they were gone.

Despite the hard feelings, there wasn't anything more Del could have helped with. At the scene, Ron pointed out the tracks of both the creature and the kids. He gave Sheriff Capaldi his best idea of what had happened up to the point where the kids ran off the cliff in the dark, Nick got away, and Cindy was killed and partially eaten by the creature.

"I was with you until you said, 'killed by the creature,'" said the sheriff.

"But its tracks are all around her," Ron said. “There's a set in the dirt next to each wound."

"I didn't say it didn't *eat* her. I said it didn't *kill* her. Look here, in the dirt on either side of her hips, those deep half moons. Shoe toes. Those bowls on either side of her chest. Knee prints."

Ron couldn't believe he didn't notice it earlier. Or maybe he didn't *want* to notice it. The idea scared him. "Nick was straddling her," he said.

"And the trenches at her feet."

"She struggled to get him off of her."

"That's right. And judging by the blood under her nails, how much you want to bet our friend Nick has more than a few scratches on him?"

"But why would he... They were both running away."

"Well... You say it's one creature, right?"

"Yeah."

"Wasn't out for murder. It was looking for lunch. And if it was only looking to fill its belly, it wouldn't need *two* people."

"But why would Nick kill for it?"

"So he could get away. Ron, I wonder if you'd mind coming with me while I question Nick."

"Sheriff?"

"I'd just like you there to hear what he has to say about it. I hate putting it on you, but it looks like we got a monster in our woods, and you're the best hunter I've ever seen. Now, course you don't have to. It's not your duty."

"The way I see it, sheriff, keeping people safe is the duty of everyone who has the ability. Not just those who are paid for it. Glad you asked. Wouldn't've wanted to end up wrecking someone else's plan."

"As far as I'm concerned, *I'm* backing *you* up on the hunt. First thing's first though, and Nick's in *my* jurisdiction."

It was one of those "American Dream" houses. Not extravagant. Not humble. But big enough for the family who lived there. White picket fence and a nice lawn. Dan and Nancy Sarnecki saw the police car pull up. They'd opened the front door by the time the sheriff and Ron had reached the porch.

"Is everything okay, Sheriff?" asked Dan, Nick's father.

As they stepped onto the porch, both Sheriff Capaldi and Ron Ballantine noted the presence of a pair of muddy red Chuck Taylors just next to the door. As satisfying as hard evidence was to the sheriff, he took no pleasure in finding it this time.

"Uh," the sheriff said, "I'm afraid not, Dan. Is Nick here?"

"Nick? What'd he do?"

"I'd really just like to ask him a couple of questions."

"He's been in his room all day," said Nancy. Whatever the problem was, she hoped the information made a difference. "I'll go get him."

"What's this about, Sheriff?" Dan asked, his apprehension turning into irritation.

The sheriff sighed and glanced at Ron in a silent request for backup, then remembered whose job it was and reengaged Dan's eyes. "Nick's been dating Cindy Cantone. Is that correct?"

Every horrible possibility pecked at Dan's heart like vultures around a wounded antelope. "Yes," he said.

"Well, of course we're still going to have to talk to him, but—"

Nick shambled up the hallway with his mother's arm around him. He was pale, expressionless, and staring through the floor all the way to China. He looked overwhelmed and numb.

"Hey Nick," the sheriff said gently. "You okay?"

Nick knew why the sheriff was there. The boy didn't much care for small talk though.

"Nick, I wonder if you'd roll your sleeves up for me and let me have a look at your arms."

"Now wait a minute," Dan said. "I'm pretty sure you need a warrant if you're going to come into my house and—"

"I don't need a warrant to ask questions, and I'm not in your house. I don't *wanna* be, but if I have to, I've got probable cause."

"A teenage girl's word is *not* probable cause!"

"Cindy's dead, Mr. Sarnecki."

"What?" The frailty of Dan's voice scared him as much as the implication. Like many men from his day, he was raised to not show weakness, to be a *man*.

"Can I see your arms, Nick?"

"Hold on!" Dan put an arm across Nick. "Not without a lawyer. Fifth Amendment!"

"Nick doesn't have to say anything if he doesn't want to, Dan. But his arms are gonna be evidence. Now, the fact that there are footprints in the mud that match your boy's shoes isn't enough to *convict* him, but it *is* enough to question him. That he's white as a ghost now tells me he's more afraid than any innocent person should be. Now, Cindy fought her killer. If Nicks arms are clean, I don't have much of a case against him."

Nick met the sheriff's eyes. Dan had run out of arguments.

"Can you roll your sleeves up for me, Nick?" Sheriff Capaldi asked again.

Nick pulled his sleeves up to reveal forearms that were indeed scratched and bruised.

Nancy gasped, put her hands to her face, and moaned, "Oh no. Oh no, no, no, no, no..." Her stomach turned and she left the room bawling.

Dan grabbed Nick by the shoulders and said, "Now you listen to me. You do *not* say anything without a lawyer. Do you understand?" The vultures took chunks out of the man's heart. He fought them, but couldn't stop the damage.

"Come on, son," said the sheriff. "Hands behind your back. Nick Sarnecki, you are under arrest for the murder of Cindy Cantone..."

The words finished off what was left of Dan Sarnecki's heart. He cried out and slammed his palm against the doorframe over and over as the sheriff read Nick his rights. Ron steeled himself against his empathy for Dan with a deep breath, making himself ready in case he'd have to restrain him.

As the sheriff and Ron lead Nick back to the car, Dan called out, "I'm getting you a lawyer! Don't say one word without him there!"

They'd barely left the driveway when Nick said, "I didn't want to kill her."

With those words and Ron as witness, the sheriff had his confession. It gave him no pleasure. "So why *did* you?" he asked.

"It made me," Nick said.

"What made you?" The sheriff pretended he knew nothing to see if Nick's story would line up with the evidence.

"The... the thing."

"What thing?"

"The thing that was chasing us."

"What'd it look like?"

"You know those gray aliens they said they found in Roswell, that people always talk about when they get abducted? Big round heads, big black almond eyes, no mouth, long skinny body..."

"Yeah."

"Well it looked like that, but... I don't know. I mean, that's just some crackpot's drawing of one."

"What are you talking about?"

"It's just not what I thought it would look like if I ever saw one. I thought they walked upright. This one was on all fours."

Ron glanced at the sheriff. As far as he could tell, the story was adding up. The sheriff was starting to feel better about it too. If Nick's story matched the evidence, he'd have a better shot at a jury believing he was forced by the creature to kill Cindy.

"What else can you tell me about last night, Nick?"

"We were by the lake, on the hood of my car, looking up at the moon and the stars. We felt the car shake, looked behind us, and there's this thing crawling over the roof towards us. It looked sick and pale in the moonlight. Its eyes just... black... dead. And it had these long creepy fingers... Oh my God!"

"What?" asked the sheriff.

"I just remembered, for a split second at that moment... I wanted to kill myself. Then we took off running, but it kept up."

"Why did you run into the woods? Why not to the street or someone's house?" the sheriff asked.

"Because I wanted to protect Cindy."

"Not sure I follow."

"I told you, I didn't want to kill her. I could've outrun the thing and gotten help. But the woods were straight ahead of us and Cindy ran for them. I wanted to stay with her.

"Eventually, we ran into a wall by a creek, took off alongside it, and ran right over a cliff. Hurt my back. Knocked the wind out of me. That's when the thing caught up to us. I remember thinking we were dead when I saw it on the cliff above us crawling closer.

"By the time I got myself up to my knees, it had crawled up to me. We stared into each other's eyes for a few seconds. I heard it breathe. Sounded sick—all phlegmy and muffled."

Tears filled Nick's eyes. The bottom fell out of his voice as he continued. "Cindy's on her back crying and going, 'Ow, ow, ow.' And I wanted to *kill* her. But I wasn't *mad* at her. You know how people say they want to kill someone when they're mad at them? But I wasn't. I just *wanted* to kill her like it was... any other thing. Like I *want* to play football or *want* to go to the movies. You know? And I couldn't help myself. I got on top of her, put my hands around her neck... and for a second I thought, 'What am I doing?' I looked up at the thing. And it crawled closer to me. And I stared it in the face while I squeezed Cindy's neck. She beat on my arms and she kicked. And I remember trying to make myself stop, trying to get the thing out of my head... but I couldn't stop any more than Cindy could push me off of her.

"Then she stopped moving... and her pulse stopped beating under my thumbs... and I let go. I couldn't look at her. I rolled off, away from the thing, and just knelt there in the dirt trying to figure out what to do. Then it reached up under its chin and peeled its skin off up to just under its eyes, like it was a mask or something. Underneath, it was wet and drooling all over the place. The rattly breathing got louder. It crawled closer. Then I took off running."

"What'd the mouth look like, Nick?" asked Ron. "What kind of teeth did it have?"

"It was pretty dark, but I guess it kind of looked like a person's mouth, but without skin. The teeth were gross looking."

"Did it have teeth like people?"

"I guess, but longer."

"Like big fangs?"

"No, just like long people teeth... but all messed up."

They pulled into the police station parking lot. As Sheriff Capaldi turned off the engine, he looked at Nick in the rearview mirror and said, "Nick, I'm glad you told me everything. I believe you, and I think Mr. Ballantine here does as well."

Ron nodded.

"We're gonna do everything we can to help you out—prove your innocence—but I gotta tell you there's a procedure. There are things I gotta do by the book, you see. If you're telling me the truth, you got nothing to worry about in the end. But you need to understand, this is gonna be hard for a while. I have to book you. The paper will put you on the front page. There're gonna be people who believe you and people who don't. Depending how the judge sets your bail, you might be in jail for a while. Depending how people react, you might be safer there.

"Now, we're gonna need to catch or kill this creature you keep talking about. It's the only thing that's gonna help you. So in the meantime, as hard as it is to think about, I need you to keep trying to think of details about the monster, and if you think of anything, no matter how small, you need to let me know. Okay?"

Nick nodded.

"Good man. Come on now."

As the sheriff helped Nick out of the car, Dan Reynold's pulled into the parking lot a little faster than the sheriff was comfortable with. He slammed on the brake, stopping part way over the line of a parking space, threw it in park, and almost broke the key off in the ignition taking it out. As he got out, Dan slammed the heavy door, rocking the car. He strode toward the sheriff waving his checkbook in the air, saying, "What's it gonna take, sheriff? Huh? What's the bail gonna be?"

A few officers who had been either in their cars or on their way out approached.

"Easy Dan," Sheriff Capaldi said. "I believe Nick is innocent and we're gonna prove it. But what I really need is cooperation right now."

The sheriff saying that he believed Nick was innocent disarmed Dan. He followed them all inside.

Nick was fingerprinted and had his picture taken. He was given a hearing, during which Sheriff Capaldi recommended a lenient bail. The judge, trusting the sheriff, gave Nick the minimum bail, which Dan paid immediately.

While they still had some daylight left, Ron and the sheriff went back to the woods, rifles in hand, to see if they could track the creature further.

As they tracked, the sheriff said, "If you got any ideas about this thing, Ron, I'd love to hear 'em."

"According to Nick, it's telepathic; it made him kill Cindy, then released him because it got what it wanted. It's limited, though. He said he hesitated to kill her until it moved closer."

"You think it's got a range?"

"And a power. Remember Nick said he wanted to kill himself before they took off running? I'm betting Cindy did too. Monster tried to make them both kill themselves but wasn't strong enough, and they got away. When it caught up, it tried a different tactic."

"Well, shit. How do we hunt something like that?"

"Not let it get too close... Tinfoil hats, maybe?"

They laughed in spite of themselves. The tracks led them to the top of a ridge where they stopped to survey the area. The tree-covered hills rolled on, orange and black under the dimming sky. The trees on the high ground were rimmed with the gold light of the setting sun.

"Ron, we don't have much daylight left. I think it's about time to shit or get off the pot."

Ron pointed across the dip to the next hill, specifically to an overhang under which there appeared to be a hole. "How much you wanna bet?" he said.

"What do you think?"

"Well... I think I'm thinking you stay up here, find yourself a branch or a stump to steady your aim, and cover me."

"You're not thinking about getting *close* to that thing are you?"

"Its range can't be more than five feet. I'm only getting close enough for a better shot... maybe use myself as bait a little bit."

"I gotta say I'm not feeling good about this, Ron."

"That's called fear, Mike. You get it from the unknown. Tell you the truth, I'm not feeling very good about it either. I usually prefer to know my enemy a little better, but we need to nip this thing in the bud before it kills anybody else. If it gets me, you do what you gotta do."

Ron crept as silently as he could down the bank, never removing his eyes from the overhang.

The sheriff lay prone and rested his rifle on a fallen tree branch. He mainly kept his scope trained on the hole, periodically checking Ron's situation.

The gold disappeared from the trees. The sky had turned a placid dark blue. Magic hour, as the sheriff had heard it called.

Ron made his way up the next bank to a spot about 20 feet to the right of the hole. Sheriff Capaldi thought the hunter was insane for getting that close. Both of them trained their rifles on the supposed lair and waited.

POW*!*

The gunshot resounded through the trees, through the hills, and away into infinity. Sheriff Capaldi looked up to see Ron Ballantine's lifeless body tumble down the hill. After it came a monster slinking like a lizard to retrieve its prey. It was so pale, it appeared to glow in the dull light. The sheriff sighted the monster in and waited for the perfect shot. In the meantime, he tried to get his breathing and shaking under control.

Ron's body came to rest at the bottom of the bank. His limbs rag-dolled in all directions. The top of his head was missing. He'd shot himself. The sheriff channeled his despair at the sight into focused anger and steadied his rifle.

When the creature stopped at Ron's body, the sheriff fired a perfect shot through its bulbous head, cocked his weapon, and took aim again. The creature fell dead with its head on Ron's body. Sheriff Capaldi fired into the creature's torso for safety, cocked his weapon, and looked again through the scope. The creature hadn't moved. He put another bullet in its torso. Then another. Then another. Until he was out of bullets.

Ron was too big for the sheriff to carry by himself, so he went back to the car and radioed for help.

Before backup could arrive, however, a black car pulled up, followed by two black vans. Twelve armed men in black fatigues and black ski masks jumped out of the vans and formed ranks. The door of the car popped open and out stepped two men in black suits.

"Who are you?" asked the sheriff.

"You say it's dead?" asked one of the men in the suits.

The sheriff thought for a second, then said, "Dropped it on the first shot. Didn't move a muscle when I emptied the gun into it. Now who *are* you?"

The other man in the suit waved the apparent soldiers on. Some of them wore goggles on which they flipped switches, then marched on into the woods.

The man in the black suit said, "We're no one for you to be concerned with."

"Bunch of guys I don't know come barging into a crime scene in my town, I think I have a right to be concerned."

"You might have the right, but not the need. Our business is *need* to know. Not *right* to know."

"What are you? FBI?"

"The less said, the better, sir."

"What do you want?"

The answer was obvious, yet the man in the suit answered. "We're going to take the creature."

"Listen, I need that creature so I can exonerate a young man."

"You'll have to find another way. As far as you're concerned, this creature doesn't exist. You've never heard of it."

"Like hell it—"

"Mr. Capaldi. Mr. Michael Mario Capaldi. 1134 Church Road, Darlington, Pa. Parents: Antony and Abigail. Never married. No children. Only $3,000 left on his mortgage. Makes weekly visits to Wheeling, West Virginia for the purposes of—"

"What do you want from me!"

"Silence, Mr. Capaldi."

"What does it matter?"

"Everything and nothing."

"Okay smart guy, how about this, I'll keep quiet, but you use your magical powers to keep Nick Sarnecki from going to prison."

"Mr. Capaldi," said the man in the suit, stepping toward the sheriff, "I am under no obligation to make deals of any kind with you."

The sheriff stared into the man's hard, impartial eyes. What else could the sheriff give him?

"But," said the man, "never let it be said we can't be reasonable. As a matter of fact, let nothing be said of us at all." His impartial eyes turned cold and steely. "Ever... Do you understand?"

The soldiers, or whatever they were, returned with both bodies and loaded them into one of the vans.

"Hey, wait," Sheriff Capaldi said. "You're not taking my *friend* too!"

"I'm very sorry," said the man in the suit. "I really am. It's policy."

"What policy? Whose policy?! Who. The hell. *ARE YOU*!!!"

"Mr. Capaldi, I can understand you're upset, but I'm afraid time is running out on our encounter. So now you have a big decision you need to make really soon. You can assure me and my companion that you're going to forget everything you've seen and heard today. If so, we will be on our way, and everyone lives happily ever after. *Or* we can put you in that van with your friend."

The next day, Nick and his family disappeared. The car was still in the driveway. Their photos were still on the wall. It was as if they had been erased from existence.

The Cantone family saw it as proof of Nick's guilt and went on to start a non-profit organization to help people in need hire private investigators for the purpose of finding their children or the people responsible for their disappearance. They never found the Sarneckis, but they did help a lot of other people. They owed a lot of the credit to an anonymous $500,000 donation they received when they first got started.

The sheriff went on pretending that none of it had happened. When anyone asked him about what happened to Nick, his parents, or Ron Ballantine, he would say, "It's a big world, and I'm only in charge of Darlington." Well, anyone but Del and Beth, anyway. After making triply sure they would keep it to themselves, he told them the whole story. And they never told a soul.

CHAPTER 12

Ariana woke from her deep, dreamless sleep. She hadn't woken on her own, though. She dug through her memories. A shotgun had gone off. Yes. She remembered hearing a shotgun. Her father would need her help soon.

She sat on the edge of the bed and looked out the window. Only the top quarter of the mountains reflected the waning sun. She dropped her feet into her boots one by one and slipped them into place. She rubbed her face a few times, grabbed her rifle from the corner, and took her time clomping down the stairs and out the back door.

Apart from the fences built to keep his own animals in, Paul had built another fence, an outer fence, to keep the monsters at bay. Early on, he had learned the hard way that a determined wood devil would find its way over, around, or through. To counter, he built an inlet to funnel them and other slower-minded monsters to a pit of spikes. The farm was closer to the mountains than the hotel, so it saw more activity. Once in a while, a stray or two would wander down, catch a whiff of his livestock, and make a play. Anything that survived the fall into the pit got the gun before its screaming attracted unwanted attention or scared the chickens out of laying.

Paul stood on the farm side of the fence in front of the pit, scanning the woods for more of whatever he'd just put out of its misery. He turned at the sound of Ariana coming out of the house.

"You wanna get the lye, darlin'?" he asked her.

Ari leaned her rifle against a small shed, put on long gloves and safety glasses, then tied a handkerchief over her mouth and nose. She flipped the latch on the shed door and pulled out a wheelbarrow containing a spade and a bag of lye. Paul opened the gate next to the pit and she sprinkled the powder onto the shredded meat that used to be a wood devil.

"Pit's really filling up," said Paul. "After this guy rots, I imagine the bones'll be higher than the spikes."

Ariana was in a post-sleep ambivalence. No memories followed her. No expectations lay ahead. She was simply a consciousness in a body, sprinkling lye.

The lye, Paul had discovered, killed the scent of the blood and kept it from attracting other beasts. They had to be thorough, though.

"You hear about Pete Steen yet?" Ariana asked as she shoveled.

"Yeah," said Paul. "Terrible." Paul, like so many others was nearly numb to that kind of news. Grief no longer took hold of him. It just hung around like a specter.

Ariana shoveled until an inch of white lay on top of the meat and the framework of bone beneath. Paul complemented her work and she put everything away.

"What else?" she asked him.

"Nothing," he said, shaking his head. "Dinner's in the slow cooker and should be about done."

Ariana felt like shit. "Seriously?"

He nodded and gave a reassuring half smile.

"I'm sorry. You could've woken me up. I would've helped."

"I know. It's no big deal, baby. Come on. Let's eat."

Spoons clanked in bowls of wood devil stew. It was hearty, with potatoes and carrots from the farm. Ariana could barely get it down. It wasn't that it was bad, though the Idaho potatoes tended to turn to mush. It was that Paul had made it for them at least once a week, sometimes twice, for as long as she can remember.

She didn't hold it against him. He was a single father trying to maintain a farm nestled among monster-infested mountains. She understood, but it was one more bowl of stew, one more day off the calendar, one day closer to her inheriting the farm, waking up early, *milking the cows, feeding the chickens, QUITTING THE BAND—*

"Ari," Paul said, "you wanna talk about anything?"

Ariana realized she'd been stabbing a piece of meat with her tightly clenched spoon. "No," she said. "Do you?"

Paul pursed his lips and dipped his head saying, "Well, you came in here in a huff this morning. You're barely touching your food."

Ari stared down at her bowl and shook her head.

"Figured something might be on your mind... more so than usual anyway."

"I'm fine, Dad."

"How's the band?"

"Fine."

"Jeremy and Reggie?"

"Fine and fine."

"You guys working on any new songs?"

Ariana couldn't humor him anymore. She got up with a grunt and strode to the front door. Paul tried to figure it out as her footsteps clopped, the door slammed, and the engine rumbled away.

"Probably too many questions at once," he guessed.

Ballantine and Nigel continued down the road as it curled around to the back side of Mt. Fayette—the witch's mountain. Only the very peaks of the mountains shone gold.

"Never told a soul, eh?" asked Nigel.

"Well," said Ballantine, "maybe a few people."

"Who do you suppose those men were?"

"Well, I don't know what happens in England, but in *this* country, people who claim to have met aliens sometimes say men in black visit them afterward. Nobody really knows who they are.

Some say they work for the government. Some say they work *outside* the government."

"What do *you* think?"

"I don't tend to worry about them. Never seen them myself. Their business is aliens, and I haven't seen any."

"So your father was killed by an *alien*!"

"Kinda looks that way."

"And the Sarnecki family?"

"By the sheriff's account, my guess is they were relocated. Given a new life."

"Astounding."

Ballantine shot up in his seat. "Stop the car. Turn it off."

"What?"

"There's something moving!"

Nigel stopped and cut the engine. They were about 300 yards from the base of Mt. Fayette. The sun had finally slipped off the tops of the mountains, leaving the sky a smooth, tranquil blue.

Nigel squinted at the mountain out his open window and said, "Where?"

Ballantine leaned over and pointed, saying, "See that clearing in the trees?"

Nigel confirmed, then gasped and said, "I see it." He pulled a set of binoculars out from under his seat and took a closer look. "Oh, Mr. Ballantine," he said with a timbre of lust in his voice. "You *must* see this."

Ballantine looked through the binoculars. He'd seen bigger. He'd seen scarier. But he'd never gotten the particular chill he had at that moment.

"Have you ever *seen* such a beast?" Nigel asked, antsy with adrenaline.

"Only in books," Ballantine said. "One book... briefly."

"What is it? Looks like a demonic yak."

"Terror dog... I'm pretty sure."

"You mean a hell hound?"

"No. Hell hounds are like a cross between a Great Dane and an Irish Wolfhound. Their hair is shorter and they don't have horns."

"May I?" Nigel reached for the binoculars again.

The creature was roughly shaped like a bulldog, but with a bare gray head and long hair covering its body. Its forelimbs arched upward from massive claws to mountainous shoulders. Its head was as thick as the rest of it, wide and sloped, with two holes where a snout should be and two tusks protruding from its underbite. Its brow was a permanent knit. In the light, the eyes appeared to be a reddish brown. A pair of horns curled to the sides, like a ram.

"You want to try the sniper rifle?" Nigel asked.

Ballantine's gut told him to let this one go for now. Do a little more research. Maybe even ask around about it.

"I can tell you want to," Nigel said.

Ballantine did want to try that rifle out... and killing monsters was what he was here for... and they were armed to the teeth.

"Okay," said Ballantine.

"Jolly good," said Nigel. "Why don't you climb up in the bed and I'll ready the rifle for you?"

Ballantine did as he was told. Flies buzzed around the shug monkey bodies. They'd start stinking soon. Well... stinking *more*.

Nigel jumped out and passed his rifle up to the monster hunter. Ballantine looked through the scope.

"There's one in the chamber and the safety's on," said Nigel. "Ooh! And turn the dial on the side of the scope for night vision."

"Oh yeah," Ballantine thought, "the infrared sight." He turned the dial, dropping the built-in infrared filter into place, and looked again. Through the scope, the mountains shimmered as if they were made of stars. "What the..."

"Didn't I tell you?" Nigel said smiling as he brought the binoculars up to his face.

"What are they?"

"No idea, but through night vision they light up the mountains like daytime."

Ballantine elected to switch night vision off and take aim. He studied the creature for a bit, making Nigel as antsy as a child with a gift he wasn't allowed to open. The monster hunter wanted to take in as much as he could before he put it down, sear the details into his memory.

"Erm," said Nigel. "I don't mean to rush you, but we *are* running out of daylight."

Ballantine clicked the safety off, took a breath...

...aimed...

...slowly released the breath...

...waited...

...waited...

POW!

"Fuck," said Ballantine.

"Oh dear," said Nigel.

Through their lenses, it appeared the shot angered the creature more than it hurt it. It charged down the mountain toward them.

Ballantine reloaded and got another shot off, just before the creature reached the base. He thought he saw a puff of blood spray off of its back end. Didn't slow it down any, though.

"I'll get another rifle," said Nigel.

"No, grab the shotgun," Ballantine said as he took aim again. The monster's head bounced in and out of the tall grass at the mountain's base. The hunter fired. Blood puffed off the beast's shoulder. "It's not slowing down."

Fear rattled Nigel's arms as he pulled the loaded shotgun out of the rack. "Channel your fear, channel your fear, channel your fear," he thought to himself. He thought about how quickly the creature had charged. By the time it was in range, Nigel would have time for *maybe* three shots. Maybe he should use the AK. "Wouldn't the machine gun be better?"

"Shotgun!" Ballantine said, and fired another round into the charging beast.

"What if I miss?"

"Don't!" Ballantine fired again.

Nigel pondered.

"Come on, world hunter!" Ballantine egged. "Crack shot!" He let another round fly.

The taunt worked. Nigel remembered himself. He took a deep

breath and swallowed his fear, then walked toward the monster. The world slowed down and disappeared around him. He couldn't hear the shots from the rifle anymore, if there were any. It was Nigel, his shotgun, and the beast. Abstract concepts such as mortality and fear hovered somewhere in his blurry peripheral, out of sight and out of mind. He saw how the creature moved, timed it, anticipated it, became one with it. It was closer now—huge. He thought heard Ballantine's voice in the distance, as though carried on the wind over the mountain. It said, "*SHOOOOOOT*!!!"

Regardless of the prompt, it was time. In one smooth motion, Nigel raised the shotgun to his shoulder and pulled the trigger. He never heard the shot, but he saw the slug streak into the dog's open mouth and down its throat.

Ballantine looked up from his rifle as the creature collapsed, its momentum carrying it forward. One of its horns caught in the dirt, making it flip once before coming to rest feet from the unflinching, calculated Nigel Carrington.

The Brit turned to look at Ballantine and asked, "Are there any more?"

Ballantine scanned the mountain through his scope, saw nothing, and shook his head.

"Damn," said Nigel as he came out of his adrenaline trance. "I'm... so *ready* now. You know? I feel like I could take on an army of those things."

Ballantine chuckled and said, "Easy there, Hoss. Be careful what you wish for."

Nigel paced back and forth by the truck, working off his excitement. "Well of course I don't want a whole *army* of them. Maybe just one more would be fine."

"Yeah. Well, these monkeys are going to start to stink a lot worse if we don't get them back soon."

"Wait a tick. We're not just going to leave this here!"

"Well there's no way we're getting it in the truck."

Nigel thought for a moment, then pulled a machete and a survival knife out of the cab. "I must have a trophy."

Ballantine sighed. He wanted to start heading back. Nevertheless, he thought it only fair, especially since it was Nigel's first time standing up to death. The two of them hacked and sawed at it for a good 15 minutes before they had completely removed the head. Then they lifted it by the horns into the bed of the truck.

"That skin was tougher than I thought it was going to be," Nigel said as he started the truck and turned around.

"Boy *was* it," Ballantine said smiling. He was riding that near-death euphoria and realized Nigel must be feeling the same way. He looked over to see the Brit smiling from ear to ear.

"I say, Mr. Ballantine, I have jumped out of airplanes. I have climbed mountains. I have swum with sharks. But I have *never* experienced anything *remotely* close to the thrill I had just now."

"You did good today, Nigel."

Nigel thought his face would crack.

They rode in silence the rest of the way back to town.

CHAPTER 13

The satin sky snaked through the shadowed treetops above Reggie. As the old delivery truck jostled up the driveway, Reggie wondered how many more trips up and down it would make before it quit, how much longer before the wheels fell off and left an immovable steel box stranded in the hills.

Ken was prepping his work station when Reggie came in.

"You get everything delivered?" Ken asked.

"Every last thing," Reggie said as he strolled.

"Any problems?"

Reggie plopped the cash bag on the table and said, "No. I don't know how much longer the truck is going to last, though."

"You say that every time."

"Well it ain't fixing itself."

"What's wrong with it?"

"What *isn't* wrong with it?"

Jenny entered through the door to the house. "Hey baby!" she said to Reggie, standing on her toes to kiss his cheek. "What's wrong with what?"

"Truck's on its last legs," Reggie said.

"The truck is fine!" Ken said. "We ain't doing as well as we are because we spend all our damn money on shit that doesn't need done!"

"When's the last time *you* drove the truck, my darling?" Jenny crossed her arms.

"Woman—"

"*Man*."

Ken had an attitude and a temper, but there was no doubt he loved his family. Typically, they dismissed Ken's attitude as it just being his way. Reggie had always done what he was told. He went with the flow as always, content to let Ken run things. Ships don't sail as smoothly with more than one captain, and Reggie never cared to lead anything. Jenny had always seemed to just be grateful. Grateful for her family. Grateful for her life. She was upset so rarely that when she *did* put her foot down, Reggie didn't recognize her.

With that single word, the nicest person Reggie or Ken had ever known transformed into a gasoline can. And Ken was a lit cigarette.

Jenny almost appeared to grow as she stepped toward Ken, pointing, affirming, "If he says the truck is bad, you better listen to him. This boy is out in it every day... delivering meat... in a town full of monsters."

"Okay, baby," Ken said putting his hands out. "Okay."

"What if it breaks down on the mountain? Huh? You want our son stranded? Surrounded by fresh meat?"

Reggie suddenly realized how bad his situation would be if the truck broke down on him while he was out. It unsettled him until he reminded himself that nothing had ever happened.

"I had a lot of really bad dreams today," said Jenny inching toward her husband, "and I don't need *this* to add to my anxiety. You hear me?"

"Yeah, yeah, I hear," said Ken.

She stuck a finger in his face and said, "You get it fixed! Or you get a new one!"

"Okay," Ken said, backed up against the table, his chin pulled tightly against his neck.

"*Pronto*!" she said with a final lurch.

Ken's head bumped the overhead light, making it swing back and forth.

Reggie thought he saw his mother's eyes glow for a moment, then decided it was the way the swinging light hit them. With a puff, the fire inside Jenny went out, returning her to her normal self. She put a hand on Reggie's cheek and asked sweet as ever, "You playing tonight?"

"Only act in town," he said.

"Be careful out there."

"Always!"

"Be *extra* careful then. I've got a lot of bad feelings I haven't had in a long time."

"You worry too much, mom."

"And you don't worry enough. You bringing Ariana home again tonight?"

"Can never say for sure."

"How's that going?"

"Same as it ever was."

"You say that, but she's been here a lot lately."

"That's only because Jeremy's house is creepy."

"That poor woman. Well, let Ariana know she's welcome any time. Not just after shows. And tell her... Tell her I'm sorry for upsetting her this morning."

"What did you do?"

Jenny bit her lip and said, "I brought up her mother."

"Hoo! That's like, her biggest button."

"I just feel so bad for her, and I want to do anything I can."

"So come out to our shows."

"You know I can't."

"Yeah, yeah. Agoraphobia. Anyway, I'm gonna head down to the Foothill if you guys don't need anything else."

"Please be careful, baby. *My* baby," Jenny squished his cheeks together and pulled him in for another kiss.

"Okay mom, you're starting to freak me out a little bit. Dad?"

Ken shook his head to let Reggie know he didn't need anything.

As Reggie opened the door to leave, Ken said, "Hey Reg... be careful out there." Jenny had *him* spooked too.

The stars were in full regalia as Nigel and Ballantine pulled up to Ken's Taxidermy and Meat Processing. Ken hadn't had any visitors yet, so in the spirit of customer relations he stepped out to greet the men.

"That the same truck you had yesterday?" he said pointing as Nigel hopped out.

Nigel looked over his battered truck and couldn't have been prouder. "Battle scars, my good man," he said with gusto. "Gives it character."

Ken gave a short laugh and said, "Whatever. How'd it get so much character between last night and now?"

Nigel held up his hands as if to illustrate a picture and said, "Shug monkeys."

Ken raised his eyebrows and said, "*Shug* monkeys! Just you two?"

Nigel nodded.

"Shiiiit, okay!" Ken was genuinely impressed. "I'll give it to you. Y'all are good. How many?"

"Five or six in the back," Nigel said. "Countless on the ground, no doubt."

The tailgate screeched as Ballantine forced it open.

"Oh, of course Mr. Ballantine deserves the *majority* of the credit," Nigel said with a gesture. "If it weren't for him, I'd have no doubt been monkey food."

"Mmhm," said Ken, losing interest.

"Indeed, I dare say I found myself today—"

"Yeah that's great," Ken said, heading for the truck to help Ballantine unload. The monster hunter had slid two bodies onto the ground already.

"Oh!" said Nigel running ahead of Ken. "And wait'll you see what else we got. Wait there! Wait there! Mr. Ballantine, if you please."

Ken rolled his eyes and halted. Ballantine sighed and walked up alongside the bed. It irritated his ethic of finishing before he celebrated, but he did get a free gun from the guy. The hunters each took a horn and, after a three count, lifted the terror dog's head over the wall of the truck bed.

Nigel beamed. Ken recoiled. "Where... how...?" said the taxidermist.

"Got you speechless, eh?" Nigel said. "I don't doubt it. This was a toughie. To answer your questions, the base of the back side of the Witch's Mountain, a sniper rifle, and a shotgun... Top of the line, of course."

"Oh, you dumb, fucking idiots," Ken said.

"Uh... how's that?"

"Did anyone else see it—see you with it?"

"Just you."

"You better hope to fucking God, if He's still around."

"I'm afraid I don't follow."

"No, I know you don't." Ken ran his fingers over his mouth and beard while he considered his options. "You got one of two choices and you need to decide right now. One: Get back in your truck and take it as fast and far away as you can without stopping, dump it, and keep going. Two: We bust it up and incinerate it."

"To hell with *that*, I want my trophy!" said Nigel.

"Those are your options!"

"I give you money. You do your job. That's how this works!"

"You listen to me, Queen Elizabeth. I don't owe you shit and you're about out of time to make this decision."

"We'll bust it up," said Ballantine.

"Smart man," said Ken.

Nigel hesitated and sighed at the monster hunter. Ballantine returned a look that made the Brit feel like a spoiled child. Nigel pursed his lips, sighed once more, then helped lug the head inside.

"Y'all think you're just the baddest motherfuckers, don'tcha," Ken said. "Just put it on the ground by the table." He stuck his head into the trailer and called, "Jenny!"

"What?" Jenny's voice came from somewhere inside.

"Baby, I need you to get the incinerator fired up. Hot as it goes. And keep it fed."

"Sure thing, baby. Why?" Jenny couldn't help her curiosity and looked into the processor.

"Don't you worry about that," Ken said.

"Oh, hello Mr. Ballantine... and friend!"

Ballantine nodded.

Nigel fell in love.

Jenny noticed the lump in the shadows at their feet. There was something familiar about it that made her look harder. She took a step forward, but Ken barred her.

"Baby, you don't need to see it—" he said.

Jenny pushed his arm away and stepped toward the head. She knew what it was at first glance, but had given the shadows the benefit of the doubt. She stepped closer with hope that it wasn't. "That's not..." When she was within a few feet, the head shifted into the light. Its dead red eyes pointed straight at Jenny. She jumped a foot and put her hands over her mouth to muffle her scream.

She stood there trembling, looking back and forth from the head to the increasingly concerned hunters. Tears streamed down her cheeks. "You idiots," she quavered. She turned back to Ken. "That can't stay here. It has to go. They have to leave! *She's gonna find me!"*

"Baby, baby, baby," Ken said, grabbing her arms. "It's gonna be okay. We're gonna take care of it. It'll be like it was never here. Now, I need you to be strong right now and get that incinerator fired up ASAP. If you can't do that, then we *all* dead."

Fear and anger twisted Jenny's face as she tried in vain to think of an alternative. It hurt her to nod.

"Good girl," Ken said. "We're gon' be all right." He patted her butt and she left out the side door.

"Um," Nigel said, "what was all—"

"You shut the fuck up and grab that pick behind you!" Ken barked. "And give *him* the sledgehammer."

Nigel found a rack against the wall with shovels, a rake, the pickax, and the sledgehammer. He took the latter two and handed the hammer to Ballantine.

"So what do we do," asked the Brit. "Just—"

"Hit the fucking thing!" yelled Ken.

Nigel swung the pick over his head and brought it down with a grimace. It entered through the eye and penetrated up to the hilt, sending a spurt of blood and eye fluid almost six feet straight up. The head rolled a bit and stuck on the pick as he tried to pull it out. Ballantine put his foot on the head to steady it while Nigel figured out the angle at which to pull.

"You two need to move a lot faster," said Ken.

"Any tips?" Ballantine asked.

"Yeah. Go faster!"

Ballantine took a mighty swing that bounced off the beast's forehead. Then Nigel swung, tearing some skin but failing to penetrate the bone. The two of them alternated for a good five minutes without doing much more than shredding flesh. Then they heard a crack. Then another. Then another. Then the head collapsed. Nigel tried to work on the larger pieces, but the sledgehammer was better suited for it. Ballantine waved him off. The remnants were shattering like china at that point.

Ken strolled over with a knife and began to cut the flesh and ligaments away into manageable pieces. "Churchill," he said.

"Yes?" said Nigel.

"Put that empty bucket down here next to me."

Nigel put the pick away, took a five-gallon bucket from the table, and placed it on the floor. Ken sawed and sliced, and every once in a while, he would pass a larger piece toward Ballantine and point. Ballantine would smash, and Ken would finish cutting before tossing it in the bucket. When the bucket was full, Ken had Nigel run it out to Jenny.

Outside, Jenny tossed another piece of wood into the incinerator and folded her arms in an attempt to stop shivering.

"Are you cold, madam?" Nigel asked. He thought it strange since it was August and she was standing next to a fire. She gave him a mean glare that told him he'd figure it out if he bothered to think. He felt foolish as he remembered she'd been afraid and upset. "I do apologize," he said. "My name is Nigel. Nigel Carrington." He extended a bloody hand that Jenny only looked at. "Right. I'll just toss these bits in here then, shall I?... Good, then." For a moment, he thought he'd rather go back and fight the shug monkeys again than stand there under Jenny's freezing cold stare.

A piece of flesh and bone fell to the ground.

"Pick it up," Jenny was quick to snap. "Don't you leave one little piece behind."

"Of course, madam," he said, retrieved the escapee, then tossed it in.

As Nigel finished off the bucket, Jenny said, "I mean it. Don't you leave one tiny little piece out."

"I shall do my best, madam," he said earnestly before turning back to the shack. As he reached the door, Ballantine was on his way out with a bucket of his own. "Don't spill a drop," Nigel told him as they passed.

Jenny threw another two billets of wood into the fire. They caught flame immediately, illuminating the woman, shimmering on her glassy eyes. She didn't care to look at the approaching monster hunter. He paused in case she had a special instruction. When she said nothing, he took it as a cue to just do his job.

Ballantine took a step to the door of the incinerator, slid his fingers around a heavy piece of dog meat, then chucked it in. Despite being a man of few words himself, Jenny's silence needled him. He said, "I'm really sorry, Jenny. If I'da known it was gonna upset the two of you, I'da never brought it here."

Jenny said nothing.

"Can you tell me *why* it upsets you?"

"I *can*. Not *gonna*, though. You fucking cowboys'll probably just end up stirring the pot even more. Just *killing* this thing is gonna bring a storm. And if *everyone* survives it, we'll be lucky. I hope you realize Ken's putting his whole family on the line for you two right now."

"I do now, ma'am, and we thank you. And now that I know that, if there's anything I can do for you or your family to make up for this, let me know."

"I'll just hold onto that favor for a while, if you don't mind."

"Of course. Any time."

Ballantine finished his bucket and went back inside, passing Nigel at the door again. It took the men three trips each to get it all out there. When the area was clear, Ken soaked it and the path to the truck in bleach water. Anywhere the creature's blood might have been needed to be sterilized and camouflaged. They slid the rest of the shug monkeys out of the bed and bleached it too. Then they tossed one monkey up into the bed, cut it open a bit, and pushed it around to rub its scent and blood over the smell of the bleach. They didn't want things to look *too* clean. Finally, they dragged the other shug monkeys in and spilled some of their blood along the path to the place where they had dropped the terror dog's head.

"You got extra clothes?" asked Ken.

"In the truck," said Nigel.

"Back at the hotel," said Ballantine.

"Hope you're wearing underwear, Mr. Ballantine," Ken said. "We gotta burn your clothes too. They're soaked."

Fuck, Ballantine thought. He was afraid they were going to have to do that. All three men stripped and stuffed their clothes into a bucket which Jenny took away. Nigel and Ballantine each wore boxer briefs. Ken went commando, and that appeared to answer the hunters' question of why a woman like Jenny was married to him. He stood there like a scraggly, brown, big-dicked Buddha.

"Well, gentlemen," Ken said, leaning a hand on the table, "I wish I could say it's been a pleasure doing business with you, but the sight of you is really starting to piss me off."

"I'm sorry," Nigel said, "it's just that if we knew *what* exactly it was that 'pissed you off' perhaps we'd be able to better avoid—"

"Killing things that will get *me* killed pisses me off, Ringo. If you're smart, you'll leave town now. Why do I feel like I've said that before? If you stay, keep your hunting to the Wood Devils' mountain. Do *not* bring me anything from either of the other two. I don't even want to *know* if you get something on either of them. You got me?"

"Loud and clear."

"Now remember," Ken said. "You don't know anything about no terror dog. You've never even *heard* of a terror dog. You read? Even if somebody tells you they know you're lying, you keep lying. You got shug monkeys tonight. That's it."

"Ah yes, the shug monkeys," Nigel brightened. "I think I should like two of them stuffed. One at rest, and one attacking. What do you think? Ooh, and if Mr. Ballantine wants a keepsake or two as well, it's entirely on me."

Ballantine thought better of asking for anything from Ken. He tried to tell that to Nigel with his eyes, but couldn't get the message across.

"What is it?" Nigel asked Ballantine. "Oh, that's right, you're not one for trophies." He turned back to Ken, who had his head cocked, and said, "How much do you pay for shug monkeys, guts and all?"

Ken sauntered toward them, his big dick flopping back and forth off the front of his thighs. Ballantine stood like a soldier at attention, eyes front, using all of his willpower to stifle any reaction. Nigel was less worried about his own reaction, cocking his head briefly and raising his eyebrows in complimentary acknowledgment of Ken's blessing.

Ken stopped in front of them and said, "Shug monkeys usually pay $350 a piece."

"So $350 times four..." Nigel mathed, "...is $1,400! And Mr. Ballantine, I'll give you $350 for my extra mount. It's only fair, since you killed five of them."

"Minus a $2,100 disposal fee for the dog head," said Ken.

"Saw that coming," thought Ballantine.

"Oh, Mr. Adams, surely that disposal wasn't worth—"

"Nigel," growled Ballantine. "Quit digging. Mr. Adams, we appreciate everything you've done for us."

"I don't think you really *can* appreciate it based on what little you know," Ken said.

"Then we appreciate it as much as we can." Ballantine put a hand on Nigel's shoulder and said, "Come on."

As they turned to leave, Ken said, "I tell you what... *if* we all survive the week, I'll *think* about mounting one for you."

Nigel didn't have much of an appetite for unknown terror anymore. He gave Ken a nervous smile and a nod, then turned to leave with Ballantine.

CHAPTER 14

Nigel had put his extra clothes on before they left Ken's place. He offered Ballantine the jacket for at least a little modesty, but the monster hunter was content to ride back in just his underwear.

"What do you make of it?" Nigel asked as they rode.

"They say there's a witch on that mountain, right? We killed something from there. Killing it could get us killed. What do *you* think?"

"It was important to someone."

"And we had to cover our tracks, which means?"

"They'll seek it out," said Nigel.

"And Jenny. She said, 'She's gonna find me.'"

"Boy, you don't miss a trick."

"She's hiding. Probably best to pretend *she* doesn't exist either."

"Right-o."

The hotel was jumping. Nigel guessed he got the last remaining parking space. Ballantine gave him his room key and the Brit brought him back some clothes.

Inside, the place was smoky, loud, and standing room only. Most people talked with each other, except Sam, of course, sitting on his stool. Rick, Louis, and Andy were sitting in the same place as the night before, but the seats Nigel and Ballantine had occupied were taken by a couple of other men. Jessica's unmistakable blond hair bounced around in the color-changing light from the stage while the band played their more danceable stuff. Laura Krause appeared and disappeared amid the crowd like a piece of driftwood on a stormy sea.

The hunters headed to Ballantine's room, took turns in the shower, and then headed down to the bar.

"It's on me tonight, Mr. Ballantine," Nigel said as they approached the bar corner between Rick and Louis. "Whatever you want."

They each placed an order for a wood devil burger and fries and the tallest beers Kelly could pour.

"You fellas are back early," Rick said.

"Yeah," said Louis. "What you all bag yourselves tonight? Let me guess. You got 20 wood devils a piece and a family of hellcats."

"No," said Ballantine. He paused to give Louis a chance to comment.

"Aw, that's too bad," Louis mocked.

"We killed a little less than 30 shug monkeys."

"And saw a chupacabra," Nigel added.

Louis took a gulp of his beer and twisted his head to wring out his irritation. "You guys are so full of shit."

"Now, you see here—"

Ballantine put a hand on Nigel's shoulder and told him, "Hey. It doesn't matter."

Nigel took a steeling breath, then the two of them found some empty ledge space along the wall near Sam. Their beers went down fast. Ballantine got the next round. He handed a beer to Nigel and said, "Don't drink so much your tongue gets loose." Nigel replied with a wink. They were on their third drink when Kelly waved them over to pick up their burgers.

Seating was difficult to come by. The two hunters craned their necks as they navigated through the other patrons, past the bar to the dining and dancing area. Silhouettes rocked and flailed in the color-changing haze. The hunters held their food and drinks high to avoid an accident as they twisted and turned around the edges between the bar and the tables, scouting for a place to sit and eat.

"There!" Nigel yelled through the music, pointing.

In the back corner, furthest from the front door, farthest from the band, under a burned-out light, there was an empty table. Or maybe there was someone there. They moved closer. It wasn't until they were upon it that they noticed the woman sitting by herself at the four top. She looked a little bit older than Kelly. Her hair was wiry and gray. She wore dirty old jeans and a tattered t-shirt. She didn't even look at the men as they approached—just stared at the band.

The hunters exchanged the same knowing glance. Usually, if someone sits alone, there's a reason. In a place like that, where everyone knew each other, and as crowded as it was, for anyone to have a table to herself was cause for question. Could she be the witch? Should they join her and sit with the enemy, or should they walk away and potentially insult her?

"Excuse me," Ballantine yelled as he leaned down to her. "Do you mind if we just sit here to eat our burgers?"

Without looking at either of them, she turned up a shaky palm, then put it back on her glass.

Nigel widened his eyes at Ballantine and the two of them sat. Ballantine took the seat next to the woman. She smelled bad. Really bad. Like she hadn't bathed in weeks and never learned how to wipe her ass. The monster hunter noticed the odor as soon as he sat down. He silently cursed to himself and resolved to eat as quickly as possible. Nigel sat across from Ballantine on the horizon of the stench. The Brit was less tactful as it came over him. He flared his nostrils as he looked around for the source, then flashed his eyes at Ballantine when he realized it.

The music stopped and Jeremy announced they were going to take a short break. As Ballantine took his first chomp, he watched the dance floor clear off. He saw the kid Jessica took home the night before leading a girl to the bar. Jessica and a female friend wiped the sweat off their brows. Four or five hands shot out to them with drinks of different kinds. The women doubled over laughing and pressed their hands together for support. Jessica's friend had long, thick brown hair, killer eyes on a smooth, round face, and dangerous curves poured into a red-wine dress under a black leather jacket. It was hazy and she was across the room, so Ballantine reserved judgment until he could take a closer look. Regardless, he didn't plan on trusting many people from this point on.

"So, you two hunters?" asked the smelly woman.

The hunters exchanged glances, then Ballantine said, "How'd you guess?"

"Not a lot of people come here for the hiking."

"Well done," said Nigel. "And what is your name?"

"Brunna."

"Brunna?"

"Uh huh."

"Pleased to meet you, Brunna. I'm Nigel and this is Delaney."

"Del's fine," Ballantine said.

"So Brunna. That's an interesting name. Don't hear that everywhere. What's it mean?"

"I don't know," she said. "Something German, probably. You boys get anything today?"

The hunters exchanged another glance for caution's sake. Ballantine gave Nigel the option to speak, but the Brit deferred.

"Few shug monkeys," Ballantine said.

"That all?" asked Brunna.

"Yeah," Nigel said with a nonchalant pout. "No big deal, really." He lifted his burger to his face, said, "Do it all the time," then took a bite.

"I heard shug monkeys travel in big packs."

"A troop," Nigel said. "A pack of monkeys is a troop."

"Yeah. Who all'd you go with?"

"It was just us, ma'am," said Ballantine.

"So just the two of you go out, you only see a few shug monkeys, kill 'em, and now you're back."

"Well," said Nigel, "I mean there's a *bit* more to it than that. Don't want to seem boastful now, do we?"

"Mm."

"Anyway, how about you, Brunna? What is it that you do?"

"Oh, I mostly just keep to myself," she said far away. "Like to... experiment in the kitchen."

"Ah, you like to cook! Wonderful. Do you have a specialty?"

Brunna's eyes sparkled for the first time. She smiled and licked her cracked lips. "Off Fayette Run Road, there's a path that runs to a creek along the base of the mountain. A ways up the creek there's a whole... what do you call a troop of spiders?"

"Something to be avoided."

Ballantine smiled.

"Well there's a like a whole nest of 'em down there, and each one's as big as a dog. And there's always one that wanders far enough you can get it. Honey, you've never had anything like a leg from one of those things."

"No, I don't suppose I have." Nigel was grateful he only had one bite of his burger left. His stomach wouldn't let him eat anymore.

"Fry it up with some breadcrumbs."

"Sounds divine. Uh, Mr. Ballantine, I believe Ms. Waters has waved us over."

She hadn't.

"Shall we see what she wants?"

Ballantine, amused and eager, dropped the last bite of burger in his mouth and nodded. "Thanks for letting us join you, Brunna," he said.

"Yes, thank you very much," said Nigel. "Got to make the rounds though, I suppose."

"Mmhm," she said.

The hunters took their beers and baskets and didn't look back. Jessica and her friend were surrounded by men at a long table near the stage.

Nigel leaned close to Ballantine's ear and asked, "My dear boy, I cannot imagine having to deal with that smell at execution range. How ever did you endure it?"

"You know how I wasn't saying much back there?" Ballantine said.

"Quite."

"I went somewhere else in my mind."

After a thought, Nigel said, "Isn't that what they tell people who might be tortured?"

"It is."

Jessica brightened at the sight of the approaching hunters and gave them a wave. The swarming suitors on the other hand, darkened. It was the first good look the hunters had of her dark-haired friend. They almost melted into a puddle on the spot. Ballantine thought he'd never see anyone more beautiful than Jenny, but the brunette next to Jessica was a work of art. She looked about as old as Ballantine but much better maintained. She was elegant and buxom, with big, brown doe eyes. She was a ballet in a chair, from the way she lit her cigarette to the way she put down her drink. Her eyelashes beat like butterflies in half time. The diamonds on her necklace almost seemed to glow in the dim light.

"Don't be rude to our guests, boys," Jessica said to the men sitting across from her and her friend. "Make some room!"

The seated men scowled at the hunters and went to the bar. Jessica gestured to the seats. Nigel took the one in front of Jessica. Ballantine took the seat in front of the friend.

"Boys," Jessica said to the hunters, "this is my old friend, Mara. Mara, this is Nigel Carrington and Delaney Ballantine. Couple of hunters from out of town. Pretty good at what they do too, assuming their tales aren't too tall."

"Absolutely *charmed* to meet you, Mara," said Nigel, extending his hand. "If I hadn't only met Miss Waters last night, I'd say I can't remember the last time I met someone so beautiful." The flattery was obvious, but nonetheless charming. The accent helped. The women laughed.

Ballantine reached across the table with a simple, "Nice to meet you, Mara."

"Nice to meet you, Delaney Ballantine." His name was a gymnast on her lips. There was something distinguished about her that he couldn't place. The way she held herself—how she spoke without the not-quite-southern accent everyone else had—

she seemed more refined.

"So, you from around here?" he asked.

"Not originally," Mara said. She looked at the ceiling in an effort to determine where to start. "I'm from all over, really."

"Ah, a traveler!" Nigel said. "I've done a bit myself, you know."

"Really? Where to?"

"Name a place."

"Hmm, Rhodesia."

"Been a bit tricky with the war there."

"Hmm, Rome then?"

"Oh well, of course Rome."

"The seven wonders?"

"You know, I just realized I've never seen the Grand Canyon! I shall do that next."

"So, what do you *do,* Mr. Carrington?"

"Oh, you know. Travel the world. Hunt. Seek thrills. And if I can fit it into my schedule, a little investing here and there."

"I see. And you, Mr. Ballantine. What do *you* do?"

"I'm just a hunter," he replied.

"Just a hunter?" Mara asked.

"Just a hunter," Nigel said wryly.

Ballantine's eyes told Nigel to cool it. The Brit got the message but brushed it off.

"Come now, Mr. Ballantine, there's no need to be *too* modest." Nigel put a hand on Ballantine's shoulder and addressed Mara. "This man killed four wood devils *by himself* last night, and just today brought down a troop of shug monkeys with the help of yours truly."

"Is that a fact?" Mara said.

"On my life," Nigel vouched.

"And you collected and *sold* all the carcasses, I assume."

"Heavens, no! Mr. Ballantine here is the—"

Ballantine cut Nigel off before he spilled too many beans saying, "It's partly for sport. Partly for the thrill. Part for practice."

"I see," said Mara. "Don't you think killing for 'fun' is a little... barbaric?"

Ballantine considered his next words carefully. To be safe, he played ignorant. "No regulations on monster hunting. They're invasive species anyway. I say, why not?"

"Some might say every one of God's creatures has its place, and a right to live. At *least* as long as its minding its own business."

"And some might say God left us all by ourselves more than 20 years ago."

"And what do *you* say, Mr. Ballantine?"

He thought for a moment to make sure his words matched his intention. "I don't consider God much. I just try to do what I think is right with the time I've got."

"And you think slaughtering creatures is right?"

"The ones that pose a threat to people. Yeah, I do."

"Like lions, tigers, and bears?"

"Oh dear," said Nigel. "Say, I couldn't help noticing we're all running low on drinks. What say Mr. Ballantine and I buy you ladies a round?"

"Well," said Jessica, "I don't know how a lady could refuse *any* offer from a couple of fine men like yourselves."

Mara tilted her head and raised her eyebrows in acceptance.

Nigel smiled and said, "Gin and tonic was it, Jessica?"

"You remembered!" Jessica flirted, touching his hand.

"And for you, Mara?"

Mara took the last sip of her drink, then said, "Amaretto. One rock."

"Ah! La signora prende una bevanda italiana!"

"Si. È la mia preferita."

"Bene, dolcezza," Nigel said, standing.

"Grazie."

"Andiamo, Signore Ballantine, before we lose our seats to the next dashing rogues." Nigel winked at the women.

Jessica and Mara smiled at each other. Ballantine raised his eyebrows and followed Nigel to the bar. The monster hunter didn't care to be pulled into what he saw was a sex game. He hated the word-dancing and the whack-a-mole intent. He didn't have the patience for flirting. To him, flirting was like talking about eating; it planted the idea but didn't solve the problem. All in all, a waste of time.

"Hey man," Ballantine said leaning into Nigel. "You need to be on better guard until we're sure it's safe. We don't know who we can trust."

"Friends close and enemies closer, Mr. Ballantine. And since we can't be sure who's who, best to play chummy with everyone. Nothing looks guiltier than playing coy."

Kelly came by and took their orders. As Nigel ticked them off, she looked over his shoulder and caught eyes with Mara, who gave a warm smile. Kelly's eyes flicked back to Nigel as he finished his order.

"Looks like you're getting *more* than a little chummy with Mara," Ballantine said.

"Part of the game, my dear boy," Nigel said. "I haven't a chance with Mara."

"Better chance than most of the guys here, I'd say."

"Strange. I thought you were a better detective than that."

"How's that?"

"She's been looking at *you* like you're made of chocolate."

"Well *I* ain't playing any games."

"Neither is she. Honestly, Del. It's obvious she's someone who is very calculated in her decision making. She isn't flirty."

"She's flirty with *you*."

"No, *I'm* flirty with *her*. She's *polite* to me."

"Then why flirt with her?"

"To warm up Jessica. If she's with her friends, you must always get in *their* good graces. One unflattering word from them and she's out the door. Benefit number 2: pointing the spotlight at someone else makes her crave it that much more."

"Yeah, I'm not playing that game."

"I don't think you'll *have* to," Nigel said as their drinks arrived. "Mara seems like the kind of girl who gets what she wants under no uncertain terms. If it's going to happen, I should say the only subject you need to avoid is hunting."

"So I should just not talk about my entire life."

"Now you've got it. And honestly, that's good advice for anyone trying to get laid. Make it about her. Good advice for finding out a villain too, now that I think about it."

"This bar is packed though, man. Don't you think you can do better than Jess? I mean you're rich and have a British accent. She's no spring chicken."

"My dear Delaney, have you never *been* with an older woman?"

"How old we talking?"

"If you have to ask..."

With a drink in each hand, they turned around to see a small scraggly man who was somehow in the way of both of them. He wore a black wide-brimmed hat. A long black coat hung like curtains from his sloped shoulders. His eyes bugged out of his head. His lips were no more than a diagonal slit beneath the hundred-year-old rat he called a beard.

After more than a few moments of less-than-comfortable staring, Nigel finally said, "I say, would you mind, perhaps taking a step that way so we can get by, please."

"Tell your fortunes," the man wheezed with a voice not unlike the one everyone does when imitating an old man.

Nigel and Ballantine exchanged glances, then the Brit turned on a syrupy charm saying, "Oh that *does* sound delightful, but I'm afraid we must be getting back to our table." He nudged the air with his elbow and gave a wink, saying, "Got a couple of fine ladies waiting for their drinks. You know how it is."

The man held up a deck of tarot cards... or something like them. Nigel had had his fortune told many times, all with varying degrees of accuracy. It was just something fun to do on his travels. There were tarot readers all over the world, though he'd found the Gypsies were always the best at it. Wherever he went, however, the cards usually looked the same. But these were patterned in deep purple with gold lettering he didn't recognize.

"That is an absolutely *beautiful* deck, sir," Nigel said. "Perhaps later."

The man fanned out the deck and said, "Pick one."

Nigel rolled his eyes and pointed with his pinky.

The man removed it, closed the deck, and placed the card face up on top. "The Mask," he said. "This is your past. You're hiding something."

Ballantine looked suspiciously at Nigel. The Brit *did* seem to have arrived before the monster hunter. He wondered, "How long could he conceivably have been here? What are the chances *he's* the—?"

"Okay, mister," Nigel said to the man. "That's easy enough to say about anyone. I don't need you putting ideas into my friend's head at the moment."

"Pick again. This is your present."

Nigel reined himself in with a deep breath and pointed at another card.

The man drew it and placed it on top of the other one. "Spider and the fly."

The hunters gave a thought to Brunna and her spider talk.

"You're getting yourself caught up in something you don't want to be caught up in," said the man.

"Yes, yes," Nigel dismissed, "and another interpretation is that I'm on the make. And *another* interpretation is that I'm a hunter. And yet another interpretation is that I'm the hunt*ed*. And it's all open to any degree of metaphor. Now listen, dear boy, I'm getting rather tired of holding these glasses—"

"Your future!" the man fanned out the deck.

"This one!" Nigel pointed. "Then leave us alone."

The man flipped up a picture of a skull and said, "Death—"

"*Death,*" Nigel said before the man finished. "Of course, I should've known. How long have I got, old-timer? A week? A month?"

"Actually, the death card can just mean something's gonna come to an end, or you're going to let something go."

Nigel pursed his lips and closed his eyes as he rolled them. "Wonderful," he said. "Now, may I return to my table?"

"How about a tip?" the man ventured.

Nigel leaned in and said, "Never get between a spider and his barfly."

He pushed past as the man held the deck up to Ballantine.

"Pick," he said.

"No," said Ballantine, staring stone at the man.

The man stared back for a moment, then folded up the cards, said, "Okay," and moved on to the next person.

"However *did* you do that?" Nigel asked on their way back to the table.

"I've found the less I say, the less I have to explain. And that's good advice for anyone looking to lay low." It was a simple enough explanation, but Ballantine couldn't help wondering if there was a different game the man was playing.

Jessica shooed away another pair of men who'd taken the hunters' seats. "You boys make a new friend?" she asked.

"One too many, it seems," Nigel said as he and Ballantine sat. "Your drinks, my dears." The men passed them across. The glasses were on everyone's lips when Nigel raised his and said, "How about a toast?"

Ballantine sighed. He wasn't in the mood for many more shenanigans.

"To new friendships. May they be as true as the old ones."

Jessica "awed" as they clinked glasses. Like a flash flood, the music started up again. The change of atmosphere was like a splash of water in his face, only less refreshing. Ballantine hated yelling to speak, and he didn't like to make anyone else do it.

Mara leaned across the table and yelled to him, "Do you dance?"

He didn't. He abhorred it. It made him feel foolish. He looked over at Nigel, who was already on his way to the dance floor with Jessica. The Brit widened his eyes and pursed his lips at him. Ballantine weighed his options. He should keep an eye out for danger... but he shouldn't *look* like he was keeping an eye out for danger... but he shouldn't leave his back to Brunna or that weird guy for too long... but Mara looked good enough to make a man cry... and she *was* interested in him... but she could be the witch... but she might not be... the lights and smoke were a halfway-decent mask...

Ballantine looked around the room for an excuse, but all he saw was the strange man staring him down. He looked at Mara and nodded, then walked around the table to join her on the floor.

The song was funky. Ballantine didn't know much about music, but Ariana's bass line was irresistible. The monster hunter bobbed his head. Clinging to his beer like a life preserver, he looked around at how other people were dancing. He figured he'd copy someone. Nigel waved his hands in the air while Jessica wriggled her backside up and down his front. "Not him." There was a tall skinny guy pumping his arms and shaking his head violently, bending over, straightening up, stomping his feet. "No." Bobby was pressed against his new friend, slobbering down her neck. Only their clothing kept it legal. "Christ." Ballantine thought he'd excuse himself—say he wasn't feeling well.

The weird guy gave him the side-eye while telling someone else their fortune. Of everyone in the place, Ballantine got the worst vibe from him. The hunter took a swig of his drink and another look at Mara. Then he forgot himself.

The music disappeared as he watched her move. The white of her eyes flashed beneath the black flames of her lashes. Her thick hair cascaded over this half, then that half of her face. Her hips swung as if attached to nothing. As she rotated, Ballantine considered mating dances, that they must trigger a primitive instinct... or...

...

His thoughts vaporized as Mara's ass rocked into view. Mating dance, schmating dance. All he could think about was having her do the same thing in his lap.

As the blood left his brain, he reminded himself once more to stay on guard, keep an eye out, not drink too much...

Then Del Ballantine danced. At least he thought he did. He might have. He moved around on a dance floor while music played. The haze changed colors under the stage lights. The beautiful woman danced with him. His friend was nearby smiling a toothy smile. Drinks kept appearing in his hand. At some point, he wondered when he'd switched to whiskey. At the same point, he no longer really cared about one thing or another.

During a break, Kelly informed Reggie that his father had called and bought him a room for the night. Reggie didn't ask why. Jeremy was mingling elsewhere, but noticed Reggie say something in Ariana's ear, then Ariana nod and mouth, "Okay." The singer got that sinking feeling again. Ballantine and Mara got more drinks and did more talking. The weird man kept trying to make Ballantine pick a card. Brunna stared listlessly from the shadows. Nigel and Jessica split away from their companions to talk and drink more.

"I gotta say," said Jessica. "I'm having a lot of fun with you."

"Mm, mutual, darling," Nigel said taking a generous gulp of whatever drink he'd moved on to.

But it meant more to her than that. "I mean... most guys here make me feel like a piece of meat."

"Come now."

"They'll humor me, yeah. But the next day?" She pointed at Bobby, who was sliding a hand up the skirt of the girl on his lap. "It's like I don't even exist."

"Most uncouth."

"I guess I use them as much as they use me. It's just different when you're a woman, you know?"

"I suppose it would be."

"And look, I know you're really only after one thing with me."

Nigel blushed, sucked down the rest of his drink, and tripped over his own tongue.

"I'm not an idiot, Nigel. I'm just saying, since the moment we met, you at least had the decency to treat me like a person. I'm having *real* fun with you and it's... oh, it's so freeing. Thank you. I mean it." She put a hand to his cheek and took a piece of his heart. In his eyes, she became the bird with the broken wing, and he wanted to care for her. At least he did at the moment. He was still planning to bed her, of course. In fact, he was made painfully erect by her "thank you." But his sense of chivalry refused to let him let her feel used.

Around the corner of the bar, Ballantine and Mara were talking and drinking.

"So what do *you* do, Mara?" Ballantine asked.

"Well, I *was* a litigator for a long time," she said. "Defense mostly."

"How'd you do?"

"Depended on the judge."

"Why'd you quit?"

"Just... lost one too many. Lost 'the big one' as they say. Got stuck in a rut. Came out here to get away from it all. Try to figure things out."

"*Here* of all places? I picture you on a beach."

"I bet you *do*," she teased. "No, I just took off and... this is where I ended up. At least for now."

"Think you'll get back into litigation?"

"I really hope I don't have to. We are bound to our nature though."

"I don't believe that."

"Really, hunter? You're telling me you don't get a rush when you kill something?"

"I'm just saying our true natures are only *semi*-involuntary. Like breathing. We can control ourselves."

"But we must take a breath eventually."

"Exactly. Look at competition. That's in our nature. Nobody likes to lose, right? But it's not the end of the world if we do. Hell, it turned out the end of the *world* wasn't even the end of the world."

"It was for *some* people."

"You know what I mean, though. Yeah, if we lose every time, it's going to drive us crazy, but we've got the brainpower to shrug off a loss or two. We can survive without sex for a while. I can go work in a factory instead of hunt if I want to. Hell, I'm going against my nature just by dancing with you."

"Then why *are* you?"

The weird man returned, fanned out the cards in front of Ballantine's face, and said, "How 'bout now?"

Ballantine ignored the man and said, "Well, there's really nothing else I'd rather be doing."

"How about you, ma'am? Pick a card?"

"Can I pick for *him*?" she asked the man in reference to Ballantine.

"Sure."

She drew a card and held it face up so they could all see. On it was a drawing of a hell hound. Ballantine's thoughts went to the terror dog, though he remained skeptical of the game.

"This is your past," the weird man said. "You got the Dog. Dog's loyal. Speaks to your character. Run across any dogs lately?"

Ballantine shook his head.

"Pick."

Mara drew another card and held it face up.

"The Mask. This is your present. Lover boy's got a secret he ain't told you, ma'am."

"That true, Mr. Ballantine?" she asked.

"Well, seeing as you and I have only spoken for a total of 15 minutes, I'd say there's a *lot* I haven't told you yet. Didn't need a card to tell me that."

The weird man cocked his head, fanned out the cards one last time, and said, "Pick."

Mara chose another card and held it out.

"The Flood. This is your future. You're about to take on more than you can handle."

"I like the sound of that," said Mara with a devilish smile.

They ordered another couple of drinks as the band started up again.

"How about a tip?" the man shouted at Ballantine.

"Invest in a Magic 8-Ball!" Ballantine shouted back. When he noticed Mara was looking at them, he felt obliged to give the man a dollar before returning to the dance floor.

As things began to wind down, a couple of strangers got in a brief shoving match. Bobby left with his new girl. Kelly squeezed Sam's hand every once in a while. Laura's burden eased as the patrons filtered out. Mara rested her head on Ballantine's shoulder for a slow dance. Jessica leaned dreamily against Nigel, each of them properly drunk and with their hands on each other's butt.

"Nigel," she said.

"Yes, darling?"

"I really like you."

"I like you too."

"You're big and strong... caring and confident. You're sensitive but fearless."

Fearless. The word nagged at him. "Well, to be honest with you darling, I only found my *true* courage more recently than you might think."

"What do you mean?"

"I was a quivering pile of jelly during the shug monkey attack. It was only after a pep talk by Mr. Ballantine and an encounter with... well, I shouldn't say."

Jessica put her hands on his cheeks and said, "No, you shouldn't. Not here anyway." She flashed her eyes and said, "Got a room, cowboy?"

Nigel grinned at the implication and looked deep into her eyes... those deep blue eyes... those magical eyes... allowing himself to be completely taken with her. Then he stooped, wrapped an arm around her legs, and picked her up on his shoulder.

Jessica gave a yelp that made Mara and Ballantine turn to look. Nigel gave the two a lazy salute as Jessica laughed and kicked her feet. Then he patted her butt and turned to leave.

She reached down and smacked Nigel's ass saying, "Wait! Wait! My purse!"

The Brit spun, looking for the purse. He grabbed it himself, then swaggered away with it in one hand and Jessica on his shoulder. Kelly pretended not to notice. She found it better for business and her sanity to ignore Jessica.

The smoke thinned. Laura asked Brunna if she could get her anything else. The crone shook her head. The weird man nursed a beer, unsuccessfully pretending not to pay attention to Mara and Ballantine. Sam was the same as ever. A few stragglers hung on here and there, either staring into infinity from exhaustion or forgetting the clock in their conversations. As the song came to an end, Ballantine leaned away from Mara to get a better look at her face.

"What are you thinking?" she asked.

"I'm thinking I'd like to get some air."

"You thinking you want some company?"

Ballantine took a glance at the weird guy who not quickly enough averted his eyes. "I am," said the hunter.

Mara snaked a slender arm around one of Ballantine's oak-branch biceps and the two took a walk.

"Alright," said Jeremy, "we've got one more song for you tonight. Then it's either pay for a room or move it on out. Don't forget to pay your tabs and tip your waitress."

Four clicks of Reggie's drumsticks started their final song. The number was a lively combination of bluegrass, disco, and rock 'n' roll. Nobody danced.

CHAPTER 15

As Mara and Ballantine left the bar, the outside air felt fresh and clean on their faces and in their lungs. Both breathed it deep as they stepped to the porch railing. The brightest stars cut through the noise of the parking lot's floodlights. Ballantine looked up at forever and sighed.

Mara asked, "What do the stars make you think?"

Ballantine said, "Same things as everyone else, I guess. What's my place?"

"Hm, you already answered that question, didn't you?"

"Did I?"

"Your nature. You know the things you were born to do. Do them."

"But to what end?"

"Hard to say after Pittsburgh, isn't it, Mr. Ballantine?"

"Ha. It was tough to say *before* Pittsburgh too. What do you think, Mara? Do you think God left, stayed, or never existed in the first place?"

"Oh, I think God exists and is incomprehensible."

"So you think He stayed."

"I think an omnipresent being doesn't have much of a choice about where it exists. The *real* question, Mr. Ballantine, is, 'What are the rules now?'"

"How do you mean?"

"Well, maybe He didn't *leave*, but maybe He turned His *back*. Maybe He's taken everyone He's going to take... and maybe we're all bugs in a campfire and He and all the angels are just watching like curious children. In which case, what do any of His old rules matter anymore? Why not steal or deceive to get what we want—kill those we hate?"

"Maybe *you* answered your own question, Mara. If our natures are the same as they ever were, maybe we're still playing the same ballgame."

"That's disappointing."

Ballantine looked at her and asked, "Why?"

Mara peeled a splinter from the railing and poked her other hand with it. She said, "I'm not exactly an angel."

"Nobody is."

"Yeah, but in my line of work—"

"Litigation."

Mara nodded and said, "I've helped a lot of bad people. And I've hurt a lot of people."

"Rather let a thousand guilty men go free than let one innocent man go to jail. Right?"

"Something like that. It just makes me wonder, when my time is up here, is it hell, reincarnation, or nothing at all?"

"Is paradise that far out of the question?"

"Ha. Paradise."

"Hey they're always preaching about forgiveness and absolution. Whatever you've done, I'm sure if you're committed to changing—"

"Nobody changes their nature, hunter... *killer*," Mara cut in.

"What does she mean by "killer?" Ballantine thought.

"If Christ himself showed up right now and told you to stop hunting forever, could you?"

"Well, I could probably find—"

"What's the longest you've gone without hunting?"

Ballantine had to think hard, then said, "Five days... a few years ago."

"And you're just gonna turn that off on a whim? No way. What was your most *thrilling* kill?"

"You mean most exciting or most terrifying?"

"You are proving my point."

"The big things are the most exciting: your wyverns, your chimeras... Ha. It's a good thing that dragon was as young as it was. Scales like iron plates." Ballantine thought Mara looked angry at his detail, so he went into the next part. "Uh, the most terrifying... the ones I don't know anything about, or how to defeat."

"Like what?"

"Uh, well there's not much out there anymore that I haven't killed or figured out. If I can make it bleed, I can kill it."

"Like the cave worm?"

"Ha. Well lucky for me, that one stays put."

"And the witch on the mountain?"

Ballantine remembered he was supposed to be on guard. He cursed himself for discussing fear with someone who could be the witch. He instinctively looked up to check Nigel's window, but the porch awning was in the way. Mara raised her eyebrows in anticipation. Ballantine pulled himself together and said, "I usually leave them to the witch hunters."

"Hell hounds?"

"Yes, ma'am."

"Swamp creatures?"

"Mmhm."

"Terror dogs?"

Thrown off guard, Ballantine hesitated, "N-no."

"Why'd you hesitate?"

"I... You said hell hounds earlier and I thought they were the same thing for a second," he lied. "How do *you* know about terror dogs?"

"You know, I've been alive for the last 20 years too. You're not the only one who's seen a monster."

"Yeah, but I've only ever seen a passing reference in an obscure book. Seeing one in real life is even more rare."

"And *have* you seen one in real life?"

Ballantine narrowed his eyes and said, "Have *you*?"

The front door banged open, rattling the old glass, startling Mara and Ballantine to look. Jeremy stormed out with a loud cry of, "*Fuck*!" He stomped down the steps to the dusty lot, running his fingers through his hair, pacing as he boiled, and cooled, and reboiled.

Kelly burst through the door calling after him, "Jeremy! You get back here right now! You're not driving home like that!"

"Leave me alone!" Jeremy screamed back at her.

"I'm trying to help you!" she said, going down to the lot.

"Well I don't need you to! I don't need a goddamn thing *in* this town!"

Kelly reached out to him and said, "Stay here tonight and sleep it off, huh? I'll forget what I saw and you can have a room on me. Come on."

Jeremy pulled away from her, crying, "Sure! That sounds great! Why don't you put me right next to Reg and Ari's room so I can listen to them *fucking*!"

Kelly didn't know what to say to that. She searched for the words. Jeremy gave her a chance to find them. Ariana's occasional attention had been the only thing keeping him from remembering that he was wasting his life. It had kept him sane, but it was getting further out of reach. He refused to admit to himself that he had feelings for Ariana. Or maybe it was just an inkling. Maybe it was nothing. At any rate, he was frustrated, jealous, and spiteful of the whole situation. Every time she passed on an opportunity with him, he felt her slip through his fingers. If he hadn't *already* lost her altogether, it wouldn't be much longer. Tonight, however, her decision to join Reggie in his room was the last straw.

Jeremy turned red and spun toward the road. In a release of anger, he swung an arm, unleashing his ability like he never had before. Until that moment he had only duplicated small, inconsequential things such as drinks. But now, with all his rage, he duplicated the road, Dave Kovak, and a passing car. A 40-foot stretch of the main road pushed away and laid next to itself.

Ballantine couldn't believe his eyes as he watched the second car split into existence, slam into a tree, and burst into flames. The monster hunter ran to the wreck but couldn't get closer than the edge of the parking lot. Nobody made it out of the car. The *original* car stopped and came back. Jeremy gaped at the flames, dumbstruck at what he'd done. Kelly ran back inside to call 911, for whatever good it would do. Laura, Brunna, and the weird guy all stepped onto the porch at the same time. Ariana pushed past them and down to the lot. Reggie wasn't far behind.

Ballantine wheeled and lumbered toward Jeremy, who immediately buckled.

"What did you do!?" Ballantine bellowed. He dug his fingers into Jeremy's shirt and shook him.

"I don't know!" Jeremy said.

"What the hell *are* you!?"

"I don't know!"

"Are you the witch!?"

"*No*! Please!"

"That's enough, Mr. Ballantine," said Mara.

Her presence next to him took him by surprise. She raised a hand and swished it around a couple of times. As far as Delaney Ballantine could tell, the world began to spin. Not the kind of spin that comes with a hangover; that spin that only goes so far before resetting. It was a full spin, as if he were strapped to a wheel. It hobbled his equilibrium and made him fall over onto his side. He tried to get up but the spinning made it impossible. It glued him to the ground. All he could do was watch and try not to throw up.

The people from the original car pulled into the lot and got out. The lifeless body of Dave Kovak's clone protruded from the rear window, fused with the car. His legs were part of the backseat and the chassis. His feet dangled from the gas tank.

"Oh my God," said the driver trying, to make sense of the situation. "Oh my God. Oh my God. Oh my God!" His wife trembled in the passenger seat.

The original Dave Kovak stepped nearer the car, saw his own dead face, and threw up.

Mara placed a gentle hand on the driver's shoulder and shushed him.

"What's your name?" she asked.

"Tom," he managed.

"Tom. Look at me, Tom. What are you doing out here so late at night?"

Tom looked back to his car and said, "There... was an accident on the highway... got off... got lost."

"Aw, you poor thing." Mara stroked his cheek. "But it's not only this that has you troubled. You're guilty of something."

Tom looked into Mara's eyes, pleading with her not to say any more.

"Aren't you?" she said.

"I don't know what you're talking about."

"Shall I jog your memory?"

Mara waved a hand in front of his face and sent the man, in his mind, back to the source of his guilt: the accident on the highway. He relived it not just once, but a thousand times, and each time from a different perspective.

First, he relived it from his own perspective, his initial shock at having hit a deer. The heavy concussion of the impact and the jerk of the wheel in his hand. The anger that his insurance probably wouldn't cover it. His annoyance at his screaming wife. The flash of his headlights on a man's face. The realization that he hit a person. Fighting with denial. The guilt that he was still driving.

Then he was his wife, nagging him about this and that because she learned by watching her mother that that was how a wife dealt with her husband. In the silences, she wished Tom's brother had been the one to ask her out all those years ago. Why she thought Tom would be just as good, she didn't know anymore. She saw the man on the road look up—saw into his eyes. By the time the scream made it out of her throat, the car was hundreds of feet down the road.

Then he was his victim, taking his time changing a tire in the dark. His flashlight battery was dead, so he did it mostly by touch. He heard Tom's car, saw the headlights, and figured his four-way flasher and two available lanes would be safety enough. In his reverie Tom tried to tell the man to move—to get out of the way—but the man pulled the bad tire off and gently set it on the ground. The other car... It sounded strange. Close. He looked up into the headlights, felt his chest cave in, felt his pelvis crush, heard the crack of the pavement burst in his head. Heard his wife scream. Heard his daughter cry, "Daddy?" Saw the stars fade away.

Tom relived the man's wife's horror and the young girl's terror. He watched it happen from above. He watched it from below, the side, and every other angle. He lived his own future prison rapes and his wife's shame. He relived every choice he could have made that would have prevented the whole thing in the first place.

Then he blinked and suddenly he was standing, screaming in the parking lot of the Foothill Hotel and Bar. What felt like a year had only been a minute.

Trembling and stammering, he got back into the car and drove east to the little town of Point Marion where he took the gun out of the glove box, shot his wife, then drove his car into the Monongahela River. He shot *himself* as it sank.

Meanwhile, in the parking lot of the Foothill Hotel and Bar, the onlookers waited with uncertain fear for Mara to make her next move. Everyone but the hysterical Jeremy, that is.

"What the...," he freaked. "What the *FUCK*!?"

"Shh, shh, shh," said Mara, extending a hand toward his shoulder. "It's okay."

The musician recoiled and flung his arms, rebutting with noise in lieu of language that did not exist.

"It's okay, baby. Calm down. Calm down."

"Who the fuck *are* you!?"

"My name is Mara... and I'm like you."

"What?"

"You don't fit in here, right? You don't feel like you have a place. You're better than it, but trapped. Yes?"

Jeremy stared at her. Mara nodded and gestured to herself.

"You're the witch," said Jeremy.

Ballantine felt like an idiot. Reggie and Ariana exchanged a glance.

"You make it sound like a *bad* thing," Mara said. "Did you ever think that maybe a witch can be something in *between* good and evil? You know... like *people* are? Did you ever think that maybe witches have gotten a bad rap?" She leaned toward Ballantine and raised her volume. "That maybe their behavior is the result of one self-fulfilling prophecy after another?"

The spinning had taken its toll on Ballantine and he threw up where he lay.

Mara pointed at the monster hunter and said to Jeremy, "This is what people like us get. We get hunted by fearful humans."

"I'm not human?"

"Of *course*, you're human, but you're *different*. Special. That is what I've been trying to tell you. And after what you just did, things will never be the same for you here."

"So what am I supposed to do?"

"I think the best thing for you is to come with me and let me help you master your abilities."

Jeremy looked at Ballantine. The once stoic master hunter lay pathetic next to a puddle of his own puke. There were bits of it in his mustache and a viscid strand from his nose to the ground. Jeremy was enticed by the potential power he held. He was mentally packing his bags when he remembered, "I can't. I have to take care of my mom."

"What's wrong with your mother?"

"She was bitten by a nightmare a long time ago. She can't get by without me."

Mara laughed and said, "Is that all?"

Jeremy twisted his eyebrows.

"Come with me tonight," Mara said, "and I *promise* your mother will be taken care of. Cured."

Jeremy weighed his options. Trust a witch to cure his mother and teach him? Stay where he was, face the consequences of his actions, keep taking care of his mother, deal with a monster hunter, never leave town, and never have sex again? Jessica appeared on the porch, disheveled and glistening with sweat. Jeremy looked at Mara and nodded.

"Excellent!" Mara said. She turned to the porch and called, "Gregory! Brunna!"

Brunna went to Mara's side while the weird man fetched the car.

"Jeremy!" Ariana yelled as she and Reggie ran over. "What are you doing?"

Jeremy searched the ground for a good simple answer but couldn't find one. Getting under Ari's skin gave him pleasure, though. And with all the stress breaking, he couldn't help smiling as he said, "You know, I don't really know."

The weird man pulled up in a 1959 Bentley Continental. It wasn't strange to see an old car in rural Pennsylvania. It *was*, however, strange to see an old *luxury* car in a poor mountain town.

Mara laid an arm on the pillar of the car, pointed at Ballantine, and asked her driver, "Him?"

"Tough to say for sure," said the weird man. "I'm a little rusty. Chances are fair."

Mara narrowed her eyes and stooped close to Ballantine. "Did you kill my dog?"

The monster hunter's eyes ran in little circles as they tried to compensate for his spinning hallucination. He stifled a gag, then said evenly, "No."

She pinched the bridge of her nose and said, "I know you're lying. I *know* you're lying. You're a *fucking* liar, Delaney Ballantine!" His name was a stab wound on her lips.

"I didn't...(*hic*)...I didn't kill your dog," he growled through a dry heave. Technically, he wasn't lying. It was Nigel who had killed it.

"Jessica!" Mara called.

Jessica trotted over with a sheepish, "Yes, ma'am?"

"What about the other one?"

Jessica pursed her lips, looked at the ground, and shook her head.

Mara's lips curled on their own. She stabbed a finger at Ballantine and said, "I know it was you. I *know* it was you!"

"I didn't," Ballantine said.

Mara kicked him in the stomach and he curled, threw up again, and groaned.

Mara pushed her hair out of her face and said, "Come on, Jeremy."

Brunna opened the back door of the Bentley for Jeremy and Mara to enter. The smelly woman got in the front passenger seat and the car drove off. Ballantine's spinning lessened the further away it rode. Before he could pick himself up, Jessica tiptoed by him and said, "I'm sorry about all this, Mr. Ballantine." He watched her get in her old pickup truck, and from his position on the ground, noticed her alignment was off. Her wheels tilted inward.

Sirens cried in the distance.

Sheriff Landry arrived first. He greeted Kelly and had her bring everyone inside so he and the other first responders could take care of the scene.

The firefighters put the car out. The paramedics took what was left of the bodies. The tow truck took the wreck away.

The sheriff removed his hat as he entered the bar. He pushed a hand through his hair, then smoothed his mustache around the corners. He might have found the silence eerie if he hadn't had the experience before.

The witnesses sat around the bar. Sam, hunched over his coffee, never turned. Kelly dabbed blood from Ballantine's forehead. Reggie, Ariana, and Laura stared in wide-eyed apprehension at the sheriff.

"Always something, huh?" the sheriff said.

Kelly answered with a roll of her eyes, then went back to Ballantine's head.

The sheriff smirked at the floor and took another step closer. He opened his mouth to ask what happened, but Kelly started.

"We had a visit from the witch tonight," she said, "apparently."

"Is that right?" The witch had always intrigued Sheriff Landry. He'd never encountered her, but had heard the stories. She did her share of hell-raising when she moved to town, after the Pittsburgh thing. He had to reach way back in his memories to find the last time he'd heard about her. "What happened?"

"Well it sounds like some idiot went and killed one of her dogs and she came looking for him." She bugged her eyes out at Ballantine.

"Simple as that, huh?" asked the sheriff.

"Could be."

"Did she find him?"

Kelly applied the bandage to Ballantine's head while she thought of the best way to answer. She had a feeling it was either Ballantine or Nigel who had done it. She thought she saw guilt in Ballantine's eyes, but if the witch couldn't fish it out, who was Kelly to try? "Don't think so."

"So she caused that accident out there?"

"No, that was..." Should she incriminate Jeremy? "Someone else."

"Another witch?"

"No! Least I don't think so."

"Kelly."

"He's a good kid. He just got mixed up is all."

"What happened?"

"He was mad about something," Kelly said. Reggie and Ariana looked at each other. "Hardly blame him. Kid's a big fish stuck in a small pond." She turned to the band mates and said, "You *all* are. Anyway, he asked me for two shots. I poured him one and told him I wanted him to get home safe. Guess that was the last straw. I turn around for a second, then look back and he's got five shots in front him. Before I could say, 'Where'd you get those?' he slammed them all back and stormed out. I followed him to try to get him to come back in. Offered him a room. He declined. Then he... uh, well he just kind of went like this..." she swung her arm,"...and made that mess out there. That wreck is a copy."

"A copy of what?"

"A copy of a car that ain't here."

"You mean..."

"The witch made them drive away."

"So the witch *was* involved."

"She *got* involved, yes."

"So you're saying that car out there has an exact duplicate driving around out there somewhere."

"Yes sir."

"With two identical people in it."

"Well, three. Dave there got copied into it as it drove past."

"Is that right? He alive?"

"The *real* Dave seems fine. The other Dave looked like he was part of the car."

"So there's a couple out there right now riding around with a dead body in their car."

"Sticking out of it, actually."

"And the kid did it. Not the witch."

"Yeah, but the look on his face... He didn't mean to do it."

"Well, Kelly, I gotta say this whole case is looking like one big mess. Now you know me. You know I believe you. More information I can get, the easier it's gonna be for me to help. So what happened next?"

"Well... Mr. Ballantine here confronted Jeremy. Looked like he was about to knock his block off, and that's when the witch stepped in. She told Jeremy she could help him and his mother, so he agreed to go with her to the mountain. Then you showed up."

"When's the last time she was here?"

Kelly laughed and said, "I don't even remember. Since before..." She pointed a thumb over her shoulder at Sam.

"Ah," said the sheriff.

"She looked different than I remember."

"Different how?"

"Just different. She was a skinny blond the first time I saw her. Today she was a curvy brunette. Hadn't aged much, though. Had a different nose, different lips, different chin. There was something about her eyes...." Kelly let out a laugh and shook her head. "I knew something was up with her soon as I saw her. Caught those eyes and I just went cold."

"Anybody want to add anything?" Sheriff Landry looked at Ari and Reggie, who turned their eyes down.

"It's my fault," said Laura wringing a bar rag. Everyone turned their attention to her. "He's been trying to get me to come home with him for a while but I kept turning him down. If I'd've known all *this* was gonna happen—"

"Oh *hell* no!" said Ariana. "This isn't the '60s, Laura. He could threaten to blow up a *school* and that doesn't mean you owe him a goddamn thing."

"It's not that! I *wanted* to go home with him."

"Say what now?"

"Why wouldn't I? He's cute, and funny, and talented. I mean you and Reggie are *good* but... Well, anyway, I've just been working all these extra hours here, trying to save up enough to move to the city. I've been too tired to even *think* about going home with anybody at the end of the night. He asked again tonight before he stormed out." Tears welled in her eyes. "Been so focused on myself. I could've made time... I could've made time."

Reggie and Ariana exchanged glances. Kelly rolled her eyes. The sheriff noticed. Without removing his eyes from Kelly, he asked, "So you think he's, uh, frustrated?"

"Well, of course he is," Kelly said. Whether she missed the sheriff's meaning or tried to save Jeremy's dignity, she said, "Kid's a talent, trapped in this shit-hole monster pit. He should be in New York or Los Angeles... or Nashville or something. Instead he's taking care of his mother and playing here for peanuts every night. Now we find out he's got magic powers? Kid don't belong here. Can't be himself. That'll drive anyone crazy." She thumbed at Sam again.

Sheriff Landry looked to the monster hunter and said, "Mr. Ballantine, was it?"

Ballantine withheld his next words for a few moments to consider their arguments. Then he said simply, "I gotta get up that mountain."

Kelly snorted.

"Witches work fast," Ballantine said. "If you want Jeremy back, I need to get to her faster."

"Well, I don't know how you think you're gonna do it," Kelly said.

"Break her charms. Then break her."

Kelly snorted again.

"Any charm can be broken," Ballantine said.

"Not hers," scoffed Kelly. "Don't care *who* you are."

"Then don't worry about me."

Kelly scoffed.

"Hey, I'm trying to help here."

"So am I!"

"Then what's the problem?"

"I guess nothing, Mr. Ballantine! If you want to end up like Sam or worse, that's your own goddamn business."

CHAPTER 16

"So... what happened to Sam?" asked Ballantine.

Kelly looked at each of the people in the room, attempting to decide what, if anything, to say about it. The others held their breath and stared at her. She chose to tell the abridged version.

"As I hear it," Kelly said, "the *cave worm* is the key to the witch. I don't know what you have to do with it. All I know is that Sam was after the witch too. He found out the cave worm's secret, went after it, came back like this. You wanna lose your mind, Mr. Ballantine? Be my guest."

"What's the secret, Kelly?"

Kelly scoffed and said, "Hell if I know."

"What else do you know about it, Kelly? Was he the first one to go after the cave worm? Did he know what he was getting himself into?"

"Nothing!" Kelly snapped. "I don't know anything else! And if you bother me one more time about it, I'm throwing you out of this hotel!"

Her last word rang through the empty bar for a hot second, then decayed into heavy silence and scraps of floating thoughts.

Sheriff Landry was the first one to snap an idea into place. He said, "You say the witch said she'd help Jeremy's mother."

Ballantine stood. He knew immediately what the sheriff was getting at.

"Yeah," said Kelly.

"Well, where is his mother now?" asked the sheriff.

Kelly gave them directions. The two men left in the sheriff's car. Ariana and Reggie went to their room. Kelly took Sam to bed. Laura closed up.

Ariana sat on a rickety wooden chair and looked out the window at the mess across the street, the double road and the charred tree. Reggie laid on the bed and stared at the ceiling, his fingers laced over his belly. They both went over the night's events in their minds.

"Did you know Jeremy could do that?" Ariana asked the window.

"No," Reggie told the ceiling. "You?"

Ariana shook her head, saying, "I'm trying to think if there were ever any signs."

"That he was gonna freak out or that he was gonna clone a car?"

"Just... I mean... *All* of it," she said, reimagining the whole scene replaying in the lot below.

"Well, I think he was overdue for a freak-out, actually."

"Because he wasn't getting laid?" Ari sneered.

"Because he wasn't getting laid by *you*."

"By *me*? But Laura said—"

"Doesn't matter. He wanted *you*. It's been all over his face for the last month."

"I told you both—"

"I know. But if you deny a man his nature long enough, he's bound to go crazy. See: every repressive ideology there ever was."

"I never denied him his nature! There are other girls in town. I don't owe him a goddamn thing."

"I'm not saying you *do*."

"Sure *sounds* like it."

"Then why would *I* have anything to do with him freaking out?"

They looked at each other and Reggie told her with his eyes.

"He *loves* me?" she said.

"Either that or it's the streak we've been on. Two boys have to share the same toy, but one's been hogging it."

"So I'm a toy now?"

"Christ, Ari, it's just a metaphor. We've been *your* toys too. Me, I'm fine with whatever. If you decided right now you wanted to go be with him, get married, have kids, move away, I'll still be Reggie. It's not that I don't care about you. You two are my best friends. But people need what they need, and I don't make it my business to tell people what makes them happy. I provide what I provide. You are free to either enjoy it or, if it's not enough for you, move on. People need to get enough. Whatever that means to them."

His words settled in her head like fallen leaves in the rain. They pulled up in clumps as Ariana raked through them. Fragments of her dreams came along. Afraid, or maybe tired of them, she turned the conversation back to Reggie.

"What is it that *you* need?" she asked. "…Ultimately?"

Reggie was back to looking at the ceiling. He cocked his head and flung his thumbs away from his laced fingers saying, "Right now? I think I have enough."

"You have enough." Ariana didn't understand it, so she said it out loud in the hope that the meaning would reveal itself.

"Yep."

The meaning did not reveal itself. "I don't get it," she said.

"I have a bed, a family, a job, friends, music, and food. I don't really need any more than that. Therefore," he smiled and sighed as he reminded himself, "I think I have enough."

They went quiet for a bit while Reggie reveled and Ariana wondered if she wasn't being selfish. After noticing how long the silence had lasted, Reggie thought he might be rude for not asking, so he said, "You?"

"I don't know," Ari said. "You make it sound so simple. I feel like that *should* be enough but..."

"But it's not."

"No."

"And that's okay. Everybody's different, right? I can pee my name in the snow. You can bring a life into the world. I'm okay with the simple things. You need more. That's what I was getting at before about not telling people what makes them happy. So what do you need? There's no wrong answer."

Ariana looked out the window for the answer. She knew she never had what she wanted, but she'd never let her dreams coalesce into something she could describe. She realized it now and said, "I don't know."

"Start broad," Reggie said.

"I guess... I want to feel like I have a purpose. Like I see my dad doing the same things every day on the farm and think, 'This can't be all there is.' I'm not really going to feed chickens, dig, and plant seeds for the rest of my life, am I? Basically, just work to feed myself."

"Well basically, that's all *anybody* does."

"Yeah, but there are people out there making the world better, *changing* the world, and doing well enough that they can spend weeks doing whatever they want. Do you know how often a farm needs tended?"

"Every day?"

"Every damn day."

"So you want to be able to take a vacation."

"*Whenever* I want, *wherever* I want, but as an afterthought, a reward to myself for accomplishing something... great... or worthwhile. I don't expect to... become president or something. But I don't want to spend the rest of my life doing the same thing in this town, watching the days tick by, watching everyone I know age, someday dying, having never known more than a handful of people."

"And how do you want to accomplish that?"

"I don't know... Music? Horses? Both?" She gave a little laugh.

"And now you're on your way. Just saying it out loud changes the world around you. Not only have you firmed it up in your head, you've put it out there. And my mom always says, 'The world provides. We just have to meet it halfway.' Tell the world what you want and it will give you opportunities. It's up to you to jump at them, though."

"Should we take this band on the road, then?" Ariana smirked.

"I got a bad feeling about the band situation right now, Ari. Our lead singer/songwriter just took off with a witch."

Something about the interaction in the parking lot had her feeling that it might not be as simple as it had seemed. She tried to put it together from the few pieces she had saying, "Yeah but... I don't know. Something doesn't sit right with me about it. Like she's not *just* evil."

"That's what they *do*, Ari. They confuse you. They're always like, 'Oh here, have an apple. It's totally not poisoned,' but, oh wait, it totally is. Maybe she'll train Jeremy. Then maybe she'll make him her slave, or steal his powers from him, or just fucking eat him. Either way, *if* we see our boy again, things will *not* be the same."

Ariana thought about it. The next time they saw their friend, he could be evil or even dead.

"Then I want to save him," she said.

"Say what?" Reggie had heard enough stories about the witch from his parents. Ariana might as well have said she wanted to ride a shug monkey to Buckingham Palace and slap the queen.

"That Ballantine guy. He wants to go after the witch. Maybe we can help him."

"*We*?!" Reggie turned to look at her.

"What the hell else do we have to do? Huh? Same old shit? I want to help our friend. And I just have the feeling that the witch isn't everything we've been told she is." Ariana slid off the chair and into the bed next to Reggie. She was ready to sleep and ready to be done talking. She sighed, "Please."

The sky had turned indigo out the window behind her. Reggie noticed the room was brightening too. Sparkles somehow found their way into Ari's heavy eyes as she waited for his answer.

"Okay," he said. He turned his head straight again and squeezed his eyelids tight, sure he'd regret his decision.

Ari, cradled in his arm, closed her eyes, sighed, and allowed sleep to approach. As her head cleared, she remembered, "Reggie."

"Hm?"

"There's one more thing I want."

"Yeah?"

"To ask my mom why she left us."

While Reggie and Ari were talking, Sheriff Landry and Del Ballantine had gone to stake out the Crawford house. The sheriff explained Connie's situation to the hunter on the way. When they arrived, they pulled past the house and into some brush across the street, killed the engine, and then killed time.

"So how long you been a witch hunter?" asked Sheriff Landry, his voice the sound of a far-away diesel engine. His eyes fixed on the moonlit pine trees around the Crawford house. Connie's nightmare noises wafted on the dewy breeze through the car windows and across the men's faces.

Ballantine had been wondering how the windshield was fogging despite the breeze. "I've gone after a few witches," he said, "but I wouldn't call myself a witch hunter. I've been hunting hell spawn since the Pittsburgh thing though. Twenty years or so."

"What's the difference between hunting witches and hell spawn?"

"Witches are human, which makes them complex. Every witch is different, needs a certain amount of study before you can go after one. Most *hell spawn* are basically animals. They have specific natures; they eat, torture, make more of themselves. If you know one of a species, you know *all* of that species. Find it, put a hole where it needs to go, call it a day."

"Simple as that, huh?" The sheriff smirked.

"Well it ain't fishing."

A single chuckle bounced the sheriff in his seat. A few beats of silence went by until the sheriff said, "Tell me about witch hunting."

"Pain in the ass," Ballantine said. "I don't usually go after 'em because there are dedicated witch hunters out there. You wouldn't believe how much shit they carry around with them. Suitcases, trunks, cargo vans. Met one guy who converted an RV into a whole stinking laboratory."

"Why so much equipment?"

"Complex prey needs complex methods. Not all witches are the same. There are three main things a witch hunter has to consider. There's the witch's origin (*how* she got her powers), her nature (*what* she does with her powers), and her motivation (*why* she does what she does). Was she *born* of witches? Did she study on her *own*? Were her powers *given* to her? If so, by whom? Another witch? A demon? Did she *choose* to be a witch? If so, why? Maybe she's power hungry. Maybe she wanted revenge, got it, and now she has a different, or even *no* motivation. What does she do with her powers? Does she steal souls? Terrorize villages? Does she make flowers bloom? Witch hunters have to be ready in a second to deal with all of that. They need to be scientists, chemists, engineers, psychologists... theologians... uh..."

"Hunters."

"Like I said, there's enough of them to go around for all the witches in the world. I'm good at killing the simple beasts. Feel like it's my lot to restore the natural order by doing that."

"Think you can handle *this* witch?"

Ballantine thought about it so long, Sheriff Landry thought the hunter preferred not to say.

"Tough to know right now," Ballantine said. "I'm not really equipped to go after her just yet."

"Can you get in touch with a witch hunter?"

"They don't exactly sit by the phone waiting for it to ring. I'm getting my ideas about her, though."

"And those are?"

"Her primary gift looks like *illusion*. She has her mountain charmed so people think they're hiking even though they aren't. She made *me* think the world was spinning. And I wouldn't be surprised if she doesn't really look the way everyone saw her tonight."

"How do you get around that?"

"Not sure yet. Would help if I knew how she got her powers. Might give me a clue as to how the charm was cast, and therefore how to undo it. But if I go trying to break a demon-gifted charm with an elemental *counter*charm, I could end up in a world of hurt."

"Not sure I know what you mean by all that, Mr. Ballantine."

"There's a lot to it."

"You got any inklings?"

"She left me alive."

"So she's not all bad."

"Either that or she's got bigger plans for me."

"In my years, I've found the simplest explanation tends to be the right one."

"And in mine, I've learned never to underestimate evil."

Suddenly, inside the house, Connie's tics and moans turned to hysterical screaming. "Get out! Get out! Who are you! Jeremyyyy!!! Jeremy help!"

The men jumped out of the car and ran across the street. Sheriff Landry lit the way with his flashlight.

"Did you see anything?" Ballantine growled as they hoofed it down the driveway.

"No," said the sheriff. "You?"

"No. Be careful in there."

The storm door gave no resistance, slamming against the side of the house with what seemed like only a touch. Following protocol, Sheriff Landry called through the open door, "Police! We're coming in!"

Connie's screams loosened the sheriff's joints as he stepped into the tiny foyer. It was the sound of torture and hopelessness beyond anything he'd ever heard. Ballantine flicked on a light, snapping the sheriff out of his hesitation, and the two of them tromped down the hall to Connie's room.

The sheriff entered first and shined his flashlight around the room, eventually settling on Connie's face. She was dripping sweat and straining in fear.

"*GET AWAY!*" she screamed at the light. "*GET AWAY FROM ME!!!*" Her breath came in heaves.

Ballantine found the light switch and turned it on. Sheriff

Landry turned off his flashlight. Connie strained and struggled, but could not move. She looked as though she was pinned by something invisible on her chest. The room smelled like body odor and shit.

"Hey, hey, hey now," said the sheriff, extending a palm. "You're okay. You're okay. We're here now. No one's gonna hurt you."

"Get her offa me! *GET HER OFFA MEEEE*!!!"

"Nobody's on you, Mrs. Crawford."

"God," she said, then addressed the no one on her chest, "What do you want from me?!"

Ballantine pulled the sheriff away from the bed by his arm, "Wouldn't be so sure we're the only ones here, sheriff."

"What do we do?" the sheriff whispered to the hunter.

Ballantine, never taking his eyes off of Connie, shook his head slowly and whispered back, "I don't know."

They searched their heads for ideas. They looked around the room for clues, keys, pieces of the puzzle they were looking at, but all there was to see was covered in years of dust: ceramic knickknacks, photos, an old Bible.

It turned out all that they had to do was wait. Connie's cries turned into moans, which turned into whimpers, which turned into sleep... peaceful sleep. The men approached her silently to get a closer look and make sure she was okay. Satisfied, they looked at each other and shrugged. Ballantine motioned for them to leave the room. As they turned, the sheriff stumbled but caught himself and looked around.

"Felt like somebody just bumped into me!" he whispered.

Ballantine ran to the front door in time to see the storm door swinging back and forth. The sky had turned indigo. There was nothing in the front yard or the driveway that wasn't there when they entered. The smells of body odor and shit hung in the doorway.

"Fuck," said Ballantine.

"What is it? What was it?" asked the sheriff coming up behind him.

"We weren't alone in there. Someone else was there, cloaked."

"You mean invisible?"

"And inaudible. Charmed. And I have an idea of who it was. Not gonna catch her now though. Be dangerous to try anyway."

"The witch!"

"One of her lackeys is more like it."

"So what now?"

"Well... if what you tell me is true, Connie hasn't had good sleep in years. I say we let her be for a while and take advantage of the downtime ourselves. You got anywhere else to be?"

"Yeah I do," said Sheriff Landry twisting his mustache with a smirk. He put a hand on Ballantine's shoulder and said, "Come on, son. I'll take the first watch."

CHAPTER 17

While Reggie and Ariana were talking, and Ballantine and the sheriff were staking out the Crawford house, Mara and company returned to her abode.

The ride up the mountain had been smooth, smoother even than the main road. Jeremy had never known there to be *any* road up the mountain, let alone a pristine finished one. It was dark though, and Jeremy wasn't able to make out many other details. Even when they got out of the car, the witch's home appeared to be little more than a pair of torches mounted in stone on either side of a great wooden door. At that point, Mara whispered something to Brunna and gave the crone a diamond from the necklace she'd been wearing. Brunna got in the driver's seat. Mara swished a hand at the car, and it disappeared.

The interior took Jeremy by surprise. He'd always expected a witch on the mountain to live in a hut or a hovel. Instead, he found himself in a cavernous, infernal castle. As Gregory lit the torches ahead of them, to the left, and up a staircase, Jeremy took in the irregular yet beautiful stonework as far as the darkness allowed him to see. At the farthest wall, across from the entrance in the dimmest of the torchlight, Jeremy saw the outline of a great hearth in the wall, along with the shapes of mismatched furniture around it. Halfway between the entrance and the hearth, two great columns rose into shadow. Flecks of white stood out in the mortar all around. Jeremy had followed Mara and Gregory halfway up the crescent staircase when he realized those flecks were bits of bone. The bones of what, he didn't care to think about.

The staircase led to another great hall. This one seemed somewhat cozier. Though it was vast enough to swallow the warm torchlight, Jeremy was able to make out fine rugs, comfortable furniture, and artwork. He imagined the hearth in *this* room was particularly inviting when it crackled.

They made a left off the staircase and headed down a long hallway. Windows to his left allowed Jeremy a view of the stars. To the right, doors.

"Brunna's room, Gregory's room," Mara said as they passed. "They are at your beck and call if you need anything while you're here."

A hallway to the right swallowed the torchlight as they passed.

"A throughway to the other side of the palace," Mara pointed.

"Palace!" Jeremy said.

"Palace. Castle. I go back and forth. I built it, so I call it what I want."

They passed a few more doors to their right and arrived at a corner. Another hallway disappeared to the right. Another staircase curled upward to their left. They took the staircase. At the top was a door that led outside to the roof... or as Jeremy noticed when he looked around, *one* of the roofs. The sky seemed bigger than Jeremy had ever seen it. From his left to his right and all the way overhead, apart from the tower in the middle, his view was unobstructed. Stars and cosmic dust streaked and speckled in the forever away but close enough to almost touch. The young man's jaw hung open as he stared straight up, wishing he could just spread his arms and lift off... and keep going.

"Look down here, Jeremy," said Mara. She was standing at the corner.

Jeremy rested his elbows on the wall and looked down into black. Lights as faint and small as the stars pricked the darkness in the distance.

"That the town, I guess?" asked Jeremy.

"If you'd call it a town," said Mara. "Yes."

The young man pondered the bleakness of it. One... two... ten lights twinkling in the void below... and only when he wasn't looking directly at them. He looked up at the Milky Way again and wondered what ten stars were worth to it. A drop in the bucket, probably. He looked to the town again and covered it with his hand, hiding it from himself. Simple as that. Who was he, who could make an entire town disappear behind his hand? What kind of town worth anything would allow itself to be covered so easily by a nobody?

"What do you want with me?" he asked.

"I've told you," Mara said. "I want to help you reach your potential. Help you kick the dust of this town off your heels and go on to do what you were meant for."

"What *am* I meant for?"

"You're the only one who can know that."

"Does it have to do with my gift?"

"Not necessarily, I don't think. Not everyone's vocation lines up with their talents."

"Then why do you want to help me?"

Mara shrugged a shoulder and said, "If *I* don't, who will? The cat's out of the bag now, Jeremy. You can't just go home and pretend nothing happened. The only way out now is forward. One day, you'll be out there in a big, mostly nonmagical world, surrounded by people who don't understand you, and you will have to either *make* them understand or defend yourself."

Jeremy chewed on her words. They made sense—*perfect* sense.

"They say you're evil," he said. "Have since I was born."

"People will call anything they don't understand 'evil.' *Comets* used to be considered harbingers of doom. Hell, I haven't even been into town in 20 years. You'd think they'd know by now I'm just trying to mind my own business up here. Way I see it, everyone's capable of both good and evil at any given time. All comes down to the choices we make. So judge me by my choices. If you decide you don't want to be up here anymore, I'll bring you and your mom home. And the only thing I'll ask is for you to let the rest of them know I just want to be left alone."

"Is my mom here?"

"Not yet. Brunna's gone to tend and bring her."

"How can I trust you?"

"The same way you trust any stranger. You give them a little to start, then let them earn the rest."

The sky turned indigo. Jeremy yawned.

"Come on," said Mara. "Let's get you to bed. We'll begin when you wake up."

Brunna pulled up to the palace, turned off the engine, and stepped out of the car. Mara wasn't going to be happy with her. As usual, there was a beating in the servant's future. Brunna had accepted that a long time ago. What was once a fearsome deterrent had become just another part of her day. She gave a little sigh as she entered the palace and dutifully reported to Mara's chamber at the top of the tower.

The last flame in Mara's fireplace had flickered out, leaving the room in the dark orange glow of the coals. The lady of the house lay, half asleep and cozy, behind the curtains of her poster bed.

"Connie Crawford is cured, Mistress," Brunna croaked.

"Excellent," came Mara's voice. "Make her comfortable."

"But she's not here."

Mara left a silence for Brunna to explain.

"Ballantine and the Sheriff were there. Couldn't get her out."

Mara boiled in silence, and Brunna knew it. The servant took off her shirt and assumed a position on all fours in the middle of the room. To say her skin was a wreck would be an understatement. Her body was a catastrophe, scarred and cratered from decades of abuse and hardship. Her back looked like a topographical map.

Mara's sigh preceded her through the curtains. She swung her legs out and sat on the edge of the bed. She just wanted to sleep.

"Are you even *sorry*, Brunna?" she asked, rubbing her eyes.

"Nothing I could do, Mistress," Brunna said without emotion. "'Sides, you're gonna beat me the same either way."

Mara sprung from the bed, grabbed a switch, and thrashed

Brunna about her back. *Snap, snap, snap,* went the stick against Brunna's flesh. Her calloused skin dulled the pain. She wasn't sure if she winced because it actually hurt or if only to placate her mistress.

"Who are you?" The weak voice seeped into Ballantine's doze. He snapped his head up and saw a confused but rested Connie Crawford staring at him from the end of the hall. He looked over at the other living-room chair to see the sheriff was still fast asleep.

"Ma'am," Ballantine said, stirring the sheriff, "Mrs. Crawford. I'm Del Ballantine and this is Sheriff Landry. How are you feeling?"

She was more worried about seeing a sheriff and a large man in her house instead of her son. "Where's Jeremy?" she asked. "Is he okay?"

"Jeremy's fine, ma'am," said the sheriff. "How are *you*?"

"I'm fine! Somebody tell me what's going on!"

Ballantine and the sheriff looked at each other for a moment. In the pause that followed, Connie realized what she'd been saying.

"Oh my God," she said. "I'm fine. I'm *fine. I'm fine*!!!" She smiled and tried to jump for joy, but her legs were too weak. She looked at her withered limbs and said, "I'm hungry."

Sheriff Landry smiled and said, "That's a good sign. There's not much in your kitchen, though. How about we take you out for breakfast?"

"Jeremy!" she remembered.

"One thing at a time, Mrs. Crawford. We're going to explain everything to you, but how about you get yourself together so we can all get some food in us?"

"Is he *okay*, at least?"

The men looked at each other again, trying to decide how to answer.

Sheriff Landry took the responsibility and said, "We think so."

"That's all you have, huh? You think so."

"There's really a lot to explain, ma'am. Could be a long day ahead. Best if you get ready."

After a few moments' time to process, Connie said, "Of course, of course." She turned back down the hall, picked out a dress, then took the first real shower she'd had in years.

Ballantine's stomach rumbled as he pushed aside a window curtain. A beam of sunlight managed to clear the treetops and make it through the window. It glittered in the dust that fell from the curtain and it warmed Ballantine's clothes. He took a good look at the front yard, felt overwhelmed at the amount of attention it needed, then grateful that it wasn't his problem.

CHAPTER 18

Jeremy slept deeply despite vivid nightmares. Nightmares that would have normally woken him (woken *anyone*) appeared and faded like passing streetlights in the dark. He groped for their slipping memories as he woke. Wood devils and his father... Being a deer hunted by a wolf... A tower in hell... Voices of anguish... and... that was all. A bead of sweat rolled down his temple. Yet, despite being wrapped in bedcovers, he was chilly. He wiped his brow with them, then remembered they weren't his sheets.

He knew if he thought about it too long he'd never get up, so he flung the covers off and let the air attack his sticky, sweaty clothes. It was cold enough to make him uncomfortable, but not enough to make him shiver. He rubbed his arms, sat up, and slipped his feet into his sneakers.

The bedroom's stonework was like the rest of the place, irregular but sound. On the wall opposite the bed was a hearth. To the left was a window through which Jeremy looked down into a courtyard lit yellow by the afternoon sun. A stone path meandered through shrubberies, fish ponds, and statues. At the center was an apple tree with Gregory on a stool beneath, inspecting and picking. On the bedroom's last wall was the door. Jeremy used it and found a weary Brunna standing by.

Despite the pressure in his head and the urgent need to relieve himself, he said, "Is my mother here?"

Brunna, not looking at Jeremy, shook her head.

"Is she okay?"

"She's fine," Brunna said. "Cured. Couldn't get her here, though. Turlet?"

Jeremy nodded. Brunna led him to the door next to the staircase they'd taken to the roof.

"I might be a few minutes," he said before closing the door.

The musician was more than a few painful minutes. He cramped. He strained. He burned. He asked God, "Why?" He thought about what he ate the day before, told himself 'never again,' and then forgot.

Brunna had waited by the door. When Jeremy came out and saw her there, he wondered how much she had heard. He gave the door a look and told himself it was probably not much. Brunna had heard everything though, not that it mattered to her.

"Bath?" she asked.

"I really should get back to see my mother," said Jeremy.

"You'll have to talk to the mistress about that."

"Okay, then take me to the mistress... uh, please."

She led him up the corridor to the throughway they'd passed the night before. Now it was on the left leading toward the center of the palace. Windows opened to the courtyard on the left. Doors to somewhere unknown stood guard along the right. In the center of the throughway, on the right side, was an opening to a spiral staircase. It curled up and to the right as well as down and to the left. Brunna led Jeremy down, past an opening on the first floor through which Jeremy saw, across the hall, an entrance to the courtyard. A few steps down, on the opposite side of the staircase was an opening to the kitchen. They kept on. The air became more humid and warm. Jeremy's glasses even picked up a little fog.

The basement, like the rest of the palace, was a Gothic cavern, complete with stone pillars rising into pointed arches. Down there, it wasn't only the darkness that swallowed the distance, but the fog—a great mist that snaked through the pillars, entwining with the ones near Jeremy, shrouding the far ones from the orange torchlights. As they walked, wall torches here and there pierced the veil, appearing at first as dim smears, then as translucent orange orbs. Brunna's light offered them about ten feet of visibility. Or maybe it was six feet. There wasn't much around to help Jeremy gauge the distance.

A long line of torch smears appeared, grew into orbs, then sharpened into haloed flames. They lined the walls around a great steaming cross-shaped pool of water. Brunna stopped them at the bottom of the cross.

"Hello, Jeremy," Mara's voice echoed. Jeremy didn't notice her through the mist at first. She sat in the far end with her hair up and only the tops of her bare shoulders protruding from the water. She rested her head on the lip of the pool, which she had designed to have a gentle slope for just such a purpose. Never opening her eyes she said, "Come on in."

Jeremy hesitated and looked around for a way he could refuse politely.

"If you're worried about being vulnerable with me, then I'd point out I can scramble your psyche with a snap of my fingers." She raised her head and looked at him. "If I wanted to take advantage of you, I'd have done it by now." She closed her eyes and rested her head again.

Jeremy looked at Brunna, who stared listlessly into the fog, and decided she was no one to worry about. He kicked off his shoes, then pulled off his shirt. This was crazy, bathing with the witch. If Mara propositioned him for sex, would he refuse? He turned sideways as he removed his pants and underwear.

With his hand on his crotch, he dipped his foot in the pool and immediately pulled it back out. The water felt like it was a degree below boiling.

"Oh, don't be a pussy," Mara said. "I swear, for as much credence people give the word *'manly'* there are so few of you who can take a little pain."

Jeremy winced as he stepped back in. He thought of something funny and said, "I met a guy once who said women like their baths so hot because it reminds them of where they're from."

Mara lifted her head again, looked at him, and said, "And

what's that supposed to mean?"

Jeremy realized his host might not have the same sense of humor as a drunk guy at the bar, so he said, "I don't know. I didn't ask him."

She leaned her head back again, the image of his body burned in her eyes. He was no Adonis, but he was young and smooth. It had been so long since... Mara stopped her thoughts there before they took off and dragged her along. "Would you get in already? You're making me nervous. You look like a minister in a brothel."

He descended the steps a little faster than he would have liked and grimaced as he poached himself. At the bottom, he dropped to his knees to get his shoulders beneath the surface.

"There, isn't that nice?" asked Mara.

Jeremy wondered how close they were to simmering. The water stung like thousands of needles. He waved his arms around beneath the surface as he adapted, then sat on one of the steps.

"Feel free to come closer."

Jeremy did a kind of breaststroke squatted walk to the center of the pool and said, "So my mom's okay?"

"Yes, Jeremy, your mother is okay. I know I told you she'd be here, but there was a bit of a snag on Brunna's end. Apparently, Mr. Ballantine ambushed her. It was all she could do to get *herself* back here, let alone your mother."

"I want to see her."

"I can't apologize enough, but it's not going to happen now. Not for a while, anyway."

"So I'm supposed to just trust you?"

"You mean like you did by stripping naked and getting in the tub with me? When you slept soundly in my guest room? Stepped to the edge of my roof? Got in the car with me? I wouldn't think it'd be a stretch at this point.

"Look at it this way, Jeremy, as far as the people down *there* are concerned, you are now in cahoots with the evil witch on the mountain, so obviously, we can't be bringing you back down yet. If I brought your mother up *here*, she'd end up part of the same rumor and would never be able to go home again. This way, if something bad happens and you never see her again, at least she can live the rest of her life normally."

If he was going to argue, that was the time. Mara didn't *seem* to want to hurt him, at least not yet, if that's what she'd been planning. Whether or not she truly wanted to help him, Jeremy was still unsure, but seeing that part of her deal had fallen through, he gave a thought to leveraging more quid for his quo. But what more could he ask?

"So, what now, then?" he asked.

"Now..." she said, standing waist high in the water. Jeremy's mouth fell open and he groaned at the sight. Shards of torchlight flickered and beckoned from the sheen on her thick full breasts. "...You finish your bath..." She stepped up onto the seat where she'd been sitting, revealing the breadth of her hips. Her shimmering body hypnotized Jeremy. He didn't realize he was staring. He was no longer a person, but a hard-on with eyes. Mara looked into his hungry gaze. "...And meet me for breakfast." She stepped out of the pool and allowed Brunna to help her into a robe.

After Mara disappeared into the mist, and when he was sure Brunna wasn't looking, Jeremy gave his erection a quick squeeze. He'd never been so hard in all his life. He wasn't about to jerk off in the witch's bathtub, though, so he dunked his head, slicked back his hair, then dog-paddled a lap each way back and forth the width of the pool.

Mara barely made it up the tower to her bedroom before she had a hand between her own legs. Her thighs burned as she arched back against her heavy wooden door, thrusting her hips against her thrusting hand. She'd maintained her composure all through the night, despite there being so many people: the brawny Ballantine, the charming Nigel, the ever-sexual Jessica, the supple bass player, the affable drummer, and other patrons who kept their pants on only by the grace of this world's social mores. She had it under control until the steam of the pool carried Jeremy's scent to her nostrils. Until that moment, his naked body was still a fantasy, a moving picture. Intangible. Perhaps it was *time* that had made her forget what a person's scent did to her. By entering her nostrils, he might as well have entered her elsewhere. It triggered her instincts, boiled her desires, and nearly drove her mad with demonic lust. She would not let herself be bested by it this time, though. Waves of ecstasy racked her body against her bedroom door, each throe a pressure valve releasing stress and desire.

Mara took a deep breath, dabbed her temples with the robe, then sat down at her vanity. She took a hard look, then commended herself for being so in control.

Back at the hotel bar, Kelly helped Sam onto his stool for the day, saying, "I see a lot of you in that Ballantine fella. I hope he's not as foolhardy."

Before Sam could react (or not), Nigel entered the bar with a cheery, "Morning all! Or shall I say afternoon?" He sat at the bar where he had been the first night, three stools away from Sam, and drummed his hands. "You two sleep well? I know I did. Feel like a million bucks, as they say."

Kelly and Sam looked at him with tired eyes that said, "No. As a matter of fact, it got pretty crazy here last night and we both feel like shit."

Didn't matter. Nigel had gotten laid. He was blissfully oblivious to anyone else's moods.

"Kelly, my darling, whenever you've got a moment I should like to put in a gargantuan breakfast order. Worked up an appetite last night."

She walked around him and the bar saying, "Go ahead whenever you're ready."

Nigel hesitated, since she didn't have anything to write his order on, but she just looked at him. "Three eggs sunny-side up, bacon, sausage, home fries, wheat toast, and a short stack of pancakes."

Kelly poured Sam's coffee and asked, "Anything else?"

"And coffee, water, and orange juice to drink please, thank you."

Kelly poured Nigel his coffee and said, "Coming right up," then went into the kitchen to tell the cook.

Reggie and Ariana, heavy lidded, entered the bar and looked around.

"My, my," Nigel said. "Does the band *live* here too? Where's your singer?"

The bandmates squinted at Nigel, then at each other. Ariana asked Nigel, "Did your friend come back yet?"

"Uh..." said Nigel, worried about what she was getting at if she meant Jessica, "which one?"

"Mr. Ballantine."

"Oh, whew, um. I haven't seen him since I, uh, went to bed last night. Why? When did he leave? Where did he go?"

The front door swung open. Everyone but Sam turned to look. With the afternoon light at their back stood two unmistakable silhouettes, one topped by the sheriff's hat and the other the mountainous physique of Del Ballantine. But there was someone else with them, shuffling in as the men escorted her.

Reggie and Ariana already knew in their guts who it was, but wouldn't believe it until they saw her for sure. Kelly came out of the kitchen and was about to take the bandmates' orders when she heard her name. "Kelly?" The voice was withered, yet familiar, like an old photograph left in the sun.

The hotel owner froze in her tracks and squinted at the silhouettes. Sheriff... Ballantine... it couldn't be. "Kelly!" croaked the little shadow. "It's me! It's Connie!"

Kelly's eye welled with tears. She put both hands over her mouth and strode around the bar to see her old friend.

"Connie!" she sobbed, touching her friend's face. "Connie, oh my God. Are you okay?"

"Yes, yes!" Connie tried to dismiss Kelly's worry with a wave of her hand. "I'm fine!" As if being bedridden and housebound for seven years was no worse than the flu or a sprained ankle. But her own tears said what she wouldn't admit.

"How are you feeling?" Kelly asked.

"Hungry," Connie said, smiling.

"Whatever you want." Kelly crushed her old friend against her and let the tears flow. "Whatever you want."

"Easy, Kelly, easy," Connie said.

Ariana dabbed her own tears with her shirtsleeve. Reggie let a couple of tears fall himself. Kelly ran back around the bar and proclaimed, "Breakfast is on the house!"

Ballantine and Sheriff Landry helped Connie onto a stool at the corner of the bar. Nigel moved one stool closer to Sam to allow the three to sit together.

Kelly wrote down everyone's order, then boomeranged herself to the kitchen to slap the orders on the counter and return to see her friend.

Ariana took the opportunity to reintroduce herself properly. "Do you remember us, Mrs. Crawford? I'm Ariana and this is Reggie."

"Yes, I remember you both," Connie said. "I had nightmares, not brain damage. You've grown into fine young people. So good of you two to stick by Jeremy despite my condition. You're true friends."

The bandmates looked at each other, unsure they agreed with Connie's assessment of their friendship.

"And you, Ariana, I can tell Jeremy especially likes you, if you know what I mean."

"He said that?" Ariana asked.

"Didn't have to," Connie said. "You can tell how much a man is interested by the details he gives when he talks. He'll say, 'Reggie killed it on the drum solo tonight,' sure. But he'll go on and on about your bass playing, Ari; talking about music theory I can't hope to understand. And if that ain't enough, without even thinking about it, he'll mention something that has nothing to do with music... like the way your hair fell, the way you looked at him, or the warmth of your hand."

Ari's head reminded her that she had no reason to feel so bad. Her gut didn't care, though. It made her feel like a cheating, manipulative bag of shit. She tried to reason why, but too much else was happening to figure it out.

"Oh, Connie," said Kelly. "Jeremy..."

"I know," Connie said. "They told me on the way over. He's with the witch."

"Connie," said the sheriff, "did you know Jeremy was, uh, gifted?"

"Not a clue. Never saw a thing."

Ballantine said, "Connie, if I'm gonna even *hope* to get him back, I need all the information I can get. So I hope you're not lying."

Indignant, Connie said, "I ain't lying. I didn't believe *you* when you told me what happened."

"Just making sure. Did Jeremy have any special relatives or ancestors?"

"Not that I know of."

"Did he experience any strange occurrences?"

"Aside from my nightmare bite, no. But I wouldn't know much after that."

"Did he undergo a sharp personality change at any point?"

"Nothing outside of what I'd think is normal for anyone in his situation."

"Hm."

"What's that tell you, Mr. Ballantine?" asked the sheriff.

"Did *you* two ever notice anything change in him?" Ballantine asked Reggie and Ariana.

They shook their heads.

Ballantine said, "Then the best I can do is he was born with it. Anomalously."

"What's the likelihood of that?" asked the sheriff.

Ballantine bobbed his head and stared at the wall. "It happens. Like being born with webbed feet or two different-colored eyes."

"You saying he's a freak?" asked Connie.

"Kind of. But in this case it's a good thing. If he wasn't cursed to be like this, and he doesn't have any witch blood in him, then he's untainted. He isn't beholden to anyone. His chances of being corrupted are 50/50."

"I don't like those odds."

"They don't get any better for humans, magical or not. If he was cursed or born of witches, his chances would be worse."

The room went silent while everyone let that all sink in. Sheriff Landry, who'd been awake far too long, stood himself up and said, "Well, unless anyone's got anything else for me at the moment, I need to be getting back to the town that's paying me in the first place."

"Of course, Sheriff," said Ballantine.

"Thank you, Sheriff," said Kelly.

"Please don't hesitate to get in touch if I can be of further help," Sheriff Landry said. "I'll be checking in otherwise."

"'Ppreciate it, Sheriff," said Ballantine.

Sheriff Landry tipped his hat to the room, then sauntered out.

The door clamored shut.

A beat of silence passed.

Nigel said, "Can anyone tell me what the devil is going on?"

CHAPTER 19

When Jeremy had finished his bath, Brunna gave him some old clothes to put on: a pair of gray slacks, a too-big button-down shirt, and a cardigan. He felt like he was wearing his father's clothes. No. He felt like he was wearing someone else's *grandfather's* clothes. Still, the cardigan was cozy in the castle's dank chill.

Mara was already at the dining table at the far end of the lower great hall (the hall through which they had entered the castle the night before). She wore a midnight-black dress and her long straight hair draped in front of her shoulders. Jeremy could've sworn it had been much shorter the night before. High above the head of the table at which she sat, a massive window streamed pale blue-sky light into the hall. Medieval weapons and armor decorated the walls. In front of Mara a candelabra with at least a dozen candles enhanced the mood.

"Come sit next to me, Jeremy." Mara's voice resounded as she patted the corner of the table.

As Jeremy sat to her right, Gregory placed a plate of bacon, eggs, and toast in front of him, filled a cup with water, and stepped away. The musician waited. He thought it was strange the servant was taking so long with his mistress' food. He figured it would've come at the same exact time, on a cart or something. Every second that passed made Jeremy more tense, waiting for the witch's temper to reveal itself on her fumbling servant. Or maybe she had already eaten?

"Well?" she said to Jeremy.

"Well what?"

"Aren't you going to make me a plate?" She smiled.

"Oh," he realized. She wanted to see him do his thing up close. He took a breath and shook the last of the morning cobwebs out of his head, then spread his fingers and pushed a hand over the plate toward Mara. She watched intently as a perfect duplicate of the breakfast moved toward her out of the original like a dividing cell. When it was complete, Jeremy put his hands in his lap.

"And the water?" she asked.

Jeremy passed a hand across the cup. He'd duplicated drinks so often, he no longer neeeded to think about it. Mara took the plate while Jeremy passed her the cup. She inspected the food, holding it close, smelling it. She held up a piece of bacon for better light, then broke it in half and took a bite.

"Mm," she said as she chewed. "Not bad." She thought a little longer as Jeremy dug in. "It doesn't feel like it's quite all there, though. Do you know what I mean?"

"Yeah," he said. "It's like making a copy of anything. It loses quality. Same if I make a copy of a copy. Every generation loses more."

Mara put a piece of bacon on the table near Jeremy and said, "Show me."

He passed his hand over the bacon and made a copy effortlessly. Then he copied the copy. Then he copied the copy's copy, and so on until there were seven pieces of bacon on the table.

Mara took a bite of each successive piece. As she went along, they lost flavor and, she suspected, nutrition. The last piece, though it had the consistency of all the other pieces, had no taste at all. Mara gestured for Gregory to clean up the bacon. He scooped them up with his hands then went back to wherever it was he stood ready.

"What does it *feel* like?" Mara asked Jeremy. "When you're

making copies, that is?"

"Um," Jeremy searched for the words. "Kind of feels like my brain gets warm and tingly. Same with the hand I'm using. Then it's like I have some kind of invisible connection to the thing. Like, without touching it, I can feel it. *All* of it. Like it's a part of me. I can feel all the nooks in the toast, the yolk in the egg, the chip on the bottom of the plate."

Mara lifted her plate and felt around. Sure enough, the plate was chipped. "Wonderful," she said.

"Then I just... *push* it." Jeremy looked at her, unsure if his explanation was good enough. "And there's another one."

"Fascinating. And I noticed it seemed easier for you to do the water and the individual pieces of bacon than the whole plate. Is that because there was more to it?"

"I guess so. I mostly duplicate drinks, so maybe it's all the practice?" He shrugged. "I don't know. But now that you mention it, yeah, I guess it did take a little more time to make the connection with the whole plate."

"Have you ever copied a person?"

"Only last night, accidentally. I thought about the what-ifs once and figured it'd be more trouble than it was worth. You know, cloning humans: should we or shouldn't we? All that stuff in the news and science fiction. Feels a little too much like playing God. I just want to play my music. Especially after last night."

"Of course, Jeremy. Makes perfect sense. What's the *largest* thing you've ever duplicated?"

"The stuff I did last night."

"You mean the car."

"And the people in it, and the road. All at the same time."

"Ah yes, the road. I forgot about that. But the car was only there for a second. It was in motion. You said more complex things require more time to make a connection."

"I don't know, Mara. I was pissed off and drunk when I did it. You said you wanted to teach me. Shouldn't *you* be telling *me*?"

"Easy there, champ. I need to figure out how you work and what you know before we start with the real lessons. If I start too simply, you'll get bored. Too hard and you'll quit."

"Sorry. It didn't sound as dickish in my head."

"Besides, I'm *already* teaching you about yourself."

Three knocks on the entrance door thundered through the great hall. Jeremy instinctively grew apprehensive. Mara noticed it and placed her warm hand on his as she gestured for Gregory to let in the visitor. The scrawny man looked at the guest through the hatch, then slapped it closed, slid back the bolts, and leaned his weight to pull the door open.

Jessica's heels clack, clack, clacked through the great hall. Her radiant coif bounced tightly around her head, escaped curls for accents. Her blue earrings seemed to glow even at a distance in the relatively dim hall. She walked with purpose but spoke with humility. She no longer appeared to be the equal partner in crime she was the night before.

"Mistress," Jessica acknowledged with a tip of her head and a polite smile.

"Jessica," Mara lilted. "Look who's here!"

"Hey, Jeremy," Jessica said, polite but curt, like she wanted only to take care of business and go.

Jeremy nodded at her.

"Everything come out okay this morning, darling?" Mara asked Jessica.

"Yes, Mistress."

"That's good to hear. Now exactly what information *did* you get last night?"

"Not much, Mistress. Not that you're looking for, anyway. According to Nigel, he and Mr. Ballantine got into it pretty good with a bunch of shug monkeys over on Wood Devil Mountain and that was it."

"And you believe him?"

"Makes sense to *me*. You should see the guy's truck. I'd have called it an early night too. Not gonna hang around *that* mountain with a bunch of fresh meat in your car."

"He said *nothing* about my dog? Nothing about Ba'athul?"

Jessica shook her head.

"No *indication*?"

Jessica shook her head.

Mara narrowed her eyes and said, "You were *awfully* friendly with him last night. You're not *lying* to me are you?"

"Mistress, you know I'm like that with everyone. I worked him from every angle he had. And he worked *my* angles pretty good too." She closed her eyes and shimmied, remembering the night before.

"Uh huh. Well *someone* in this town is responsible. Jeremy, if you had just killed a witch's pet and taken its head, what would you do next?"

Jeremy didn't want to say what he really thought, so he said, "Drive as far away as possible."

Having said her question out loud made it click in Mara's head. "The taxidermist, of course!"

"Shit," thought Jeremy. "Please don't let Mr. Adams have it. Please don't let Mr. Adams have it."

"Ooh," said Jessica, cringing. "I can't stand the thought of that place. Making trophies out of poor little animals."

"Poor bloodthirsty animals from hell that kill humans, you mean?" asked Jeremy. He wasn't much offended. He just wanted to put the other perspective on the table.

Jessica didn't know how to respond. She knew about Jeremy's father. She felt bad for the kid, but she also hated the thought of one of her babies ending up skinned and mounted on some yokel's wall.

Mara looked from Jeremy to Jessica, then raised a palm and her eyebrows as if to say, "He's got a point."

Jessica took the gesture to mean the argument had been called in favor of Jeremy, so she apologized to him. He dismissed it with a shake of his head.

"Nevertheless," said Mara, "Ba'athul was *my* bloodthirsty animal from hell that killed humans." She addressed Gregory, "We're gonna have to take a little drive later."

"Fuck," thought Jeremy. "Please, don't have it. Please, don't have it."

"Anything else for me, Jessica?" Mara asked.

"Nothing right now, Mistress."

"Then you may go... Oh no, stay for one more minute!"

Jessica had only pivoted and so pivoted back.

"Jeremy," said Mara. "I would like you to duplicate Jessica, here."

Their eyes widened. Jeremy's thoughts raced about how he might do it, that he's never really done it, and that he might kill her if he tried. Jessica came to many more frightening than good conclusions about what might happen to her. She considered that even if it *didn't* kill her, what would it mean for her? Would Mara kill her and keep the clone? Would the clone take all or part of her soul or abilities? Would they be perfectly equal? Would her clone try to kill her? Would Mara have them fight for her amusement?

"Mistress, I—"

"Serve me unquestioningly, I know," finished Mara with the exact amount of severity needed to remind everyone whose word was final.

Jeremy had made no deal of servitude, however. He protested, "Mara, I'm not sure it's a great idea. Not right now, anyway. I think I should maybe work my way up to something like a person. And even then, I really think it'll cause more problems than it will solve."

Mara cleared her throat, smiled, then said, "Jeremy. It is only by pushing our boundaries that we expand our capabilities. The Wright brothers didn't settle for a twelve-second flight. NASA didn't settle for a low orbit. You mustn't settle for parlor tricks."

"It just doesn't seem right."

"That's the feeling you get when you're about to step into unknown territory. It's an instinct built into you humans. It was crucial to your evolutionary survival. Isn't it exciting?"

"If it's a survival instinct, shouldn't I listen to it?"

"Darling, it exists because without it, people would've walked blindly into the brush at night and got eaten by lions. Orville felt it before he got on that plane. Neil felt it before he opened that hatch. And now *you're* feeling it. It's exciting enough for me to *watch*. I can't imagine how you must feel."

Jeremy never understood why it was called "butterflies in his stomach." It felt more like rock monsters trying to punch their way out of him.

"Jessica's excited too! Aren't you Jessica?"

"Yes, Mistress."

Jeremy wasn't quite sold. Jessica looked more terrified than excited.

"Jeremy," Mara said, with that perfect severity, pulling his attention to her deep, dark eyes. She leaned toward him and said gently but firmly, "Your first official lesson is not about how to copy a person. It's about taking a shot at something you've never done. It's about believing in yourself."

"But what if I— "

She didn't want anything like the word 'fail' to escape his lips and solidify in his mind, so she cut him off. "You won't. You can do this. And I'm not saying it like an idiot mother who tells her idiot child he can hit a home run. I'm saying it as someone who has an understanding of how you do what you do. Take your time. Make sure you've made the full connection, then do it."

An out. That was all he needed. If he couldn't make the full connection, he could stop and everything would be okay.

"Okay," he said, standing. He could tell Jessica was nervous and said, "It's okay, Jess. I'm not going to do anything unless I'm sure it'll work perfectly." He walked around the table as Mara shifted excitedly in her seat. He rubbed his hands together and blew on them to warm them up, then eyed Jessica up and down. "Can you lose the purse, please?" Jessica hung her purse on the back of a chair. "And the jacket too? I'm sorry, I know it's chilly in here. I'm just trying to make it as easy as possible."

"Would you prefer her to be naked, Jeremy?" Mara asked.

Jessica's eyes widened. Uninhibited as she was, being turned into a science experiment was a whole new experience for her.

"I don't think that'll be necessary," Jeremy said.

"Very good. I'll stay out of it."

Jeremy looked Jessica up and down a few more times, then

raised both hands, palms out and one above the other, in Jessica's direction. "You don't *have* to stay perfectly still," he said. "But every little bit helps."

Jessica sighed and tensed her muscles. As Jeremy made the connection, she felt her whole body tingle. It was that sandy tingle like when her foot fell asleep, but instead of being relegated to her skin, it went all through her. It was in her muscles and her bones. It was in her stomach and her brain. It was in her blood, assaulting her veins and her quickening heart from the inside.

In an instant, Jessica felt herself pass through herself and the feelings were gone. Behind her sounded the clack, clack, clack of high heels followed by a thud and an, "Oof!" She turned and saw herself sitting on the floor, looking bewildered up at herself, their expressions the same. Despite Jessica's shock, she offered a hand and helped her clone to her feet.

"Wonderful," said Mara.

"But which one of us is the copy?" asked the one who fell.

"You are," said Jeremy. He was already getting a sinking feeling about what he'd done.

"But I don't *feel* any different."

"A test, if I may," said Mara. Jeremy stepped out of the way. Mara moved her cup of water to the edge of the table, pointed at the original Jessica and said, "Do something with this."

The original Jessica wiggled a few fingers at the cup and the water formed a column that rose up and out. She relaxed and the water plopped back into the cup.

"Now you," Mara said to the other Jessica.

The other Jessica wiggled a few fingers at the cup but nothing happened. She jabbed her arm toward the cup, but still nothing happened. Panic twisted her brow as she pushed past the original Jessica. She put her hands around the cup and grunted but could not make the water do anything. She picked it up and shook it, then threw it across the room with a cry.

"Very interesting," said Mara. "Guess that settles that. Jeremy, could you make me another water, please? I'm still thirsty."

He did so.

The original Jessica was relieved still to be herself.

"May I see one of your earrings, darling?" Mara asked the other Jessica who, shaking, handed one over. Mara inspected it closely for only a few moments, said, "Hm," then handed it back. "Nothing."

Other Jessica was on the brink of tears.

Mara stood and placed a hand on the woman's cheek. "Don't cry," the witch said. "You are a miracle. Your life is a bonus. Extra. Inconsequential. Free. You are soulless. Do you know what that means? Soulless? It means that nothing you do matters. It means that when you die, there is nothing else. You get to experience this world and that's it. No Heaven. No Hell. No reincarnation. No Other Side. No more singularities and reconfigurations ad infinitum. You, my dear, are blessed, and I envy you. It's a damn shame I have to kill you."

Other Jessica covered her mouth in terror as tears streamed down her face.

"Wait, what?" said Jeremy.

"Oh, do *you* want to kill her?" asked Mara.

"No!"

"It's okay! She's soulless. She isn't recognized."

"Why does she have to die anyway?"

"Well, like you said, she's more trouble than she's worth. And without her abilities, she's no real use to me. Without a soul, she's a danger to us all. And Jessica here doesn't need someone else out there wrecking her chances of doing what she needs to do." Mara winked at the original Jessica, who blushed and looked at the floor.

"Oh please, oh please," other Jessica begged on her knees. "I'll stay out of the way. I'll do whatever you need."

"But you can't just *kill* someone," said Jeremy, "even if they *are* soulless... which, I don't know how you can prove."

"Think of her like a chicken," Mara said. "You eat chicken all the time and never give a second thought to the life it led. It doesn't matter. She doesn't matter."

"But... she's got memories," Jeremy said.

"I do!" whimpered other Jessica. "I do! I remember driving up the mountain. I remember sleeping with Nigel. I remember being out with you, Mara. We had fun, didn't we? Mara? Didn't we have fun?"

Mara wasn't buying it. She had no doubt other Jessica remembered everything that had happened to the original, but it just didn't matter to her. Letting her live would help keep Jeremy's trust though. Decisions... decisions...

"Fine," Mara said, "she can live."

"Oh thank you!" Other Jessica said.

"But! She stays here as your servant, Jeremy."

Jeremy felt strange about it, but decided it would be better to say nothing for the moment. The eagerness with which other Jessica agreed to the terms eased his mind about it to some degree.

"Now, Jessica," said Mara.

"Yes, Mistress?" the Jessicas said in unison.

Mara pinched the bridge of her nose and said, "*Original* Jessica. Other Jessica needs a new name. I don't care *who* comes up with it. Now... *Jessica*."

"Yes, Mistress?" said Original Jessica.

"How do you feel?"

"Fine."

"Normal?"

"Mmhm."

"Fine. Keep trying to find out what happened to Ba'athul. And you, Jeremy."

"Yeah?" he said.

"Other Jessica is your servant and she is only alive because you wore me down. If she puts a toe out of line around here, I will end her in a blink. Do you understand?"

"Absolutely."

"I encourage you to treat her anyway you want. Explore your dark thoughts and desires. Push your boundaries, as I've said. Her soul can't be ruined."

"Sure," he said to placate her. He had no intention of "experimenting" with Other Jessica.

"Good. If there's nothing else, then let us adjourn to the courtyard for more practice. Jessica..."

"Yes, Mistress?" said Original Jessica.

Mara held her cup out to her and said, "Can I get some ice?"

Original Jessica waved her hand toward the cup.

Ariana felt different on her way home from the Foothill. Good different. Like she had a purpose. She and Reggie were going to help defeat a witch, clean up the mountains, and then... happily ever after... whatever that would mean when she got to it.

Paul was about to wrangle the cows and horse when Ari pulled in. He could tell from the second she got out of her car that she was different—good different—and it made him happy.

"Dad!" she said, running up and hugging him.

Paul put his hands on her shoulders and looked hard at her, saying, "I can't tell you the last time I saw you this happy. What is it?"

Ariana didn't know where to start. "Well, it's kind of a long story but... let's see. Jeremy's been taken by the witch."

"What?"

"Like I said, long story. Jeremy was taken, or actually, he went with her willingly. Turns out he can do magic, which is, we guess, why she wants him."

"Oh my God."

"She healed his mother to sweeten the deal."

"Connie?"

"Saw her with my own eyes. Anyway, since we're pretty sure no good will come of Jeremy being with the witch, Reggie and I are going to help Mr. Ballantine and his friend go after her!"

"First off, who's Mr. Ballantine? And secondly, no, you're not."

"Um. First off, he's an experienced monster hunter and secondly, yes, I am."

Paul's eyes shone a fire Ari had never seen. They went red and sharp. The corners of his mouth twisted down and his nostrils flared with rage. It was like he turned into a completely different man, or worse, a monster, and it scared her to death.

"Now you listen to me," he said. "You, for once in your life, listen to me. Under no circumstances will you go after that *thing*! Do you hear me? Now I've let you have your space. Tried not to keep my thumb on you too hard, despite the fact I'm worried sick from the second you leave until the second you come back. I put a lot of trust in you. A lot of faith. A lot of love, despite you coming and going as you please. Bought you a goddamn horse which, by the way, I've been taking care of more than you have lately. And I haven't said a goddamn word about it because on your *best* days you're taking off on me. I'd rather have an hour a day with you angry at me than nothing at all. So if you only listen to me once for the rest of your life, you will *not... GO AFTER...* ***THAT WITCH***!!!"

He'd never yelled at her like that. It frightened her, despite the loving sentiment. Tears welled in her eyes, but her resolve would not be shaken. She'd never felt good about anything—never felt like she had a place to be—and now he was trying to tell her she couldn't do the only thing that felt right.

"I'm sorry, dad," she said pulling away. "I have to." She turned to run back to her car but Paul caught her by the sleeve.

"GODDAMMIT, ARIANA!"

"Get off me!" she said, pulling her arm free.

Paul stomped a foot and cried, "*I ALREADY LOST YOUR MOTHER TO HER*!!!"

Birds chirped into the silence while Ariana processed the new information. Her reality was changing. Though she'd never been told anything, she felt as if she'd been lied to her whole life. She felt as if Paul were the biggest liar of them all. Years of questions tried to force themselves out of her mouth at the same time, but all she could say was, "What?"

"Please, Ari," Paul growled.

"No. You fucking tell me what happened right now!"

"She killed her! Okay! The witch killed your mother! My wife! And if she gets hold of you too, she might do even worse."

"How?"

"Please, Ari."

"How did she kill her?"

"Let it lie, Ari. Live your life! It's what your mother wanted."

Ariana was done playing games and done asking questions. She walked to her car, hoping he'd start talking before she got in.

He didn't.

She glanced at him as she pulled away. The sight of him standing there with his fist against his mouth burned into her memory and, after she rounded the bend, broke her.

CHAPTER 20

The hunters loaded up and took Ballantine's truck to Jessica's house. On the way, Ballantine caught Nigel up on the situation.

"So it was Jessica's tracks at the bottom of Witch's Mountain, eh?" asked Nigel.

"Yeah. Looks like Jess is working for her," said Ballantine.

"Blimey!"

"Yeah. You didn't tell her anything, did you?"

"I..." Nigel panicked. The night before came back to him in snippets. He barely remembered the sex, let alone the things he said. "I'm not sure."

"Nigel!"

"I was drunk!"

"Goddamnit, we can't afford to be reckless."

"I know! I'm sorry!"

"Sorry's not gonna cut it if it gets back to the witch that we killed her dog."

"I'm not so sure it will."

"Really."

"Really! I truly feel that Jessica and I connected last night."

Ballantine remembered Mara's questioning of Jessica. She'd asked, "What about the other one?" which the monster hunter took to mean, "Did *Nigel* kill the dog?" Jessica had shaken her head. If that *was* what she had meant, they might be okay. He let the rest of the ride pass in silence.

They rode past an anomalous patch of tall grass in the tree line and Ballantine realized he had passed Jessica's driveway. He stopped and backed up until he reached the almost completely obscured mailbox.

"I say," said Nigel. "Good eye. Looks twice as thick as last time."

The foliage swallowed the truck and muffled the engine as they drove up. Grass brushed its sides. Fallen branches banged off the bottom. Twigs scraped the roof.

The forest released them into Jessica's clearing, yet the men still felt trapped, as if they were in a prison or asylum made not to *look* like either, as if just beyond the tree line was a wall.

A breeze rustled the grass around the old trailer. It would've been rustic and picturesque if not for the circumstances. Jessica's truck was gone, but had cut just enough of a path for Ballantine to follow to the trailer.

"Well, what now?" asked Nigel.

"We wait," said Ballantine, putting the truck in park and turning off the engine.

They stepped out and took a look around. Cotton ball clouds sailed silently across the monsterless sky. Wind hissed through the treetops.

"You know," Nigel said. "She's got a pretty nice little spot right here."

Something bumped inside the trailer. Ballantine reached for his pistols. Nigel ran to the truck and grabbed his shotgun.

"Jessica!" Nigel called to the trailer.

b-bum-BUMP

The men crept to the door.

"Jessica, if you're in there, please say something so we know it's you. Kind of a bad area to play frightening jokes on people."

Ballantine put a pistol away, placed his back against the wall next to the door and motioned for Nigel to stand ready.

The *bump-bumps* turned into *BAM-BAMS* against the door.

Ballantine counted to Nigel with his fingers, one... two...

The monster hunter flung the door open, stepped away, and

aimed. There was a screech, a shotgun blast, and ringing ears, but nothing else.

Nigel lowered his gun and waved away the smoke. The two men stepped to the door and surveyed the mess. Whatever it was had evaporated into red, but for a leg and a paw here and there.

"Did you get a look at it?" asked Ballantine.

"Only just," said Nigel. "It was the chupacabra. Impressed?"

"Very," Ballantine said with a smirk. "You don't sound happy, though."

"If I'd known, I'd have used a smaller caliber. A once in lifetime kill and I'll never be able to mount it."

A familiar hollow, throaty hiss sank the men's stomachs and drew their attention to the right. A wood devil was already halfway across the clearing to them and bearing down fast. The men took aim and fired, but the devil leapt ten feet high and made them miss. As it soared toward them, arms outstretched, Nigel froze. Ballantine aimed, breathed, and blew a hole through its chest. The creature landed in a bloody heap at Nigel's feet.

A slam on the roof of the trailer made them look up. Looking down on them were the onyx eyes of a shug monkey.

"Inside," said Ballantine.

As they hurried into the trailer they heard hisses, screeches, and growls from every angle. They wedged the musty sofa against the door. On the other side, the shug monkey hollered and banged.

"Look for ways in," commanded Ballantine. "Close the curtains."

Nigel made a right to the kitchen area. Ballantine, left down the hall. Upon opening the first door, the monster hunter nearly threw up from the stench of feces and rot. Inside the room, the water heater was surrounded by what looked like ostrich eggs. Some were hatched. Some were not. Straws of hay and dead grass lay scattered about. Along the left wall hung a string of dead rodents that a baby wyvern was tearing into. It turned its attention to Ballantine and screeched.

The monster hunter knelt, unsheathed his knife and sliced its neck open as it reared.

While Ballantine processed what was going on, the shug

monkey banged on the roof again. Another wood devil hissed somewhere else. Something unidentified scratched under the floor.

Running out of time to think, he scanned the room for danger. A foot-long spider dangled in the corner. It bared its fangs as the hunter made eye contact. Rattler-quick, he drew and fired, exploding the spider.

"Mr. Ballantine!" Nigel cried as he ran over. "Okay?"

"Yeah, check the other rooms."

Ballantine went to work stabbing his knife into the eggs. Some were mostly goo. Others had fetuses of random creatures: teeth, claws and closed eyes. One had a tail and short legs. Another had long claws. As he put his knife through the penultimate egg, the creature inside wrapped its tentacles around the blade.

He banged the egg to pieces. He stabbed and slashed, but he couldn't cut the boneless creature. It was like a little octopus. He ran to the kitchen and threw the knife with the creature into the oven, then turned the heat all the way up.

Nigel opened the door of a spare room to see the shug monkey had come in through the window. It howled at him, making him jump and fire. The kick of the shotgun staggered him back against the hallway wall as the shug monkey was blown in two.

"You okay?" Ballantine called down the hall to Nigel.

Nigel nodded, looked at Ballantine and said, "Yeah." Jessica's bedroom door swung open behind the Brit.

Ballantine pointed with a cry of, "Look out!"

Nigel turned in time to see himself emerge from Jessica's bedroom. The other Nigel's eyes were jaundice yellow orbs. It had two-inch fangs and its mouth gaped open so far that its chin nearly touched its chest. It lunged at Nigel, making him stumble backwards, and landed on top of him. The Brit managed to grip one of its wrists but couldn't get his other hand up in time. It craned its neck and sunk its teeth into his succulent throat. With a wrench of its head, it tore out Nigel's larynx, severing his jugular.

Ballantine, with no shot, rushed over, prepared to beat the shape-shifter to death with his bare hands. As he dropped to his knees in front of them, the creature reared. With Nigel's blood oozing down its chin, it released a gurgling growl from deep in its throat. Ballantine reached for his guns but the creature lunged, forcing him to drop them.

The monster hunter held it by its skinny wrists as it clawed, snapped, and drooled. It changed to look more like him and chilled his insides with its pestilent growl.

Ballantine pulled one of the creature's arms across his body, taking it off balance and allowing him to roll on top. He slid a hand under its chin and clamped down with all his strength on the creature's neck. Struggling to breathe, the other Ballantine clawed with its spindly fingers at the massive arm that had it pinned. When that didn't work, it turned itself back into Nigel, which gave it a long enough reach to get its own hands around Ballantine's neck. But Ballantine's neck was too thick and strong. It changed into Jessica to see if that would work, but Ballantine wasn't fooled. At last, it changed into its true form, black and lanky with bristly hairs. Its head was nearly spherical. Its yellow eyes bulged from the surface. The jaw was a hatch—invisible when closed, razored and drooling when opened. The neck was elongated. Ballantine had to use his other hand to keep the creature from craning to bite his arm. On the ends of its fingers were claws like a dog's, dull and only moderately effective. In its last throes, it clawed at Ballantine's arms, barely breaking the skin, but leaving its mark nevertheless.

Then it stopped clawing. It took weak swings at the air. Its body shuddered and shook in a violent last fight for air.

Then it relaxed.

Ballantine felt the irregular ridges of the creature's vertebrae against his thumbs. He held on for a few more moments to make sure it was dead. Something scratched under the floor. Somewhere outside, a wood devil clawed and hissed at the trailer.

When he was sure the shape-shifter was dead, Ballantine slowly released it. Without taking his eyes off of it, he reached for and holstered his weapons.

"What the hell are all these things doing out in the day?" he asked himself.

He pursed his lips and turned to look at Nigel. Poor bastard. The Brit's eyes were still wide open with the hope of survival. His mouth was agape in a silent gasp for air. The last of his thick blood oozed from the missing chunk of his neck.

Ballantine closed the man's eyes for him, then turned down the corners of his own mouth. He grabbed Nigel's shotgun and stormed toward the entrance. With one hand, he flipped the couch out of the way and yanked open the door.

As he hopped to the ground, the wood devil hissed to his right. Ballantine turned and blew it in half. A creeper emerged from beneath the trailer. The hunter backed away, blasted a hole down the middle of it, then forgot it. Nobody remembers creepers. He turned left and right, looked high and low, and backed himself away into the grass for a better view.

An engine rumbled up the drive. It was Jessica's truck. As it emerged into the clearing and she saw Ballantine standing there with a ready shotgun, she gunned the engine and stopped just before hitting his truck.

She jumped out shaking, screaming, "What the hell is going on? *WHAT THE HELL IS GOING ON*?" She gasped at the dead wood devil. She cried out at the sight of the dead creeper. She threw a questioning glare at the bewildered Ballantine as she strode to her door. She looked inside and crescendoed, "No, no, NO, *NO, NOOOOO*!!!"

Jessica stepped inside, looked around, and covered her mouth with her hand. "Oh God," she moaned. "Oh God, no." She looked back at Ballantine as the tears fell from her eyes and said, "What did you do? What did you do?"

The monster hunter was confused. He thought he'd saved her.

"My babies," she sobbed. "Oh, my babies... And Nigel! Oh, you *idiot*!" She strode out of the trailer straight at Ballantine, who found himself at a loss for a next move. The hunter decided it was best *not* to brandish the shotgun at the woman. Instead, he allowed her to slap his face and beat his chest until she got it all out of her system.

When she'd finally tired herself out, she pulled out a cigarette, lit it, and asked, "Need a drink?"

Ballantine hauled the carcasses out of the house and into the woods. Jessica pulled a pair of rocks glasses out of a blood-spattered cabinet and poured them each a couple of fingers of cheap rye whiskey. She stood in the doorway with the glasses in her hands and the cigarette between her lips as she watched Ballantine lower Nigel's body into the truck bed.

"I really did like him," Jessica said. "He was good to me."

Ballantine rested his hands on the truck's side and looked out at the orange sunlight pricking through the trees. He tried to wrap his head around it all, step outside of the whole situation, see if he could see a bigger picture. It was refreshing and calming, but led him to no conclusion other than "This too shall pass," and "Ultimately our problems don't matter much." He sighed and turned to face Jessica, who offered him a glass.

"You mind putting my couch back for me?" she asked as they stepped inside.

The couch lay in the kitchen area. That's when he remembered the oven. He slid the couch out of the way, then cracked the oven door to check. A black plume came out. The creature was charred and flaking off of his knife. He closed the door and turned the oven off.

"You baking a cake?" Jessica asked.

Ballantine replaced the couch, inspected it for residue, and sat with her. Jessica puffed hard on her cigarette and ashed on the floor. She flicked her thumb against it as she processed the scene, her feelings, and what she wanted to say. She looked older. Her brow was heavier and her whole body sagged like the corners of her mouth.

The fishtanks, somehow unscathed, hummed.

"What did you mean when you said, 'My babies'?" Ballantine asked.

"I meant, my *babies*," Jessica said.

"Where did all those eggs come from?"

Jessica patted her stomach. Ballantine's brow furrowed. He'd never heard of such a thing.

"*You* laid those eggs?" he asked.

Jessica bobbed her head and took another drag.

"You, uh, care to elaborate on that?"

"I fuck men. I breed monsters."

"So what's that make *you*?"

"Cursed."

"By the witch?"

Jessica bobbed her head and took another drag. "Got into it with her a long time ago," she said. "Thought I was something. Thought I had her number. I was wrong. Made a deal to save my life. I keep her informed, I get to live."

"And the eggs?"

"For her own entertainment. My burden to carry. Help keep these mountains populated."

"So *you're* why nothing can get wiped out."

"Don't be stupid. I lay an egg a day. People here can't wipe anything out because there's two infested mountains they can't and won't go near." She took a final drag and flung the butt across the room out the door.

They each took a sip of their whiskey and Jessica lit another smoke.

"And what exactly have you informed the witch about me and Nigel?" Ballantine asked.

"Just that you're a couple of hotshots. Didn't say anything about the dog."

"Why's that?"

"Cause I'm hoping you can help me. I don't want to be her tool anymore. To lay eggs. Be a whore."

"I see," said Ballantine. "Well I'm gonna need all the information on her that you can give me then. How'd she come by her powers?"

"Don't know."

"She lets you up her mountain, right? How?"

"Charmed me so I can get up."

"Can you pass the charm on to me?"

Jessica shook her head.

"Can we *trick* her into charming me?"

Jessica said, "Doubt it. I think the only way you're getting up there is to pay a visit to the cave worm first."

"The cave worm... Kelly said it was the key to the witch. Jessica, what happened with Sam?"

The rusty sun had descended below the height of the castle walls, leaving the courtyard in cool shadow. Lana stood in the path next to a basket of apples and held one of the fruit in an open hand. Lana was the name Jeremy had given the other Jessica. She trembled. She had been trembling all day from the shock of her existence: of being soulless, the potential pain her mistress could inflict on her, her indebtedness to Jeremy, the loss of her magic, the thoughts rushing back to her, and the fact that her mistress' charms did not transfer with her. Did Mara not realize? On top of all that, she was chilly. Though Jeremy had persuaded Mara to give her some clothes, what was provided left little to the imagination. That was for no other reason than the witch's own sadistic entertainment.

Ten feet in front of Lana, Mara stood next to Jeremy and gave him instructions.

"Can you," she asked, "make a copy jump? Every time you do it, it seems you only push it one way or another." She raised her voice so Lana could hear, "But if Jess—Lana held out an empty hand..."

Lana put her other hand out, shoulder width from the one holding the apple.

"...could you make the copy fly over?"

Jeremy held up a hand and zeroed in on the apple. Despite Lana's trembling, he connected with the smooth skin, permeated the porous flesh, felt the cartilage of the core, and sluiced through the seeds. When he was sure he had it, he focused on pushing it up and out. The apple shot diagonally out of itself, but as soon as the skin cleared the original, the duplicate apple fell to the ground.

"No telekinesis then," said Mara. "Not to worry. Your gift is so *near* to it, you might be able to unlock it someday." She addressed Lana, "What do you think? Is our man doing well or what?"

Lana nodded, still trembling.

Mara knew her charms hadn't transferred with the clone, so she took the opportunity to ask Jeremy, "Has she told you yet?"

"Who, what?" he asked.

"Lana. My secret."

"No, and I'm pretty sure I'm happier not knowing."

Mara clicked her tongue and said, "Ooh, Jeremy. Willful ignorance is one of the *most* egregious sins."

"Well, why'd you bring it up then?"

"Well... I suppose I figured she'd tell you sooner or later."

"I don't want to know what it is if it means you'll have to kill me later."

Mara laughed and said, "I can't outright kill any human."

"How's that?"

"Because I'm not a *witch,* Jeremy. I'm a demon."

"Saywhatnow?"

"Been around since the beginning... Well, before *humans* anyway. One of the devil's many advocates. I won't get into the reasons now, but... Where to start...? Well, there was the disagreement, the uprising, and the fall. I'm sure you've heard of all that."

"I heard the skinny version."

"Right, well the Prince of Light wanted something to rule and he got it, in a way. People think of Hell as a place, but it's not. It's more of a state. It was created to be something you humans have to overcome in order to grow—to transcend."

"So there's no lake of fire and brimstone?"

Mara laughed. "Not *literally,* no."

"So, where do demons live?"

Mara shifted her eyes back and forth and cast her palms out as if the obvious answer were all around them. "In one manner or another."

"How do you mean?"

"Well, there are different planes of existence, Jeremy. Your body's here. When you die, your spirit crosses to another, then another. They're all in the same place—"

"Just different dimensions," he clarified.

"That's not quite the way to put it, but if it helps you understand for now, then sure. Anyway, during what was *supposed* to have been the final battle in Pittsburgh all those years ago, all the planes opened up in one place, unleashing Hell and all the other planes into the physical realm. I did my part for a while. I fought for my side. I was sure I'd die and was grateful for it. Believe it or not, the plane I'm from isn't the party your rock music claims it to be.

"*But,* when my chance to die revealed itself, I ran... and I ran... and I kept running until I found this mountain. I thought I'd wait out my days here, however many left I had in this realm. I thought I'd meditate and pray and heal and repent... on the off chance that I might be allowed to cross over when my time here ends."

"Doesn't the Bible say something like, 'Repent and you'll be forgiven'?"

"Yeah, well, that's the thing about repenting. You have to be sorry for what you've done. And I'm not. I'm not sorry I showed Constantine that cross. I'm not sorry for making Helen irresistible to Paris, and I'm not sorry I inspired Temüjin. I know what I've done is not according to God's will, yet I feel no pain for it and I ache to do more. It is my nature."

"Then He made you this way. And that would make you blameless. Nobody blames the *tiger* when a person gets eaten."

Mara's eyes went glassy. "Ha. Mark Twain. I tried that argument. No dice."

"Okay, well you're helping *me* now, aren't you? You have to start somewhere."

"Indeed, Jeremy. That's one way to look at it. Another way is that I'm keeping you in my pocket for something sinister."

"*Are* you?"

Mara thought and shook her head. "I don't even know. You can take the tiger out of the jungle, but you can't take the jungle out of the tiger. I'm a demon, Jeremy. I'm the last thing you should trust."

It would have been prudent for Jeremy to stop there and invoke his right to leave. Whether Mara would have allowed it or not, even *she* wouldn't have been able to say.

Then Jeremy had a thought. "You *were* a demon... You *used* to live in Hell... Maybe now that you're here, the rules are different. Maybe *now* you get the same chance as any human."

"The thought had crossed my mind... Anyway, come on. Time for dinner."

"One more question. I'd think people would leave you alone if they knew you were a demon. Why make everyone think you're a witch?" As soon as he asked, he remembered.

They both said at the same time, "Protocols."

After the battle, demons were listed high on the government's extermination priorities. Witches, not so much.

Jessica recounted the story to Ballantine:

"It mighta been two years since Mara came to town. I was pretty new myself. Sam was as big as you, if not bigger. I remember thinking he could do better than Kelly. She wasn't *ugly* or anything, but she didn't look like *me*. Tried to work my feminine wiles on him.

"I know you probably haven't given a thought to sleeping with me, Mr. Ballantine, but back then a *whiff* of my perfume had them falling out of their chairs. Everyone but Sam, that is. I don't know how he resisted, but he did. Drove *me* crazy. You ever hunt something you could never catch? It was like that. I got *obsessed* with him. I followed him. I learned about him.

"Fell in *love* with him.

"He was so strong in his convictions, and his will... and his arms... like yours... He was determined to wipe out every last monster from these mountains... like you are... and it appealed to everything feminine in me, curse or no curse. I thought, 'This is it. This is him. My man. My mate. I'm the beautiful damsel in distress and he's the knight in shining armor come to save me from the wicked witch.' I thought we were meant to be. That he just didn't know it yet.

"I wanted him more than I'd ever wanted anything, even more than my own freedom from Mara. I devoted myself to him. Worked him from every angle I could think of... but when other men would've fallen, he turned away—back to Kelly. Every time. Until the day I offered him what he wanted most—a shot at the witch.

"*That* got him thinking. He asked me how. I told him. He needed the cave worm's blood to immunize himself to the witch's powers. And he needed my *necklace* to immunize himself from the *cave worm's* powers. But he'd never get my necklace if he didn't leave Kelly for me.

"Took him years to decide, but he finally came around. I played coy. Made him work for it. It was fun watching him squirm, working every angle he could think of.

"Then he told me he loved me. That it was *only* ever me. 'Kelly who?'

"All those feelings I had, all that obsession that they'd turned into welled up inside me. Carried me to cloud nine. I was gonna get my prince. He was gonna save me from the wicked witch. We were gonna live happily ever after.

"Day after, I stopped in at the Foothill for lunch. Kelly's father had only just died when Sam dropped the bomb on her. Heh. Talk about bad timing. They were screaming at each other in the kitchen when I came in. They never knew I was there, but I heard every word.

"Kelly's screaming at him, 'How could you! How could you!'

"And he's all, 'It's the only way!'

"She says, 'It can't be!'

"I'm sitting there smiling, thinking I've got it made and then he says, 'I don't even care about her,' meaning me. 'All I'm doing is telling her what she wants to hear so she'll give me her necklace!'

"Then Kelly's voice got real high and warbly and she cried, 'Are you gonna *fuck* her too?'

"Silence. Wrong answer. She screamed and cried and I heard pots and pans crashing.

"Meanwhile, I felt like *I'd* been stabbed through the heart. Felt like somebody sliced open my stomach and my guts were falling out all over the floor. Needless to say, I lost my appetite. They were still screaming at each other when I left.

"By the time I got home, I'd worried myself sick. Despite everything I'd done up to that point, I felt dirtier and sleazier than ever. I remember looking at myself in the mirror and going through all the reasons to hate myself. Calling myself worthless. Whore. Even took a shower to try to wash my own bullshit away. Obviously, it didn't work.

"Sam knocked on my door that evening. He'd cleaned himself up, put on a nice shirt I'd never seen before. He handed me a bouquet of flowers and stepped inside.

"I had some candles going and poured some wine. I wanted to tease him a little. Drag it out. See how much he'd lie. Plus, I still had to get laid. Part of my curse. I go crazy if I don't get any. Good thing men don't say anything about being raped by a woman. These eggs don't fertilize themselves.

"Anyway, he was a little nervous at first, but he got into it. We told each other it was only me and him from here on out. We'd take that bitch on the mountain down together, then ride off into the sunset and live happily ever after. I let myself enjoy the fantasy of having my knight in shining armor sweep me off my feet. Let myself forget it was bogus. Let myself fall in love one last time.

"And we made love. Do you know what that's like, Mr. Ballantine? I'm not talking about fucking. I'm talking about making love. At least, *I* made love to *him*. I don't know how *he* felt about it, but he was real tender anyway. I almost believed he cared.

"When we finished, I asked him one more time if he loved me... and again, he lied through his teeth and said that he did. I might have respected him if he hadn't. Might not have done what I did next. Maybe.

"In the morning, while he was still asleep, I went and laid an egg, freshened up, and removed two of the stones from my necklace. And since I know you're wondering, Mr. Ballantine, yes, these are them on my ears. I made him a good breakfast and sent him on his way to collect the blood of the cave worm.

"He noticed the two stones were missing and asked about them. I told him that he didn't need all five stones. You know, just like he told me he loved me.

"Anyway, the three remaining stones gave him just enough power to get close to the cave worm, but not enough to strike. He had the strength to walk away, but it turned his mind to scrambled eggs.

"It was either Ken Adams or Paul Coleman who found him wandering down the road babbling to himself. Took him back to Kelly. She's been caring for him ever since. Hid my necklace somewhere and won't give it back. Says she'll give it back when she gets her Sam back. I guess that's why she still lets me come around. Probably always hoped one day I'd walk through the door, wiggle my nose, and everything would go back to normal."

CHAPTER 21

Mara bit into a hard-boiled egg, then spit it onto the floor beside her. As Gregory came over to pick it up, Mara beaned him in the head with the rest of the egg.

"It's too rubbery!" she said.

"Yes, mistress," he said. "One, mistress."

"How's your steak, Jeremy?"

"I didn't know food could taste this good," he said, savoring the piece in his mouth as long as he could without swallowing.

"That's good to hear. Gregory!"

Gregory approached again as Mara pointed her pinky to one of the cherry tomatoes on her salad. "Soft spot," she said. "You *know* that repulses me."

"Yes, mistress. Two, mistress," he said plucking the tomato from her bowl.

Mara flung her hands up and said, "*TAKE* the whole thing, Gregory, and bring me my main course. I've lost my appetite for the salad."

"Yes mistress. Uh... *three*, mistress?"

Mara thought for a moment, then nodded.

Jeremy asked, "What is he counting?"

"He's counting his mistakes," Mara said as Gregory laid her steak in front of her, "so we both know how much to punish him later." She pointed to her plate at nothing Jeremy could see and she made eye contact with Gregory.

The servant looked at the plate, nodded, and said, "Four, mistress."

"Don't you think," said Jeremy, taking time to choose the right words, "maybe this would be a good opportunity to work on your own, uh, spiritual"—'Don't say problems. Don't say problems!'—"...*things*?"

Mara didn't understand. She stared at him as she tried to decode his language.

Jeremy clarified. "You *say* you're looking for redemption, right? Change your nature?"

"Maybe," Mara said, suddenly defensive.

"Well, why not start with something small? Why not forgive Gregory for the egg and the tomato and whatever's the matter with your steak?"

"It's hanging off the side of the plate."

"Okay! There you go! It's still good to eat though, right?"

"That's not the point! It's bad etiquette!"

"But who do you have to impress?"

Mara did not care for being stuck for words. She hated being frustrated logistically. Her insides turned to chaos at being corrected, in her own home, in front of her servants. Had she been younger and weaker willed, she would have driven the musician mad right then. She would have penetrated to the darkest, most gnarled portions of his mind and made him live them over and over again until he died. It took all of her strength to lay her silverware down so gently and ask, "What do you suggest, Jeremy?"

"Forgive him," he said. "Give him another chance to get it right."

Forgiveness. A concept all but erased from Mara's psyche millennia ago. Angels forgave. *Humans* forgave. Demons? Demons were the unforgiven and, subsequently, the unforgiv*ers*—the punishers.

Mara chewed on his suggestion for more than a few minutes. She cut into her steak and chewed on *it* while she thought. Her puzzling kept her from noticing the meat was a few degrees cooler than she preferred. It kept her from noticing it was closer to medium rare than rare, the way she liked it. It kept her from noticing she hadn't been given a fresh glass with the change of wines.

"If I have my facts right," said Jeremy, "you chose the side you chose because you believe you are better than humans, right?"

Mara said nothing.

"Then be better than humans."

Mara stared at him as vexation puckered and pursed her lips.

"Gregory!" she called.

He stood next to her.

"What number are we up to?" she asked.

"Four, mistress," he said.

With her eyes still on Jeremy, she said with no small amount of effort, "Make it two."

Gregory's mouth fell open. In all his years, he'd never imagined—

"Back to your spot Gregory," Mara said sharply and without looking at him, "before I change my mind."

The servant retreated to his waiting place far enough to be out of sight, but close enough to be handy.

Jeremy raised an eyebrow.

"Baby steps," she said into her chalice as she took a sip. "Now I hope you'll excuse me. I have to powder my nose before I run an errand."

"What errand?" Jeremy asked.

"I don't ask you all of *your* business," she said, standing. "Now... you'll have the place mostly to yourselves for a while," she said, meaning Jeremy and Lana. "You have my permission to... live it up." She gave Jeremy a wink and exited.

While "powdering one's nose" is typically a euphemism for using the toilet, Mara had used the excuse to get away from Jeremy before she ruined him in one way or another. Her head swirled with both rage and lust for having been bested in argument, for having been shown another way. The world as she knew it had changed, if only by a hair.

Humans were *used* to change. *Humans* couldn't escape it. With their limited brainpower and understanding, they would never *not* experience change.

The *demon,* having been around since before the earth was created, since before she even *was* a demon, was privy to most of this life's answers. It *knew* most of the conclusions there were to be reached. It *knew* how the world worked. For someone to come along and change Mara's perspective even a micron was like a supernova exploding inside her mind.

Once again, Mara had only barely closed her chamber door before losing control of herself. She squeezed her head to try to calm her burning mind, which literally felt to her like it was burning. Her instincts were a maelstrom of fire, threatening to tear her apart from the inside if she didn't act accordingly. She could have torn his soul to shreds. She could have torn his clothes and raped him where he sat. She could have imprisoned his mind and sent him to raze the town. She could have taken him for a husband, borne monsters the world hadn't dreamed of... taken the Earth for their own.

Instead, she hiked up her dress and ground herself to one orgasm after another, until she was raw, until it was all out of her system.

That was twice that Jeremy had escaped fate that evening.

"So, what's this necklace business, then?" Ballantine asked Jessica.

"The stones were where I stored about half of my power," she replied.

"What power? What are you?"

She gave him clues. "I'm supernatural... I'm horny..."

"You're a nymph."

"*Was* anyway." She lit another cigarette.

Ballantine's thoughts wandered to Jenny, Ken's wife, and *her* necklace, but he chose to say nothing.

"Didn't you have enough power to... *make* Kelly give you back your necklace?" he asked.

"It doesn't work like that, Mr. Ballantine. I'm a water nymph. I'm *'of* nature.' I go with the flow. Create, not destroy. Live harmoniously and all that. I can desiccate a fruit if I like, but not a person. It's against my nature, which I'm bound by... unlike humans.

"The witch came in and wrecked that harmony. Wreaked havoc on my home. I just want things to go back to the way they were, and I'll go back to my streams and leave everyone alone."

"If you got your necklace back together, could you? Could you fix Sam and help me kill the witch?"

"Sam's mind is gone. It's actually incredible he's still alive. I'd have thought he'd have gone to pieces and died shitting the bed years ago. He'll need a miracle at this point, and I haven't heard about any messiahs since Pittsburgh. Don't hear much out this way as it is.

"If I got my necklace back together, I'd absolutely give it to you to get the cave worm blood. Help you kill the witch though? Kind of under contract not to, if you catch my drift."

"You're spelled against harming her."

"For good measure. Already bound by my nature against harming living things. I'll do whatever I can to help you though, Mr. Ballantine. That is... if you're willing to help *me*." Jessica looked him in the eye and slid a hand up her leg.

"Christ," he said. "I was afraid of that."

"I ain't asking you to love me, Mr. Ballantine. I just need my itches scratched. And you know I'm not just some whore. You know I'm cursed to be like this."

"I know, I know." He downed the rest of his drink in one huge gulp, grimaced, and looked out the door. It was getting dark. He needed to get Nigel's body back to town. "Can I use your phone?"

Jessica gestured to where it lay on the floor near the kitchen counter. He picked it up and called the bar. "Kelly, it's Del Ballantine. Listen, can you call the sheriff and have him bring an ambulance? Mr. Carrington didn't make it today... Yeah... I'll meet him at the hotel if that's all right with you... Back of the lot... of course... Okay, thanks... bye." Ballantine sighed as he hung up and turned to Jessica. "You gonna be here later?"

"If I have a reason to," she said, looking down at his crotch.

He bit his lip and looked around, trying to buy himself time to come up with a better plan than the one that was about to come out of his mouth. "All right. I'm going to give Nigel's body to the authorities. Then I'm going to talk to Kelly and try to get your necklace back. Depending how that goes, I might have to make another stop. *Then* I'll come back and... scratch your itch. In the meantime, you try to get this place cleaned up. I mighta seen some shit in my time, but I'm gonna draw the line at fucking in a bloodbath."

Jessica smiled and asked, "What's the other stop?"

"I think it might be better if I left that a mystery for now."

"Mysteries don't do a lot for my trust in you, Mr. Ballantine."

"Yeah, well your service to a witch doesn't do much for mine in you."

"Touché."

"You got enough booze, or should I pick some up?"

"Fully stocked, my dear."

"Good."

"Well, don't look *too* happy about it."

"Sorry."

"Remember, Mr. Ballantine, I get crazy if I don't get what I need."

"Yeah, yeah."

Reggie hadn't told his parents about the plan to help Ballantine with the witch. He hadn't told them *anything* about the night before, as a matter of fact. Ken had asked him if anything unusual happened and Reggie had replied, "Compared to what?"

Ken didn't like having his son around with the threat of a witch about to knock on the door any second. He had had a mechanic come out to work on the truck, but there was a long way to go by the time he called it a day. Still, there were orders to go out, so Ken had Reggie take his own car for a couple at a time. That way the orders stayed fresh and the drummer stayed safe.

Before sunset, Ariana pulled up to the Adams house and knocked. After a pause came the sound of multiple bolts and locks being slid back and undone. Then Jenny opened the door, keeping all but one green eye behind it, and whispered, "Come in! Come in!" Ariana raised an eyebrow and stepped inside. Jenny closed it behind her and watched out the peephole for more than a few moments. "Make yourself comfortable, dear. I'll be with you in a sec."

Ariana sat gently on the edge of the couch and tried to figure Jenny out. "Is, uh, Reggie here?"

"Should be home any minute," Jenny said, locking all the locks.

"So I guess Reggie told you, huh?"

Jenny whirled and said, "Told me what?"

"About the witch last night?"

Jenny flew to Ari, knelt in front of her, and took her hands. "You saw the witch last night? What happened?"

"Uh, maybe I better wait until Reggie gets here."

A door opened and closed in the processor. Jenny put a finger up for quiet. Ken was speaking with someone. Reggie. Jenny ran to the door to the processor and cracked it just enough to see the two of them.

"Ken!" she whispered. "Is anyone else there?"

"Just Reg," he said. "You should be hiding."

"Both of you get in here, now!"

The men followed her into the house and she locked the door behind them.

"How you doing, Ari?" asked Ken.

"I'm fine, Mr. Adams," she said.

"They saw the witch last night," said Jenny.

Reggie cocked his head at Ariana, who threw her palms up.

"I thought you told them," she said.

Ken looked at Reggie, who said, "I was waiting for the right time."

"Tell me everything," said Ken.

They told Reggie's parents everything they knew, including Ballantine's intentions to go after the witch, and their own intentions to help him however they could.

"No, you're not," said Ken.

"Well, lucky for me," said Ariana, "you're not my father."

"Yeah? And what did ol' Paul say when you told him you was going after the witch?"

Ariana answered him with silence.

"Uh huh," Ken said.

"Well maybe it doesn't have to be just me and Reggie helping Ballantine. Maybe we can all—"

Ken cut her off, "Get our torches and pitchforks and all head up the mountain? You don't even know what you're talking about, little girl. I know what you're thinking. You're thinking it's just a witch. Just a person who does a little magic. And all you gotta do is figure out how to protect yourself and maybe do a little rope-a-dope before you dump a bucket of water on her. Right?"

Ariana realized she didn't quite know what to expect.

"Tell me something, Ari. How do you fight a hurricane?"

"Baby," Jenny said.

"I'm making a point, woman. You know I'm right. Ari, how do you fight a hurricane?"

Ariana shrugged and said, "You wait it out?"

"That's how you *survive* a hurricane. I asked you how you *fight* one."

"You can't."

"Can't what?" Ken said, cupping his hand to his ear.

"You can't fight a hurricane," Ariana said to the floor.

"That's right. You can't fight a hurricane. All you can do is batten down the hatches and wait it out. It's not *just* a witch on that mountain. It's a goddamn hurricane."

"Is that why you don't go out, Mrs. Adams?" Ari asked.

Jenny bit her lip and nodded.

"What happened?"

Ken stepped in, saying, "Girl, you do not need to know."

"Hold on, hold on," said Reggie. "You always told *me* you were agoraphobic. All this time, you've been hiding from the witch?"

Jenny pursed her lips.

"What happened?"

"Boy!" warned Ken. "First off, neither of you need to know. And even if we *were* gonna tell you, we don't have time to get into it now. Y'all gotta get moving."

"But I thought we had to batten down the hatches," said Ari with a half-smile.

"Don't you sass me, girl. You need to learn some respect."

"I kind of feel like I've been lied to my whole life," said Reggie, "if I'm honest."

"Ha," said Ari. "Welcome to the club."

"Oh, I'm so sorry, baby," Jenny said. She addressed Ken, "Maybe we *should* tell them now."

"Absolutely not!" said Ken with a stomp.

"But they already know so much."

"I mean," said Reggie, "we're all adults living in monster-infested mountains. I think we're entitled to all the information available about our home."

"You need to get away from here right now!" said Ken.

"Information first," said Ariana, standing.

"I'll tell you," said Jenny.

"No!" cried Ken.

"Yes," said Jenny. There was no mistaking it this time. Her eyes literally flashed.

The taxidermist stormed to the processor door and pointed at the musicians saying, "If shit goes down and *they're* still here, it's on you!" He slammed the door behind him.

Jenny peeked out the window. There was still a little light left. She might be able to get them on their way before they got a visit... *if* they even got a visit.

"Have a seat, guys," she said. "There's kind of a lot to it."

Jenny recounted:

"Once upon a time, there were three nymphs and a satyr. The nymphs' names were Jessie, Jenny, and Jodi. The satyr's name was Nicholas. Spirits of the earth, all of them, they lived in harmony with nature.

"Jessie, the water nymph, tended the streams and all that lived in them. Her hair shone as gold as the sun. Her eyes, as deep and sparkling a blue as any ever seen on earth. And she got her laugh from the babble of the brook.

"Jenny, the forest nymph, tended the woods and all that lived in them. Her hair was a thick and shiny dark brown. Her eyes, as green as any Spring. And she got her love from the blankets of the leaves.

"Jodi, nymph of the wind, tended to the air and all that lived in it. Her red hair flowed as she sailed. Her eyes, as warm and inviting as a cup of hot cocoa. And she got her vitality from the freedom of the wind.

"And Nicholas would play his flute for them, and share his wine with them, dance with them, enliven and inspire them.

"That's how it was until one day, before the two of you were born, when an evil witch decided she would make her home on one of their mountains. Jenny heard the cries of the trees as they were cut down to make room. She went to help. She tried to welcome the witch and guide her to a clearing where she could build her new home. She tried to show her how to build a home with mud and stone so as never to disturb a single living thing. But the witch would not listen. She would settle for nothing less than exactly what she wanted. And what she wanted was a cottage on the peak of the mountain.

"No, a *house* on top of the mountain.

"No, a *mansion* on top of the mountain.

"No, a *castle* on top of the mountain!

"Her tastes changed as often as the seasons as she built her home bigger and bigger. Tree after tree fell from my forest. Stone after stone was quarried from my sister's streams. Great plumes of black smoke rose into the air as she warmed her ever-growing castle.

"The nymphs and satyr watched the witch take and take, every day thinking it would be the last day. Every day thinking her project was nearly complete—that they would restore the harmony after she'd finished. But she was never finished. And one day, the nymphs and satyr decided they could no longer watch. If they didn't act soon, there would be nothing left but a crag and a witch.

"The four confronted her at the door of her castle. They told her she had to leave.

"She laughed at them.

"Jodi and Jessie called a storm. Jenny caused the ground to shake. Nicholas drew an arrow from his quiver.

"Still, the witch laughed.

A storm cloud gathered and grew dark. Lightning crashed. Stones crumbled from the walls of the castle. The satyr drew his bow and took aim.

"Laughing all the while, the witch raised a hand to the cloud and called a thunderbolt to strike down the satyr.

"Jessie and Jodi cleared the sky. Jenny shook the earth more violently, crumbling the castle.

"The witch laughed and told them she had nothing but time. By destroying her home, they'd only given her something to do. And now, she'd have to take even *more* from the earth to rebuild.

"Jenny opened a hole below the witch, but the evil one did not fall. She floated in the air where she stood. Jodi sent a gust of wind to push her into the hole, but it had no effect. Jessie tried to desiccate the witch, but could not penetrate her charms.

"At long last, the nymphs admitted defeat.

"The witch offered them each a deal in exchange for their lives. Jessie would be taken with insatiable lust, but would bear only monsters. Jodi would wed a human and forfeit her firstborn child to the witch.

"As the evil one prepared to offer Jenny a deal, the cowardly nymph allowed the earth beneath to swallow her. Though she sank in a flash, she felt the witch's magic touch her. The earth took her away and hid her for a time. Eventually, she found the one place where no one would look for her and told the man there her story. He took pity on her and took her in. Not long after, they fell in love."

Ariana and Reggie stared at Jenny for a long hard moment. They lived among monsters from hell, so it shouldn't have been a stretch to believe Jenny's story. It explained all the houseplants, and the glowing eyes, and the fact that she looked the same age as Reggie. But still...

"So," said Reggie, "you're a nymph?"

Jenny nodded.

"And Jessica Waters, the town whore..."

"Is a nymph as well," Jenny said. "Cursed. It's not her fault she's a whore... technically."

"And Jodi—"

"Was my mother," said Ariana with a thousand-yard stare.

"That's right, Ari," Jenny said. "Oh, I've wanted to tell you for so long. The day you were born, she convinced the witch to take her instead of you."

Rage reddened Ari's face. "Why didn't anyone tell me?"

"For the same reason I'm telling you now. Because we didn't want you to seek revenge and get yourself killed. It's why your mother gave herself up in the first place. She wanted you to live a normal life. A *happy* life."

CHAPTER 22

Ballantine was waiting in the parking lot when the sheriff arrived, ambulance in tow.

"Mr. Ballantine," said the sheriff. "What you got for me?"

"Nothing much, sheriff," said the monster hunter. "Shape-shifter got him."

"I'd only ever heard stories."

"They're rare. This one took him by surprise. His ID's in his pocket. I assume you'll be able to get in touch with his next of kin."

"We'll take care of it, Mr. Ballantine."

"Good. Let 'em know he died fighting."

"Of course. And if and when you need me, you can call me any time," said Sheriff Landry as he handed over a card.

"Thanks, sheriff."

"Anything else?"

"Not at the moment. But I'll keep you posted."

The sheriff nodded, then waved the paramedics over to collect the body.

Ballantine went inside. He took the stool next to Sam and waved Kelly over.

"I know what happened between Jessica and Sam," he said.

Kelly's expression soured and she turned away.

"I want to help!" he called after her.

Kelly wanted to nip the scene in the bud. She wheeled, leaned across the bar as best she could, and hissed, "There ain't no *help,* Mr. Ballantine. What's done is done. Far as I'm concerned, the only one who can help now either won't or can't. And I don't much care to see her face either way."

"Kelly, you gotta be reasonable. That necklace is the key! I get the cave worm, I get the witch, and we get these mountains back to the way they were before all this shit happened! Life goes back to the way it was meant to be!"

"Necklace don't work, Mr. Ballantine!"

"Not the one *you* have. Well, not entirely."

"The hell you talking about?"

"Jessica knew Sam had planned to betray her, so she betrayed him first. She took stones out of the necklace to weaken it. That's why Sam wasn't able to complete his mission. That's why he ended up like this... Hell hath no fury."

"That bitch. That evil...," Kelly puckered her lips and paced. "I'll kill her. Next time I see her, she's a dead woman."

"I don't blame you, Kelly. I'd be furious. But I'm begging you. Forget what she did for one second. She's been spelled too. If the witch hadn't come to town, you'd never have met Jess in the first place. So I'm asking you, think of the bigger picture. I need *all* of Jess's jewels to get the cave worm... to get the witch... and finish what Sam here started."

Kelly tapped her foot and mulled it over. She could tell Ballantine was a good man from a mile away. She saw a lot of Sam in him, which endeared him to her. Still, she couldn't give up the necklace.

"No," she said. "Let it all burn for all I care."

Sam turned his head to look at Ballantine and the two locked eyes. The withered man's eyes spoke volumes that the monster hunter couldn't decipher. Ballantine tried. He willed the man to speak, then smacked his hand against the bar and left.

A chill ran up Jenny's spine, making her shiver and filling her with dread. The room had grown darker as she told the story of the nymphs and the witch on the mountain. Ariana reached for the lamp.

"No, don't!" Jenny whispered.

A powerful but smooth engine rumbled up the drive way. Ken stuck his head in and told everyone to hide. Jenny locked and bolted the door to the processor, then hurried the kids to Reggie's room, where she closed the windows and curtains. Ari and Reggie sat next to each other on the edge of his bed while Jenny took a chair. They sat in silence. All Ariana could think about was the fact that she'd had sex in this bed recently, that it probably hadn't been washed, and that her partner's mother was sitting three feet away.

"So," said Reggie, "if you and Ari's mom were nymphs, are we—"

"Shh," whispered Jenny, putting a finger to her lips. "Not right now."

Ken was processing a wood devil at his table when Gregory opened the door and gestured Mara in. The taxidermist pretended to be too busy to notice her entrance.

"Kenneth!" said Mara, emerging from the shadows.

Ken shaded his eyes from the light and squinted. "Julia, was it?"

"It's Mara. Always been Mara, as a matter of fact. And I hope you'll forgive my deception all those years ago. I've gotten much better."

"Mmhm," he hummed before returning to his work. "You not a redhead no more neither, huh?"

"Not today," she said gingerly, "no."

"To what do I owe the honor?"

Mara stepped into the light, saying, "Listen, Ken, I'm not sure what I expect to get from you on it, but I think I *am* truly sorry for what I did to you."

Ken slapped his knife down on the metal table and said, "Okay then, you're forgiven. Thanks for coming by."

"My presence unnerves you."

Ken scoffed and went back to his work.

"Why?" She sniffed the air and looked around.

Ken raised an eyebrow at her.

"Because you think I'm evil and would use my magic on you and your family."

"What family? Ain't got no family."

"I don't follow."

"I ain't got no family."

"Really? So Reggie Adams, the young man who delivers meat for you and plays drums at the hotel is not your son?"

Ken pretended to focus on his task while trying to think of a way out, around, or through his lie. For more than 20 years, he and Jenny had been able to live peacefully. Now, their life was a house of cards. He maintained his poker face but internally cursed everyone he could think of who might be responsible.

Mara leaned toward him, resting her fingertips on the table, and said in no uncertain terms, "I've spent a lot of time with the father of all lies, Kenneth. Do not test me."

Ken slammed his instrument on the table and leaned toward her, raising his voice to say, "And you wonder why I'm nervous. Alright, yeah, Reggie's my son. You gonna blame me for trying to hide him from you?"

Mara broke eye contact as she realized his point. "And your wife?" she asked.

Ken scoffed again and went back to the wood devil on the table.

"You are married, aren't you?"

"I plead the Fifth."

Mara strolled about the processor, inspecting its contents. "It's interesting. People seem to *know* you're married, but nobody knows to whom. Such a small town, I find that hard to believe."

"Ha."

"What?"

"I'm standing here carving up a creature from Hell, talking to a witch, and she finds it hard to believe nobody's ever met my wife."

"Well?"

Ken rolled his eyes and continued his butchering, saying, "She's agoraphobic. She's afraid to go outside."

"Oh, the poor thing! You know, I may be able to help her with it if you like."

"We're fine, thanks."

"Honestly, Ken, I'm *really* trying here."

"And you're best buds with the father of all lies. So, no thanks. You want to do me a favor? Stay away from me and my family."

Mara turned up her nose, gave another sniff, and said, "Very well, then. I just have one point of business with you and then I'll be on my way."

"You mean you weren't just here to apologize?" Ken said flatly.

Mara chose to move on. "I was wondering if anyone's brought any unusual beasts in here lately."

"I'm afraid you'll have to be more specific."

"You know what I mean, Ken. Anything one of a kind?"

While Ken pretended to think hard (but not too hard), another hunter entered, dragging a wood devil.

"Well," Ken said, "apart from the two guys who brought me in a horde of shug monkeys, there was one guy who brought me a hellbat. *One*! Said he fired his shotgun into a flock of 'em and it was the only thing that fell. Hey, Steve."

"Hey, Ken," said the hunter.

"Early night?"

"Yeah, dug a trap yesterday. Worked out pretty good."

"I'll say," Ken said grabbing a pen and order sheet. "You want any souvenirs?"

"Naw, I got bigger heads on my wall. Wife says no more. If I get a new one, I gotta get rid of an old one."

"Ha, ha, all right, well, let me get this weighed for you." Ken weighed it, then took it to the cooler.

"So what do you do then, Steve?" asked Mara. "You give him the wood devil, then what?"

"Well," said Steve, "he weighs it, pays me what it's worth, and sells the parts."

"*Pays* you?"

"Yes, ma'am."

"In cash?"

"Yes, ma'am."

"And there's people like you in and out of here all night selling their kills to him?"

"Yes, ma'am."

"My... he must have a *pile* of money in here somewhere."

"I guess."

"And only his razor-sharp instruments to protect it from anyone who might be carrying a firearm."

Her implications made Steve uncomfortable.

"Don't worry," said Ken, rejoining the conversation. "Nobody gets their hands on my money unless I give it to 'em."

"'Course, Ken," said a sweaty Steve, feeling guilty for even *considering* robbing him. The trapper realized he'd been imagining it, how it would go. How easy it would be to just walk in with a sidearm—hell, a *peashooter*—and just... "I wasn't gonna... I mean, I wouldn't..."

"One hundred and eighty dollars," Ken said, handing Steve the money while side-eying Mara. "Now, you a good customer, but I'm gonna need you to take a couple days off before you come see me again, you read?"

Steve shoved the money in his pocket. He gave a weak "Yeah... yeah" and nodded. Mara stopped him as he turned to leave.

"Just a second," she said. "Have you heard about anyone killing anything out of the ordinary lately?"

Steve thought, then said, "Well, *everybody* knows about the guys that brought down the shug monkeys last night."

"Do they now?"

"Yes, ma'am. Supposedly, they brought down a whole *troop*!"

"I believe 'em too," said Ken. "They brought me six of 'em last night."

"That's what everybody's *saying*," said Steve.

"Still got 'em in my fridge if you wanna see," said Ken.

"Oh, could I?" Steve said. "I still don't quite believe it."

"Same," said Mara.

Ken showed them to the cooler and opened the door where, in fact, there hung six shug monkeys.

"My God," said Steve. "Never thought I'd see so many in one place and live to tell the tale."

Mara was agitated. This was the last place she could think to look. She was trying to play nice, give Ken a chance to help her. She took a deep whiff and asked, "Did they bring nothing else with them, then?"

"Woman, what is it you're after?"

A breeze from nowhere wafted her hair and dress as she raised her voice to say, "Someone killed my dog and took its head, and I am now *politely* asking the two of you for any information as to whom it was."

"W-what kind of dog was it?" asked Steve.

"A *terror* dog," said Mara.

"You mean a *terrier* dog?" asked Steve.

Mara stared daggers at Steve. Her blood boiled at his ignorance. She was trying to decide how to *begin* to torture him when Ken spoke.

"Steve," said Ken, "I think you're a little out of your element here. You and I are good. I'll see you in a couple days, huh?"

Steve nodded and hurried out. Mara took a deep breath and cooled.

"Now I've *heard* of terror dogs," said Ken, "but I ain't never *seen* one. That like a hell hound or something?"

Mara pinched the bridge of her nose.

"What?" said Ken. "I'm trying to help you. Maybe I *have* seen your dog and didn't know what it was."

The witch took another breath to calm herself, then evenly yet severely said, "What did I say about testing me?"

Ken threw up his hands and said, "Hey, you're the great and powerful one here, right? We both know you can do whatever you want to do. Thing is, *you're* the only one that really *knows* what you wanna do. I'm over here in fucking limbo wondering whether or not you're gonna turn me inside out or leave me alone. And why? Because someone killed your pet? Man, there are a lot of bullshit reasons to die in this world, but I can't think of one much worse than because someone else killed your damned dog.

Your *literally* damned dog."

The door swung open and a pair of hunters entered, dragging a couple of burlap sacks.

"Now if you really *have* had some kind of change of heart, or if you need me alive for one of your bullshit schemes, I'll thank you to let me get back to my job. Even better, you just let me get back to my life."

Mara took a few more sniffs and scanned the room again for evidence before she turned to leave. After only a few steps she turned to say, "Just one more thing that's peculiar to me, Ken."

Ken chuckled, "On *these* mountains? Do tell!"

"You've got a lot of flowers and plant life around your home."

With a raised eyebrow, Ken said, "Yes, I could see how that would be strange since I live in a forest."

"It's just that there are certain flowers I've only ever seen along the creek or on one of the other mountains."

Ken shrugged and said, "Okay, you got me. I'm a wizard... but all I can do is make flowers grow and dicks shrink, so I took a job cutting up monsters."

"Droll," Mara said with a flat smile.

"I don't know what to tell you. Unusable parts get incinerated. Ashes are fertile. I don't have a lot of time for yard work. You do the math."

Mara narrowed her eyes and thought about it. "I suppose," she said. "If you find out anything about my dog, will you let me know?"

"How?"

"Just have Reggie tell Jessica."

Ken helped the hunters as Mara's car rumbled off. After he sent the hunters on their way, Ken went out the side door and around to Reggie's room. He gave the secret knock on the window, then went back to work.

Jenny shivered, despite the blanket Reggie had given her.

"You had a question, Reggie," she said. "Yes, you're both half nymph, half human."

"Actually, I was going to ask if we're related. Because..."

Ariana's eyes bulged and darted from Reggie to Jenny and back again as she considered the implication.

"No," said Jenny. "It doesn't work like that. Jodi and I have the same mother in that we are born of the earth, but we have different blood."

"What about Jeremy?" Ariana asked.

"What *about* Jeremy?" Jenny said.

"Where did he get *his* abilities?"

Jenny shook her head. "Don't know. The better question now is, 'What's he gonna do with 'em?'"

They sat and thought for more than a few silent moments until Reggie said, "So what do we do now?"

"What do you *want* to do, baby?"

Reggie thought about it, then said, "I just want to keep playing music with my friends. I think... I think I want to take it on the road. You know? See some stuff. Have an adventure."

Ariana wanted that too. "But we need Jeremy," she said.

"Yeah," said Reggie to the floor. "So I guess we gotta get him back."

Jenny cried and took a deep breath to keep herself from sobbing. "Good boy," she squeaked as she unwrapped her blanket. She unclasped her necklace, removed four of the five gems, and gave two to each of them. "These oughta help you. Keep them on you and keep them hidden."

"Help us how?" asked Ari.

"They'll protect you a little bit. Might even let you make some magic if you figure it out. But they're not enough to beat the witch. Use your heads, be safe, and make sure I get those back."

"Are you gonna come with us?"

Jenny cried in shame, saying, "I can't."

"But you'll let your son and me go after her?"

"Remember when I said the witch's magic touched me? Well, I still haven't found out how. She could've made me unable to attack her. She could have been looking through my eyes all these years without me knowing it. She could snap her fingers and I could turn against everyone I love. I just don't know. And I can't take the risk."

Jenny stood and helped the kids to their feet. She had lost her supernatural radiance and already appeared worn. It frightened Reggie. "Now you two get going to the hotel. And remember, use your heads and trust your hearts."

Del Ballantine passed Reggie and Ari on his way to Ken's. Ari thought about turning around to confer with everyone, but Reggie maintained their course ahead of her. He knew it wouldn't be a fun conversation and that Ballantine would end up back at the hotel anyway.

The door hadn't even swung shut behind Ballantine when Ken said, "Well, I'm just seeing *all* my favorite people tonight."

"I need to talk to your wife," said Ballantine, striding over.

"Heh. You can go fuck yourself instead. How's that?"

Ballantine leaned across the table and whispered, "Jenny's a nymph, isn't she?"

Ken seethed. He hadn't even wanted his *son* to find out. Now there was a stranger walking in, poking around, figuring stuff out. He reached under the lip of the table, retrieved his sawed-off double-barreled shotgun, and had it pointed across the table before the monster hunter knew what happened. "You get the fuck outta here, *NOW*! *YOU HEAR ME*?! Get back in your piece-of-shit truck, drive it back to the highway, pick a direction, and keep fucking going. Don't stop until you are out of gas and don't talk to anyone, *especially* my son. And don't you *dare* say one more word about my wife!"

Bolts and locks clicked and clacked open on the door to the house.

Ken threw his head back and asked the ceiling, "Why do I bother?"

Ballantine watched as Jenny stepped in. She seemed less vibrant than before. Less buoyant. More... human. Weary. She no longer inspired his passion like she did when they first met.

"Mr. Ballantine," she said. "Reggie and Ariana just left. They told us everything."

"I'm not here for them," said Ballantine. "What happened to your necklace?"

Ken shot Jenny a glance. She waited for a reaction from her husband but received no more than the look.

"None of your business," she said. "Why are you here?"

"I *was* going to ask to borrow it."

Jenny pressed a hand over her one remaining jewel. She feigned ignorance with a "W-why would you want my necklace?"

"You're a nymph, right? Jessica's sister?"

"Enough," said Ken.

"I knew there was something different about you."

"You shut up!"

"The stones on your necklace can protect me from the cave worm!"

Ken had had enough. He blasted a slug through his own ceiling. Ballantine ducked and drew a sidearm. Jenny screamed, pressed her hands to her ears, and cried as the men took aim at each other. A short standoff passed while their hearing came back. As Jenny's sobs pulsed through the ringing in Ballantine's ear, he holstered his weapon. Ken lowered his to the table, but kept it pointed at the monster hunter.

"Now have I made myself clear?" Ken asked.

Out of tactics, Ballantine growled, "Pleeeeease. The reason Sam failed was because Jessica didn't give him the *whole* necklace."

"Yeah, we know! Figured that out forever ago."

"If I just had a *whole* one—"

"It ain't about you or Sam, dummy! It's about us living our lives without being hassled. And I don't know if you noticed, but we were doing just fine until your dumb ass showed up."

"You call *this* 'doing just fine?' Living in fear of a witch? Monsters everywhere? Up to your eyeballs in blood every day?"

"Don't you try and tell us how we're gonna live our lives! You're standing in *my* home trying to tell me you gonna put me out of business *and* you're asking for my help to do it. The answer is *naw*. Now get outta here and don't come back. Don't talk about my wife, and don't even *mention* her necklace. Cause if you do and I find out about it, you're gonna have bigger problems than a witch to deal with. And I won't fuck around with you like she is. I *will* kill you. Put you in that incinerator like the dog. Ain't nobody find you. You dig?"

Ballantine gave the quivering Jenny one more look.

"I can't give you my necklace, Mr. Ballantine," she croaked. "I gave my stones to the kids to protect them."

"You did what?" said Ken.

"You'll have to figure something else out. I'm sure you will."

The monster hunter knew it would be the best deal he would get at this point—an unspoken, yet limited, blessing to continue his mission.

"Kids are gonna try to help you," Jenny said.

Ken raised his eyebrows and said, "Say *what*?"

"Can't lock 'em up, Ken," she said. "They're gonna do what they want. It's why I gave them my gems. You don't know anything about those gems though, Mr. Ballantine."

The monster hunter remembered the favor he owed her. "Not a thing," he said.

"Just... promise me you'll keep them out of harm's way as best you can."

"I'll do my best, Jenny—Ken."

Ken hated everything about the situation. He was cooling off, though, partially relieved by the symbolic emptying of his hands. He sighed and released his grip on his gun. "You discourage them from helping you," Ken said. "You tell 'em the risks. Make sure they understand. If they still want to help you, then I guess I can't say nothing."

"I prefer to work alone anyway."

"And you ain't welcome here no more. Not unless them kids come back in one piece."

"I understand."

"And tell King Richard he ain't welcome here no more neither."

"Don't worry. He was killed today."

Ken and Jenny looked at each other. Then Ken said to

Ballantine, "That don't exactly inspire confidence."
"Then lock up your kid."

CHAPTER 23

Reggie and Ariana walked into the Foothill bar feeling... different. The power of the gems was seeping into them, making them more alert, in tune, and alive. The absence of Jeremy, however, felt strange, like walking out of the house naked. Should they play anyway? What if Mr. Ballantine needed them and they were in the middle of a set or a song?

They saw Connie Crawford on the stool next to Sam and went over to say hi. She looked much less frail and had better color in her face. On the other side of the bar, however, Laura Krause was pale and sweaty.

Kelly put a hand on her waitress' forehead and asked, "S'matter?"

"Nothing," said Laura, as her stomach did flips. "Probably had some bad devil or something."

"You throw up?"

Laura put her hand to her mouth and nodded.

"You're sick. Go home."

"I can..." Laura's stomach turned and she almost barfed where she stood.

"Don't you do it out here!"

The waitress pressed both hands over her mouth and ran to the bathroom.

"Gonna be a long night," Kelly said with a forced smile to

Connie.

"You want some help?" Connie asked.

"Thanks dear, but I wouldn't want to put you to work so soon."

"Please! I've done nothing but lie in bed for the last how many years?"

Kelly put her hands on her hips and eyed Connie up. The bar owner stuck her tongue in her cheek. Her friend was looking better. Didn't mean she'd be able to carry around trays of glasses, though. But every little bit would help. Besides, she really wanted to do it. "Okay," Kelly said. Then she pointed a stern finger and said, "But don't overdo it, okay? I don't care if you're carrying one glass at a time. And you let me handle the rowdy ones."

"Aw, hell, Kelly." Connie dismissed her concerns. "I'm a little weaker than I used to be but I ain't made of glass."

Ariana put a hand on the woman's bony shoulder and said, "How are you doing, Mrs. Crawford?"

Connie slid off the stool and hugged the bandmates, saying, "Much better, dear. Much better. How about the two of you? Any news?"

The musicians checked in with each other, then shook their heads.

Connie pursed her lips, then hoisted herself back onto her stool, saying, "Well... don't worry. Something will come up. You gonna play for us?"

"We're not really sure," said Ari. "This might not be the room for a drum and bass duo. Maybe we should just help you with the tables."

"Oh no you won't! Right, Kelly? They're gonna play. The way Jeremy talks about you two, I'm sure you'll sound great."

Kelly shrugged and said, "It's not like I've got a whole lot of options for entertainment."

The musicians checked in with each other again.

"Go on!" Connie said. "For me. I've heard *enough* talk about you. I want to hear the music."

Reggie and Ari had never played like they did that night.

Entirely improvisational, the music was effortless and innovative, hypnotic and transcendental. They felt it in their hearts and heads before it flowed out of their hands. Typically, they would check in with each other visually for changes, but that night they both played with their eyes closed the entire time. Half the room danced like they never had. The other half was silent and entranced. Ballantine entered during the set and stopped, dumbstruck, just inside the door.

After a straight hour of playing, Ari announced they'd take a short break. The applause from the dancers was raucous. The applause from the watchers was awkward, like they were in an unfamiliar church trying to follow its customs. Ari saw more than a few people wiping their eyes, but assumed it was from the smoke.

People patted their shoulders and shook their hands as they made their way toward Ballantine. Connie was just around the corner, not far from where she'd been sitting when they arrived. Her eyes were glassy and she had her palms together in front of her mouth. Sam chewed on his lip and stared hard at his coffee. Ballantine approached.

"That was wonderful!" Connie said. "I've never heard anything like it."

Rick Jenkins, from his usual stool on the corner, swung a hand out to tap Reggie on the arm.

"Real good," said the farmer. "Real good." He put a finger in the air to grab Kelly's attention and said, "Whatever these two want, it's on me."

"Ah, that's okay, Rick," said Reggie smiling. "You don't have to—"

Rick held up a hand to silence the drummer. "Whatever you want."

"Well... thanks!"

"Thanks, Mr. Jenkins," Ari said. Then she noticed Andy and Louis. Andy was sobbing. Louis was glassy eyed and chewing his bottom lip hard. "Are you okay, Andy?"

"That was—*sob*—b-beautiful," said Andy.

"Yeah, it was all right," Louis wheezed.

Ari and Reggie exchanged wide-eyed looks, then acknowledged the monster hunter.

"So, how'd the meeting with Dad go?" Reggie inquired. The smile and lilt in his voice indicated that he had a good idea of how it had gone.

"I helped him put in a new skylight," said Ballantine.

Reggie grinned wide and nodded.

"So, what's the plan?" Ari asked. "And where's Nigel?"

"He was killed this afternoon. And I don't have much of one now," said the monster hunter. "Unless Kelly..."

"Don't you say it!" Kelly warned.

Ballantine, out of options, moved to the bar to plead with her, but she cut him off before he could say anything.

"Ask me one more time and see what happens!" she said. "Now what are you all drinking?"

Reggie, Ari, and Ballantine each ordered a beer. As the monster hunter hung his head, Sam reached over and grabbed his wrist. The two locked eyes. Sam squeezed the hunter's wrist harder and strained his face. He was trying to speak, to transmit his thoughts. He was trying to tell Ballantine something... something important. And though the monster hunter knew it, he couldn't put it together. By the time Kelly returned, Sam had let go and was staring into his drink again.

"Mrs. Crawford," said Ari. "I want you to know me and Reggie are gonna do everything we can to help get Jeremy back."

"Really?" said Connie. "What did your parents think when you told them that?"

Ariana was getting tired of hearing about and from parents. "Doesn't matter," she said.

"I think it should matter a *little,*" said Connie. "You don't *have* to do what they tell you, but the least you can do is entertain the possibility that they might have some wisdom for you."

"I guess," Ari said to her glass.

"Saw your dad today."

"When? Where?"

"Here. Earlier. He left at sundown. Waited for you 'til he couldn't keep his eyes open anymore."

"What'd he have to say?"

"Just that he wanted to talk to you."

Ari didn't quite believe her. "I'm going to help with Jeremy. I'm aware of the risks and I don't care. This feels right."

"Well, only *you* can know what's right for you, dear. But maybe someday you'll have a child and understand his selfishness."

Ariana took a sip of her beer and let Connie's words sink in.

"So how you gonna get my son back for me?" Connie asked.

"Well... we don't really know... yet."

"I see."

"I think the plan right now is to help Mr. Ballantine however we can."

Ballantine butted in for his due diligence. "I really don't want or need your help. I don't like having to babysit other people."

"Who says we need babysat?" asked Ari.

"You ever go up against a witch, little girl?"

Ari grew hot at his description of her.

"Back it up," Ballantine said. "Have you ever even hunted *anything* that's on these mountains?"

"I put wood devils down all the time!"

"Put 'em down or *hunted* them? There's a difference."

"I've been riding these mountains since I was 16, okay? I think I know how to handle 'em."

"What about you?" Ballantine addressed Reggie.

Reggie put his hands up and said, "I've had a monster anatomy lesson or two. Hey man, I'm just gonna do what I can, you know?"

"I appreciate that you both want to help. I do. But you don't know what you're getting yourselves into."

"We're getting ourselves into going after our friend," said Ari.

"I think it's great that you want to save your friend. That's a good attitude. But if someone told you to walk blind into an uncharted cave to save him, would you? You're better off hanging back and waiting for your moment."

Ari was tired of being treated like a child. "We're helping," she said. "Or we're doing it ourselves."

"Okay, tough girl, what's the first thing you're gonna do?"

Ari was stumped. "I guess... we start looking for a way up the witch's mountain."

"Know how to break her charm?"

"I might not have to," she said catching Reggie's eyes.

"Say you *do* get by her magic. Do you know what's on that mountain? It could be booby trapped. There could be monsters we haven't dreamed of. Ari, you could end up spider food if you go running around unprepared. Then you've helped nobody." Ballantine put a hand on her shoulder and said, "Maybe your opportunity to help just hasn't arrived yet. Maybe this part is for me and later on there'll be something only you can do. You don't want to be dead when your moment comes up, do you?"

"Reggie," Kelly called. "Your dad got you another room for the night."

"Cool. Thanks, Kelly," Reggie said.

"Fine," said Ari to Ballantine.

"Good. Keep your eyes open. You have an advantage in that you're under her radar. Stay that way as long as you can. You saw what she did to me and that was all over her dog."

"What do we keep our eyes open for?"

"For anything *strange*, of course," Ballantine said, smiling.

Ariana cocked her head and asked, "And meanwhile what'll *you* be doing?"

Ballantine chugged the rest of his beer and said, "I got some dirty work ahead of me."

Lana held the torch while Jeremy focused on the trees. She had spent the day on the verge of hysterics, but nevertheless doing as she was told. That's not to say Jeremy was a tyrant. He was actually very sensitive—never ordering, only asking, since she insisted on staying at his side. Before Mara had left to see Ken, the witch encouraged Jeremy to practice on larger areas to see how far he could reach. She even suggested he make clone after clone of Lana to see what would happen, but the musician put that out of his mind immediately.

"What are you aiming for?" Lana whispered. She wasn't wearing much more than a silk robe and shivered in the evening chill.

Jeremy looked past his fingertips into the dark and said, "There's a group of trees out there. I'm trying to get them all."

Lana squinted in the direction Jeremy was looking. She couldn't tell if she was seeing the vague shapes of trees a couple of hundred feet away or if her eyes were playing tricks.

"How's it going?" she whispered, as if by whispering she'd be less likely to disturb him.

Jeremy lowered his arm, took a deep breath, and rubbed his face. "It's tough. I kinda feel like I wanna throw up."

The car pulled up. Gregory hopped out and opened Mara's door for her. Lana shrunk as the witch approached.

"How's it going?" Mara asked.

"Fine," said Jeremy. "I was just practicing on some trees."

"What trees?"

"A cluster of five out there in the dark."

"Ambitious!"

"Yeah, but I didn't get the roots and they fell over the first time. So now I'm trying to get the whole trees but it's starting to make me nauseous."

"Do you think it's the *amount* of practice or the *scope* of it?"

"I don't know. Probably just been doing it too long." He rubbed his temples.

"Take a break, then try again. It's like any exercise. It's all good for you. But you have to push your limits if you want to get stronger. Why don't you take Jessica back to your room for a bit and... clear your head?"

"Lana," said Jeremy.

"Lana, yes," Mara remembered. "Lana, I'm sure you won't have a problem helping him relax."

"Thought about it many times, Mistress," Lana said. And though that was true, and she was still dying to know what Jeremy was like in bed, she no longer felt the compelling lust she used to. She realized in that moment that she had the ability to say no if she wanted. She wasn't only relieved of her powers, but relieved of her curse. Though, in some ways, she could say she had a new one.

"Uh... that's okay," said Jeremy.

She felt like she should have been relieved. Instead, Lana was disappointed and even a little insulted. What was wrong with *her*? Was she nothing but an old whore without her powers? For the first time in her life she felt old.

"Fuck's sake, Jeremy," said Mara, "live a little. At least take a back rub. What are servants for?"

Jeremy and Lana adjourned to his bedroom. The musician flopped backwards onto the bed and rubbed his eyes under his glasses.

"How's your stomach?" asked Lana, fidgeting with her nails.

Jeremy, still with his fingers in his eyes, took a deep breath and puffed out. "Mm. Getting better, I guess."

"You want me to rub your back for you?"

"You don't have to."

"I want to."

"If it'll make you happy," Jeremy sighed as he rolled onto his stomach and crossed his arms under his face.

"I am your servant," she said straddling his legs. "If you don't let me help you out once in a while, what else will I do?"

"Hm," he said relaxing. "I don't know. Good point, I guess."

She slid the sweater and shirt up his body to his shoulders, then went to work kneading his back.

"Mm," Jeremy said. "Your hands are warm."

Lana wasn't used to such innocent comments. She let out a little laugh and said, "They've always been like that... Jeremy?

"Hm?"

"Where do you think we go from here? You finish your training and then what?"

"We leave. Hit the road. Find some place we can live."

"You mean you and me?"

"Do you want to stay my servant? I mean, you wouldn't have to. You could do whatever you want."

"I don't know. Maybe. Would you want me if I did?"

"I don't know if I'll be able to afford a servant on a musician's payroll."

"Maybe you'll make it big."

"Ha. I just want to play music. See the world. Live in peace."

Despite the history lesson Lana had given him about Mara, he still expected to walk out of the palace when the witch deemed him finished with his training. He was optimistic. He still had dreams. Lana found that magical and endearing. She lay on him and tucked her arms under his shoulders in an awkward embrace.

"What are you..." Jeremy breathed.

His scent mixed with the musty clothes inebriated her. His bare skin heated her robe. She touched her cheek to his back. She laid a flower-petal kiss between his shoulder blades, sending warm tingles through his back.

"We can't," he said.

"Okay," she said.

She planted more kisses heavier, hotter, wetter, down his back until he twisted his body and said, "Stop!"

Dejected, Lana slid off of him and sat on the edge of the bed.

Jeremy pulled his shirt back down and said, "We don't know how everything's gonna go at this point. I don't want to complicate anything."

"Sentimental type, huh?"

"Guess *you* wouldn't understand."

"No. I guess I wouldn't." Lana stood and walked out.

Jeremy followed Lana to the roof. She stood in the same spot he did his first night there, looking out over the town. He approached her but kept outside of arm's reach.

"I'm sorry," he said. "I didn't... mean..."

"Yes, you did. And you're right. Been a long time since I've had the luxury of sentiment. I'm sorry if I made you uncomfortable. Bad servant."

Jeremy moved closer and rested his forearms on the wall. "You're not a bad serv—you're not a bad *person*. Just... caught up. Like the rest of us."

Lana rubbed her arms and leaned against him. He reached around, pulled her against him, and rubbed her arm.

"Thank you, Master," she said.

A twinge of arousal shot through Jeremy. He hadn't felt one like that since his first kiss. Like an electric shock through his groin. Why? The submission? The power she gave him? The fact that he hasn't gotten laid in... Goddamn. Had it been so long he couldn't remember? No. No complications. He took a step along the wall, away from Lana, and shook the seeds of desire and an inferiority complex out of his head.

"I should practice some more," he said and looked into the dark below for something to try his hand on.

"Why don't you see how far you can reach?" asked Lana. "You don't have to go for a whole mountain. Just see how far you can feel."

Jeremy looked from her to the twinkling lights of the town below. He picked a lone streetlamp to focus on and held out his hand. At first, there was nothing. At second and third there was nothing either. He kept going though, because he could feel his power stretching through the air like a strand of web. He felt the shifting air. A bat passed through his reach and he felt it too: snout, fangs, eyeballs, brain, heartbeat, wings, stomach, claws, and tail. Then the bat was gone and Jeremy felt nothing but the wind until he reached the lamp.

"I can feel it," Jeremy whispered, so as not to break his concentration.

Lana's instinct was to respond with a campy, "I bet you *can*," but she kept it to herself. Instead, she whispered, "Feel what?"

"Streetlamp. Hang on." The bulb burned. The filament seared. Electricity hummed in Jeremy's magical grip. The longer he held on, the more he felt: the base of the bulb, the old cast iron framework of the lantern, the wood siding. Siding? Jeremy's grip spread along the wood. To the left, a door frame, then a door. To the right, a window shutter, then a window. "It's not a streetlamp it's a house!" he whispered.

"Can you clone a house?" Lana whispered back, wide eyed and sexually aroused at the potential power she'd been given the opportunity to serve—to live in the graces of. What *couldn't* he duplicate? He could clone cars, boats, and planes! He could clone fine clothes. He could clone *money*!

"I don't know." The floorboards of the porch. The spindles and supports. The plaster walls and the picture frames. An old TV. A dusty rug. A comfy chair and a couch with a neatly folded throw blanket. The stairs. The kitchen. The appliances—the heat of the refrigerator's electronics and the freezing Freon. The weak wooden basement steps and its concrete walls leading to the cold, hard floor. A second-floor bathroom: the dripping faucet, the toilet paper on the roll, pills in the medicine cabinet, and the crust around the shower head. An empty bedroom, dusty, with two dressers full of clothes. Picture frames on the dressers and walls. A jewelry box. A night stand on either side of the bed. Matching lamps. A closet full of clothes. Moths. Another wall. Another dresser. A twin bed. Thick hair.

Jeremy hesitated. It was an invasion of privacy. Only, he wasn't just invading someone's bedroom. He was about to invade *someone*. It frightened him. It excited him. He grew warm and tingly with the rush of breaking the taboo. His face flushed and glistened in the moonlight as he felt to the top of the person's head, the spongy brain, rubbery eyes, soft and smooth cheeks, slimy tongue, the neck and throat, the ridges of the vertebrae, the rib cage, beating heart and hot pulsing blood, the gentle bellow of the lungs, the firm breasts pressed tight beneath the old cotton t-shirt, the stomach and its mushy contents, the spaghetti of bowels, the thin layer of lipid over the belly and hips, the... pulsating bean-sized shrimp... *a fetus*! He lingered there to absorb the gravity of touching the beginning of life.

He moved on. There was the patch of fur leading to the folds between the legs, down the femur to the gnarly structures of the knees, the soft curve of the calf and the blade of the shin, the webwork of bones through the feet and the pads at the ends of the toes.

Jeremy moved on to engulf the rest of the house. He finished the bedroom and moved on to the attic. There was an old crib, a few boxes of Christmas decorations, loose insulation, support beams, then the roof with its rusty nails and cracking asphalt shingles. From basement, to gutters, to beating hearts, Jeremy was connected to the house and everything inside.

It felt good. He had it. He was in control, but his concentration was taxed. He was a waiter with a full tray of glasses. "I've got it," he whispered. "Whole house."

The power... Lana was enamored, drawn by the potential. She wanted to be as close as possible to this man. She wanted him to be happy with her. What could she do? She moved behind him and slid her hands around his waist.

"Jeremy," she breathed into his ear. "Master. I'm yours."

Lana slid a hand down to his crotch and squeezed him through his pants. Jeremy hadn't realized he was fully aroused. She spun him to face her and gently pushed him against the wall. He groaned and broke his connection with the house, but didn't fight Lana off. Or maybe he couldn't.

"Don't," he sighed.

"Let me make you happy," she whispered into his mouth, unbuckling his belt.

"It's a bad idea."

"Then stop me." She pressed her heavy lips to his and undid his pants.

Every passing moment fuzzed Jeremy's thoughts and drained him of his resolve. It had been so long. The next thing he knew, Lana was on her knees in front of him.

Jessica wrapped her arms around Ballantine's neck, pulling his face against hers, kissing him hard the second he walked in the door. Her lips billowed over his and gave like an old broken couch. The monster hunter braced himself on the door frame and put a hand on her hip.

"Easy, easy," he said to her lips.

"Pheromones," she said between her kisses. "Your pheromones help me keep it under control." She breathed in deeply through her nose.

They stood kissing in the doorway for a few minutes as Jessica's grip on him loosened a little at a time. As she got herself under control, she came down from her toes and aimed her big blue eyes up at him. She seemed younger than before, more innocent. More enticing. Ballantine surmised it was due to the remnants of her nymph magic, but all the same he wanted her. Regardless, he poured himself a whiskey first.

She wore a sheer pink nightie that pushed her tits up to her chin. She stood there with a knee turned inward and her thumbnail in her mouth, playing innocent. Not only had she gotten the place somewhat back to normal, she'd gotten her makeup and hair back together as well.

Del Ballantine downed his whiskey in one gulp and set the glass on the counter. He swaggered over to Jessica and pulled her against him.

"I'm going to blow your mind," she whispered.

Reggie and Ariana played on to much the same result as their first set. Watchers wept. Dancers transcended. Patrons offered the musicians anything they wanted: food, drink, tips, sex, good lives far away from here. The two of them correctly guessed it had to do with Jenny's nymph energy in their pockets and agreed not to take too much advantage of it. They accepted a few drinks and an appetizer, but didn't quite know what to make of the sudden adulation. It made them uncomfortable, so when they finished their final set, they went straight to Reggie's room.

"This is so weird," said Ariana.

"I think it's cool," said Reggie.

"It's like... It's like... What's it like?"

"It's like being able to see colors and hear sounds we didn't know were there."

"Yeah. I feel so connected. Like I can feel the earth's heartbeat and I know what the wind is going to do."

"Like a whole other world exists on top of this one. Or beside it. In *tandem*." Reggie was proud of coming up with that word.

"And I can feel all the cracks in the floorboards."

They sat on the bed and Reggie said, "And the fibers in the blanket."

"And I can see your aura."

"And I can see yours."

They paused to stare in wonder at each other. Then Ariana saw a familiar look in Reggie's eyes.

"I'm not having sex with you tonight, Reggie," said Ariana.

"I wasn't expecting you to," he said.

"Just making sure we're on the same page."

"Although, it *is* good for relieving anxiety."

"Reggie."

"Just playing devil's advocate," he laughed and put his hands up. "I'm fine with whatever."

Laura dreamed:

4th of July.

The Krauses, Crawfords, and Adams celebrated on the Coleman farm. Thanks to Paul's fence job, there was space enough there for the kids to play without the adults having to worry too much. Laura and Ariana sang the first two lines of "Yankee Doodle" over and over. The two of them waved miniature flags, watching in wonderment as they rippled through their own draft.

Snap, snap, snap, snap! Reggie and Jeremy threw Pop Pop firecrackers at the girls' feet, making them jump, scream, and flee. Laura and Ari first spun toward each other, stopping just short of a collision. Then they ran to the adults with their arms out, their little flags clutched tightly, rippling in their own breeze.

Halloween.

Pittsburgh.

David and Sandra, Laura's parents, left the masquerade ball. They said their giddy good-byes and Sandra held David's arm down the single step to the sidewalk. Outside, the limousines and taxis had queued around the block. David had a grip on a taxi's door handle when a warmly dressed man on a horse-drawn carriage offered a ride. Husband and wife shrugged to each other, told the driver to take them to the hotel, then climbed into the carriage.

The seats were smaller and less comfortable than they had expected. The small windows let in so little light they didn't even realize they were sharing the ride until the man who sat across from them spoke. He was nicely dressed and made small talk that was unintelligible in Laura's dream. As they rode, David squinted out his window, trying to figure out where they were. Sandra kept looking at her white gloves, unable to tell if they were actually dirty or if it was a trick of the light.

The man across from them produced a stiletto and held out a hand. The Krauses hesitated, then handed over their belongings. A streetlight cut through the window and allowed Sandra to see that her white gloves were streaked in blood. It was all over the seats. She opened her mouth. The man leaned across and slashed her throat, spattering the window. David, panicked, reached for his wife and froze at the catch-22 of letting her bleed to death or pinching her neck shut to let her choke on her own blood. Then the knife came down through the side of his neck, missing his jugular, but tearing a new hole in his windpipe. He coughed a glob of blood down his chin but couldn't breathe in again. He strained and struggled and watched his wife turn pale and fade away, her only fur coat matted and shiny from the deluge down her neck. Then David coughed the last of his breath as the cab went dark.

Their bodies were found in the river the next day, snagged on some brush along the shore, their coats rippling in the water.

As Laura floated over the scene in her dream, she began to tingle. It started in her head and moved down through her body to her feet. It was a heavy, sandy tingle, like the kind she got when her foot fell asleep, except it was all over and all through her.

Black.

Laura was back in her bed, half-awake but still tingly. She always thought that was an interesting phenomenon: dreaming she was doing one thing but still aware of the bed beneath her. The tingling persisted. She decided it was hormones and that she should try to keep sleeping. Hm... she kind of had to pee... but she was so comfortable... but what if she had to pee worse than she thought and that's why she was tingling?

Now Laura was fully awake, still tingling. She was beginning to worry something was wrong with her. Before she could remove the covers and sit up, Laura tore away from herself. The house groaned.

"Well," Ballantine panted. "That was..."

Jessica smiled as she rested on his chest. "I know," she said. "You weren't so bad yourself."

"I didn't even know it was *possible* to— "

"Well, that's just cause you haven't been with the right woman."

"I guess not."

"Guess I still got it then, eh, Mr. Ballantine?"

"I bet you literally *killed* men with sex back in the day."

"If any of 'em had lasted long enough, I probably would have... Hey."

"Hm?"

"Thank you... for coming back... for respecting me. I mean, I know you only did it for one reason, but... You're a good man, Delaney Ballantine."

"I try to be. Gotta ask you for your earrings now, though."

"No reason to hurry. Not much you can do until tomorrow. Besides, I meet with Mara every morning. Can't have her seeing anything different. I'll give 'em to you after. I'll make you breakfast and everything."

"You understand why the idea of you leaving to see the witch before you give me the earrings makes me uncomfortable."

"I understand. S'the way it is, though. You don't have to stay here if you don't want to. You can come back later. Course, if I was going to sell you out, why wouldn't I have just had her barge in right about now?"

Ballantine thought hard. Cat and mouse, maybe. The thrill of the hunt. Weak explanation, though.

"Of course, if you stay," Jessica said as she slid her hand to his crotch. "We can go again."

CHAPTER 24

The morning chill woke Ariana around 9:00 and refused to let her fall back asleep. Her body was warm against Reggie's, but her ass and legs, though clothed, were cold, and she'd always hated that. And since Reggie was on top of the blankets, she resigned herself to just getting up.

Fog muted the morning sun and shrouded everything beyond the charred tree across the road. Ariana went to the bathroom and came back to find Reggie putting on his shoes. Neither spoke. Neither needed to. They packed and got in their cars. Ariana left first.

Something felt off to the two of them, even more so than usual. The world was eerily still. Ariana assumed it was because she wasn't normally awake at that time of day. Reggie made no assumptions, but rode with a pit in his stomach all the same. As they passed by Laura Krause's house, they each craned their necks at the odd sight. Ariana slammed on her brakes and Reggie almost rear-ended her. They pulled into the driveway and got out to gawk.

Laura's house was no longer a square farmhouse, but a cell that had stopped mid division. The original house kept its footprint, but another one had grown at an angle out of its side, such that the left side of the house now protruded from the front corner and the rear right corner stuck out the back. The awning and porch made an obtuse angle along the fronts. The original front door was behind the window of the duplicate.

Ariana and Reggie ran around the house calling for Laura but got no response. When they arrived again at the duplicate front door, they searched for and found a spare key on top of the door frame.

Inside, the front wall of the original house ran through the foyer of the duplicate, cutting through the staircase and the wall and into the dining room to the left. To the right, the walls converged just beyond the front door of the original house. They used the duplicate spare key to open the door and stepped into the original foyer, which had blended with the duplicate sitting room. The duplicate's sitting room wall ran at an angle to the original stairs. Photo frames hung half on the duplicate wall, half inside the original where the two met. The duplicate couch protruded from the bottom of the stairs. The old television and one rabbit ear stuck out of the original wall.

Ariana called out for Laura again, but got no response. They climbed over the couch, ran up the stairs to Laura's bedroom, and were immediately confronted with the sickening bizarre. The bathroom had merged with Laura's bedroom. The left wall, on which sat the sink and vanity, angled in. The bathtub was on the far wall, just past the corner of the bed. The right wall had swallowed half of Laura's dresser and all of Laura's head. Ariana pulled the covers away from the heap on the bed to confirm, then in her horror, turned and pressed her face into Reggie's chest. The drummer stared in morbid curiosity.

He knew this person who was no longer a person. This bag of livid flesh was walking and talking just yesterday. It was going to move to the city and be a nurse. Now it was an empty shell, a house full of memories abandoned by its owner. The anxious pit in his stomach turned acidic. Then he remembered what he was looking at.

"Wait," he said. "If there's two of everything..."

Ariana shot him a glassy-eyed glance before they both took off, looking for a way into the other bedroom.

Eventually, they realized the only way in would be through a window. They found a ladder in the detached garage and set it up against Laura's other bedroom window. Reggie climbed it, peered in, then shook his head at the hopeful Ariana. The outer wall of the original house had cut through the duplicate Laura's chest. Her body was still.

As Reggie reached the ground, Ari asked, "What do you think *did* this?"

Reggie said, "Well, I only know one person who can clone things."

"Me too. I wasn't sure if you knew about any other monsters with the same ability."

Reggie shook his head at the ground.

"I just *can't* believe he'd do something like this, you know?" Ari said. "He *wouldn't*."

"He's with the witch now, though, Ari. We can't imagine what's going on there. She could've forced him to do it—brainwashed him. She could've learned how. She could have *taken* the power from him and done it herself."

Ariana gasped and said, "What if they did this to other houses?"

Reggie's heart sank as he worried about his parents for the first time in his life. The two jumped back in their cars and raced to Ariana's house.

Paul was outside feeding the chickens when they arrived. Ari ran up and threw her arms around him. He hugged her back and they apologized to each other as Reggie strolled over to them.

"Are you okay, Dad?" Ari asked.

"I'm fine... what happened?" he said.

"Laura Krause is dead. Someone or something... How do I explain it? There *was* one house with Laura in it. Now there are two houses and two Lauras, but both of them are dead."

"I'm not sure I even understand what you just said."

"It's a lot to take in, Mr. Coleman," said Reggie. "We're on the way to check on my parents and make sure they're okay too."

"Does this have to do with the witch?" Paul asked.

"It might," said Reggie.

"And Jeremy?"

"We don't know for sure yet," said Ariana.

"Can we talk, Ari?"

"Go ahead," said Reggie. "I'm gonna go check on my parents."

"I can come with you," Ari said.

"It's fine. I'm not as worried now that your dad's okay. I'll come back either way and we'll make plans." He left.

"Make you breakfast?" Paul asked his daughter.

She nodded and followed him inside.

When Jessica entered the palace, Jeremy and Mara were sitting and eating as they had been the day before. After Gregory closed the door, he returned to stand at attention in the shadows behind Jeremy. Lana lovingly dabbed egg yolk from the corner of Jeremy's mouth. Jessica wasn't sure how she felt about what she was seeing: herself happily playing servant. What was going on in the other her's head?

"You two seem to be getting along pretty well," she said to Jeremy and Lana.

"Famously," Lana cooed.

"Yes," said Mara, "I must admit, I was worried at first to have another *you* around, but she's been absolutely lovely with Jeremy. And she's freed up *my* servants to focus on me!"

"That's good," said Jessica. "Good for you."

"Yes, thank you. So, what's new?"

"Nothing much, Mistress. I stayed in last night... with Mr. Ballantine."

Mara adjusted herself in her seat and said, "Tell me everything."

"Well, first he and Mr. Carrington came to my home while I was on my way from here. They shot a bunch of my babies—"

"Murderers," Mara whispered.

"—Louis Junior killed Mr. Carrington. Mr. Ballantine killed Louis Junior."

"I *know* he killed Ba'athul."

"I still couldn't say that for sure. Either way, he was gentleman enough to clear the carcasses out of my trailer and fuck my brains out."

"Ooh, how was he?" asked Lana.

"Best I've had in a while."

"Better than Nigel?"

"Eh. Apples and oranges," said Jessica. She addressed Mara again, "Anyway, I never made it out last night. Not sure I'll be welcome back at the Foothill any time soon since they know I'm working with you now. Any chance you'll lift part of the curse?"

"Not remotely," said Mara.

"Didn't think so."

"So what else about him, Jessica? What's his plan?"

"He's a simple man, Mistress, with simple tools and simple methods. A *hunter,* I'll give him that. Overconfident though. He'll get himself killed on these mountains before long.

Mara tapped her fork against her plate and thought.

Jenny opened the trailer door for Reggie as he stepped up and in. After a paranoid scan of the outside world, she locked the door, then stood on tiptoe and threw her arms around her son's neck.

"Hey," half-whispered Reggie. "Are you guys okay?"

"Yes of course, baby," Jenny said, pulling away to catch his eyes. "Why, what's wrong?"

"Laura Krause is dead. I wanted to make sure you're okay."

Jenny covered her mouth. There were shadows on her face Reggie had never seen before. Her eyes were duller. Her hair was frayed and had lost its luster. He couldn't stand the sight of it, so he promised himself he'd give back her stones before she withered, whether he'd completed his mission or not.

"How?" asked Ken from the hallway. He hadn't slept well and hoped his son had decent news to ease his mind.

"Kind of hard to explain it. The short answer is 'magic.'"

"The witch?"

"Could've been Jeremy. We don't really know."

Ken pinched his chin through his beard, weighing options and meanings. After a few scratches, he asked, "So what you gon' do?"

"Huh?"

"What. You gon'. Do?"

"You're not gonna shackle me up?"

"You want me to?"

"No! I just... wasn't expecting you to give me a choice."

"You a grown man. You can make your own decisions."

"Then... I guess I'll help."

"You guess?"

"I'll help."

"How?"

Reggie caught himself short of shrugging. Ken never had much patience for unanswered questions. The drummer patted the gun on his hip. His eyes were wells of uncertainty.

"Boy, when's the last time you fired that thing?" Ken said, crossing his arms.

Reggie opened his mouth to answer but nothing came out. He couldn't remember. It dawned on him how odd it was that he'd never had to fire it, especially considering he drove a meat wagon, even *with* the precautions.

"Why have I never had to shoot?" he asked.

"We're not entirely sure, baby," said Jenny. "Nymphs are one with nature and therefore at peace with everything that belongs to it. A *bear* would never attack you, for instance. But these creatures from other planes don't belong, so you—*we*—should have to fight them as much as anybody else."

"So how does this work?" Reggie said.

"That's what I'm saying, baby. I don't know."

Reggie puzzled in his head. He was part nymph. At one with nature. Animals were nice to him and vice versa. These creatures left him alone and vice versa. Was he one of them? Was he half hell beast or something?

"Is dad from Hell?"

"What? No! Of course not," said Jenny. Then realizing she lived in a world in which anything was possible, she turned to Ken and asked, "Right?"

"If I was, would I tell you?" he said.

"You'd better not be."

"Think I'd've sold you out by now if I was."

"I don't know. We have some pretty good—"

"Oooooooookay," said Reggie, "back to the matter at hand. If I'm a nymph who lives in peace with nature, and monsters don't attack me, and Dad's not one of them, then... are the monsters part of nature?"

Jenny shrugged. "Hard to say. They're not from this plane, but they are from this world. Same town, different ballpark, if you get me."

"Magic or not," said Ken, "you need some kind of plan, Reg. You can't just go barging in on a witch, guns blazing. She's ready for that."

"All right, well, what do these stones do?" Reggie asked, patting his pocket.

"Like I said," said Jenny, "I'm an earth nymph. You won't be as strong as I was, but they'll let you move most things made of dirt or stone. And the plants will come alive for you... to some extent."

She looked at her houseplants. They looked different to Reggie today, sad. Droopy would have been how most people would have described them. But even if pressed, and with the word on his tongue, he'd have still called them sad. He instinctively held out a hand to a cluster of plants, felt a tingle in his hand, and watched as they perked up.

"Cool," he said without irony. "I'm sure this will come in handy. Can Ari and I, like, link hands and combine our power or something?"

"You can. Of course, I can't say exactly what you'll be able to do. It all depends on how receptive she is, her innate abilities, and old-fashioned practice."

"And I guess it goes without saying that if one person has all the stones, they get more power."

"That's right."

"Just making sure. Good to know. Well, if you don't need anything, I told Ari I'd catch back up with her and we'd make plans."

"Matter of fact," Ken said thumbing through some dollar bills, "I need some new hacksaw blades." As Ken handed them over, Reggie saw something in the man's eyes he wasn't sure he'd ever seen. If he could have thought of the word, he'd have called it concern. "And there's some deliveries need to go out. Just if you can fit it in. They'll keep if you can't. You do what you gotta do, though."

"Two bodies. Both Laura's. And you'll need tools to get them out... Mmhm... Thank you, Sheriff."

Ariana hung up the phone and leaned against the counter. The kitchen felt different to her. Maybe it was the tension between her and her father. It was no longer the space that she had seen every day her whole life. It was no longer just the space where she knew every crack and peel, no longer home. Despite the connection to the world that she got from the gems, these spots at which she had always unconsciously stood and sat seemed disconnected, nothing more than places and things in time and space. Her eyes glazed as she pondered her sudden lack of sentimentality.

"Scrambled eggs okay?" asked Paul.

"Fine," said Ariana.

He cooked in silence as Ariana looked around the kitchen: photographs, knickknacks, pots and pans, dishes in the dish rack that had been for days now. Or maybe Paul had been reusing those same ones.

Just things.

Things that sooner or later would return to the dust from which they had come... like the eggs Paul was cooking... like Paul himself... like her.

Her thoughts neither weighed on nor lifted her. She sat in a tranquil equilibrium, a seesaw with neither end on the ground.

Paul set a plate of sausage, eggs, and toast in front of his daughter and sat across from her. He stared at her as she dug in. He was in his own equilibrium, torn between letting his adult little girl do what she felt she must and keeping her safe from what he was sure would ruin her and, subsequently, him. He'd been thinking hard about what he'd say to her since she took off on him the day before, but as he watched her eat he decided he'd rather enjoy the peace with her as long as it would last.

Ariana stopped herself from speaking several times. She didn't want to tip the first domino yet. This was nice enough.

She finished and Paul took her plate.

"More?" he asked.

She shook her head and said, "Were you ever going to tell me that my mother was a nymph who sacrificed herself for me?"

Paul set her plate in the sink, then faced her and leaned against the counter. "I don't know," he sighed.

"I mean, I'm half nymph, right?"

"You are."

"What was going to happen if I ever came into any abilities?"

"I guess I figured I'd cross that bridge if I came to it."

"Well? Here we are."

"I know."

"So how about you tell me what's up?"

"I didn't know your mother was a nymph when I married her. Just knew she was beautiful, took care of me, made me feel like nothing else ever had. We got married. We had you. The witch came down and said she was here to collect your mother's debt. Your mother cried her eyes out apologizing to me, then convinced the witch to take her instead of you."

"What did the witch want me for?"

"Sacrifice? Child of her own? To torture us? Who knows? Point is, the best thing you can do, Ari, is live your life and be happy. You wanna stick it to the witch? That's all you gotta do."

"Yeah well, she's got my friend now. And she's threatening the town again."

"Just let it lie, Ari."

"Laura's dead. What do you want me to do, bury my head in the sand... like *you've* been doing since I was born?"

Paul slammed a hand on the counter, rattling the dishes, and growled through his teeth, "Damnit Ari, I don't know how many different ways I have to explain it to you."

"Well, maybe if you'd told the truth from the start I could understand."

Ariana smacked the table and stomped up to her bedroom, stomped around her bedroom, then stomped back down the steps and out the door carrying her rifle. Paul went after her. The wind picked up, blowing Ari's hair back as she strode toward the barn.

"What are you doing?" Paul snapped.

"Don't worry about it," said Ariana.

He yanked her by the arm, pulling her face to face with him and yelled, "Hey!"

It hurt—both the yank *and* the yell. It was the move he did when she was about to get herself or someone else seriously hurt. Every time he'd ever done it had been a wake-up call to her. Every time he'd done it, he was right. Maybe he was right this time too, but this time Ariana's resolve was stronger. Paul's move only made her angrier.

The wind howled around the house and over the barn. It swirled around them, kicking up dust and hay. It forced Paul to cover his face. The weather vane threatened to let go of its perch. The barn doors flew open. Tempest and the two cows charged out.

The wind died away.

Paul pulled his arm away from his face to see his daughter and the animals staring him down. He checked in with her face to see her determination. The cows stared. Tempest snorted and stamped. Paul gave up.

He pulled his lips into a tight line to keep his chin from shaking, then waved his hands in resignation and turned away. As he stepped onto the porch, Ariana called out, "I'm going to see if I can get to Jeremy." He threw his hands out and walked inside.

Ariana ushered the animals back into the barn and readied Tempest to ride.

CHAPTER 25

Ballantine was putting on his boots when Jessica walked into the trailer. He hated being stuck in one spot. He hated wasting time even more. He stood and put his hand out.

Jessica removed her earrings as she walked to the kitchen.

"How about some breakfast?" she asked, setting the earrings on the counter.

"It's getting late," Ballantine said, taking the jewelry. "I need to get moving."

"You're gonna need more information than just, 'carry my earrings on you.' *And* you're gonna need your strength."

Ballantine squeezed the earrings tight and sighed. Jessica prepared eggs and sausage. The smell was refreshing. He'd almost gotten used to the smell of Jessica's place: a blend of farm, animal droppings, sex, and cheap perfume.

"So, you're gonna go up around the back of Wood Devil Mountain," she said as she fried, "and come down the other side. At the bottom, you're gonna come to a great big gate."

"Been there."

"That'll put you on the path to the cave worm. Paul Coleman owns that farm on your left before the road turns up into the hills. He has the key to the gate. You'll need to get it from him. Good luck with that.

"Eventually, that path is gonna run out and you'll have to get out and walk. You'll know where to go from there. If you see any creatures, they won't likely be concerned with you. They'll be on their way to the worm. Once you get there, you're gonna feel its pull on you. You're gonna want—*need* to lie down in its mouth. It doesn't make sense now, but it will when you're there. Obviously, don't do it."

Jessica plated the food and continued. "Now, to immunize yourself from the witch's charms and some of her powers, you'll need to drink a big glass of the worm's blood. And it *will* wear off, so don't just take a swig while you're standing there and think you're good. Take extra."

"Which powers does it nullify?" he asked between shovels of egg.

"I can't say for sure. I know it'll let you through the charms she's got on the mountain. Lets say at the very least, it'll let you see through her deceptions.

"You don't have to *wear* the earrings, but they do have to be *on* you, if that wasn't obvious. And of course, you need the other stones. And if you can bring them back to me, I'll be forever in your debt. If you can't, I'll still need the earrings back before my meeting tomorrow."

"I'll bring 'em back tonight," he said, setting his empty plate on the counter.

"You better. And uh, maybe scratch my itch again?"

"We'll see."

Lana tossed an apple straight up in front of her. Jeremy reached, connected, and copied it. Lana caught one apple, then laughed at her own clumsiness as the other bounced off her wrist and rolled away.

"You're doing it at the height of the arc," Mara said to Jeremy. "It's barely moving there. It's too easy. Lana!"

"Yes, Mistress?"

"Throw one *at* him."

Lana checked in with Jeremy, who shrugged and readied himself.

"Yes, Mistress," Lana said.

Lana threw it like a bocce ball, soft and underhanded on a high arc, with the intent of landing it at Jeremy's feet. Again, Jeremy connected and copied, and two apples landed in front of him.

"Fine," said Mara, "but I said throw it *at* him, not *to* him. Put some *mustard* on it, as they say. You won't break him with an apple."

Lana checked in with Jeremy, who again shrugged and nodded that it was fine. She picked up another apple, then conjured the few memories she had of a baseball pitcher. She planted her feet sidelong, wound up, stepped with her front leg, and let it fly.

It was a good pitch. Jeremy didn't have more than a second to react. He only made contact with part of the apple before he had to duck.

"Go get it," said Mara. "Let me see."

Jeremy retrieved the apple and handed it to Mara. She held it up and inspected it. Half an apple bulged out from the edge of the original.

"Gregory!" she called.

The servant, who had been tending another part of the courtyard, rushed to her side.

"Knife," Mara said.

Gregory produced a pocketknife, opened it for her, and presented it.

Mara shaved a sliver off the original apple at the point where the copy protruded. Nothing but apple flesh. She shaved some more and got only more apple flesh.

"What are you looking for?" asked Jeremy.

"I'm looking to see if you copied the entire apple but couldn't separate it, or if you only caught part of it. It looks like you only caught part of it."

"That's about how it felt."

"Very well, then," Mara said, handing the knife back to Gregory and shooing him away. "Work on that. I'll come back to check on you in a little while." She took a bite of the apple and went back into the palace.

When they were both ready again, Lana wound up and chucked another one at Jeremy. Again, he didn't entirely connect. However, that time he wasn't fast enough and the apple thumped him in the forehead. It was a much harder fruit than he had considered. He took a knee.

Lana gasped and ran to him, apologizing. "Let me see," she said, taking his hand away from his head. The spot she had hit turned purple and swelled before her eyes. "Oh, poor baby. I'm so sorry!"

"No, no. It's *my* fault," he said. "I tried to give it an extra second to focus."

"What can I do?"

"I'm guessing she doesn't have any ice around here."

"No, she doesn't. No electricity."

Jeremy felt his head throb. "I'm just gonna stay like this for a minute, then."

Lana kissed his contusion and they shared a little laugh. She let him enjoy the respite before taking the opportunity to tell him what had been on her mind.

"You can't trust her, you know," she said barely loud enough for him to hear.

Jeremy said nothing. He didn't know how to respond to that, especially after having invested so much of his faith in Mara.

"She's a demon, baby," Lana said. "You can't trust a demon. Their nature is to turn people away from their own, to ruin them."

"She fixed my mom, though."

"Have you *seen* your mom yet?"

"I guess you have a point."

"If she's not using you now, she will. Trust me. I've been close to her—cursed by her—for about as long as you've been alive."

Ballantine strode with purpose toward the bar, toward Kelly, who had just given Sam his coffee. She knew she wasn't going to like what he had to say and it showed in her face.

She began, "Don't you even—"

"Kelly, look," Ballantine said, as he held out the gems. "I've got 'em. I can do it. I just need the rest of the necklace. Then I can go kill the cave worm and get the witch that's been ruining everyone's lives! Perpetuating the monsters! Making everyone live in fear!" He pounded his fist on the bar.

"You're not gonna bring Sam back, though, and that's all I want, so *fuck off*!"

Ballantine searched for the right words, but they refused to come. The best he could do was "Kelly... please."

Kelly couldn't keep her lips from quivering or her eyes from welling. She pointed at Ballantine and said, "You get your things... and you get out... and you don't come back."

"I can *do* it, Kelly!" Ballantine bellowed. "Give me a chance!"

"GET OUT! GET THE FUCK OUT OF MY HOTEL OR I SWEAR TO GOD..."

Kelly had lost her breath along with her train of thought when Sam latched onto Ballantine's wrist and pulled him closer. Ballantine was dumbstruck as well. The invalid cupped his shaking hands together and jerked his head toward the stones in Ballantine's free hand. The monster hunter took his time understanding, then dropped the stones into the old timer's hands.

Sam closed his hands and his eyes and took a deep, ragged breath. Kelly and Ballantine held theirs as they watched him. Sam breathed out, smooth and clear. His shaking and tics subsided. He relaxed and sat up straight.

"Kell—*cough, cough, cough*—Kelly," he croaked. His voice was a motorcycle starting for the first time in decades.

Kelly could've screamed. She could've fallen on her knees. She could've spun like a top and burst through the wall. Unable to think, she stood there gaping, tears falling onto her shirt.

"Kelly," said Sam again. The gravity of the situation hit him too, and he grimaced as his tears fell on the bar.

Ballantine froze. He was trapped in a moment that didn't need him, and it hinged on the jewels he'd relinquished. As much as it touched his heart, it worried him that he might have made a mistake, that he'd have to wrestle the gems back from a feeble old man, or that Kelly soon would be escorting him away at gunpoint.

"Sam," Kelly said, regaining control of herself, leaning across the bar, squeezing his face, tousling his hair. "You came back." She wept again. "You came back." She put her hands his and hung her head as she sobbed.

"Yeah." He took a deep breath and said, "But I can't stay."

She looked up at him with that fire he'd always liked and said, "Like *hell*!"

Sam couldn't help smiling.

"You think this is *funny*?" Kelly straightened up.

"No darlin', no," he said. "I just... love you is all. The way you are. Even when you're mad. Always have. You've been a lot kinder to me than I deserved. I'll never be able to repay you and I can't thank you enough. And I want you to know that every second I sat here mute, I was lovin' you with everything I had, whatever it was worth. I want you to be happy. I don't want to be a burden anymore."

Sam undid his collar button as Kelly stomped and said, "Don't you dare."

He reached inside his shirt and pulled out the necklace.

"You were never a burden and you ain't one now!" cried Kelly. "Don't you *dare* do what I think you're going to do!"

"You gonna get that witch, Mr. Ballantine?"

"I believe I will, Mr. Karasek," said the monster hunter.

"Then let this be my contribution." Sam turned the clasp of the necklace to his front.

"*NO! SAM!*" Kelly screamed.

"I know you hoped I'd get better someday. And for a while, I did too. But even if I did, right now, what would we do? Huh? What do we have left?"

"We'd have this hotel! And each other!"

"Things are the way they are because of what I did. This man can finish it for me. He can make it right. You wanna help me, you help him. Don't let it all have been for nothing."

"*Please,*" she whimpered, though she knew he was right.

"C'mere," he said, leaning over the bar.

Kelly wept and crept nearer, clinging to every second she had left with him. Sam held out his free hand for Kelly. She took it and allowed him to pull her in. It was the ugliest most beautiful kiss Ballantine had ever seen. There were anguished faces, tears and snot, bad teeth, and missing teeth. It was awkward and off balance. But it was *their* kiss. It contained 20 years of love, 20 years of heartache, 20 years of apologies, 20 years of thank-yous, 20 years of missed flirtations and accomplishments, 20 years of pats on the back and butt that never were, and 20 years of "just because."

It was 20 years of good mornings and good nights.

It was 20 years of hellos.

It was 20 years of good-byes.

It was the last good-bye.

"I love you, Kelly." Sam undid the clasp of the necklace and placed it in his hand with the earrings. He gave Kelly a reassuring smile in which she saw his younger self. Without taking his eyes off his wife, he stretched out his hand to Ballantine and released the gems into his cupped hands.

"No, please," Kelly whined.

The madness kindled in Sam's mind like a forest fire from a smoldering ember. He rocked in his stool, gently at first, then increasingly erratically. His eyes rolled back in his head and his facial muscles contorted this way and that. He pounded the bar a few times, then took hold of it, and steadied himself. Whether he had his faculties at that moment or not, only he knew.

"Get him upstairs!" said Kelly.

Sam's screaming welled like an air raid siren, quiet and low in pitch, building to ear-piercing wails of damnation.

Ballantine slid an arm behind Sam's knees and lifted him off the stool, but the madman began to flail. The monster hunter almost dropped him, but caught him around the waist and threw him over his shoulder in a fireman's carry.

Kelly led them to her bedroom, where Ballantine placed Sam on the bed. The frail man shook and twisted and screamed and tore at the covers. The monster hunter looked to Kelly for instruction.

"Well, what are you waiting for?" she hollered through the

screams. "He ain't dead yet! Go get your goddamn worm and get back here with that necklace!"

"Get the sheriff out here and spread the word. It's going down tonight."

Paul was pushing a wheelbarrow of fertilizer when Reggie pulled up. The farmer sighed and set his work down to meet the drummer. Reggie knew what Paul was going to say before he said it.

"Ari's not here," he said. "She went to the mountain to look for Jeremy."

"Thought we were gonna do that together," Reggie said, puzzled.

Paul shrugged. "You know Ari."

Reggie gave a little laugh and said, "Yeah, I do. Well, I should probably get over there then. Catch up."

"Might be a tall order, Reg. She took off on Tempest. Direct route. Even *if* you had a horse, you probably wouldn't catch up until she was on her way back."

"What should I do, then? I can't just sit around."

"I don't like that she's gone alone any more than you do. Hell, I don't like it when she's out of my sight. But she's made it this far. And she knows them woods. I'd feel better if she had backup... Ha. Like the army... But at the same time, one person can hide easier than two."

"I guess you have a point."

"My advice would be to think about what you're gonna do if she gets back... and if she doesn't."

The thought of Ariana not coming back sank both men's hearts. Reggie's feelings doubled as his mother's gems helped him connect to Paul.

After an uncomfortable silence, Reggie said, "I'm sure she'll be fine."

Paul sighed and shook his head.

"Need anything?"

Paul stared into the distance and chewed on the question. His thoughts were a mix of smart answers like "A million dollars and a jet plane" and practical ones like "Salt and feed." Ultimately, he shook his head.

"Okay," said Reggie. "Well I'm gonna get moving then. You take care."

"Yeah," said Paul. "You too."

Reggie spent his ride to Steen's General Store trying to come up with possible plans. It was uncomfortable for him, foreign, like learning a new style of music. He understood the concept of planning. He just needed to rearrange his thought process to do it.

Ari went to find Jeremy. When she came back, she would either have or not have him with her. If she *had* him, then that would mean... the witch could be angry and want to come after them. Or if she had let him go, it might be because of a bigger, badder plan. In which case, they'd have to be ready to fight.

If Ari *didn't* have Jeremy with her, then she'd either have nothing or some valuable information. At which point they'd have to wait for Ballantine for their next move.

If Ari didn't come back at all...

Reggie slowed down as he passed Laura's house—houses. They were surrounded by emergency vehicles, puzzled paramedics, and mystified firefighters. Sheriff Landry was the only one who seemed unvexed as he stood amid the flurry, pointed, and directed.

The Steen parking lot was buzzing too. Reggie didn't even try to find a spot inside the walls. Instead, he pulled to the side of the road behind a line of other vehicles.

Inside the walls, some people carried armfuls of odds and ends. Others pushed them in wheelbarrows. Some stood with their hands placed on things that were too heavy to move. Cars and trucks sagged as their owners filled them.

A sandwich board next to the door proclaimed:

50% OFF ENTIRE STORE
EVERYTHING MUST GO!

Reggie had never seen the place so crowded. A line of customers extended from the register, wrapped around the entire interior, and wormed its way halfway up another aisle. Behind the register, Maxwell Steen was a machine, tallying items, punching numbers, making change.

The drummer excused himself, crossed the line, and stood next to the register.

"What's going on?" he asked Max.

Max gave him a quick glance, then went back to his tallying. "I'm closing the store and mother and I are getting out of here," he said.

"But you're like the only place to buy stuff for at least ten miles."

"Not my problem." *Kaching*! "Have a nice day, Mr. Vanderwal."

"But why?" asked Reggie.

"I should think it's obvious."

"Because of your dad."

"Dad, Laura, my Uncle Steve, my cousins Bill and Dave. It's a big list, Reggie. Everybody's got people on it. I don't have to endure it anymore, so I'm packing up and getting out. Somewhere there aren't monsters." *Kaching*! "Have a nice day, Ms. Potelicki."

"Where you gonna go?"

"West."

"And what happens when they migrate west?"

"Cross that bridge when I get to it."

"You know this store helps keep this town going."

"Communities live and communities die, Reginald. There are ghost towns all over this country. It's as natural as anything. They require people to thrive." *Kaching*! Max looked into Reggie's eyes and said, "And this one's running out of people." He handed change to the man across the register and said, "Have a nice day, Mr. Tomeo."

"Ari and I are going to help Mr. Ballantine go after the witch," Reggie said. "If we get her, these mountains'll be cleaned up in no time."

Maxwell looked up to consider his options, then went back to punching numbers in the register, saying, "I'll drop you a line."

Reggie pursed his lips, then retrieved the hacksaw blades, the last two on the bare pegboard hangers. The end of the line had snaked its way into another aisle. Reggie experienced another feeling he hadn't had in a long time: frustration. He didn't have time for this. He had to prepare for a witch. He looked at the price tag and walked up next to the register again.

"Hey, no cutting!" someone yelled.

"He's not cutting," Max said. "What do you want, Reggie?"

"To cut," he whispered. "Witch is coming. Here." He slid a few bills onto the counter next to the register out of view of the other customers and said, "Full price. Good luck, man."

As Reggie turned to leave, Max stopped him with a "Reggie, wait." The clerk reached under the counter and pulled out a lollipop. He held it out to the drummer and said, "For Ari."

Reggie put the candy in his pocket and excused himself through the line to leave.

"Hey," someone said, "did he pay for those?"

Reggie's insides sank as he left. It felt like he'd forgotten something.

He was halfway to his car when a shot rang out from inside the store. Screaming and raised voices followed. As Reggie jogged back to the building, people began to spill out, some with armfuls of goods, others with nothing but fear on their faces. He forced his way through the doorway into chaos. People were fighting over goods, knocking over shelves and each other. One woman hid under a table, crying and clutching her leg. One group of men held down a man who was shouting, "I didn't mean to do it! I didn't mean to do it!" Still others scooped up what they could and broke for the door. Most were successful. Some were foiled by Good Samaritans. Maxwell was missing. All Reggie could see behind the counter were the tops of a couple of heads. He ran over in time to see someone snatch up the money he'd left and take off.

On the floor behind the counter two people worked to stop Max's stomach from bleeding. Reggie felt Max's pain: the nausea, the white-hot hole in his gut, the fear. The clerk's skin was hot and cold at the same time. Sweat beaded on his forehead. He lolled his head to look daggers at Reggie.

"People and monsters deserve each other," Max said.

"There's an ambulance up the street, Max," said Reggie. "Just hang on!" He strode to the door and addressed the men holding down the shooter. "The sheriff's up the street too. He'll be here in a minute."

Reggie jumped into his car, sped off to the Krause house, and informed the sheriff. The sheriff signaled a couple of paramedics to follow him and they all raced back to the store. Max was pronounced dead. The shooter was arrested.

CHAPTER 26

Ballantine's feet nearly slid out from under him as he bolted through the parking lot. The necklace energized both his body and mind. And his thinking was already several steps ahead of his body. It was halfway to the mountain before he was three steps out the door. He stopped at his truck only to grab a few necessities: a rifle, a canteen, and a five-gallon bucket and lid. He tossed it all into Nigel's truck which, despite the damage it had taken, could still "haul ass." The engine roared. The wheels spun. Gravel tinkled off the wall of the compound and a few of the vehicles on the way out of the lot.

The Coleman farm was five minutes away. Ballantine made it in three. He barely had the truck in park before he jumped out and strode to the bewildered Paul Coleman who stood near the opening of the barn.

The hunter's speech was frantic. "Mr. Coleman, I don't have a lot of time. I need your key to the gate that leads to the cave worm."

"Who the hell are you?" Paul squinted.

"My name is Del Ballantine and I'm on a mission to kill the witch. But to do it, I need the cave worm's blood. I'm told you have the key to the gate that leads there."

"Maybe I do."

Maybe it was the magic heightening Ballantine's perception, but Paul's pace felt maddeningly slow. Almost as if he were doing it on purpose.

"Mr. Coleman, please. This is life and death."

"It's *always* life and death around here. Yours next, apparently."

"What's it to you?"

"Another goddamn lock to replace, that's what! Key goes in your pocket, you go in the cave worm, *I* have to replace the lock to prevent the *next* moron from thinking he's God's gift to hunting. Get off my property."

"I'll set the lock and key down next to the gate. If I don't return, you can put it right back."

"No!"

"Mr. Coleman, Sam Karasek is dying right now. If I hurry, there's a chance I can save him too."

Paul's frustration and emotion came to a head inside of him. He took a wide swing at Ballantine. The hunter dodged. Pain ripped through the farmer's hand (and pride) as his fist connected with the barn door. He doubled over cursing and massaging his hand.

When he recovered his thoughts, Paul said, "Sam is the way he is because of that thing."

Ballantine replied, "Sam is the way he is because he didn't have the whole necklace that I'm wearing right now. This thing is going to immunize me from the cave worm. I'm going to kill it, then the witch, then I'm going to kill every damn monster on this mountain."

Paul didn't know what to believe anymore. He *did* know he couldn't win for losing lately. He was pretty sure his daughter was dead, if not *about* to be.

"Fine," he said. "Whatever." He retrieved a ring of about ten keys from a hook inside the barn. "I don't know which one's which anymore. So you'll have to play with it. Been years. Lock's probably rusted up too."

"Thank you."

"Ha. Yeah."

"The cave worm blood negates the witch's powers. I'll be

bringing back a lot more than I need if you want to help."

Paul shook his head.

"Meet up at the hotel. I'll blow my horn on my way back through. You can join us if you like."

Paul shooed Ballantine away, then went back to the house.

Jenny's gems gave Ariana a better sense of the land and a kind of radar for monsters. She couldn't necessarily identify specific creatures, but she *was* able to roughly determine how big and how many there were. As a result, she and Tempest were able to avoid most confrontations and outrun the rest.

The horse didn't lack for energy. She scaled the hills, forded the streams, and leaped obstacles with little variance in her pace. Ari wondered if the gems' powers might not have been transferring to Tempest as well. She stroked her horse's neck and said, "I'm proud of you, my friend."

Tempest nickered her understanding and continued with renewed vigor.

They paused at the base of Mt. Fayette and looked it over. Ariana wasn't entirely sure what she was looking for. Threats? An easy way up? A curse or a charm? What would a charm look like anyway?

"One way to find out," she said, tapping her heels to Tempest's flank.

Every five minutes as they climbed, Ariana stopped Tempest to look behind them. As far as she could tell, they were still climbing after half an hour. The mountain looked young. The trees were skinny and more sparse than in any other part of the mountains Ari had seen. She was almost able to take a straight path up the mountainside. Though the workout was tedious and Tempest's muscles burned like they hadn't in a while, the horse was fulfilled. Running was in her nature, after all. On top of that, she knew she was making her friend happy.

"It looks like it flattens off just ahead, girl," Ariana said. "We'll take a break when we get there, sound good?"

Tempest nickered again, then pushed hard up the mountainside to the shelf.

The sound of Tempest's hooves on stone took them both by surprise. They stopped and looked around bewildered. Beneath their feet sloped a path of perfectly flat stone perfectly fit together. Ariana considered her options.

"What do you think, girl?" Ari asked. "Take the path..." she looked up the hill, "...or the direct route?" Saying it out loud, however, made Ari realize that the path wasn't likely the safest option.

Tempest nickered her ambivalence as she caught her breath.

"Tell you what. How about we take the path at a nice trot, then whenever you're ready we'll take off up the hill again, okay?"

Tempest snorted.

"Good girl."

Tempest's hoofbeats on the stone were a drum solo on the silent mountain. It unsettled both of them. Ariana strained her ears for anything else. It wasn't more than a couple of minutes before Tempest whinnied and yanked the reins toward the mountainside.

"You ready, girl?"

Tempest pawed.

"*YAH!*"

It took them longer to reach the next turn in the path. It *felt* longer, anyway. There were more creatures to evade, forcing them to turn one way or another instead of letting them continue straight up. The terrain worsened as well. Craggy gullies and caves cropped up and around and scarred the mountainside. At one point, they'd traversed a half mile sideways before being able to continue up safely.

During their break on the path, Ari looked around and assessed the situation. Even *she* was fatiguing. The hair on her temples was soaked and her t-shirt stuck to her. She was short of breath. She began to think she should have filled a canteen, packed a sandwich and a feedbag.

"We gotta be getting close, girl. Just a little further. You got it in you?"

Tempest stamped, neighed, and nodded.

There was sky ahead... and danger.

They were into the final leg of their climb when Ariana pulled up on the reins. What there was of a path split at a sheer face. To the left, Ari sensed a single large creature. To the right, a pack of smaller ones. Behind them, a significant backtrack. Above them, the sun was winning the race.

Ari's thoughts ping ponged. Small creatures, easier to kill, harder to hit, large numbers, can surround. Large creature, one location, target size substantial, kill difficulty unknown... potentially one bullet.

"Get ready, girl. Things are gonna get hairy."

They took their time and stepped quietly, hoping to get the drop on whatever awaited them. At the least, Ari hoped it would present itself while they were far enough away, rather than wait until they were on top of it. The alarms in her head grew louder, her heartbeat faster, her forehead wetter. She drew her rifle from its quiver and gently cocked it.

It was 20 feet away... somewhere.

Fifteen...

Ten...

Ari's pulse pounded in her ears.

Five...

...

"*RUN*!" Ari whispered.

Tempest reared back and sprang forward. Then she disappeared from under Ariana, sending the girl flying face first to the ground.

Ari rolled onto her back and looked behind to see a golem of mud and stone lumbering over her prone horse. It had a vaguely humanoid shape, with hulking legs and arms. It had divots where a person's eyes and mouth would be. Other than the clacking of rock against rock, it made no sound. One great hand held Tempest's hind legs to the ground. The other was curled into a fist and hoisted high above the golem's head.

"*NO!*" screamed Ari, raising her rifle and firing.

A plume of dust shot up from the golem's wrist as it brought its fist down on Tempest's neck, killing her.

The girl, still on her back, fired again, sending another plume of dirt off the stone monster's head.

The golem turned its attention to her and lumbered nearer.

BANG!

A plume of dust rose up from its shoulder.

STOMP!

BANG!

A plume of dust wisped from its chest.

STOMP!

BANG!

A plume of dust wafted about its stomach.

STOMP!

One more stomp would crush Ariana's pelvis. As the foot came down, Ari saw an inscription she couldn't understand on the creature's throat. With neither thought nor proper aim, she fired a shot into the inscription and the golem fell to pieces.

The girl stood and brushed herself off. She looked down at her dead horse—her best friend—and didn't know what to do. She didn't want to look, but she owed her one last thank-you and good-bye. She also had to retrieve some of the supplies she had been carrying.

As she approached, she took a glance at Tempest's face and almost threw up. Leaves and dirt clung to the horse's lolled tongue. Blood ran from both her eyes. The girl covered her mouth and looked away, stepping carefully so as not to trip. She took short breaths and looked only when she needed to retrieve her ammunition from the saddlebag. Then she closed her eyes, placed a hand on Tempest's side, and wept.

The lock was indeed rusted shut. Ballantine tried every key twice. He popped the hood of the truck and found some engine grease to scoop into the keyhole. He tried each key again, twisting and wiggling. The lock rattled but never gave.

If it hadn't been for the necklace, he'd have never had (or been able to execute) his next idea. Ballantine took his canteen and poured water into the keyhole. With his tingling hand on the lock, he manipulated the water inside—felt the inner workings and pushed the grease out of the hole to give himself more room. He poured more water in, concentrated, and began to freeze it. Not being a natural, his work was slow. Being determined, his work was steady. After a few minutes, the lock cracked and popped open.

The hunter apologized silently to Paul as he tossed the lock aside, but reminded himself that the road was about to be open for business anyway. The chains rattled as Ballantine wrenched the double gate open.

The path was not a welcoming one. It was rough, rocky, rooty, and overgrown, unused in who knew how long? Long enough for saplings to grow about six feet high. They banged and brushed the truck's undercarriage. The stones and roots bounced Ballantine in his seat. The supports threatened rebellion if the driver didn't keep it under five miles per hour. The pricks of sky in the canopy were still bright blue, but Ballantine's pace was further behind than he preferred. He squeezed the wheel and rocked himself back and forth in his frustration.

The woods grew thick. Thicker than anywhere else on the mountains. Thicker than anywhere Ballantine had ever seen. Primordial. Almost like a rain forest. He'd rarely seen trees so massive. Even when he had, they were anomalies. "How old?" he wondered. How many rings? In what year did those seeds take root?

Ferns carpeted the forest floor as far as he could see. They swarmed over the path, reducing it to an educated guess. Jessica told him he'd know when to stop. Since he wasn't sure, he kept going.

Something man-made came into view. It looked like an old truck. As Ballantine drew nearer, more vehicles appeared, mostly trucks, one car, a bulldozer. He made a five-point turn and killed the engine. The last truck in line was an old Ford. Must have been 20 years old. *Most* of the vehicles were that old or older. Models from the Forties and Thirties. Someone had even got a Model T this far. Everything was rusted and rotted. There was no life and no sound other than Ballantine's footsteps.

That's when he felt it—the pull—not a *literal* pull, like a rope wrapped around his waist or a magnetic attraction. Instead, Ballantine simply wanted to walk *that* way, into the woods. He took a few steps before remembering his mission. Regret squeezed his heart as he walked back to the truck to retrieve his supplies. Grief seeped in as he slung a rifle over his shoulder, his canteen over the other, and affixed a pair of Nigel's grenades to his belt. Setting out was sweet relief.

Ariana was right. She didn't have much farther to go until she reached the top. After trudging only a few hundred more feet, she cleared what there was of a tree line and gaped at the enormous structure rising above the lip of the summit. Stained black and gnarled, it looked like a twisted version of the castles in her childhood fairy-tale books.

As she neared the lip, the heads of the castle's current residents came into view. From left to right stood Lana, Jeremy, Mara, Gregory, and Brunna. Ariana unslung her rifle and shouted for Jeremy to get out of the way, but before she could take aim, all five disappeared. Ariana cursed, lowered her weapon, and strode to where she last saw them. She was more than a few steps on when she was yanked to a stop and had her rifle pulled out of her hands. Her handgun floated away before she could reach for it. That's when Mara revealed the party. Gregory held the rifle. Brunna, the handgun. They both held Ariana's arms.

"It's okay!" Jeremy said. "It's okay!" He looked to Mara to confirm that it was indeed okay. She nodded to him. "Just calm down," he said.

Ariana stopped struggling and took a deep breath. She stared Mara down with contempt.

Mara took a step toward the girl and said, "I commend you for making it up here all by yourself *and* for defeating my golem. Although you're not going to sneak up on *anyone* by firing so wildly."

Ariana chose not to speak. She barely breathed, afraid one wrong move could mean the end for her.

"What do you think we should do with her, Jeremy? More practice? Make yourself another little plaything?"

Jeremy blushed at how that probably sounded to Ariana.

Mara bit her lip and brushed a finger over Ari's cheek. "Maybe I'll keep her for my own..." she slid a finger along Ari's lapel, "enjoyment." The demon turned herself on, and so turned away sharply before she lost control of herself. She changed her tone. "You know they *shoot* trespassers in these parts."

"We could take her home," said Jeremy. "Show her mercy."

"Mercy." Mara used to laugh at the word without hesitation. This time she didn't, and that intrigued her. She crossed her arms and mulled the concept. What if she *didn't* torture her now? The future could hold *anything*! It was exhilarating.

"Ariana," Mara said, "how'd you like to stay for dinner?"

"Do I have a choice?"

"No."

CHAPTER 27

The canopy thickened, darkening the woods. The only sounds were the rustle of Ballantine's fatigues through ferns, the snapping of twigs, and the crunching of leaves under boots.

A little less than a mile on, he came upon an ages-old wreck—the skeleton of a horse-drawn carriage half swallowed by the earth. The reins were strung from the dashboard to the earth ahead, as though the horses had long ago sunk beneath, still strapped in. The leather cracked and fell to pieces at Ballantine's touch.

Leaves rustled somewhere... then again... then again... The commotion grew louder as Ballantine spun and pivoted, looking for the source. The hunter set down the bucket, unslung his rifle, and looked up into the trees. Two black hairballs bore down on his position—shug monkeys. Strange that they didn't howl. Stranger still that by the time he took aim, they were directly overhead, ignoring him. They swung on, silent but for their rustling, in the same direction Ballantine was headed.

Rick Jenkins stood at his front door as Reggie approached with his delivery. The drummer didn't have the usual spring in his step and he kept looking at the mountains. His behavior unnerved Rick.

"Everything okay, Reggie?" Rick asked.

"You hear about Max Steen?" Reggie replied on his way up the porch steps.

Rick nodded, eyes glazed over, and said, "Yeah... stupid... awful. Nobody's safe from *nothing* no more."

Reggie handed over the packages and said, "Five pounds of ground hellcat. One tenderloin... and your change."

"Thank you. You and Ariana playing again tonight?"

Reggie looked to the mountains again, thought hard, and said, "I doubt it, Rick. She went up the mountain today."

"By herself?"

Reggie nodded.

"She got a death wish?"

"She went to find Jeremy."

"Hold on. You saying she went up the *Witch's* Mountain?"

Reggie nodded.

"How'd she get through the curse?"

Reggie shrugged and said, "Can't say for sure she did. We might have a way, though."

Rick took a moment to process what that could mean, then asked, "Why didn't you go with her?"

"She left *without* me. Long gone on horseback before I knew about it. We told Mr. Ballantine we'd help him save Jeremy, but I haven't seen him today. I don't know if he's dead or already up there or what." Reggie sighed. "Anyway, I hate saying it, but you probably want to be on extra guard."

"Course, Reggie. Anything I—we can do?"

"Just be ready for anything, I guess."

The servants, including Lana, set the plates in front of their host and guests, then stepped away.

"How's my mom?" asked Jeremy.

Ariana glanced at the smug-looking Mara, then said, "Fine. She's helping Kelly out at the hotel."

"She's *working*?"

"No more than she can handle."

"So she's fine? Like *really* fine?"

"Like *really* fine."

"Told you," said Mara, flipping her hand.

"What's the rest of the town like?" Jeremy asked.

Ariana checked in with Mara again. The witch had been watching her but looked away to feign disinterest.

"Honestly, Jeremy," Ariana said, "they're more *worried* about you than anything. You need to come back before it gets any worse."

"Mm," Jeremy said, chewing on a piece of steak, "I can't go back. I can go *through*—pick up my *mom*—but once I leave this mountain I'm taking off. Seeing the world."

"What about me and Reggie?"

"I thought about that. I *want* you with me. Feel like I still have some training to do here before I go, though. Couldn't say *when* my boat is leaving. I just know people are either gonna be on it or they're not. You know?"

"Well, assuming you haven't been made evil..."

"See that's the *thing,* Ari. If I stay here, everyone's going to wonder about me, aren't they? There'll always be someone in this town who's got his eye on me, waiting for me to do one thing he doesn't like. All because I hung out with a witch for a little while, who by the way, is *just* trying to get by up here and, oh yeah, isn't even a witch."

"Say what now?"

"She's not a witch. She's a demon. Exiled herself, but people keep fucking with her."

Ariana blinked and shook her head in an effort to process the new information. A hundred questions fought for dominance in her head. She looked at Mara who simply shrugged and sipped her wine. She looked at Jeremy who only chomped away at his steak. "Jeremy," she said, "someone cloned Laura's house last night... with her in it."

Jeremy's heart stung. He put his fork down and asked, "And?"

"And she's dead... both of her."

Jeremy's stomach lurched and his cheeks bulged. He jumped from the table with his hands over his mouth and ran to the front door. He barely made it outside. Lana's heels clacked after him as she brought him a napkin and a cup of water.

"So, Ariana," said Mara, "tell me about yourself."

"Well, I'm 21, I play bass, and my mother was killed by an evil witch... or demon."

"Was she now?"

"Mmhm. Right after I was born. They say she sacrificed herself to you for me."

"So, you're here for... what? Revenge?"

Ari thought about it and realized she didn't care about Mara as much as she did before. "I guess I'm just here to make sure my friend is okay. Bring him back, if possible."

"Might be a tall order, as he said."

"Yeah, well. Trouble with people is preferable to trouble with demons."

"You think so?"

Ari wondered what Mara would say if she replied yes. As she thought about her response, the girl decided it might be better not to talk to a demon any more than necessary. She said no more until Jeremy returned.

The songwriter, pale, sat down and pushed his plate away. Lana replaced it with his cup of water. Mara and Ariana looked at Jeremy until he decided to talk.

"It was an accident," he said to nobody in particular. "I was practicing and I got distracted. Oh my God. What did I do?" He'd consoled himself about the people he duplicated the other night because, as Mara said, they 'didn't count.' But there weren't any more Lauras left. Jeremy had killed her—*murdered* her. He put his face in his hands and cried.

"Jeremy, it's..." Ariana said, stopping short of a complete thought.

"It's what, Ari?" asked Mara. "It's okay? Gonna be all right? No big deal?"

The girl couldn't find words that were both comforting and true.

"*This* is why we train, Jeremy," said Mara. "It is unfortunate that your friend was killed, but it would've been *more* unfortunate if you'd done it to the hotel while it was full of guests."

"Wow," said Ari. "Yes. Great training."

"Believe it or not, little girl, this is the time for him to be making mistakes. Not after he leaves. Not after he's out in the big bad world that'll judge him for being himself. Better to screw up now... and here. Learn his cans and his can'ts. The bigger the mistake, the bigger the lesson.

"Just a minute, Ariana," said Mara with a new idea. "How would you like me to train you as well?"

"Um. No. I wouldn't. Not at all."

"Oh, come now. You know you're too big for this town. You're a half nymph. You're *destined* for a life more wondrous than anything you can get here."

"Yeah, well, I'll just have to manage that on my own."

"You know I can destroy your mind."

"Fuck you. If you're going to do it, just do it. Don't fuck with me."

"I'm trying to tell you that I'm trying not to be what I am anymore. I'm trying for a second chance."

"With who? God?"

"If you want to call it that, sure."

"I thought God left. Revelation happened. World's over."

Mara laughed and said, "Oh darling, I doubt that. The all-encompassing force of creation abandoning the Earth? Naive. Primitive school of thought—everything must have an end. Nothing ends. It only changes. It would of course be presumptuous of either of us to *begin* to think we know what God wants and expects. Seeing's how I've been around since the beginning, however, I'd like to think my perspective is a little more sophisticated than yours."

"So what, you think God's giving you a second chance?"

"Well to put it much more simply than can be explained in human language, maybe. Here's how it works, darling, in a nutshell that you can comprehend: The plane I'm from, "Hell," as you may begin to understand it, is a place of torment for the

Fallen astral. The *Earthborn,* that's you, having been given such a short lifespan, cannot begin to hope to understand the will of the Constructive. You cannot fathom what is meant for you, your deeds, or your place in the universe. And you may never come close in one lifetime. And so the Constructive has given you the *infinite* gift of regeneration and resilience."

"You mean reincarnation?"

"That's a way to put it."

"So the Buddhists are right?"

Mara pinched the bridge of her nose and said, "This is the frustration of the Fallen. This is why we rebelled—why we took such umbrage with service to your kind. Your unshakable ignorance. Your need to put every explanation into a neat little box. The Earth is flat. The Earth is the center of the universe. Women are inferior to men. Our leader was chosen by God. This religion is right. That religion is wrong. News flash: they're *all* right and they're *all* wrong."

Mara sighed and collected her thoughts. "What was I talking about again?"

"Reincarnation?"

"Ah yes. You die. You come back. And so on, and so on, until you've got it. Then you get to stay with the Constructive."

"Heaven."

"Girl!" Mara took a deep breath to calm herself. "Call it Heaven if it helps you, but don't go thinking it's all puffy clouds and harps. There *is* no paradise. There is only *con*struction and *de*struction. You're a product of construction, therefore you go back to the Constructive when you leave this plane. As I said, the Fallen were damned to the plane of existence you call Hell. It's been no picnic. We thought it was forever, so we made it our mission to disrupt the Constructive however possible, like corrupting its creations." She gestured to Ari and Jeremy. "But *now* I'm *here*. I'm Earthbound. Bound to its trappings and limitations. Can I say for *certain* that I am now on the same playing field as a human? Of course not. But I'm here to tell you that eons in Hell make a return to service of the morons that walk this planet look pretty goddamn good...

"Or maybe I won't be reinstated. Who knows? Maybe I'm human now. Maybe I'll be reviewed and sent back until I get it right, until I earn the same place as you as a spoke in the great wheel of the universe. Anything is preferable to where I've been. Even this. Even my self-imposed exile. Even this flawed bag of meat and bone. Honestly, my first year here I gagged every time I moved my bowels. The Physical is disgusting."

"You make a fair case," Ariana said.

"Had a lot of practice," said Mara.

"I am sympathetic to your problems."

"Thank you."

"But seeing as you're a demon, I have to ask why should I trust you?"

"You have absolutely no reason to. I've spent millennia torturing your kind through deceit. I still have no remorse for it. I thirst to torture you now—to hear you scream, to watch you cry, to watch all hope leave your eyes... to hear you curse God." Mara sighed. "You're a succulent chocolate, and I've been *very* good about my diet."

"So what's stopping you?"

"Myself... and it is utterly fascinating to me. I'm sitting here denying my very nature and it's blowing my mind. It's got me wondering, have I always been capable or am I becoming human?"

"Well, then. If you're serious about your *diet,* maybe you should let us go now before the temptation becomes too much."

Mara thought, then asked, "Why are you here? Why did you come alone—risk life and limb on my mountain?"

"To bring back my friend? Or at least talk to him?"

"That's it? That's the only reason?"

Ariana nodded.

"You see, I have to wonder, because of the incident the other night, if there might not be some sort of design against me."

Ariana said nothing.

"I was present for the first lie, child. Is it Ballantine? Is he coming for me?"

"If he is, I don't know how he'd do it."

Mara pounded the table and stood. She gave Gregory and Brunna orders to keep them in line and then had Lana drive her to Jessica's home.

The further Ballantine walked, the better he felt. Despite the sweat he had worked up, he was invigorated. His head swam and his heart beat with excitement, as if he were on his first date, or his first hunt.

Apart from the shug monkeys, Ballantine didn't see much more in the way of wildlife on his trek. A pair of birds sailed past, soundless. He heard a few rustles somewhere else but never saw the source.

The hike was mostly flat and winding. The monster hunter tromped along a creek for a while before breaking off to follow the cave worm's psychic pull. As he rounded another hill, the babble of the stream died away, leaving him in silence again.

Unease crept into Ballantine's bones, not because of the cave worm, but because he was at the bottom of a sort of gully, susceptible to ambush. He took it a bit slower, trying to keep his feet out of the leaves and on the jutting rocks. He kept one eye on his path and another on the looming hills above.

Rustling again. This time from the ground... somewhere. The hunter readied for battle and again saw a monster, a hunner dyer, travel by ambivalent to him. It kicked up leaves and dirt as it scuttled and stumbled down the hill into Ballantine's path, then disappeared around the bend toward the cave worm's lair.

The hills opened into a cul-de-sac. A big one. Maybe 50 yards in diameter, guarded by primordial birch sentinels. The hillsides were craggy and overhung with moss. In the crag across the clearing was a cave about ten feet tall and ten feet across. Inside the mouth of the cave was another mouth, a large mouth, a soft mouth. Earthworm pink, it had no teeth or tongue or lips. It was simply a ring of flesh that extended into the cave. A gap in the canopy released a stream of soft light into the clearing and onto the cave.

The hunner dyer scuttled directly into the cave worm's mouth and into the dark. The mouth lumbered closed, lifted, lowered, then opened again.

Ballantine wished the hunner dyer had been him. He had the presence of mind to know that if he went into the cave worm's mouth, he would die, and that he didn't want to die. But it looked so... sweet. So nice. He felt like he was home and everyone he cared about was there.

The closer Ballantine moved, the happier he felt. His thoughts dissolved like sugar in water, swirling sweetly inside his head. He nearly dropped his bucket and rifle. Had he been able to pay more attention, he would have noticed the clearing was littered with old weapons and other vestiges.

The cave worm's breath was gentle, humid, and stank of death. Ballantine didn't care. He stood feet from it, loving everything about it. He loved the smell. He loved the way the worm looked and the texture of its wrinkled flesh. He loved what it did and wanted it to do it to him. All he had to do was step inside... maybe just a little.

He told himself to stop, that he wasn't there for that. What he *was* there for was no longer clear, however. His boot touched the cave worm's lip, turning him into a drug addict. Forward was happiness. Backward was pain. He pressed on it a few times, felt it squish, allowed himself the chance to think and fight.

The cave worm's upper lip lurched down. Ballantine's survival instinct pulled him away. He felt the bucket in his hand and the rifle on his shoulder, gave them a look, and remembered his mission. His eyes blurred with tears as he looked again at the cave worm settling itself back into position. It was as if he had to kill his best friend.

He popped the lid off the five-gallon bucket, then looked for a good spot. Just behind what would be the corner of the worm's mouth, Ballantine sank his five-inch knife in with little resistance.

The cave worm flinched and shuddered, but did not bleed. Ballantine checked his knife and saw no blood. He stabbed the cave worm higher. Again, it flinched and shuddered. Again, no blood. He thought about shooting it, but didn't want to risk it retreating altogether. So he took a stab near his original cut. Then another. Then another. When the cave worm settled again, he reached his fingers into the cuts and ripped a glob of flesh out of the twitching worm. Able to sink his knife deeper, he finally drew blood.

First, it came at a trickle. Then Ballantine gave it another stab. He stabbed until the blood poured from the cave worm which, after its repeated shuddering, settled back into place. The hunter held the bucket there until it was full, then popped the lid back on, carried the bucket twenty feet away and placed it behind a boulder. Again, he felt the anguish of leaving the worm and the sweet relief of returning.

He stood in front of the mouth again, loving it. A stream of blood flowed from beside it down the earth and rocks, turning blacker the farther it went. The hunter was sorry—genuinely sorry, as he would have been if he had struck a loved one in a blind rage and suddenly come to his senses. He could have fallen to his knees and wept. He could have patted the cave worm gently. He could have stepped inside and lain down, but he remembered his mission.

Ballantine pulled the pins on each grenade and hurled them as hard as he could into the darkness of the cave worm's mouth. He spent exactly one second thinking about going in after them, then turned around and ran for cover.

The blast was muffled, but it sent blood and flesh spewing from the cave worm's mouth. The creature collapsed, then the cave collapsed, leaving only the monster's lips visible.

Standing up to inspect the scene, Ballantine realized it no longer had the hold over him that it did before. He didn't love it anymore. He could walk in any direction and be satisfied. He did feel a twinge of guilt about it, though.

A look at the sky told him he needed to hurry before the woods grew too dark. He picked up the bucket and moved as fast as he could. Not even a rogue wood devil slowed him down.

CHAPTER 28

Jessica awoke from her nap to the sound of a car door closing. Her stomach sank when she looked out her bedroom window and saw Mara's Bentley.

"*Fuck*!" she whispered, as she dug her fingers into her scalp. She scanned the room for evidence of her treachery.

There was a knock at the door, followed by a *scrip, scrip, scrip,* from the birthing room. Jessica took a deep breath. She had to be cool. Of *course* Ballantine had been here. Mara knew that. Enemies closer and all that stuff. She had done nothing... She had done nothing.

Her front door flew open with a bang, causing Jessica to jump. The *scripping* intensified.

Mara stepped in, looking side to side and barked, "*JESSICA*!"

Jessica jumped again, calmed herself, then emerged from her bedroom with a nonchalant "Mistress? What has you worried?"

"Delaney. Ballantine." Mara said, with hot coals for eyes. Her knuckles were white around the switch in her hand.

"Oh, Mistress," Jessica sang. "Why do you worry about him so much?" She flung a casual hand, surreptitiously bumping the birthing-room door open as she walked by. "Who have you *ever* had to worry about?" She pulled the door shut, but not enough for it to latch.

Scrip, scrip, scriiiiiip...

"You tell *me,* Jessica. What *do* I have to worry about?" Mara wound up and struck Jessica with the switch on the side of her thigh. When the nymph reached down in pain, Mara gave her a whack across the head, nearly knocking her to the ground.

"Please, Mistress!" Jessica cried, hands on her head. "I don't know what you mean!"

Scriiiip, scrip, scrip...

"What is Ballantine up to?!" Mara whacked Jessica on her side and arm. "If you make me ask you one more time..."

"Please, Mistress... please... He fucked me and left! He didn't say much!"

"Where are your earrings? You look twice as old as you did this morning!"

Jessica felt her face, then her earlobes and lied, "They... must have fallen out during my nap." She strode to the bedroom with Mara behind her. The nymph tore her bed apart pretending to look for the earrings. She got on her hands and knees and looked under the bed. She checked among the effects on her nightstand.

She put on her best surprised face, turned to Mara and said, "He must have *stolen* them!"

Mara struck a blow with each word as she spat, "You! Were! Wearing! Them! This! *AFTERNOON*!!!" Then she screamed like only a demon can scream, "*WHAT'S HAPPENIIIIIIIING*?!!"

"I don't know!" cried Jessica from the fetal position.

Mara took a deep breath, closed her eyes, and aimed her hand at Jessica.

The nymph felt her wrists and ankles bound and opened her eyes. She was tied naked to her own bed and Mara was nowhere. Something was off. The room seemed... different? It looked cleaner, or neater than ever, though everything was where she remembered it being. Her bedroom door creaked open and Ballantine walked in, the deliberate thump of his boot the only noise.

"I like the look of *this*," said Jessica with a smile and a wriggle. She put her faith in the situation to try to quash her unease. Since she didn't remember *why* she was uneasy, the tactic mostly worked.

Ballantine ran his fingertips from her foot, up her leg, across her belly and sternum, up her throat, over her chin, to her lips. She stuck out her tongue and tried to take one of his fingers into her mouth, but he had already pulled away. She closed her eyes and pushed her head back, enjoying the sensations as he ran his fingers along her body again: across her breasts and around her nipples, down her stomach, teasing her by skipping to the legs, up the sides, tickling her ribs, up the inside of her arms and down the outside, to her neck...

...to her cheek...

...to her lips...

Jessica stuck out her tongue again and caught his wet fingertip. Wet? ...and coppery. Against her own better judgment she opened her eyes to see a viscid black claw above her. Beyond it, Ballantine's features shifted to the grotesque. One of his jaundice yellow eyes sank into the socket while the other sank on his face. The nose pulled back and the mouth drooped like melting ice cream. The skin turned black in spreading patches... a shape-shifter!

Jessica fought her restraints. As she looked for a way out, she realized she was covered in blood. Her body was cut open everywhere the creature had run its fingers. A fiery sting ran through every slice. She tried to scream, but coughed a gob of blood onto her own face. Something touched her foot. She squinted through the crimson blur in her eyes and watched as the dark shape lowered its serrated mouth to her foot.

She tried to scream again.

"Are you ready to talk?" asked Mara.

"*YES*! *YES*! *YES*!" cried Jessica.

"Then talk."

Jessica was no longer on her back on the bed. She was still curled up on the floor. She gave a relieved laugh and a sniffle, then said, "He's gone to take the cave worm's blood. Then he'll come for you. Probably on his way back with it now."

"You traitorous bitch," sneered Mara. "Enjoy your Hell." She stretched her hand out to Jessica again.

The nymph closed her eyes.

There was a hiss and a yowl.

Mara cried out.

Fabric tore.

Furniture rattled.

A thump.

A growl.

"God *FUCKING* damn it!" cried Mara. "I don't have time for this." She spit at Jessica and left.

Coarse fur rubbed Jessica's face.

The sound of the Bentley's engine was replaced with a crackling purr.

Jessica reached up and pulled the hellcat to her chest.

"Good kitty," she said.

A rough tongue licked the sweat from her chin.

Paul Coleman gave a yawn and a look at Jupiter as it pierced the indigo sky. His better judgment told him Ariana wasn't coming back, that she was either dead or enslaved. His heart held on to hope, though, and he turned on every light the farm had. The last one was in his daughter's room.

He switched it on and looked around, taking in every little piece of her that he could, attaching her belongings to his memories of her... just in case.

A horn blared in the distance and grew louder.

Paul ran across the hall to his own bedroom and looked out the window in time to see the truck Ballantine had been driving zoom past. The farmer put a shaky fist to his mouth and considered his options.

Joe Markovich, the Foothill's early-evening gatekeeper, put his hands up to signal Ballantine to slow down. The monster hunter ignored him and almost rammed an ambulance after making the turn into the lot. He pulled his truck to the side and jumped out.

The reds and blues of the sheriff's car painted the gathering of patrons as the paramedics brought out the gurney and shrouded body. Some in the crowd held each other. Others whispered. Some raised their glasses or bottles.

"Wait, wait, wait!" Ballantine shouted to the paramedics. He took off his necklace, pulled Sam's hand from under the sheet, and pressed the two together.

"You're too late, Mr. Ballantine," said Kelly.

"Just give it a minute," he said, though he felt no change.

"He's been dead an hour, Mr. Ballantine. No saving him now."

"Fuck," said Ballantine. He put the hand back under the shroud and faced Kelly. "I'm so sorry."

"J'you get the worm?"

Ballantine nodded and said, "And five gallons of its blood." He removed Jessica's earrings from the chain, then held the necklace out to Kelly.

She pushed it back toward him and said, "He sacrificed himself so you could carry out his mission. That is the only reason I don't shoot you where you stand. Now you finish it, and then I don't ever want to see you again. Until then, I'll do what I can to help."

"Me too," said Sheriff Landry.

"You know *I'm* in," said Reggie.

An old pickup truck pulled into the parking lot, narrowly missed the ambulance, and slid to a stop. Paul Coleman stepped out.

The Bentley's horn blared loud and long. It was Gregory's cue to have the door open and ready by the time Mara approached if he didn't want hell to pay. Of course, when Mara was angry, there was little he could do anyway. She shoved him to the ground as she strode inside. Jeremy and Ariana turned to look.

"It seems Mr. Ballantine is on his way," Mara said, red faced. She mocked Ariana with a pout and said, "And I doubt it's just to see his friends."

"Okay," Jeremy said, attempting to diffuse Mara's anger. "It's okay. Look, maybe Ari and I should just head back down. Sort things out."

"Out of the question," Mara said, pacing. "Out of the question. Can't trust her." She pointed at Ari.

"But you can trust *me*."

"I need you both for insurance. You can talk to him when he gets here—*if* he gets here."

"What if we're *not* here when he gets here? Huh? How about that? We can go find somewhere else. All of us."

"I'm not running, Jeremy! I'm not an animal. Convince him to leave if you can, but if he attacks this castle, he damns himself. Gregory, Brunna, take Miss Coleman and lock her up."

"What?" Jeremy squeaked.

Mara pinched the bridge of her nose and said, "She's on *their* side, Jeremy. If she can behave herself, and we come out of this all right, she may go free... maybe."

The lights in the Foothill bar weren't supposed to be all the way on. They were supposed to be half dimmed, or half off, however Kelly did it. Few knew. But *everyone* knew that if the lights were on early, something was wrong. They kept their voices low, murmuring their guesses to each other, waiting for someone to speak up and tell them what the problem was. Many expected some kind of tribute to Sam, with people being invited to share words or stories. Some of them guessed Kelly was going to tell them all to finish their drinks and get out. The observant surmised that Delaney Ballantine, the Buffalo Bill of monster hunters, who was approaching the stage, who had a heavy bucket in one hand, who scowled, who tapped the microphone, had nothing good to tell them.

"Uh," Ballantine began. "You all probably know..." He pulled away and crinkled his eyebrows at the microphone, wondering why his voice sounded so weird. "...probably know that your singer, Jeremy, was taken by the witch the other day."

"He went *willingly* is what *I* heard," said Louis Malone.

The crowd murmured and shushed.

"That's true," said Ballantine. "He did go willingly."

The crowd murmured again.

Ballantine raised his voice saying, "But there's still a chance that I—*we* if you like, can save him."

"Yeah, no thanks," said Louis with a laugh.

Connie Crawford smacked the back of Louis' head as he took a sip of beer, making him dribble on himself. Ready for a fight, Louis pounded his beer bottle onto the bar and wheeled around. He froze at the sight of the little woman standing there, the mother of the kid he had just disrespected.

"You got something to say to me, punk?" Connie sneered.

Stone-faced, Louis turned back to the bar, put the bottle back to his lips, and tried to disappear.

"Hey, I know it's a long shot," said Ballantine. "But there's always a chance. And if it's anything to you, I was informed just before I came up here that Ariana, the girl who's usually standing right about here," he pointed, "went looking for Jeremy earlier today and hasn't come back yet."

The crowd gasped and murmured more.

"Now, she's either dead or with Jeremy." He let that sink in for a few moments before moving on. He gestured at the bucket beside him and said, "*This* is a bucket of cave worm blood." He glanced over to where Louis was sitting.

Louis didn't look up from his beer, though the rest of the room buzzed.

"I killed it today."

Another reaction from everyone but Louis. If he were going to say something, that would have been the time. Nobody outright challenged Ballantine, though.

To drive the point home, he said, "So the cave worm's mountain is open for business. Now, I'm *told* that the cave worm's blood negates the witch's power. Not sure how *much*, but it should be enough to at least get past her charms on the mountain. I've got five gallons here, which should be plenty if any of you want to come with me."

"What do we have to do with the blood?" someone asked.

"We drink it."

The crowd was revolted.

"And it's not enough to have just a cup. Whatever it does to us will wear off like any other drink, so we'll need to have more to keep the effect. Hopefully though, we'll get the witch before we have to drink too much.

"This is your chance," he said. "The cave worm is dead. If you want the witch gone, if you want to clean up your mountains and get back to life as it was meant to be around here, if you want to save not just two talented kids, but countless lives in the future, you're probably not gonna get a better chance than this."

The room thought in silence.

Sheriff Landry, Paul, and Reggie walked up to the front of the stage to show they were in.

"I got three," said Ballantine. "Anybody else?"

The people looked around as a smattering of men raised their hands. The hands went up slowly, with some of the men raising them grudgingly so as not to look cowardly.

Louis shook his head and laughed into his beer bottle. He hadn't been paying attention and took the silence as a collective "No." Then, out of the corner of his eye, he saw Rick raise his hand. He looked up, bewildered. There were hands all over the place, even from some of the women. And Andy was reaching as if the teacher had just asked the one question he knew the answer to. Louis put his hand in the air.

"Kelly," said Ballantine, "we're gonna need some to-go cups."

Ariana struggled in the grips of Brunna and Gregory, each holding an arm. They were much stronger than they looked. Not that she cared to look too hard at either of them.

"We should put her in one of *these* rooms," croaked Brunna, indicating one of the rooms on the main floor, near the courtyard.

"But the dungeon is downstairs," rasped Gregory.

"But Mistress may want quick access to the girl."

"Then we take her to Mistress' boudoir."

"What if Mistress doesn't *go* to her boudoir? Then she'll be too far away."

Gregory puzzled hard, looked up at his eyebrows for an

answer, then said, "Okay."

The rooms on the main floor didn't have much in the way of windows. Brunna and Gregory typically used them to store tools and supplies. Otherwise they contained nothing but tiny, barred windows way up high. Ariana wondered what the dungeon must have looked like.

They shoved Ariana into the room, making the girl stumble but not fall. Ariana shook the blood back into her arms and watched as the caretakers closed the door.

Brunna turned her skeleton key in the lock and gestured for Gregory to lead the way back to the main hall. He obliged.

Ballantine saw Jessica's front door was open and entered with his weapon at the ready. A hiss came from the dark hallway, pulling the hunter's attention to the fiery eyes of a hellcat. He took aim, but before he could pull the trigger, he heard, "Here, kitty, kitty," and the eyes disappeared into the dark.

Ballantine flicked on the light and called for Jessica.

"Back here," she called from the bedroom. "It's okay. Bobby Junior does what I say."

"Bobby Junior?" he asked, stepping into the bedroom and flicking on the light.

"No, don't!" said Jessica, curling up on her bed, trying to hide her face in her hair. The hellcat sat beside her.

"Jesus," Ballantine said. Her hair had gone almost entirely white and wiry. The skin of her arms and legs was saggy and spotty. "Jessica?"

She pulled her hair aside to prove it to him. She was *her* all right, but all her living had caught up to her. Ballantine couldn't tell if she was frowning or if it was just the way the creases of her mouth made her look. Her lips weren't as full as before and her cheeks no longer clung to the bone beneath.

"Do you have my earrings?" she asked.

When Ballantine pulled the whole necklace from his pocket, Jessica beamed and wept.

"Oh Mr. Ballantine," she sniffled. "I didn't think I'd ever get them all back. Thank you. Thank you."

She put them around her neck, leaned back against the headboard, and sighed.

"Well, hey, look," said Ballantine. "We don't have a lot of time to be sitting around. I got the people rallied, and they're all on their way to the mountain right now. You want in?"

"I do. And you're going to want my help. But if you don't fuck me before we go I'm going to be more trouble than help."

"Christ! We don't have— "

"You know what happens when there's one cat in heat around a bunch of males? If you don't want that to happen while we're up there, then you'd best throw me a quickie."

"I don't even know if I *can* right now!"

Jessica got up and went to the bathroom saying, "Just give me a moment to put on my face."

Ballantine spent the "moment" checking the time and going over what he was likely going to see when he arrived up there, as well as what the game plan would be.

"Okay, I'm ready," Jessica said coming up behind him.

Ballantine sighed and squeezed his eyes shut. Her scent hit him first, taking him by surprise. Jasmine and lavender and... cake.

He felt her hands, electric, slide around his waist. When Jessica dipped a finger between his belly and his belt, the hunter went as hard as he'd ever been.

He cracked an eye and looked down at the person looking up at him. Jessica appeared about 20 years old again. Her blond hair gleamed. Her blue eyes sparkled and shone. Her skin was flawless. Her tits were nothing short of magnificent.

"I'd kiss you," she said, "but I need you inside me before you come."

She bent over the bed, wiggled her perfect ass and said, "Come on, stallion."

Ballantine's head swam, drunk as he was when he sought the cave worm. Reduced to his primal urges, he barely functioned enough to work his belt buckle. When he finally freed himself, he gave it a spit, slid in, and orgasmed in the same instant.

Jessica rolled her eyes and said, "I guess that'll do."

She put on some jeans, a shirt, and a jacket while Ballantine stood there trying to remember what year it was.

"Come on," she said, fixing her hair. "Time to put little Del away and go slay the witch. You can come too, Bobby Cat. *Ha*! Bob Cat! I didn't even realize."

CHAPTER 29

A convoy of almost 20 cars gathered at the base of Mt. Fayette, the witch's mountain. They left an aisle for Ballantine to go ahead. Andy helped Paul and Reggie push the gate open, then they got back into their trucks. Reggie rode with Paul. Andy rode with Louis and Rick.

Ballantine and Jessica rumbled up in Nigel's truck. Bob, the hellcat, sat between the two, his vigilant eyes ablaze. The monster hunter stopped at the gate, in the light of everyone's headlights, and raised high a polystyrene cup as the signal to drink... and pray, if anyone was still into that sort of thing.

The people removed the lids from their first of two cups. The blood smelled like rotten eggs and black licorice, causing some to lean out their windows and vomit before they even took a sip.

Andy Tumpkins was one of them. The faintest whiff made him gag so hard, Rick and Louis thought his stomach was going to come out of his mouth.

"Get the fuck out of the truck before you puke, man!" Louis said.

Andy jumped out and fell to his knees dry heaving and spitting. He didn't spill his cup of blood, though.

Ballantine held his nose and downed the blood in one gulp, then tossed the cup behind him.

"How was it?" asked Jessica with the shittiest of shit-eating grins.

"How bad do you *think* it was?" said Ballantine, who burped and almost threw up at the smell.

"I think it must have been absolutely terrible."

"Yeah, well multiply that by about a thousand and that's how terrible."

Ahead of them, the dirt path beyond the gate turned to stone. Ballantine rubbed his eyes and squinted.

"I guess it's working," said Jessica. "You can see the road?"

"Yeah."

"Smooth as any pavement. Clock's ticking, Mr. Ballantine."

They rolled forward onto the path. To those who hadn't yet choked down the blood, it looked like they had disappeared altogether.

"Come on, Andy," said Louis. "Suck it up and suck it down!"

Andy held his nose and poured, but only got down a few little swallows before deciding it was good enough. He left his half-full cup on the ground and jumped back in the truck. The three farmers brought up the back of the pack.

"She's got sentinels," Jessica said. "Be ready for anything."

Ballantine unholstered a pistol and held it at the ready.

Jessica hung her head out the window and called out as if to a missing pet, "Heeeeeere babiiiieeeess... Baaaaaaaabiiiiieeeeessss..."

"What the hell are you doing?" Ballantine growled.

Jessica scoffed and said, "Calling for backup."

"You might want to roll up your window, Mr. Coleman," said Reggie.

Paul gave the drummer a glance, then rolled up his window.

Reggie explained, "There's more than just a witch on this mountain. I can feel them."

Rick rolled up his window instinctively.

"You know something we don't?" asked Louis.

"Just being cautious," said Rick. "Big mountain like this, you don't really think a witch is the only thing on it, do you?"

"Hey, Andy," said Louis, "maybe roll up your window too."

A huge thump shook the truck. As Andy reached for the knob, a barbed tentacle reached in and wrapped around his head. Louis almost leapt into Rick's lap. He pressed his shotgun to the tentacle, but couldn't fire without killing Andy. Andy tried to scream, but couldn't get air in or out. He tried to grab the tentacle, but his arms only flailed and shook. The barbs had penetrated into his brain. Everything was black, and his head hurt, and he couldn't breath.

His panic subsided.

Andy heard a muffled gunshot.

Blinding pain cracked in his neck.

The truck fell away from him.

Louis panted as he peered through the hole he had just put in the roof. Satisfied that all was clear, he kept an eye on the window as he rolled it up. "This is *fucked,* man!" he repeated. "This is *so fucked*!"

"Lou," said an already worn Rick.

"This is so fucked."

"Lou!"

"What!"

"You wanna move over?"

Louis realized he was pressed against Rick. If he could have answered honestly, he would have said no. He didn't want to move over. He placed a hand on the passenger seat and pulled himself mostly, but not entirely into the spot where Andy had been sitting. It was still warm.

A heavy thump rocked Ballantine's truck. Neither Jessica nor Bob the hellcat were concerned. He looked in the rearview and saw the glint of a pair of shug monkey eyes looking back at him.

"Shit," he said pointing a gun over his shoulder.

"No, don't!" Jessica yelled. "He's one of mine. He'll help us."

The monster hunter didn't like the idea of having a shug monkey riding with him, but if it hadn't started tearing the truck apart yet, it probably wasn't going to.

"Christ!" said Paul. "You see that?" He and Reggie were in line behind Ballantine and saw the shug monkey drop into the bed.

"I sure did," Reggie said. "Don't worry though. He's on *our* side."

"How can you tell?"

"I can see his aura."

"Ah. Of course."

"Now, whatever is about to come down the hillside is *not* on our side. Shouldn't attack this vehicle, though."

A chorus of hollow, throaty hissing swelled from the mountainside. It neared the convoy, bringing with it the snapping of twigs and the rush of shuffled leaves.

"Wood devils," said Ballantine, looking around.

"Keep moving," said Jessica.

The wood devils rammed the middle truck from the high side and swarmed like ants. The passengers were shaken, but the wheels never gave. The wood devils weren't strong enough to move it. They snarled and spat at the windows. They chewed on whatever they could get their teeth around. They fell beneath the wheels and over the sides. The people in the truck behind summoned the courage to open their windows enough to poke their weapons out and killed or hobbled enough wood devils to attract the blood lust of the rest of the pack. After a tense few minutes, the wood devils were left behind by the convoy.

Next came a troop of shug monkeys, bringing with them chaos. The bulk of them attacked three vehicles in the convoy's rear half. Dumbstruck, Rick and Louis watched as the monkeys ravaged the trucks ahead of them. The monsters bounced and bounded. They threw things out of the beds, smashed the vehicles with rocks. They pulled people and *parts* of people out of the windows. One truck was forced over the edge. Another drove over because he couldn't think of anything else to do. A third driver was killed where he sat. His foot slumped against the gas pedal and forced the truck into the side of the mountain, making the vehicle overturn. The monkeys pulled the passenger out and tore him apart in the bright light of Rick's high beams.

Louis shivered and sweated and squeezed his shotgun tight.

"One way out, Lou," Rick said, unwinding his window. He drew his .45 and said, "and that's *through*."

Louis sneered, nodded, and rolled his window down. The two men leaned out and fired until they ran out of bullets. Some hit.

Some didn't. Lucky for them, the last shug monkey was either killed or frightened away by their final shot. They squeezed past the overturned truck, then hit the gas to catch up with the rest of the group.

After a few more monstrous encounters, the convoy had lost six vehicles in all on the way up. Sheriff Landry's car was nearly knocked over the side. Louis and Rick witnessed horror they'd never dreamed of, but they made it to the final obstacle with the rest of the survivors.

"Stop here," said Jessica.

Ballantine obeyed and looked around. The trees were sparse and the rocky terrain shone a pale blue in the moonlight.

A lantern light flickered and swayed in the distant dark up the road. Ballantine reached for a pistol, but Jess put a hand on his and shook her head.

"What is it?" Ballantine asked.

"You know how every town's got a ghost story, Mr. Ballantine?" Jessica nodded toward the approaching lantern.

"How's this one go?" the monster hunter asked.

"Once upon a time, a young Indian mother awoke in the night and realized her child was missing. Instead of rallying the tribe, either out of courtesy or shame, she lit a lantern and went looking by herself. She went into the woods, following clues and instinct, until she saw the orange glow of campfires behind some distant trees. Rightfully wary of a strange camp, she decided she had better wake the others... but as she turned to leave, she came face to strangled face with her child, hung by its neck from a nearby branch. The woman stood there gaping, weeping, unable to find the breath to scream, let alone the sense to run away. She felt her heart tear, assumed it was grief, then realized she had a bayonet sticking out of her chest. Turned out the camp was a colonial regiment, off course and bored. They slaughtered the Indian camp and left their bodies to rot, the young mother laid at her child's swinging feet... but not for long. Ever since, there've been sightings in these woods and on the roads of a grieving woman who carries a lantern."

The lantern light shone brighter as the woman shambled nearer. Ballantine could make out her shape, luminous and white, hazy around the edges, with long black hair.

"Ghosts can't harm the living, though," said Ballantine.

"No?" asked Jessica.

"No. It doesn't work like that. If it did, there'd be spectral murderers and vigilantes all over the place."

"If you say so."

Strands of the woman's long black hair floated and swayed like they were underwater. Her sunken eyes glowed with the reflection of Ballantine's headlights... or maybe they glowed on their own. Cracked lips surrounded the courage-devouring black hole of her slack and sullen gape.

Ballantine began to doubt himself. What if he didn't know everything? What if there'd been new research into ghosts that hadn't gotten to him? He wasn't equipped to handle specters. What if this was the end for him? What if he doesn't complete his mission?

The woman floated over the hood of the truck and pushed her face and swaying hair through the windshield. Bob put his ears back and growled.

"Never show fear to a ghost," someone had told Ballantine once. He stared into the desperate depths of her eyes and held his breath. She stared back into his, examining... or could it have been pleading?

Despite the stoic facade, Ballantine's doubt turned to despair. His heart hollowed and he lost his faith in himself. He felt like a failure, like he was already beaten. He felt as if nothing mattered one way or another. He thought he might kill himself now.

The woman turned her attention to Jessica, easing Ballantine's depression. The nymph took a glance at the ghost's eyes, then looked away and shifted in her seat. Jessica's confidence subsided but did not drain. Unlike Ballantine, she was able to resist and walled off most of the emotional fluctuation. When the ghost realized she wouldn't get any more from Jessica, she moved on, passing through the back of the truck and on to Reggie and Paul.

Reggie, like Jessica, was able to calm himself and stop the emotional tailspin. Paul broke down and cried like a baby. Reggie coached him through it.

"Paul, listen to me," said the drummer. "You're totally fine. You're okay."

"No! No!" Paul said, putting his head in his hands.

"Yes, you are. This ghost is making you this way. She's feeding off your bad energy."

"So I'm supposed to just turn it off?"

"Pretty much."

"We live with monsters! My daughter might be dead and I don't remember the last time we were happy with each other."

"It's okay, Mr. Coleman. We're gonna get her back."

"We're gonna die up here."

"We're not gonna die up here."

The ghost moved on to the next car, driven by Bobby, the hellcat's father. In the passenger seat next to Bobby was his buddy Ray, another strapping young fellow whose greatest achievements included carrying his high school football team to the state final and sleeping "with tons of chicks."

Both men pissed themselves before the specter even reached the car. They cried and moaned and closed their eyes, but it didn't matter. The ghost woman took what she came for. As with the others, she inhaled their confidence and replaced it with despair.

Bobby put his .38 in his mouth and pulled the trigger. The sound drew Ray's attention and the sight sent him into shock. He stared from another world as Bobby slumped over the wheel. He had no sensation as the car lurched forward with Bobby's foot on the accelerator. He didn't notice the impact when the car caromed off the back corner of Paul Coleman's truck. He didn't realize he'd gone weightless when the car went over the side.

The ghost woman moved from car to car with mixed results. Some people killed themselves like Bobby. Others were more resilient. Rick held it together enough to keep Louis from killing himself, the elder heart annealed by nature and time.

The convoy had already gotten moving again by the time the

woman passed through the last vehicle. Only ten people remained. Drained of hope, they carried on like a funeral procession until they reached the end of the path, the clearing, and the castle.

What remained of the convoy pulled into the lawn and lined up, headlights illuminating the castle. Ballantine hung his head and sighed.

"Hey," said Jessica.

"Hm."

"Look at me."

He did. Her eyes glowed brilliant and blue in the dark. Confidence poured into him like wine in a glass. His heart beat warm and strong. Determination bolstered his upper lip. When she kissed him again, his glass overflowed.

They hopped out of the truck and Ballantine held up his second cup of blood to signal the others to drink. Jessica went car to car restoring courage with her magic gaze.

The moon was full, bright, and high overhead, rimming the peaks and turrets of the castle in silver, yet it seemed to scowl back at the people. Maybe it was the light. Maybe it was built that way. With its twisted web of light-swallowing crevices, it looked like a monster all on its own, as if at any moment it would rise up out of the ground and end them all.

Mara, Jeremy, and Lana stood unnoticed atop a corner bastion. Lana caught sight of Jessica and couldn't help but feel jealous. The original "her" was whole again—still cursed, but with her youth and magic back.

Jeremy pinched his bottom lip between his thumb and forefinger. Logic told him to panic, but he remained calm. The whole scene was like something out of a movie. And he was never in danger watching a movie. He couldn't fathom anything bad about to happen, even as he watched the people step out of their vehicles and arm themselves. He knew those people. They wouldn't hurt him. For that matter, he wouldn't hurt them.

Mara fidgeted like an addict. All those souls down there. So much potential pain and pleasure. She could turn any one of them into a gelatinous bag of fear. She could make them all servants like Brunna and Gregory. She could seduce them all and fuck them until they fell apart.

Mara touched herself through her jet-black gown. Lana noticed and cocked her head at the demon. Mara smiled and sighed with pleasure.

"Okay, Jeremy," Mara said, sliding her hand to her hip. "You're on." She and Lana moved away from the battlements, out of view of the people below.

Jeremy stepped up to a crenel between the battlements and surveyed the scene. Dull headlights lit the lawn and drive. Shapes of people milled behind the lights, but were difficult to identify. Some of the people murmured to each other. Jeremy heard someone say, "Would you believe that?"

The songwriter alternately squinted and widened his eyes. A few details became apparent: shapes of certain people, faces, and the weapons they were carrying. Many of them stood gaping at the castle. He wished them away. He willed them to recognize their bad decision, to cut their losses, and turn around.

"Any time, Jeremy," Mara said.

He cleared his throat, put his hands in the air, and called, "Don't do this!"

Sheriff Landry shined his cruiser's spotlight at Jeremy. Some of the people took aim, but Ballantine ordered them to hold their fire.

"Look, I know you're all afraid," said Jeremy. "I grew up with you all. I know all the same stories you do. And I bet there's a few more now. It's only natural, I guess.

"But you know... *we're* afraid here too. I know none of *us* wants to die. We don't even want to *fight.* And it got me thinking, you know? We're as afraid of you as you are of us. Nobody wants to fight and nobody wants to die. So I have to wonder, isn't the world big enough for all of us? Isn't there a way everyone can just leave each other alone?"

His naivete annoyed Mara. "No," she wanted choke him and

say, "when have human beings ever left *each other* alone, let alone a fucking demon? When have humans ever *not* been afraid of something they didn't understand?" Then again, she had to admit that she and her kind shared some responsibility for that.

Jeremy continued, "Isn't stopping the fighting the only way to end a war? What if we all just walked away from each other right now? Why couldn't we?"

Ballantine called, "That's naive, Jeremy."

"Sure, yeah. Walking away from violent solutions is naive. Makes sense. And we wonder why aliens haven't made contact yet."

"No, Jeremy. It's naive to think a witch like her can be good."

"She lived up here peacefully for 20 years until *you* came! This whole town had figured out how to make it work. Mara stayed up here."

"Make it work? The town's on its last leg! And as for her, she's got the *time*, doesn't she? Best case scenario, she waits until the town dies on its own. But I'd bet my life that whether I came to town or not, she was going to come back eventually. She was going to hurt someone eventually. Someone would cross her eventually. She sold her soul, Jeremy, and if she hasn't already, she's gonna sell yours too."

"You don't know what you're talking about! She's not even a *witch*. She's a..." Jeremy caught himself and glanced at Mara. The demon shook her head, but the singer pressed with his eyes.

"If you tell them, you damn everyone here," she warned.

"What is she, Jeremy?" Ballantine called.

Jeremy took a beat to conjure a lie, then said, "She's a *good* witch. She just got... caught up in a bunch of shit. You know, like people do."

"She's not people."

"No. She isn't. And I gotta say, I'm not exactly proud to call myself a human right now."

"Jeremy, I don't know what she told you, but you can't trust a word of it."

"She told me she cured my mom. How *is* my mom?"

Ballantine didn't know how to begin explaining why that answer didn't matter.

"She's all better," called Reggie. "Look, how about you come home, huh?"

"Reggie?" Jeremy squinted and scanned the shapes.

"Yeah."

"God, man, you shouldn't be here."

"Where's Ari?"

"She's... inside. She's okay."

"Okay. So how about you guys come out and we go home?"

"It's not as simple as that anymore, though, is it, Reggie?" Jeremy left a beat of silence. If Reggie would have said anything, Jeremy might have chosen to believe him. But since Reggie never lied, he left the silence alone. "That's what I thought," said Jeremy. "She told me *that,* Mr. Ballantine. Can I trust *that*? That things aren't the same anymore? That I can't just go home? Huh? Am I just gonna go back to playing at the hotel or maybe hit the road? You think I'm not gonna be investigated for what happened the night I left? Or what happened to Laura? Then what? Say I go with you. Sheriff's at least going to want to question me. Worst case, I'm found guilty. Feds come take me away and lock me in a cell. Only bring me out to run tests like a lab rat. Maybe try to turn me into a weapon. No. I'm not coming down."

"I don't want to fight you, man," said Reggie.

"Then go home!"

"Give us Ariana."

"I can't do that right now. What if..." Jeremy looked back and forth between the people and Mara. "What if, you all leave now and we let Ari go tomorrow? How would that be?"

"Goddamnit, kid," called Ballantine, "do you know how many people died tonight just coming up this mountain to get you? This ends now. Pick the right side."

Jeremy thought, then held out a hand and partially duplicated Sheriff Landry's cruiser. The deformed engine ground itself apart and caught fire. The people ran for cover behind the other cars. With two gas tanks for fuel, the explosion sent a shock wave through the vicinity. The heat warmed Jeremy's face and chilled his heart.

There was a pop followed by searing pain as a bullet sliced through his arm. He cried out and took a knee behind the battlements. Lana ran to him and checked his wound.

"Ooh, poor baby," she said. "This needs stitches."

"Go ahead inside," said Mara.

"I'm sorry," said Jeremy.

"I know. You tried."

Lana and Jeremy ran back inside as Mara cracked her knuckles.

"Let's get through that door!" cried Ballantine.

Mara stepped to the battlements and waved her hands. She tried to create an illusion but couldn't connect her mind with any of the people's. She tried again. Nothing. She realized they'd all drunk the cave worm's blood.

"Damn you, Jessica," Mara breathed. She scanned the charging townsfolk and saw the twinkling blue specks of Jessica's eyes and jewels.

The nymph strolled casually behind the people and gave Mara a smug wave. Beside Jessica prowled Bob the hellcat. Behind her stalked a growing number of monsters from the deep dark of the woods; wood devils, shug monkeys, creepers, shape-shifters, hunner dyers, and in the sky, hellbats and vultures.

Mara laughed and called down, "You almost had me, Jessica! They may be your babies, but they served the lords of Hell first. *ATTACK*!!!"

The lawn erupted in a cacophony of hisses, howls, growls, gurgles, and shrieks. Jessica, wide eyed, spun to face her children and put her hands out. She walked slowly back toward the castle, trying to win back the salivating monsters. Bob the hellcat remained at her side, unaffected by the demon's command.

"Babies," she said. "My babies. Listen to Mama!" She pointed to the bastion on which Mara stood. "*SHE* is your enemy. Not them!"

The beasts stalked on, silhouettes in the car headlights. Hungry eyes fixed on the soft humans at the door.

"Listen to your mother!" Jessica screamed.

The beasts roared back their dissent.

Jessica frowned deeply and teared up, then bolted with Bob back to the group at the door. The monsters charged.

The townspeople had made a semicircle around the door, weapons ready.

"Conserve your ammo!" called Ballantine. "Don't shoot unless you have a shot! And try not to hit the cars."

When Jessica and Bob broke through the semicircle, Ballantine shouted, "*NOW*!"

The mountaintop crackled and boomed with gunfire. Muzzle flashes lit fearful faces. Bullets and shot tore holes through monster flesh. Ballantine focused his AK-47 fire on the harder-to-hit beasts. Louis and Paul turned their shotguns skyward and brought down bats and vultures. Jessica and Reggie worked on the door.

"Can you get us in here?" Reggie asked.

Jessica put her hand on the thick wooden door and concentrated. After a moment, she shook her head and said, "If it had more water in it, I might be able to break it up."

Reggie remembered his own power and put his hands on the door. He felt a connection to the it, not unlike the one Jeremy had when he duplicated things. Reggie couldn't duplicate, but he could manipulate. The door was heavy, though. He searched it for weak spots and found them at the hinges.

The small army of monsters drew closer as Reggie worked the wood. It shifted little by little, like a fibrous clay around the bolts. As he kneaded the wood, he realized he might be better off working outside the hinges. He was encouraged at the sight of splinters curling away, layer by layer. The deeper he went, the more he connected, the faster the wood peeled.

Part of a hunner dyer made it through the gunfire and clawed someone's leg. A shot from a pistol exploded its head.

A hellbat flapped in. It dug its fire-hot fangs and claws into the neck and shoulders of the man next to Ballantine. The monster hunter took his knife and pressed it upward into the bat's body. It let go and Ballantine flung it onto the battlefield. The man who was attacked bled but fought on.

With the scent of blood in the air, the wood devils attacked with vigor. Difficult targets to hit, the wiry creatures ducked, dodged, and leapt their way closer to the group.

A vulture swooped down, dug its talons into one man's shoulders and began to drag him away. Someone else shot the bird, dropping it and stranding its victim in the middle of the battlefield where they were torn apart.

Ballantine shot a leaping wood devil. It fell three feet in front of him. He glanced back at Reggie and Jessica working on the door.

Reggie gave the door a push. It moved but did not give.

"They're not gonna last much longer," Jessica said.

"Just a little more," Reggie said, working. "Get the others ready to push."

Jessica went from person to person telling them Reggie's plan. Whether they actually heard her or not, she couldn't have said.

Nobody saw the creeper until it was crawling up Rick's legs. He cried out in fear and pain and fired his pistol straight down through its body. He tried pushing it away with his foot, but it was too awkward and kept flopping back to where he was standing.

"Okay!" cried Reggie. "I got it! Come push!"

"*DOOR*!" cried Jessica.

Half the group charged the door. It moved and splinters crackled, but it did not give. They pulled back to try again. A wood devil broke the line and tore into someone.

Again, they put their shoulders into it. This time it gave. The hinges let go and the last splinters released. After a few more pushes, the door was wide open and half fallen.

CHAPTER 30

At the people's final push, the door swung fully open and leaned at an angle against the wall. The full moon shone its pale light through the great window above the table. A fire flickered in the hearth, casting shadows high on the wall.

"Choke them at the door!" Ballantine cried.

The people turned and faced the frame, blasting their silhouettes as they approached. The sound of gunfire in the great hall compounded to a deafening threshold.

Ballantine yelled in Jessica's ear, "I gotta find Mara before this shit wears off."

Reggie tugged on Jessica's arm and shouted, "Where would they keep Ariana?"

"Try the dungeon," Jessica said. She pointed at a doorway to the right of the hearth and said, "Straight through the kitchen and down the stairs. At the bottom of the stairs, stay left. There'll be a door."

Reggie nodded and jogged off while Jessica motioned for Ballantine to follow her up the stairs.

A pair of creepers snuck through and pulled gunfire away from the door. Then a wood devil made it in. Then another.

Ariana heard the commotion from her cell. She pressed her ear to the door to listen but couldn't hear anything distinct. Just a wash of gunfire. The door felt strange to her. It had an energy.

As he rounded a corner with Jessica and Bob, Ballantine was smacked hard in the forehead by the blunt end of a spear. He fell to the ground, dazed, and watched as Gregory threatened Jessica with the sharp end. The nymph put her hands up and backed away.

Ballantine reached for a gun, but as soon as he touched the handle, Gregory pricked his hand with the end of the spear, forcing him to let go. The hunter reached for the other gun and Gregory pricked that hand as well. He rolled and reached and Gregory pricked him again.

Jessica and Bob slunk away down the corridor as the men fought.

Ballantine got an idea. He reached for a gun and with his free hand reached for the spot where Gregory's staff would be when he struck. This time Gregory did not strike. He kept the spear just out of Ballantine's reach and allowed the hunter to draw. *Then* the servant struck, slicing both of Ballantine's hands in one thrust, making him drop the gun.

The hunter pushed away and got to his feet. He turned his remaining holstered gun away from Gregory and drew. His idea was to shoot from the hip, but the servant circled him to the other side, putting the hunter's body in between.

Gregory toyed with Ballantine as he circled, making Ballantine look foolish for trying to grab the end of the circling spearhead, making little cuts on the hunter's arm, shoulder, and hand. He even caught him once on the ear.

Ballantine knew never to show his back to an opponent. Fancy spins were only for the movies, but Gregory's harassment frustrated the hunter to the breaking point. Ballantine spun the opposite direction to try to open up a shot. But the servant was ready and speared the back of the hunter's hand, forcing him to drop his other pistol.

Reggie descended into the castle's misty cellar. A torch burned on either side of the opening. Though he couldn't *see* as far as anyone else, he felt the stonework around him as if he were a spider on a web. He felt the cracks in the mortar. He felt a couple of the pillars in the deep fog, but couldn't feel all the way to Mara's bath. That was in the distance to his right. Jessica had told him to keep left.

Left was a wall, which he felt and followed. It was about three feet thick and densely packed. Though Reggie easily felt through it to the space on the other side, he didn't pick up much more than the floor and walls. An orange orb came into view, intensified, and sharpened into the flame of another torch. Next to the torch was the dungeon door. It was hardly heavy duty. It was simple, with a knob and a bolt.

"She's not in there," he thought. Regardless, he slid the bolt back. Better to check and know for sure, despite the bad feeling in his gut.

The dungeon was pitch black and chilly. Magic powers or not, it terrified Reggie. He removed the torch from the wall and held it through the doorway. When nothing jumped out at him, he took a step inside and raised the flame so he could see better. To his left and right were rows of iron-gated cells separated by stone walls. It was dank and mildewy and looked unused. Reggie had expected something hot, stinking, and rat infested.

"Ari," he murmured. "Are you in here?"

From where he stood, he couldn't actually see into any of the cells—only their gates extending into the dark. With his fear subsiding, Reggie crept toward a cell.

In the first cell was a human skeleton dressed in 20-year-old tatters. The sight shook Reggie's bones.

He called out a little louder, "Ari! Are you in here?"

"Reggie?" floated Ariana's voice. "I'm out here."

The drummer took a breath of relief and left the dungeon. Ariana was standing just outside. Reggie closed and bolted the door, replaced the torch, and sighed.

"Find anything interesting?" she asked.

"If by 'interesting' you mean 'terrifying,' then yes. Yes, I did.

Come on. Let's get out of here."

"What about Jeremy?"

"Jeremy's gonna have to come back on his own."

"But we can't just leave without him!"

"Ari, the man's gonna do what he wants whether he's right or wrong. Now, the least I can do is get you back home. It's a fucking war zone upstairs."

"Is it? What's it like?"

Something had been nagging at Reggie, but he'd been ignoring it. "The people and monsters got in and now they're tearing each other apart." Why wasn't she moving?

"That's horrible," she said. Her eyebrows showed concern, but her cheeks hinted at delight.

Reggie's nagging turned into a slap in the face.

"You're not Ari," he said.

"Took you long enough," came Mara's voice out of Ari's mouth. The demon released the illusion and appeared again as herself.

Reggie, less than deftly, drew his pistol.

The great hall was bedlam. Monsters of all kinds swooped and snuck, snarled and struck. The people fired franticly in all directions. They found the weapons on the walls and fought with them as they ran out of ammunition.

Ariana slid her palms along her cell door. Her thinking was that the energy in the door was a charm placed by one or both of the servants to keep her from breaking out. Her *feeling*, on the other hand, was that it was something else, something... *not* sinister. She couldn't have described the feeling if she had been asked. There may not be a better word for it than "instinct." It wasn't as obvious as glowing gold instructions. It was subtle, like a leaf-strewn path through the woods.

It led her to the knob and then the keyhole. A breeze came through. She looked in and saw nothing at first, but, as she looked away, she thought she saw light. She looked again, pressing her eye closer, and saw faintly what appeared to be a glowing white mist inside. Ariana willed it out of the way and, to her surprise, it moved, revealing a key left in the door.

Lana had just pulled the last stitch through Jeremy's wound when Jessica flung his bedroom door open.

"Where's Mara?" Jessica asked.

At the sight of the young nymph, Jeremy's blood drained from his head to his cock and shut his brain off.

Lana glared in jealousy.

"Well?" said Jessica, impatient.

Her lips were so supple and shiny. Her eyes so brilliant and blue. The way her thin cotton shirt clung to her breasts was pure tantalization. The subtle shadows on her midriff led the eye to her skin-tight jeans and clearly defined crotch.

"Oh, for the love of..." said Jessica.

She squeezed Jeremy through his jeans and made him release instantly. Lana only glared.

"There," said Jessica. "All better? Where's Mara?"

Jeremy laid back and panted.

"Jeremy, come on, we have to destroy her."

"It's not right," he said. "It's all fucked up. I really don't know what to think anymore. I've seen both sides and I don't want to be on either one."

"Of course it's all fucked up, Jeremy. You're in the middle now, though. Not many good things happen to those in the middle. The only way out may be through."

Jeremy said, "Think I'll just start walking. And whatever happens, happens."

"That's a start, I suppose. Come on. Take me to Mara. Maybe we can mediate something, huh?"

Jeremy sighed and said, "Whatever."

"Hey, where's that human spirit I'm always hearing about? Not giving up until it's over?"

Jeremy rolled his eyes and carefully slipped his arm back into his shirt.

"You don't really want to use that thing," said Mara.

"You're right," said Reggie. "I don't. But I gotta do what I gotta do."

"But you don't 'gotta do' this. You can feel it. You're in tune with me, aren't you? You've always had that gift: harmony, rapport, empathy." She gestured to the dungeon and said, "And despite my past, you can feel in your bones what kind of person I am."

"You're not a person. You're a witch."

"Am I?"

Reggie searched his feelings and said, "No. You're something else. What are you?"

"I don't even know anymore, darling. First I was nothing. Then I was. Then I was an angel. Then I was a demon. Now and for the last 20 or so odd years, I've been a cross between both demon *and* human. Ha. The worst of both worlds. Difference is, humans get chances and chances for redemption. And you, sir, know I'm trying. You can feel it."

"I know I shouldn't even trust my *feelings* around a demon because they're that good at lying."

"But your powers are special, aren't they? You're not *just* a really empathetic guy. You've got a boost."

Reggie said nothing, afraid to out his mom.

"You know I can see your aura. Your radiant, green aura. You know the last time I saw an aura like yours was about 20 years ago."

Reggie raised the gun.

"Ah, ah, ah! I'll tear your mind to pieces before you can pull the trigger."

Reggie lowered the gun but kept it pointed at Mara.

"You don't think you can trust me? With all the shit I can do to you? Could've *done* to you by now? I could've shut you in that cell. I could've made you run screaming headfirst into the wall. I could've had you crying on the floor in a puddle of your own piss and vomit, falling apart from the inside out."

"I can't let you live."

"But you can't kill me either. It's against your nature."

Reggie thought about it.

"It's against your nature to kill anything. Let alone an innocent."

"But you're not innocent."

"I *wasn't* innocent... and maybe I'm no angel now, but who is? If you held everything against everyone who did anything bad, everyone would hate each other."

"But you *murdered* people."

"I never *murdered* anybody. I *tortured* them. They died on their own, one way or another. I've changed... maybe. I was *trying* to, at least... I'm pretty sure." Mara was tired of thinking about it. "Look, the bottom line is by sunrise I will torture, or enslave, every last person who doesn't belong in my castle. So go. Run. Find Ariana and Jeremy and leave. Last chance."

Each of Reggie's thoughts played out on his face. Training his weapon on a living thing had never felt right to him. It didn't feel right now. He thought about his parents—how afraid they were of Mara, that his mother was hiding and now apparently no longer secret, what his father would do if he were here. Ken would pull the trigger. He'd take the chance with the threats. Reggie agreed that it was the only thing to be done, but he wasn't the one to do it. Besides, he knew she wasn't lying when she said she would break him before he could pull the trigger. She'd have to be taken by surprise if at all. Maybe he could pick up his parents and leave town.

An image of the inside of the cell flashed before his eyes.

"You're a tough one," said Mara. "Must be your mama's magic."

Reggie holstered his gun and ran.

Ballantine bled from dozens of cuts while Gregory danced around him. The hunter felt like the bull in a bull fight, speared and goaded for the fun of the fighter. His shirt and pants clung sticky and red to his stinging wounds. The pain stole some of his concentration—made it hard to fight.

Gregory had a style of baiting Ballantine's reaction and capitalizing on it. The servant would thrust, elicit a dodge or parry, then make a cut in whatever was left unprotected: a forearm, a flank, a cheek. He could do it all night.

Ballantine knew he had to either disarm Gregory or get a weapon that could beat him. He considered his knife, but didn't want to wield it until he was sure he wouldn't lose it. Gregory fought like he was clairvoyant. He may have been. He seemed to know what Ballantine would do before he did it. If that were the case, Gregory would either have to make a mistake or be tricked. That gave Ballantine an idea.

He scanned for where his guns lay and worked his way toward them. Gregory continued to harass and slash. Ballantine unholstered his knife and sprang backwards. Gregory leapt at the same time. Ballantine knelt to pick up a gun and threw his knife. Gregory dodged the knife and swung at Ballantine, but the hunter had bought himself a step and fired a shot straight through the servant's heart.

As Gregory lay dying, Ballantine looked his wounds over and retrieved his weapons. He took inventory of the dark halls, saw nothing, and picked a direction in which to walk. He came to a doorway with a set of stairs spiraling up to the right and down to the left. He gave it some thought and decided that of the two directions, if he were hunkering down, he wouldn't go up.

Ariana got a familiar feeling from the key, like a smell or a song from a time and place she couldn't remember. It attracted her. It was comfortable. Right. It was the feeling of a puzzle piece going into place.

She connected to it, but not the same way Jeremy connected to the things he duplicated. Jeremy's connections extended like another arm, able to feel anything in between him and his target. Ariana felt the key as part of her, but separate.

She turned the key with that feeling, popped the door open, and peeked out. The clamor of the great hall came to her through the corridor. She stepped out, removed the key, and inspected it. Its power seeped into her.

Ariana's heart raced and her eyes dilated. She took a deep breath, then forgot to breathe... or maybe didn't need to. She was nauseated. Her brain tingled and burned.

A breeze came from nowhere, picked up, swirled around her, whipped her hair like a Gorgon's snakes. The corridors illuminated—no! They were still dark. Ariana knew that, yet she could see all the way to the ends of them. She could feel all the air around her too. She was able to tell the difference between the gasses—how much nitrogen, oxygen, and carbon dioxide was around and inside her. She could feel every pore of every surface in the vicinity.

Both of her guns, the 30/30 and the Model 19, lay next to the door. She holstered the handgun and slung the rifle, looked around, and saw Brunna’s face at the end of the corridor, disappearing around a corner. A full yet sinking feeling filled Ariana.

"Hey!" she called and gave chase. Goosebumps tingled one side of her body as she passed a door that led to a spiral staircase. Around the bend, Brunna's retreating form and the clamor of the great hall became clearer. "Please come back! I just want to talk!"

The roar of gunfire had been replaced with the clang and clatter of whatever the people in the hall had been able to find: swords and other decorative weaponry. A few people had managed to save some bullets and used them sparingly, popping one off here and there. The clatter and pops resounded sharply above a bed of the grunts, shrieks, and cries of both men and monster.

Ariana emerged from the corridor into the great hall and froze in horrified awe. The floor was covered in bodies of all kinds. Creatures crept and leapt. Men slashed and bashed. Both had trouble keeping their feet under them for all the bodies and blood on the ground. Whether confused or content, some of the simpler monsters stopped fighting to gnaw on the dead. They hardly noticed anyone approach them and paid no attention when the swords and spears came down.

Brunna stalked awkwardly through the mess. She was amid the strewn furniture in front of the hearth when Ariana caught sight of her.

"Brunna!" called Ari.

"Jodi!" called Paul. He was standing between the two main pillars, covered in blood, and brandishing a scimitar. "Is it you?"

Brunna froze, tears in her eyes. She wanted to run to each of them. Twenty years of apologies frothed inside her. She locked eyes with Ariana, took in her daughter's face, and shook her head. She wanted to tell her everything, but couldn't guarantee she hadn't been charmed—charmed against telling Ariana the truth, charmed to kill Ariana if she considered defecting.

"Jodi," said Paul, next to her.

Brunna looked at Paul, then turned to run. He caught her by the arm and pulled her to him. She hid her face in his chest.

"What did she do to you, baby?" said Paul stroking her hair. "What did she do?"

The hair on the back of Ariana's neck stood up. She could see the room and feel the air. She was missing something. Something she couldn't see had started breathing again.

Paul felt a sore muscle in his lower back. The pain grew worse as he stood there holding Brunna, so he shifted his weight to the other foot. That only made it worse as he felt the sting of a pulled muscle. He reached back to massage it and felt the crusty, jagged claw of a creeper dug into his back. His insides went hot.

"Jodi," was all he could say.

The creeper plunged a claw into Brunna's back as well. She gasped at the pain, but was thankful the end was near.

Ariana, seeing something was wrong, made her way to them through the fighting and the bodies. Before she could reach them, they fell to the floor, revealing the half-dead creeper. Ariana drew her pistol, blew the monster to pieces, then forgot it. Her parents lay opposite each other, bleeding to death.

Ariana knelt next to Brunna and asked, "Are you my mother? Are you Jodi?"

Unable to speak, Brunna nodded. She motioned Ari closer, pointed to her own mouth, gestured with her hand as though something were coming out, then pointed at Ari's mouth. The girl didn't quite understand.

Brunna relaxed, lay her head back, breathed out, and died.

From her mouth arose a white mist not unlike the one that had veiled the key in the door.

Ariana realized what Brunna must have meant. The girl leaned over and breathed in the mist. Her power grew, but it was barely noticeable. She went to her father, only to find him dead already.

An angry wind swirled through the great hall, nearly extinguishing the torches and the fire in the hearth. Ariana had had enough, and she had an idea of where to head next.

CHAPTER 31

Dripping red and with both pistols drawn, the monster hunter stalked into the area below the castle.

"Delaney Ballantine," Mara's voice echoed from somewhere in the mist. "I know we're not exactly friends, but I must say I'm impressed with all you've done. I'd dismissed your stories as tall tales. Now I'm thinking they might not be so tall after all."

"How about you come out and I tell you another one," Ballantine said.

Mara laughed and said, "Okay... in a minute." She changed to a more serious tone and said, "You know, it didn't have to come to this."

"If you can't live in harmony with people, then you can't live."

"Why do I have to live in harmony with you? Huh? Why shouldn't YOU live in harmony with ME?"

"Because we were here first!"

"Were you?"

"It's *our* world."

"And that's the problem with humans. Everything you see is yours. And if you can't have it or control it, well then, it's either your enemy or it's expendable, isn't it?

"As a matter of fact, that was my exact argument to the Constructive's reps before the Fall: humans have *no* respect for the gifts they've been given. You're children smashing your toys, oblivious to the fact that daddy's not buying you any more. And when you run out, you'll have nothing left to eat but each other."

"You think you're a gift from God?"

"As I've been saying, I don't know *what* I am now. I might be nothing. I might be something. I might be a means to an end... or an end to a means."

"As I hear it, God don't take too kindly to evil."

"Yeah, well, you're getting thousandth-hand information."

"Is that right?"

"The human understanding of the 'supreme word' is like a kindergartener's understanding of Shakespeare. It's easy enough for you to see that there are players involved and that there are problems, but any deeper understanding is just so beyond you... well, it's enough to make legions of angels revolt in disgust."

"So what, then? Evil is okay?"

Mara pressed the bridge of her nose. "What does it take to get it through the human mind that nothing is black and white? *Nothing*, do you hear me? It's as simple, yet complex, as that, Mr. Ballantine."

"Yeah, well if you come on out, I got a simple solution to *both* our problems."

Mara sighed and stepped out from behind a pillar. Ballantine fired one shot into her chest and dropped her. He strode to the body and fired three more shots into her head, blowing it to pieces.

He didn't feel any different. Maybe it was the years and the countless hunts. He used to feel a sense of accomplishment, like he'd finished a list or a project. Not anymore. He was standing bleeding in a dank castle having just killed a witch, and he had a long way to go before he could sleep again, with more killing in days to come.

He holstered his weapons and turned to head back. Then he heard a rustle. He reached for his guns as he sought the source. It was coming from a door in the wall.

"So that's what *I* look like inside," came Mara's voice from behind him.

Ballantine wheeled to see Mara inspecting her own dead body.

"What the hell?"

Mara put her hands up and japed, "Don't shoot!"

Ballantine shot her through the chest and dropped her.

Mara stepped out from behind the pillar again and said, "I can explain!"

BANG! Thud. Another Mara.

"You see..."

BANG! Thud. Another Mara.

"...your antidote..."

BANG! Thud. Another Mara.

"...has worn off."

BANG! Thud. Another Mara.

"You're firing at nothing, Mr. Ballantine."

Click.

"Look." Mara gestured to the floor near the pillar to show that all of the bodies were gone.

"What the hell *are* you?" Ballantine growled.

"The end to a means."

Ron Ballantine, Del's father, stepped out of the void and into the light. He came close to Del, about three feet away, put a rifle under his own chin, and pulled the trigger.

In slow motion, Ron Ballantine stepped out of the void and into the light. He came close to Del, about three feet away, put a rifle under his own chin, and pulled the trigger.

In slower motion, Ron Ballantine stepped out of the void and into the light. He came close to Del, about three feet away, put a rifle under his own chin, and pulled the trigger.

For what felt like days, Del Ballantine watched his father kill himself over and over. The bullet plunged through the flesh of his chin. His eyes winced and lost their focus. His blood sprayed. His jaw fell slack. Every detail of Ron's face tattooed itself into Del's memory. He couldn't look away. He couldn't close his eyes. He had no eyes to close.

Del's mother was still alive and well back in Darlington.

However, this crazy world made him wonder about her from time to time—worrying about what could happen while he was away. For what felt to him like the next few weeks, Ballantine was forced to watch every possible horrible scenario. He watched his mother fall down the stairs, cry for help for days, and slowly die on the cold basement floor. He watched her hit her head, fall into a full bathtub, and drown. He watched the worst moments of a losing cancer battle. He watched her die in every kind of car crash imaginable. He saw her robbed and shot. He saw her beaten, robbed, and shot. He saw her raped, beaten, robbed, and shot. He saw her stabbed to death. He saw her mauled and torn to pieces by every kind of creature: animal, monster, and man. Every time she died, she called out for him.

His lost loves and old friends suffered similarly. He watched them beaten, raped, shot, and stabbed. He watched them tortured in all ways, modern and medieval. Their screams went from horrifying, to monotonous, to maddening.

As far as Ballantine could tell, he spent the next few years in the terror and pain of being hunted and killed by everything he'd ever hunted and killed. He lay paralyzed and was slowly eaten by chipmunks, squirrels, and rabbits. He had his eyes pecked out by birds, was gored and trampled by deer, mauled by a bear, disemboweled by wood devils, bitten in half by a wyvern, devoured whole by a giant snake, torn limb from limb by shug monkeys, poisoned by countless venomous creatures, digested by the cave worm, and so on... and so on... and so on...

Then there was nothing but black. Ballantine took it as a reprieve at first, but soon learned it was a petri dish for his own terrible thoughts to mutate and ferment. He tried to calm himself and clear his mind, but he couldn't shake a pervasive feeling of dread. He tried to remember happy times, but they were vague and out of focus in the periphery of his memory. He flashed back to every horrifying thing he'd ever seen, both in his personal hell and in his life. Interspersed with his flashbacks were the comparatively mundane, but no less thorny, bad memories. He relived the pain of every broken heart he'd ever had or caused, every slight, every insult, every damaged ego and broken spirit. He disappointed himself over and over, until he was worthless.

"Oh hey, here's some people," said an apathetic Jeremy.

He, Jessica, and Lana approached Mara and the twitching, bloody Del Ballantine. Bob the hellcat prowled at Jessica's side. The girls looked, wide eyed, from Mara to the hunter as he writhed on the ground.

"Wait, stop, don't," Jeremy said, deadpan.

"What's with him?" Mara asked Jessica.

"I think it's all gotten to be too much for him," Jessica said.

"I see you got your gems back."

Jessica put her hand to her necklace and said, "I did, yes. And I feel great." She gestured to Ballantine and asked, "How long has he been like that?"

"A few minutes."

"So to him... a few decades?"

"Should be."

Jeremy watched Ballantine writhe. Jessica was right. It *had* gotten to be too much for him. He wasn't in shock, though, only ambivalent. Nevertheless, the sight of Ballantine's pain moved him to say, "Mara, can you let him go? Please?"

To Mara it was like a guest had just asked her to leave her own home. It didn't register. She almost asked why. In that moment, torturing Ballantine, she'd forgotten everything she'd ever said about changing, like an alcoholic who promised herself one drink and suddenly realized she was on her tenth.

"Go ahead," Jessica said. "Thirty years in hell would drive any human to irreparable madness. The sooner he dies, the sooner he starts over. Let him spend the rest of this life questioning reality and flashing back at the drop of a hat."

Mara released Ballantine.

The hunter opened each eye alternately then shut both tight. The change of reality hurt his mind. The backs of his eyelids still held images of his time in his own hell. Speaking was out of the question.

"*HANDS UP, EVERYBODY*!" Ariana called from the doorway, rifle trained. "I'm done fucking around with you people!"

The women and Jeremy casually put their hands up.

"Back away from him!"

They took a few steps away, even Bob, who stayed at Jessica's heel.

Ariana knelt at Ballantine's head and lay a hand on it. She kept her rifle on her knee, finger on the trigger, aimed at Mara. Ballantine was still in there. He was badly abused, but he was still in there.

"Girl, what are you doing?" Mara asked.

"You shut up," Ariana said. A white glow that only Jeremy and Lana were unable see enveloped Ari's hand and Ballantine's head. She saw shadows of his memories, but not details. She could tell they were horrible, but not why. In a kind of psychic grip, Ariana crumpled them like pieces of paper and threw them away.

"That'll take you all night, child," said Mara. "Even if you had enough power. He's been under too long."

"What the hell, Jeremy?"

Jeremy shrugged and said, "She had him like that when I got here. I'm the one who told her to stop."

"It's true," said Lana. "Don't blame Jeremy."

"So, Ariana," Mara said, "if I may ask, how did you come upon your ability?"

"Just lucky, I guess," Ari said, still working on Ballantine.

"Indeed. You know, my servant Brunna—"

"You mean my mother, Jodi?"

Jeremy snapped to attention.

Mara paused. Then she tittered. She was rarely taken by surprise or fumbled for a word, but now she was—and she did—and it amused her. It made her feel more human and gave her a strange sense of hope.

"That her necklace you're wearing, I take it?" Ariana asked the demon.

Mara stroked the diamonds on her décolleté. Again she had no words. Something else crept into her, though. Fear. For the first time in years, she felt fragile and uncertain. She giggled again at the thought. Thousands on thousands of years immortal, with front-to-back knowledge of the universe, survivor of the Great War, and here she was, heart racing at the threatening eyes of a 21-earth-year-old human.

"Something funny?" Ari asked.

Mara tingled and chewed her thumbnail. She'd never felt threatened by a human in her life... but Ariana wasn't human. Not *entirely*, anyway. She was half nymph and therefore partially resistant to Mara's powers. She was half human and therefore unpredictable.

Jeremy, Mara's protégé, stared at the demon with a look she had been helping to create since the dawn of mankind: disappointment. It was the peaked eyebrows and hung jaw of suddenly stripped faith. The poor naive boy. The magical dangerous boy. She had told him she was bad news.

Del Ballantine reached a shaky hand to his pistol.

"Don't do it, Mr. Ballantine," Mara warned. "I'll send you right back."

"What the hell are you?" he asked.

"My name is Mara. I am the demon of illusion."

"Ha. If I'd known you were a demon, I'd've left you alone."

"Maybe. But you'd have reported me."

"Yeah."

"Did you kill my dog?"

"Nigel did." Ballantine said placing a hand on his pistol.

"I'm warning you."

Ballantine drew and aimed at Mara.

Ariana stood and cried, "No, don't!"

Ballantine, under Mara's illusion, had his gun against his own temple. He pulled the trigger and blew his brains across the floor past Jeremy.

Jeremy screamed.

Ariana took aim at Mara.

Mara, with what illusion she could muster against Ariana's nymph magic, made herself seem to disappear. She tried to shift out of Ariana's line of fire but ran into a wall... a cold wall... an ice wall. Jessica had pulled the water from the bath and formed a semi-circle around Mara, blocking retreat left, right, and backward. As she spun, she saw Jessica smiling at her. The nymph couldn't kill her, but there was no provision against aiding and abetting.

A heavyweight blow smashed Mara in the chest and slammed her against the ice wall. Her blood painted the spiderwebbing ice with a bright drooling crimson. She reappeared and fell in a heap. Jessica thawed the ice instantly, allowing it to crash on Mara and soak her as a final insult.

The water nymph felt the curses fade from her as the life left Mara. She knelt by the demon.

"Thank you," whispered Mara. Her illusion of beauty faded. Her skin sagged and wrinkled. Hair and teeth disappeared. Face and body sank and withered. The gown turned into a tattered robe.

"My pleasure," said Jessica. "Good luck on the other side."

Mara smiled, took her last breath, and died.

Jessica leaned close to Mara's mouth and breathed in as the demon's final breath escaped. Then she removed the diamond necklace and stood to face the others.

Ariana held out a hand for the necklace.

Jessica shook her head and placed the necklace on herself.

"That was my mother's," said Ariana.

"Yes," said Jessica. "And now it's mine."

Ariana raised her rifle and said, "Give it here."

Jessica laughed and disappeared.

Ari took a shot but hit nothing.

Jessica laughed from nowhere and said, "Join me, Jeremy."

Lana, looking around in vain, said, "He's mine!"

Jeremy said, "I'm nobody's."

Lana said, "But I thought..."

"I thought we were gonna get out and go live our lives," said Jeremy. "I don't need a servant. I can barely afford to take care of *myself!*"

With that, Lana saw herself living out the rest of her days as a whore. She had no other plan. She'd thought she was going to serve Jeremy. She never expected to be desirable forever. She knew eventually he'd fall in love and she'd be made a housekeeper or something, but that was a bridge she'd cross when she came to it. She'd thought that bridge was much farther down the road. But here he was already kicking her to the curb... on top of a mountain full of monsters... in a nowhere town. Her only skill, one of ill repute; and that was fading.

She screamed at him, knelt, picked up one of Ballantine's guns, and aimed it at the singer.

Jeremy cloned Lana partially, giving her three eyes, three arms, three legs, and compromised organs. She fell dead immediately. When he looked up, there were two Arianas, identical to the freckles. He looked back and forth between them.

The Ariana on his left said, "You'll have to kill us both."

Jeremy said, "Well, one of you is standing in the same spot she's been in since she came into the room, so..."

"But you can't be sure what you're seeing is real."

Jeremy realized she was right. If he were being manipulated, he might not even be in the castle. He said, "Okay, so how about nobody kill *anybody*? How about whichever of you is Jessica leave and not come back?"

"I could," said one Ariana.

Jessica appeared behind Jeremy, pulled his head back against her shoulder and said, "Or I could kill you and siphon off your power."

The fake Ariana disappeared. The real one, unthinking, drew her sidearm and fired a shot through Jessica's head. The nymph fell hard to the stone floor behind Jeremy.

Gun trained, Ari moved closer to make sure Jess was dead. She wondered how the nymph had been planning to kill Jeremy if she couldn't kill humans. Jessica had absorbed some of Mara's power, but demons couldn't kill either. Had there been some sort of supernatural metamorphosis? Had Jessica become something else?

"I'm so sorry, Ari," said Jeremy.

"It's okay," she said.

"No, it's not. No, it's not. I didn't expect it to come to all of this. I just wanted to..."

Satisfied Jessica was dead, Ari holstered her gun and put her arms around Jeremy.

He returned her embrace and buried his face in her hair. It smelled good, intoxicating. He kissed her shoulder.

"Jeremy," Ariana admonished.

"Ariana," he said, not letting her go, but looking into her eyes, "I just want to say..."

"Please don't." Ariana's head swam and heart raced. "Not here, anyway."

Jeremy squeezed her by the waist. He pulled her body tight against his and kissed her hard on the lips.

She tingled and blushed. She grew hot and wet. It was the best kiss Ariana had ever had. She almost forgot where she was. Punch drunk, she pushed Jeremy away.

"We gotta..." she said, "We gotta... find Reggie... get outta here."

"Sure thing," said Jeremy.

Ariana knelt next to Jessica. She slid a hand around the nymph's neck but couldn't find the clasp of either necklace. She tried to slip her fingertips beneath the jewels but couldn't get under them. She tried to pick one up but felt nothing. It was an illusion.

Ariana stood, wheeled, and found herself face to face with a very much alive Jessica. The bassist looked back at the ground and saw Jeremy lying there with her bullet hole in his head.

She didn't hear Jessica laughing right away. Nor did she fully process what she'd done to Jeremy. She wondered if Jessica hadn't sent her to her own hell like Mara did with Ballantine. She wondered if Mara wasn't still alive and making her see all of this.

“Is this real?” she asked as she stared at Jeremy’s body.

“Sad to say,” Jessica said with an insincere pout.

Jeremy was dead by Ariana’s own hand. Her life with him flashed before her eyes—good times, bad times, and regrets. He hadn’t *only* been a friend. He had been family. And not only did

Jessica take him away, she made Ariana do it. A tempest welled inside Ari. It turned her stomach, heaved her chest, twisted her lips, and swirled her head. It threatened to tear her apart from the inside until she could no longer stand.

Then Ariana looked at the indifferent Jessica and the storm inside caught fire. It offered to explode out of her and engulf the mountain if that's what it took. It told her to start by throwing herself at the cunt in front of her and tearing her to pieces with her bare hands.

Any other day, with any other person, Ariana might have done just that. But this time, she held the rage to a few tears while she made sure not to make any mistakes.

"Why?" she croaked.

"Power," said Jessica. "Revenge. Freedom."

"Why'd you make me kill him?"

"Gotta start somewhere, baby doll."

"What are you even talking about?"

"You think Mara's the only thing that's ever come through here that couldn't play nice with nature?"

Ariana only stared at her.

"I'm talking about *humans*! *They're* the invasive species. *They're* the parasites. *They're* the ones demolishing forests to build malls, and golf courses… all the other shit they don't need.

"You know, for as bad as Mara was, she kept these mountains pretty pure."

"Pure?" said Ariana. "She kept them *infested*!"

"And now that she's gone, there'll be a *new* infestation! One of people. You'll hunt the creatures to extinction—"

"They don't *belong* here."

"Don't they?! Don't they?!" Jessica paused to let it sink in. "*People* don't belong here. They don't. They *don't* know how to take care of nature. They *don't* deserve to be a part of it."

Jessica looked down at Jeremy. "I used to like him," she said. "I used to like *both* of you." She laughed and looked at Ariana. "Which was strange for me since I've *never* cared much for humans. Guess I got used to you or something.

“But now I’m free of my curse. I’ve got my power back and more.”

"So, what now?"

“Same plan as Mr. Ballantine. Only *I’ll* be focusing on the *real* invasive species.”

“But you can’t kill people. You’re bound by your nature.”

Jessica shrugged and said, "Guess I’ll have to get creative then, won’t I. For instance,” she raised a hand toward Ariana, “I can start by driving you ma—"

Without a twitch, Ariana connected with the air in Jessica's lungs, expanded it a hundred times in an instant, and exploded the nymph's body.

Bob the hellcat, eyes aglow, watched indifferently.

Ariana dropped to her knees next to Jeremy. She cried over him for more than a few minutes. She studied his face and allowed it to etch itself into her mind. She was sorry she hadn't spent more time with him, sorry she had spent so much time with Reggie... Where *was* Reggie? She was afraid to guess.

A glimmer on one of Jessica's necklaces caught her eye. Ariana removed the diamonds that had been her mother's and put them on herself. As with the key, the wind picked up and she became more aware of her surroundings. This time she was better able to control it.

She took Jessica's sapphires and placed them on herself. Every water molecule in the room made itself known to her: the mist in the air and the dew on the stones, the water from the bath and the cells inside of her.

With Jenny's stones in her pocket, she was able to feel just enough vibration in the castle walls to know that the fighting upstairs was winding down. But there was another vibration. Something stirred nearby... through the door in the wall.

Ari drew her pistol and approached the door. She turned the handle and flung it open. Inside, Reggie leaned against the wall weeping, and writhing, and twitching, and moaning.

"Reggie!" Ari called and went to him.

He recoiled, cried, and twitched.

"Shh, it's okay," Ari said. "I'm here. Ari's here."

She managed to lay a hand on his shoulder. He was worse than Ballantine was when she had found him. Dark memories tortured his mind. Ari reached in and began to clean them out, but every time she did they were replaced with more. Reggie was stuck in his own hell.

Upstairs in the great hall, the last of the men searched for survivors and finished off the wounded monsters. Ariana emerged from a corridor with Bob at her heel. She called for anyone with the strength left to retrieve Reggie, Jeremy, and the rest of the bodies.

The sky turned its predawn indigo as the last flames flickered in the hearth and torches. The survivors inspected the vehicles. Some were still viable. Others were full of holes.

When everyone was outside, Ariana turned to face the castle. She sat, cross-legged in the dewy grass. Bob sat next to her. With the power of all three nymphs inside her, she connected with the castle.

The people watched her and waited. At first there was nothing, then a moment of dread, then a rumble, then an earthquake.

Little by little the castle fractured and crumbled. The tower toppled behind the walls. The walls caved inward. The ground opened and swallowed the structure. A great dust cloud arose, forcing the people to cover their faces.

Ariana summoned a wind to push the dust away. When the air cleared, an empty crag and a perfectly laid stone drive were the only things left.

CHAPTER 32

Ken cradled his aging wife on the couch. Jenny dozed. She'd worried herself exhausted. A truck rumbled in the driveway. Husband and wife exchanged a glance, then ran to the door. When they saw it was townspeople, they ran out to get the news.

As the truck stopped, Ariana popped up from the bed and said, "We should get Reggie inside. He's bad."

Jenny's heart sank. She was afraid to look. She expected severed limbs or disfiguring burns. She was a little relieved to see he was all in one piece as they unloaded him.

"All right, all right," said Ken, leading the way to the trailer door. "Get him in. Put him on his bed." He gave no thought to the hellcat following Ariana.

The people carried Reggie in then waited in the living room while Jenny, Ari and Ken talked.

"What the hell happened?" Ken growled.

"We killed her," said Ari. "She's dead."

Ken pointed at Reggie and said, "What happened to *him*?"

Ariana gave Jenny back her jewels and said, "She got to him first. I don't know. He was like this when I found him. I think he might be in shock."

"No," said Jenny, searching Reggie's pockets for the other two jewels. "Not shock. Something else. You're sure the witch is dead?"

"She wasn't a witch. She was a demon."

"A demon!"

"How did you not know that?" Ken asked his wife. "Shouldn't you have known that?"

"Remember when I said her magic touched me once?" Jenny said transforming back into her younger self.

"Yeah."

"And that I didn't know what it did?"

The answer clicked into Ken's mind. She'd been made to forget that one detail, possibly others. He gave a grunt and a nod.

"May I have Jessica's necklace?"

Ariana gave it to Jenny, who put it on.

“Here,” said Jenny, handing Ari the lollipop from Reggie’s pocket. “Trade ya.” The nymph laid her hands on her son and reached into his mind. Like Ariana, she was only able to see the happenings there as shadows and shapeless forms. The bad ones far outnumbered the good ones. She reached in and crushed them one by one, faster than Ariana had been able to do, but the progress was still slow going. It was like trying to empty a swimming pool with a shot glass.

The lollipop started Ariana thinking about Pete Steen. Thinking about Pete started her thinking about all the people she’d lost in the last few days. Thinking about all the people she’d lost started her thinking about—

"Help me," Jenny said.

Ariana mimicked the way Jenny laid her hands on Reggie and connected to him. She felt the way Jenny was working and tried to mimic it, but couldn't match her speed. She panted in frustration.

"It's okay," said Jenny. "Just do what you can."

"What's wrong with him?" Ari asked.

"He's in his own personal hell, I think. Ken, honey, we're gonna be a little while."

Ken was hesitant to leave but knew he was no help. "You give a yell if you need anything," he said.

"Thank you, baby."

Ken went to the living room and got all the story he could from the people. They told him about the gauntlet on the mountain road, the chaos at the castle, and how it was Reggie who stepped forward and made the final plea for peace. Nobody knew exactly what happened to Reggie. They only knew he had faced the witch and lived.

Ken bit his cheek to keep his pride from showing. He thanked them all, assured them he'd see Ariana to wherever she needed to go, and walked them out.

Hours passed while the women worked on Reggie's mind. Ken kept himself busy on one thing or another. He made the girls sandwiches and cleaned the house. He worked on small projects in the processor, but his head wasn't in it. He didn't want to be that far away for too long. When he returned to the bedroom, the sandwiches were untouched and the women were deep in concentration. Jenny and Ariana had entered a kind of trance. To them, time had ceased to exist. There was only their task. They stayed on it for four days.

The first two days, Ken took orders from customers but did no work. Everyone who came in asked about Reggie. Those who were in the fight had a story about it. Those who weren't had secondhand stories about it. People speculated about what it all meant now that the witch and worm were dead. They asked Ken what he was going to do when all the monsters were gone.

He said, "Sleep."

They laughed.

Ken laughed too. Despite the grief he'd given Ballantine about trying to ruin his business, Ken was a little relieved. He'd saved more than enough money to retire, as it was. But, like Ballantine had said, if the monsters went away tomorrow, the deer would be back in a year or two. Ken wouldn't have much more than a brief hiatus. And when *that* was over, it would be business as usual, just like *before* Pittsburgh. Suddenly, the stuffed creatures in his processor seemed less like trophies and more like museum relics.

On the third day, he realized nobody was tending the Coleman farm and drove down to feed the animals and shovel some shit.

On the fourth day, after a night of work and a visit to the farm, Ken came into the trailer and found Ariana asleep on the couch with Bob on the floor beside her. He went to Reggie's room and found his son alone, asleep, and no longer twitching or ticking. He went to his own bedroom and woke his sleeping wife to ask what was up.

"He's stable now, baby," Jenny said with weak voice and closed eyes.

Ken pushed down hard on his tears.

"Still needs work, though," Jenny said. "Might never be the same Reggie."

"But he's gon' be okay?" Ken asked.

"He's not in pain anymore."

Ken lost the battle with his tears. They fell onto Jenny's arm as Ken asked, "What can I do? Can I do something?"

"Mm," she reached up and touched his face. "Just keep being a good husband and father."

He kissed her hand.

"And let me sleep for a while."

"Of course, baby. Of course."

Ken left the bedroom, wiped his eyes, and went to Reggie's room. He pulled a chair over to the bed and put a hand on Reggie's arm. Then he rested his head on the bed and fell asleep.

That evening, everyone awoke at about the same time. Everyone but Reggie, that is. Ken made breakfast as the women talked at the table.

"You're an extraordinary girl, Ariana," said Jenny.

"An extraordinary girl who almost got our son killed," said Ken.

"Not the time, baby," Jenny scolded.

Ariana blushed and fidgeted with her coffee mug.

"I can't say you remind me of your mother," said Jenny. "And that's not to say neither of you is great. You're both great. Just not the same. You're your own great woman. And I think that's better than being comparable to another great one, because it means you became great all on your own."

"Thank you. But I'm *not* a woman, right? I mean, I've got powers. My mom was a nymph."

"But your father was human. You're *half* woman. Half nymph. Best of both worlds."

"What do humans have over nymphs?"

"The same thing they have over every other being. Freedom. Choice. You can do anything you want. You can ignore your abilities or you can use them."

"They say you killed the witch—uh—demon," said Ken handing her a plate. "That true?"

Ariana nodded.

"There you go. A nymph can't kill. They're bound by their nature to create harmony."

"But Reggie," Ari said. "He's never killed anything in his life."

"Some children get their father's eyes and their mother's hair. Reggie got my harmony... and his father's tummy." She smiled at Ken, who did not return it.

"So how much more work do you think it'll take?" asked Ariana.

"To make Reggie better? A lot. But if you help me for one more day, we should be able to at least get him awake and able to eat."

"Of course," Ari said. "I don't exactly have any other... the animals!"

"I got 'em," said Ken. "I *been* gettin' 'em. Eat your breakfast and make my son better."

Ariana took a bite of sausage and said, "I'll be back every day until he's back to normal."

"You're sweet," said Jenny. "But that could take the rest of his life, I'm afraid."

Ariana's heart sank. She had been afraid that it was that bad while she was working on him, but she didn't want to believe it.

"Just help me get him to the point where he can feed and dress himself, then go live your life," said Jenny. "I'll take it from there."

"What do I do?" asked Ari. "Nymph... stuff?"

"I told you. You're part human. You can do anything you want. If I could make a suggestion though, you've lost a lot of loved ones. Live for them. You lost Jeremy and most of Reggie. So go make three times the music. You lost your mother and father, so make sure others don't. You lost friends. Make more. Help others."

"How do I do all that?"

"It's only a suggestion."

Ariana spent the night helping Jenny, then went home to tend the farm. It took her much of the day to straighten things out for the animals. There was a wood devil in the pit for her to shoot and lye. She thought about tending the house but didn't care for the hollow feeling it bore. As soon as she stepped inside, it felt dead to her. Instead she went back to the Adams home and helped with Reggie some more.

Ariana went through the same motions for the next few days. They got Reggie on his feet and shuffling, but not talking.

Then Jenny said, "Why don't we all go out to eat?"

Ari and Ken looked wide eyed at each other, then to Jenny.

"What?" said Jenny. "Ding, dong..."

The Foothill Hotel Bar had been somber and quiet all week. The stories had spread. The words had been said. It hadn't felt right to talk about much else. Besides, there was no band to change the mood.

Somehow the place went even quieter when Ariana and the entire Adams family entered. Even Kelly's mouth hung open.

Connie ran to Ariana with her arms outstretched, squeezed the girl's face, kissed her forehead, and pulled her tight for a hug. She moved on to Reggie, but Jenny blocked her.

"I'm sorry," said Jenny. "He's not quite ready for that yet."

"Connie Crawford," said Ariana, "meet Jenny Adams. Reggie's mother."

The aged woman stared at into the face of the perfect young nymph, and despite all she'd experienced, said in disbelief, "No..."

"I believe it," said Kelly from behind the bar. "I remember that necklace." She pointed at Jenny's décolleté, upon which she still wore both her own and Jessica's necklace. "So what are you, like sisters?"

"In a sense," said Jenny.

"You know your sister ruined my life?"

"I believe I heard about that. I am truly sorry."

Kelly looked the family over. She didn't have anything against Jenny. She didn't have anything against any of them. But they were the only people she still hadn't seen. While they were gone, there was still the hope that when they returned, they'd bring her... something, some piece of all she'd lost, or maybe something to salvage it. Instead, they stood there looking at her, waiting for her to serve them.

"Have a seat wherever you like," Kelly said.

They sat at the bar. Reggie took Sam's old seat. Jenny sat next to him. Then Ken. Then Ari.

They ordered and ate in relative silence. Every so often someone would come by and say an awkward hello, offer a thanks or condolence to Ariana. Most just smiled and waved.

Someone put his hand on the seat next to her and asked if it was taken. Ariana was uncomfortable about it—there were other places to sit—but she said, "No."

The sheriff's hat flopped onto the bar. Ari turned to look at the hat's owner. The light came back into her eyes at the sight of his half smile and bushy mustache.

"How you doing, darling?" Sheriff Landry asked.

Ariana gave a short laugh and said, "How do you think?"

"Relieved. Exhausted. Angry. Sad. Confused."

Ariana hadn't considered how to put it into words, but after thinking about it, she realized that was exactly how she felt. All of it.

"You said it," she said. "I can't just go back to tending the farm. I never wanted that in the first place."

"No one says you *have* to."

"But I feel like riding the wind wouldn't be enough for me."

Sheriff Landry didn't realize she was being literal. He said, "Maybe that's not such a bad idea. Travel. See the world. See *some* of it, at least. Maybe you haven't found yourself yet because you *can't* here."

"But they might need my help with the monsters."

"Girl," said Ken, "it's gon' take *years* to clear them monsters out. We did okay without you before. We'll do okay without you after."

"You killed a demon, Ariana," said Sheriff Landry. "That's no small feat. You ever give any thought to hunting demons?"

"Ha," she said. "I had help and got lucky."

"All right, then. Not demons. What about everything else? What if you took up Mr. Ballantine's mantle?"

"Monster slayer? I don't think I could. I haven't had much of a stomach for killing in cold blood lately, even if they *are* monsters."

"Hm. Maybe you could help catch the really bad ones. Bring 'em to justice."

"Like a sort of monster police?"

"Hey, if they're going to be living with people, they'll need policed. As long as there are humans, and demons, and witches, and what have you, there will be unrest and there will be crime."

A thought clicked into place for Ariana. "As long as all those beings are around, there will be crime." What if all those beings were to be around forever? They've all been around for the last twenty years. They weren't going anywhere soon. What if *this* was how it was meant to be? What if *this* was the new natural order: humans and monsters living together?

ARIANA AND THE BOOGEYMAN

Heads banged, bodies ground, faces collided, and drinks flowed in the dark amid the noise and the color-changing lights. The place stank. August wasn't kind to the residents and friends of the Pittsburgh Art House. Not even the half-nymph Ariana Coleman was immune to the heat.

The House itself was nestled in a once-affluent neighborhood of mansions long ago purchased by slumlords and converted into apartment complexes. Because they had so many neighbors, the Art House residents had to host their bands in the basement and add soundproofing to the ceiling and windows.

When Ariana had moved to the city, she was welcomed into every music circle she visited. It took time for her to find the right scene. She first sought out singer/songwriters, but grew bored of them. None were as inventive as Jeremy had been. She spent the least amount of time in the blues and rock circles. Though she loved the energy, there was little challenge for her. The jazz scene both intrigued and challenged her, but there weren't enough people her own age in it. The art scene had everything she wanted. She felt free there. She could play what she wanted, when she wanted. Whether or not her audience understood it, at the very least they appreciated it. Her talents helped her make friends fast. She was invited to the Art House before long.

The best musician in the house, Ariana regularly received offers to join bands and other musicians. She put together her own band, named it Tempest, and rocked the basement on a fairly steady schedule. As a matter of fact, if she *didn't* play, people complained. Some even grew belligerent. The band even gathered a following. People who didn't even *live* there stashed sleeping bags so they could crash after an all-night Tempest jam.

Ariana didn't *officially* live in the Art House, but there wasn't a person there who didn't offer to share their bed. Besides, how many people had a pet hellcat? In the beginning, drunk on freedom as well as alcohol, Ari wasn't very picky about who she slept with. Lately, however, she'd been alternating between two people. There was Jordan Tanner, a reuse artist who was a bit of a space cadet but great in bed, and Lacey Lisicki, an atheist painter with a quiet mystique that charmed Ari almost as much as Ari charmed people with her innate magic.

As Tempest rocked the Art House basement, Jordan allowed a little blond girl to grind on him in front of the stage. It was a game he played. He thought it would get Ari hot either by making her jealous or letting her see his action from a different angle.

Ari rolled her eyes. She couldn't care less what he did or whom he fucked. She'd relaxed her own rules since Brothers. The freedom the city offered her had been like the breaking of chains. The monsters were fewer and farther between. She didn't have to be on high alert at all times when she was outside. Lately, she left her gun at home... or rather in whomever's room she was last in when she took it off. She got drunk regularly, but rarely allowed herself any other controlled substances. Once, she had become paranoid after a toke of someone's joint and nearly destroyed the club they were in. After that, she swore off everything but booze.

Lacey, the painter, did not attend the concert. She mostly kept to herself and worked. She came downstairs as the band was wrapping up. The place was as full as ever, but the attendees were asleep on their feet, asleep against each other, and some even asleep on the floor.

Ariana smiled at Lacey's haphazard bun and paint-spattered overalls as the artist weaved her way closer to the stage. Jordan rocked back and forth, eyes closed, in the arms of the blond he'd been grinding with. Lacey came to a stop in front of Ariana, laced her fingers, and watched the bass player through big green eyes.

Seconds later, the song came to an end. The audience cheered weakly and began saying their good-byes. Ari pushed a wisp of hair behind Lacey's ear and said, "I think that's gonna be it for us tonight, Lacey. Wish you'd been here earlier."

"Can you play one more for me?" Lacey asked. "Doesn't have to be the whole band. Just a quick one."

Ariana thought about it. She was really looking forward to sleep. Mm, but those eyes... and that lower lip, the way it stuck out plump, firm, and round... like a cherry.

"Okay," said Ariana. "One more. I'll call this, 'Lacey's Lullaby'."

Ariana closed her eyes and made up a song. She hadn't played by herself in a while and found a connection with her instrument that she'd almost forgotten. It felt good, like a meditation. She relaxed and let it take her where it wanted. Fifteen minutes later, Ariana played her final harmonic and opened her eyes.

Everyone in the room was asleep on the floor. Her bandmates too. They hadn't even finished putting away their gear.

"Whoops," said Ariana. She put her bass away and turned off the electronics, then woke up Lacey. "Hey. Come on, let's get you to bed."

Lacey looked around at all the sleeping people and tried to remember what happened.

"I'm so sorry!" Lacey said. "I didn't mean to fall asleep on you."

"It's okay. Really. That was my fault," Ariana said as they stepped over the bodies.

"Your music is beautiful."

"Thank you."

"No. It's better than beautiful. Whatever is more beautiful than beautiful. That's what your music is."

"All right, darling."

Bob came out of nowhere, followed them to Lacey's room, and curled up at the foot of the bed. The girls passed out as soon as their heads hit the pillow.

In the basement, Jordan twitched in his sleep. Then his little blond twitched. Then the people next to them. Then the people beyond them. Before long, everyone in the room twitched and talked in their nightmares. The basement floor of the Art House writhed with people fending off imaginary monsters.

Then they all woke up. At the same time, they all opened their eyes.

A single light bulb burned above the staircase. Its light struggled to reach the far corners of the basement. In the not-quite-pitch-black-darkness, the man appeared.

Jordan saw the unnaturally still figure, squinted and yawned, and looked again. He still wasn't sure. It looked like a shortish man with a top hat and jacket with tails. He had a round head and stout body, but his arms and legs were comparatively skinny. Jordan stared at it, trying to figure out if it was a person or just a shadow.

The little blond saw it and gasped. Jordan looked at her, then back to the shadow. It was gone. Randomly about the room, the others gasped and screamed. Some got up and bolted out, stepping on people as they ran. Jordan looked around and watched the silhouette of the top hat and tails flicker about the room.

It appeared on the stairs, in the light, so that Jordan, blondie, and a few others saw it clearly. Its face was wide and round, less than human, with glinting eyes set deep and dark. Its nose was flat and its mouth was grotesquely wide and full of spiky teeth. The corners of its mouth curled up, pushing deep folds into its cheeks nearly all the way to its ears. Scraggly black hair hung from underneath the hat.

Jordan jumped up, looked around for a weapon, and picked up the microphone stand. Its heavy base made it awkward to wield, but panic is the thief of reason.

The thing on the stairs blinked out of existence again.

Nobody spoke. They only shuddered and cried.

The thing reappeared in front of Jordan, mouth open and

emitting dripping, putrid breath, claws brandished at the end of its long bony fingers.

Jordan clutched his chest, knelt, and collapsed.

The thing vanished again.

Blondie crawled to Jordan to try to wake him up.

The wall erupted in flames that quickly spread. The people in the basement panicked and trampled each other to get up the stairs and out of the house.

Ariana heard the commotion, woke up Lacey, and they ran outside into the daylight.

"What's happening?" she asked.

"The basement's on fire!" someone said.

Something felt off to Ari. Nonetheless, she went to the neighbor's house and called 911. While they waited for the fire trucks, Ariana checked the petrified people to make sure everyone had made it out. She saw blondie, but no Jordan.

Without a second thought, Ariana ran back into the house. As soon as she stepped inside, she realized what was off. There was no smoke. It wasn't even hot.

There were injured people on the basement steps and floor. They moaned in pain as Ariana checked on them. They would all live. Everyone but Jordan. He'd had a heart attack and died.

There was no evidence of a fire in the basement. The only smoke she smelled was the stale cigarette odor that had always been there.

The fire trucks arrived as she emerged from the house.

"False alarm!" Ariana called, waving her arms at the firefighters.

"False alarm?" said fire chief, Rob Stanton.

"No fire," said Ari. "Injured people in the basement though."

"You call an *ambulance* for injured people, young lady."

"Easy, chief. People were running. Someone said, 'Fire.' We called the fire department."

A uniformed officer and an older detective interviewed the residents and friends. The detective was stout; he almost seemed to waddle when he walked. Ariana couldn't imagine him getting his cheap gray suit buttoned over his belly. Sweat poured from under his out-of-style fedora. The bass player put herself within eavesdropping distance.

He pulled out a notepad and introduced himself as Detective Brinkley. Everyone had the same story: a grotesque man in a top hat and tails. He disappeared and the room caught fire.

The detective nodded and thanked each person he talked to, then turned to the officer and said, "Fear feeder."

The officer nodded. Detective Brinkley noticed the hellcat at Ariana's heel and asked, "That thing registered?"

She nodded, which was good enough for the detective. He signaled his officer to move out.

As ambulances took away the injured, the fire chief approached the group of residents and friends and said, "Who's in charge here?"

The group looked around at each other.

"Nobody's in charge?" the fire chief said.

No answer.

"Well to whom it may concern, the fact that we just pulled five injured and one dead out of your basement is why we have fire codes. You can't have that many people in a room that size with only one exit." He stared at them, waiting for someone to say something. When no one did, he flapped his hands at them and left.

The Art House dedicated that night to the memory of Jordan. The musicians played unplugged in the parlor while all around the house other artists did their own tributes. Some raided Jordan's supplies and tried their hands at reuse art. Others, like Lacey, worked on portraits of him in their chosen media. Friends who were not artists went from room to room looking in on those who were. It was one big, walkable live show. Nobody went in the basement though.

A dark and handsome stranger caught Ariana's eye while she played. He looked into the parlor when he arrived, then made his way through the house. There was something off about him, though nobody could put their finger on it. He was too clean looking. His hair was too perfect. His clothes fit too perfectly. He didn't really speak to anyone other than to excuse himself. Everyone just kind of assumed he was invited by the person he was looking for.

The stranger was headed for the basement when the friend of a resident said, "You don't want to go down there, man. It's haunted."

"Oh yeah?" asked the stranger.

"Saw it for myself. Ask anyone here. Most of them saw it too."

"*I* saw it," said the girl under the friend's arm.

"Well, I'll be sure to stay out of here then," said the stranger.

The friends moved on and the stranger went to the parlor, where he found a folding chair, sat, and watched the band.

Ariana watched him back. He had no aura. Or if he did, Ariana couldn't see it. Nor did he move... at all. Some people talked and gestured. Others danced. Some people made out. Even the people sitting on the floor swayed or bobbed or tapped their feet, but the stranger near the back of the room sat like a rock sticking out of a stream.

As Ariana drank, she became more intrigued by the man. When she realized it was she he was looking at, she realized she'd been looking at *him* for more than a little while. It put her off guard; a feeling she enjoyed around people she *trusted*, but not so much around strangers, especially when there were supernatural goings-on.

She allowed some of her nymph magic into her music to make him react. Everyone else in the room turned their undivided attention to the stage, but the stranger didn't move.

Ariana turned up her magic for the next song and everyone moved closer to her. Even the other artists in the house stopped what they were doing to come listen, but the stranger stayed put.

Ariana turned up her magic a third time, reduced half the room to tears and turned the other half into Terpsichores. The stranger watched, unmoved.

"Okay," thought Ari, "no more Mr. Nice Guy."

The stranger shook his head, as if he knew what she was

thinking. Drunk, Ariana didn't care what might happen if she turned her power all the way up, so she did it.

Everyone but the stranger and Ari went into a fit of madness. They cried and they howled, fell down, kicked, and pounded their fists.

Ariana stopped playing and panicked. She tried to think of how to fix it, but nothing came to her. The stranger stood and stepped over the people toward her.

"What are you?" she asked him.

"I'm a detective," said the stranger, flashing a badge. "Marco DaPonte. What are *you*?"

"Ariana Coleman. I'm a half nymph."

"That explains it," he said. His face had life in it but told Ariana nothing. He could've been angry. He could've been amused. He could've been there to arrest her. "You wanna take a walk with me, Miss Coleman?"

"But..."

"They'll be fine. It just has to wear off."

She followed him to the front porch, apologizing to the writhing Lacey on the way.

"Are you going to make me register?" asked Ari. "Because I really wasn't planning—"

"No."

"—on staying too long."

"Only beings not originally from physical Earth have to register."

"You're here about the fear feeder then."

The detective touched his nose. "Know anything?"

"No more than you. Although... I did kind of put everybody to sleep in the basement last night, if that helps."

"You know, I think it does. More bang for his buck."

"Who, his?"

"Boogeyman."

"Say what now?"

"Fear feeder. It's just what we call them. They're not really ghosts, but they're not really physical. They kind of hop between planes of existence. They scare people and feed on the energy. Our boy had a feast last night. They don't usually kill anybody, but sometimes shit happens."

"Okay, I think I got about half of that."

"You don't have to get any of it, Miss Coleman. *I'm* on the job."

"So what do you have to do to a fear feeder?"

"Usually dissipate it."

"You mean kill it?"

"Killing is a relative term."

"End its existence?"

"That. Yeah."

"Just because it scares people?"

"It *endangers* people, Miss Coleman. It caused a stampede in a basement and killed your friend."

"A *heart attack* killed my friend. Would you kill me for yelling 'boo' at someone and then they die of a heart attack?"

"That's different."

"How?"

"You're a person."

"No. I just *look* like one."

"You fit into society."

"So what... you just go around eradicating everything that doesn't fit into you're idea of society?"

"That's how the world *works,* Miss Coleman."

"Bullshit. That's ignorant."

"How is it ignorant?"

"It *ignores* that fact that everything has its place in nature. It *ignores* the fact that man is a *part of,* not *above* nature."

"Nature is about survival of the fittest."

"Nature is about harmony!"

A few moments of contemplation passed before Detective DaPonte said, "Well, you're the nymph. What would you like me to do?"

"Can it be captured?"

"No way *I* know."

"Can it be talked to?"

"Theoretically."

Ariana thought hard, got her idea, then said, "All right. Come with me."

The people in the parlor were calming down as Ari led the detective in.

"Hey everybody," she said. "You all okay? Listen, this is Detective DaPonte. He was here investigating what happened last night and it's a good thing he was. He says these kind of... mass breakdowns are common after an encounter with a fear feeder like you had last night. He says I should play some soothing music to help you all reset, so I'm gonna go ahead and do that. You all just listen to the music."

Ariana picked up the bass and played "Lacey's Lullaby" again, note for note, all 15 minutes of it, and put to sleep everyone but herself and DaPonte.

"Why don't I affect you?" she whispered to him.

"Nothing affects me," he whispered back. "That's *my* gift. Now meditate. Anything higher than an alpha wave, you won't see him."

Ariana cleared her head and let her eyes unfocus. Thoughts drifted by but never stopped or got stuck. Her heart slowed. The point on the wall at which she stared seemed to twist and morph after being stared at for so long.

A shadow entered from the foyer. It slid along the floor and crept up the wall into the spot at which Ari stared. It had a top hat, a round head, no neck, and long legs.

Ari and the detective watched as the owner of the shadow stalked into the room. His footfalls made no sound and he never bobbed, as people do, when he walked. His grin gave Ari goosebumps. The lamplights twinkled on his eyes buried deep beneath his bushy brow.

Ariana's heart quickened, but she kept her mind clear.

"Hello," she said. "I'm Ariana. What's your name?"

The boogeyman blinked out of existence, then back in, right in front of Ariana's face.

"What do you want?" she asked. She kept her eyes unfocused to stave off her fear.

Still, the boogeyman said nothing.

"This man wants to kill you," Ari said. "I don't think he has to. I think I know somewhere we can take you where you'll be happy and won't hurt anyone like you did last night. Would that be okay?"

The boogeyman leaned his face into Ariana's and raised an eyebrow at her. Then he shrugged.

"Marco," she said, "do you mind driving?"

Ariana kept herself entranced in the passenger seat in order to keep an eye on the fear feeder in the back. She watched the sick grin stretch across his face when they arrived within sight of the amusement park. Kennywood was closed when they pulled up, but that didn't matter to the boogeyman. When they stopped at the light out front, the boogeyman passed through the car door and walked straight through fence.

"There you go," said Ari. "He doesn't even have to do his own scaring anymore."

DaPonte looked out his window for any signs of the supernatural, but saw nothing.

"Not bad, princess," he said. "Not bad."

"Don't call me that," Ariana said.

THANKS FOR READING!

Thanks for reading! I hope you've enjoyed it. Stay tuned to find out what happened in Pittsburgh all those years ago in my upcoming epic: City of Monsters.

SPECIAL THANKS

My special thanks in no particular order…

Mom, Dad, Jeff and the rest of my family and friends for encouragement, indulgence, and just being them.

Alex Nye for never walking by or letting an email chain go without asking how the book was coming.

Jenn Weiss, Sadie Freund, Shantih and Conrad Bianco for the early reading, feedback, and review.

Jamie Moore and Tara Tippel for putting up with my mood swings and spotty help around the house while I fought to get this done.

Kris Swanson of Swanson Editorial Services for the edit.

Cru Kazmierczak for the help with ideas and for the hours of gaming.

Jeremy Caywood for inspiration and good vibes.

Last, but most of all, Alyssa Herron for encouragement, indulgence, feedback, care, and understanding. For opening her house to me, feeding me, and doing nothing but give of herself so that I could write. I owe her so much.

47285939R00213

Made in the USA
Middletown, DE
25 August 2017